JUST ONE KISS

"What do you mean, I don't know how to kiss? How dare you?" Amanda sputtered, twisting away from him.

Daniel tightened his grip. "I mean kissed the way a husband would kiss you, the way a lover would kiss you."

Amanda glared at him. His eyes flashed back at her. Then in one swift movement he pulled her up hard against his chest, one arm circling her waist. He tilted her head back and slowly lowered his mouth to hers, staring directly into her eyes. Amanda swallowed and tried to speak, but for the life of her didn't know what she would say even if she found her voice.

Finally Daniel touched his lips, warm and firm, to hers, and Amanda closed her eyes, savoring the feeling. She felt the strength leaving her tingling body, and leaned into Daniel for support. He licked her upper lip with the tip of his tongue, then gently nibbled on the lower one. She gasped at the sensation, and when her lips parted, he ran his tongue inside her mouth.

Amanda found she couldn't trust her legs, and she swayed. When Daniel pulled away from her, she opened her eyes, but for a moment had trouble focusing.

His voice husky, Daniel murmured, "Good night, Amanda."

"Good night, Daniel," she whispered as the door closed behind him. He was right, she thought. She never had really kissed anyone else before.

BOOK YOUR PLACE ON OUR WEBSITE AND MAKE THE READING CONNECTION!

We've created a customized website just for our very special readers, where you can get the inside scoop on everything that's going on with Zebra, Pinnacle and Kensington books.

When you come online, you'll have the exciting opportunity to:

- View covers of upcoming books
- Read sample chapters
- Learn about our future publishing schedule (listed by publication month *and author*)
- Find out when your favorite authors will be visiting a city near you
- Search for and order backlist books from our online catalog
- Check out author bios and background information
- Send e-mail to your favorite authors
- Meet the Kensington staff online
- Join us in weekly chats with authors, readers and other guests
- Get writing guidelines
- AND MUCH MORE!

**Visit our website at
http://www.zebrabooks.com**

COME WHAT MAY

Jill Limber

Zebra Books
Kensington Publishing Corp.

http://www.zebrabooks.com

ZEBRA BOOKS are published by

Kensington Publishing Corp.
850 Third Avenue
New York, NY 10022

Zebra, the Z logo and Splendor Reg. U.S. Pat. & TM Off.

First Printing: March, 2000
10   9   8   7   6   5   4   3   2   1

Printed in the United States of America

To Mary and Terry,
who have proved to the rest of us
what true love and courage are all about

Chapter 1

Camp Dennison, Union Army
Near Cincinnati
Summer, 1862

"Young lady, you could be the answer to my prayers."
General Allen pointed to Amanda Giles' bodice. "But we will
have to do something about those."

Shocked into silence, Amanda sat utterly still inside the
musty tent and watched the older man as he walked around
her, tugging on his uniform coat and muttering to himself.

Had anyone told President Lincoln one of his generals was
a lunatic? The man was deranged. Her late brother Andrew
had never mentioned that the general he reported to was brain-
sick. As Andrew lay dying, she promised him she would visit
General Allen personally. Postponing her move from Philadelphia to New York, she had kept that promise.

Clutching her gloves, she gauged the distance to the tent flap.

Abruptly General Allen stopped pacing, blocking her escape
route. He pointed his stubby finger at her again. "You look
exactly like your brother, you know. We have to try. Lives are
at stake."

Amanda had absolutely no idea what the general was talking about. Whose lives? What could she do?

"Lieutenant! Get me Captain McGrath!"

Amanda jumped when the general suddenly hollered to someone outside.

"Yes sir!" a voice replied.

Thank goodness. She put a hand over her racing heart. She could make a graceful exit when this new person arrived. Wanting to be ready, she pulled on her gloves.

The general turned back to her. "There is no alternative. No time."

Even though the general had piqued her curiosity, Amanda didn't have any intention of staying around until she could figure out what he had in mind for her. This entire situation was just too peculiar.

She tightened up the wide ribbon bow under her chin and, with a no-nonsense gesture, straightened her bonnet. Gone were the days when Amanda let other people tell her what she must do every day of her life.

She was on her way to New York City to be a sketch artist for the newspapers. She had already been published. She intended to be famous.

How could she save hundreds of lives? The general must be having delusions. Easing off the stool, she had one foot firmly on the ground when a man appeared at the tent flap, saluting the general.

"You sent for me, General Allen?" His deep mellow voice flowed over her jangled senses like warm honey.

She told herself not to gawk at the man who had just appeared. Staring wasn't polite. His well-tailored blue uniform accentuated his broad shoulders and tall, rugged physique. Russet hair, a full mustache a shade darker than his locks, and deep brown eyes complimented his tanned skin. He glowed in the gloom of the tent. She found herself holding her breath as she gazed at him.

"McGrath, come in. This young lady is Amanda Giles. Miss

Giles, may I present Captain Daniel McGrath?'' The captain
removed his hat and smiled at her.

She nodded at the captain politely, then stiffened at the way
he looked her up and down. His smile broadened into a grin.
Stunned by his striking appearance and the knowing way he
watched her, one thought leapt into her mind. *This* was the
type of man her mother had cautioned her about.

Amanda ignored the flutter in her midsection and forced
herself to speak courteously to the insolent captain. ''I'm very
pleased to meet you sir.'' She edged toward the opening in the
tent.

The captain's ungentlemanly gaze made her as uncomfortable as the general's babbling. She couldn't recall a man ever
looking at her quite that way.

Abruptly, the general reached out and grabbed her arm, turning her toward Captain McGrath.

''Miss Giles is Andrew's sister. Uncanny resemblance. Same
titian hair, same golden brown eyes. It will work.''

Pulling out of the general's grasp, she took a step toward
the captain. If she could make it around him, the entrance to
the tent was just paces away.

A frown creased Captain McGrath's forehead as he looked
down at her. He appeared to be confused, too. ''What will
work, sir?''

The general gestured toward Amanda impatiently. ''We will
use Miss Giles in her brother's place.''

''You can't be serious!'' Captain McGrath looked from the
general to Amanda. ''Send her?''

With those words the captain dismissed her as if she wasn't
worth consideration. Thoroughly annoyed, Amanda forgot for
a moment about leaving and watched as the two men glared
at each other.

Nothing got her attention faster than a challenge. Just what
made the captain think she was inadequate?

The general puffed out his chest. ''Must I remind you of the
lives at stake, captain?''

Captain McGrath's features hardened. "I haven't forgotten. But she's just a woman."

Amanda had heard enough.

Furious with both of them, Amanda addressed the general. "I have no idea what you two are talking about, sir, but I have no intention of being discussed as if I wasn't even here. My purpose in coming here today is done. I have delivered the papers and sketches Andrew said were vital."

McGrath crossed his arms over his wide chest with an air of resignation. "I rest my case, general. You can see for yourself how emotional and easily overwrought she is. She couldn't possibly be a part of the mission."

She turned and glowered at Captain McGrath, silently willing him to perdition.

General Allen appeared ready to explode. "Quiet, captain! I run this intelligence unit and I will collect information any way I see fit!"

Mission? Intelligence unit? Whatever did that mean? Amanda let her curiosity get the better of her. What if lives really were at stake? She supposed she could give General Allen a few more moments, especially if her staying would prove to irritate the patronizing Captain McGrath.

"General Allen, please explain."

General Allen looked enormously relieved at her acquiescence. Captain McGrath looked as if someone had set fire to one of his boots. She smiled to herself, pleased with the result.

The general took her hand. "Your brother had been working for months with a well-placed contact in the rebel army."

Amanda looked at him blankly. It took a moment for what the general had said to sink in. "Andrew? Andrew was working with a spy?"

The general nodded and patted her hand. "More than that. He did secret work for me, behind enemy lines."

"Andrew *was* a spy? He told me he was your aide." Amanda pulled her hand from the general's grasp and reached for the stool, afraid her rubbery knees wouldn't hold her up. The odd information her brother had dictated to her and the sketches he asked her to do for him as he lay dying now made sense.

The general's voice pulled her back to the present. "Because he looked so young, it was easy for him to pretend he was just a boy and slip into enemy territory without arousing suspicions. You are of a like size, I believe."

The general paused, as if he realized she needed time to absorb this startling information, then resumed his story. "When he expressed concern for your welfare I gave him leave to go home and see you. He was to finish a vital mission upon his return. The information we expected him to gather is essential to saving many lives. We were depending on him."

Amanda had depended on Andrew, too. He had been her best friend, and he believed in her talent. Now he was dead because he had come home to escort her to New York. Dead, not from the war, but from a case of typhoid fever. The misery of grief and guilt ate at her.

"Miss Giles, please, we need your help to get that information. We could pass you off for your brother."

Could she help? Could she do something to save the lives of men, to protect their families from the kind of misery she had so recently experienced?

Clearly exasperated, Captain McGrath interrupted. "General Allen, with all due respect I must protest. You can't expect this woman to take a man's place."

"I tell you, we have no choice!" The general squared off to face the captain, turning away from Amanda.

Amanda edged toward the tent flap as she watched the two men argue. Confused and overwhelmed, she felt as if she had fallen into the middle of a strange dream, and her only hope of waking was to get out of the tent. She needed time to think.

They were so involved in their discussion they didn't notice her leave. She could still hear their raised voices as she climbed into her hired carriage.

* * *

Back in her Cincinnati hotel room, Amanda took off her shoes and let down her hair. She sat with her sketch book open in her lap and pondered her bizarre visit to Camp Dennison. She couldn't stop thinking about what General Allen had said. Was there really something she could do, or was the general grasping at straws?

She heard a knock, and when she opened her door she found Captain McGrath standing in the hallway. Her first impulse was to slam the door in his face.

He must have read her thoughts, because he stuck out his hand and caught the edge of the door before she could close it on him.

"Miss Giles, please. I've come to apologize." Leaning a broad shoulder against the door frame, his indifferent tone sounded as if he wasn't the least bit sorry for anything.

"For what?" She stood her ground, pointedly not allowing him entry. She had no intention of being alone in a hotel room with this man, not after the rude way he had regarded her earlier.

Silent, he stood gazing at her.

"Well, sir?" Amanda returned his stare, unwilling to appear timid. He was so big, and they were alone at her hotel room door, for heaven's sake. All of her mother's dire warnings about men came to mind.

"I'm sorry if I said anything to offend you this morning."

Amanda looked him square in the eye. "General Allen told you to come here and apologize, didn't he?"

"General Allen *ordered* me to come here and apologize." Eyes flashing with anger, he threw the comment down like a gauntlet.

"You came all the way into town just to say that?"

"No. General Allen also *ordered* me to ask you to reconsider his request for your help." The emphasis in his voice underlined the fact that this was entirely General Allen's offer.

Now that she'd had time to think, she was sorely tempted to take the general up on his offer. How could she say no if lives were at stake? And she couldn't ignore the tempting opportunity to gain valuable material for her sketches at the same time.

Captain McGrath shifted uneasily at her silence. Feeling perverse, she had to admit that annoying the captain by agreeing to help also had appeal.

He was avoiding her look, and she enjoyed his discomfort at having to request anything from her. ''Do you expect me to say yes when I don't even know what you want me to do?''

Moving swiftly, he startled her by leaning forward and grasping her chin in his hand, his voice ominously soft. ''I *expect* you to be a reasonable woman and decline the general's offer out of hand.''

He might as well have waved a red flag in front of a bull. She'd show him, just as she would show everyone who thought she shouldn't go to New York and pursue a career.

Without giving the situation any more thought, Amanda drew herself up to her full height and slapped his hand away. Riled beyond telling, she fairly spit her words at the arrogant captain.

''You may go back to Camp Dennison and inform General Allen that I would be proud to work for him.''

Chapter 2

"This is probably the stupidest thing you will ever do."

Amanda Giles ignored Daniel McGrath's dire comment as she concentrated on getting up the gangplank of the paddle-wheeled steamer without tripping in her baggy trousers and too-large boots. Far below, the muddy water of the Ohio slapped and swirled below against the side of the boat.

The handsome captain had been directing warnings of calamitous consequences at her for more than an hour. She glanced over her shoulder at him, impressed by his steadfast tirade. She figured he would have noticed she wasn't paying attention and gotten tired of haranguing her by now.

He wasn't the first person to warn her about her impetuous nature. Her parents had come up with far more interesting adjectives than Captain McGrath had managed so far, but since he showed no sign of letting up, she hoped he would become more inventive as their quest proceeded.

Stopping at the top of the gangplank, she looked around to be sure their conversation wouldn't be overheard, then turned and faced the irate man.

"Captain, I understand that you are unhappy with this

arrangement, but I fully intend to see this mission through and proceed as directed by the general.''

Captain McGrath pushed back the brim of his battered felt hat with one long finger and leaned in so close to her she could see the flecks of gold in his deep brown eyes.

''General Allen's sanity is in question.'' He was hissing at her by the time he finished speaking, the skin on his face flushed by his heightened emotion.

A well-dressed couple came up behind them, interrupting their conversation. Captain McGrath took hold of her sleeve and pulled her into a deserted doorway. ''Only a crazy man would send a woman to do a job like this.''

The nerve of this man! This was not the first time he had expressed doubt about her abilities simply because of her gender. With an effort, she kept her temper in check.

''Only time will decide that point, captain.'' She knew Captain McGrath had been ordered to accompany her on this secret mission in spite of his vocal protests.

He leaned in even closer than before. ''What about your reputation? What will people think when they find out you dressed in men's clothing and traveled unchaperoned in a man's company?''

Amanda almost laughed at his change of tactics. She'd heard this argument before and had a ready answer. ''I do not care about a reputation, sir, good or bad.''

For the first time since she had met him, he looked nonplussed. ''How can you not care for your good name? How do you expect to marry a decent man without it?''

Another argument she found boring and familiar. She shrugged. ''I don't expect to marry at all. After we find the Confederate agent the general is so anxious to contact, I will go on to New York City.''

His heavy auburn brows drew together. ''Alone?'' He ran a hand over his full mustache.

She smiled at his look of disbelief. ''Yes, alone. I will travel alone and live alone. I plan to be a bohemian, Captain McGrath. Bohemians don't marry. They believe in free love.''

His hand dropped from his face and he opened his mouth and then closed it without saying anything. He was having much the same shocked reaction her parents had had before she had left home in Philadelphia. Of course, she hadn't mentioned the part about free love to them. They had been having a hard enough time with her plans without hearing that.

Amanda suspected that despite her determination to go, her mother and father might have tried to stop her if they hadn't been so grief-stricken over her brother's death. Andrew had always been their well-behaved child and they had gone into a decline after his sudden passing.

The shrill steam whistle sounded, signaling their imminent departure.

Still shaking his head over her last comment, Captain McGrath brushed past her and muttered, "Come with me," as a deck hand headed their way.

She had found a way to shock the captain speechless, and wondered how long the blessed silence might last. Amanda followed him to the door of a cabin, and he ushered her inside.

"Phew!" Amanda breathed through her mouth. Dark and cramped, the room smelled like the inside of an old shoe. Windowless, the only ventilation came from the doorway. Too small, she thought, too closed in. She couldn't imagine getting any sleep in here.

Captain McGrath threw his gear on one of the six bunks, and motioned to her to do the same. Her uneasiness about the accommodations escalated as she shrugged off her knapsack. She would have a problem staying in the confined space, but she wasn't about to admit any weakness to the captain. She took off her hat and ran her hand through her short hair.

"You cut off your hair!" He seemed more upset about that than everything else.

"Of course I did. It wouldn't stay up under this hat." Hair would grow back.

He grumbled under his breath. "Come on. We need to be out where you can be seen." He sounded resigned, as if he had finally decided to accept their situation. "Don't talk to anyone, and keep that hat down over your brow. Your disguise won't fool anyone who takes a really good look.''

Had she known her haircut would have such an effect on him, she would have shown him her short locks before they left Camp Dennison. Hopefully his new, more reasonable attitude would last through their journey, she thought as she followed him out the door.

Behind them she heard the scrape of wood against wood as the gangplank was dragged onto the boat.

They walked along the outside passage past crates and bales of goods being transported east. All she was supposed to do was stay out in the open. Both she and Captain McGrath would look for a man that resembled the sketch she had done from a description Andrew had given her before he died.

She hadn't mentioned to General Allen or Captain McGrath that she had an ulterior motive for agreeing to the general's plan. The material she could gather for her sketches would be invaluable. She had wired her editor from Cincinnati and he had offered to buy a series of sketches from her.

He headed toward the stern. She nearly had to trot to keep up with his long strides. Walking as far back on the boat as they could, they stood looking at the giant paddle wheel as it turned slowly around and around, churning up the muddy Ohio. Each slat made a sucking sound as it pulled out of the water, spraying a fine mist in their faces. The sound would cover their conversation.

Standing side by side at the rail on the lower level, she felt dwarfed by the captain's height and size. She could feel him watching her, and she concentrated on the dock workers as they scrambled to release lines holding the riverboat fast to its moorings.

''What are you going to do in New York, besides indulge in free love?'' His tone mocked her. He didn't look at her as he spoke, but down at the dock.

She didn't let his obvious mocking opinion of her plans bother her. ''I'm an artist. I will continue to submit sketches to the newspapers." She watched his profile for a reaction as he leaned powerful looking forearms on the carved railing.

He turned his head and studied her. "Andrew mentioned you could draw. I didn't know women worked for newspapers."

He had hit a sore spot. "They don't. I use my initials. They think I'm a man."

His raised eyebrows showed his surprise. "They've never met you in person? How did you get hired?"

Amanda shifted from foot to foot, uncomfortable with the turn in conversation. Wishing the newspaper would accept her work on its merits and ignore her gender, she hated the necessary subterfuge. "Andrew took my drawings to New York. They think he is 'A. Giles.' "

Her brother Andrew had been her staunchest supporter. He had come home on leave to escort her to New York, in spite of her parents' protests. The day before they were to leave, he had fallen ill. Three days later he died of typhoid fever.

Engine noise increased as the paddle wheel turned with greater speed. The boat slid away from the dock, first with a groan and then with a more steady throb. Amanda felt the vibration through the thick soles of her boots as they swung into the center of the river, settling into the current.

Increasingly uneasy under the captain's continued scrutiny, Amanda forced herself to stand calmly.

He jerked his thumb in the direction of the engine's sound. "Let's go."

As she followed him she could see that Captain McGrath knew the layout of the boat. He turned in and out of deserted little passages and by the time they came to a short metal stairway, she had lost her sense of direction.

He checked both ways to see if anyone watched them, then pushed open a door under the stairs and motioned her inside a short passageway that faced a heavy metal hatch. He grasped the wooden handle and swung it open.

Amanda flinched as she was hit with a tremendous blast of heat. The smell of smoke and the temperature of the air made breathing difficult.

"This is the furnace room." He drew her around in front of him so she could get a better view.

This must be what hell is like, she thought, transfixed. In a scene out of *Dante's Inferno*, a dozen men, stripped to the waist, cloth bandannas tied around their heads, worked to feed the fires. Their bodies glistened with sweat, and soot covered their arms. Smears of black marked pale faces where they wiped perspiration away with the backs of filthy hands.

All the stokers had well-developed shoulder and arm muscles from the back-breaking labor, but one man in particular caught her eye. He was half a head taller than any of the others, the blackest Negro she had ever seen. Effortlessly, he lifted huge shovels full of coal and tossed them into the fiery opening of the roaring furnace with a graceful rhythm, doing double the work of the other men.

Smoke burned her eyes and throat, and Amanda longed for a breath of fresh air. She was just about to turn to Captain McGrath and ask if they could leave when she thought she saw the big black man nod to him.

She shouted to be heard over the noise of the furnace room. "Do you know him? I think he's trying to get your attention."

"Come with me," he shouted in her ear, jerking her backwards by the collar of her jacket and slamming the hatch closed.

She stumbled, and he righted her, still hanging onto her jacket. Alarmed by his physical handling, she twisted out of his grip and hurried out of the narrow passageway.

Captain McGrath checked again to make sure they were alone under the stairs, then spun and pinned her against the wall with one big hand on her chest. Her head smacked against the wood siding and her hat fell off.

Heart pounding just under his palm, she grabbed his wrist and tried to push his hand away. She made no impression on his hold.

He leaned close, a look of menace clear on his face, and spoke threateningly in her ear. "How many times did I tell you not to speak out? You could cost someone their life."

She shivered both at his words and from the sensation of his warm breath against her cheek.

Chastised and shaken, she managed an apology. He was right, she hadn't been thinking.

Abruptly his hand dropped and she sagged against the wall, afraid her shaking legs wouldn't hold her up. After a few moments, her breathing returned to normal and she stooped to pick up her hat.

When she finally got up the nerve to look at him, he was standing very still, turned away from her so she couldn't see his face.

He cleared his throat. "I apologize. I shouldn't have handled you like that. Now maybe you understand why I think this is such a poor idea."

The strained silence stretched between them, awkward and heavy.

Amanda rubbed the sore spot where her head had made contact with the wall. What the captain failed to realize was she had understood from the beginning his feelings about her part in this mission. She had chosen to ignore his opinion. She ran her fingers through her short curly hair and put her hat back on.

Finally Captain McGrath leaned close to her and made a frustrated gesture at the passageway behind them, then broke the uncomfortable lull. "I brought you down here so you could see the man who nodded at me. His name is Tobias. I wanted him to know you're with me. If things go bad, you find him. He'll help you." His low voice held a harsh edge.

If things went bad? Amanda tried to concentrate on what the captain was saying. He stood so near she could smell him, a masculine scent she found unsettling. She saw the outline of his upper lip under the mustache and felt the warmth his body gave off. Taking a deep breath, she forced herself to focus on his voice.

". . . so I don't want it known that Tobias and I talk. That goes for others on this boat, too. This is the last time I'll warn you. Watch your mouth or you'll give us away." He stared at her lips.

She nodded in reply, afraid her voice would prove unsteady

if she tried to speak. He pulled back and, to her relief, put some distance between them. She wasn't sure what unsettled her more, what he was saying or his proximity.

"Let's go sit up on the bow. We make a stop in the next half hour. We can watch from there."

She ventured a question. "Do you think the man we're looking for will meet us there?" She hoped that they would meet him later rather than sooner. She wanted more material for her sketches.

Captain McGrath shrugged. "Possibly."

The general was convinced that she would look so much like her brother if she dressed in men's clothing the Confederate agent who had been working with Andrew would approach her. Then Captain McGrath would take over.

Andrew was the only one who had ever met with the mystery man. All they had to go on was a sketch she had done from Andrew's description of the agent.

Time was wasting. She needed to get busy. "All right if I get my sketch book?"

He nodded. After they stopped at the cabin and she grabbed a pad and pencil, they returned to the forward part of the ship. Captain McGrath sprawled on a bench. He looked half asleep, his handsome face turned up to the warm sun.

His casual pose did not deceive her. She was sure he saw everything going on around them. Amanda looked carefully to make sure no one could hear them.

"Captain?"

"Yeah?" He didn't move.

"Who exactly is the agent, the man in the sketch?" She was curious about what kind of man would spy for an enemy.

Head turned, he studied her for a long, unnerving moment, as if he was trying to decide what to tell her. "I don't know anything about him except that he supplied Andrew with good information. Information we need."

They didn't know who he was or where he'd meet them. All in all, the general's whole plan for her to connect up with this shadowy character still seemed rather optimistic to

Amanda. She picked up her pad and tried hard to concentrate on her sketch.

Captain Daniel McGrath watched Miss Giles as she hunched over her sketch pad, scribbling furiously. She sat cross-legged on a crate, leaning against a huge coil of rope, oblivious to everything but her drawing.

Damn General Allen anyway. The man was insane to think his stratagem would work. He had made his authority clear when Daniel protested using Miss Giles in the scheme. Daniel remembered the general's words clearly. If the captain failed to follow the orders, he would face a court-martial.

Daniel wanted to smack Amanda on her nicely rounded bottom and send her back to her family where she belonged, but he wasn't willing to risk his future by disobeying a direct order.

After giving the situation a lot of thought, Daniel figured he could go along with the hare-brained scheme for a couple of reasons. The general's plan had little hope of working. The agent they were to contact was bound to notice something amiss and not risk an encounter. And they were fairly safe because they were in a very public place. As long as she kept a watch on her mouth. A slip like the one in the furnace room in front of the wrong person could spell trouble.

He hadn't meant to be rough with her. Afterwards she had looked scared, so he hoped he had gotten his point across.

The soft curve of her cheek glowed in the late afternoon light. Never before had he encountered such a stubborn, willful female. Free love. Ha! He wondered if she had any idea what she was talking about.

Andrew had mentioned his family. Amanda had been raised in a respectable household. Had her father lost his mind to let her go alone to live in a place like New York City?

Despite all her talk of being independent, Daniel had the feeling that he needed to protect Amanda, a feeling he didn't like. In his line of work he didn't even need a partner, let alone a ward.

He must have made a noise, because she glanced up at him. When he didn't say anything, she went back to her drawing.

The facial resemblance she bore to her brother Andrew was remarkable, but Daniel remembered how she had looked when she came to camp to deliver Andrew's papers and reports, the graceful curve of her slender waist and enticing roundness of her full breasts under her fashionable dress.

She could be taken for a boy sitting there, he mused, her female curves hidden by her loose clothing, but as soon as she moved no one who was walking behind her would doubt her gender.

Smiling, he also remembered the incredulous look on her face when General Allen had informed her that her brother had been spying for the Army Secret Service. Her pretty, full mouth had dropped open in surprise, her big eyes round as saucers. The battered old hat she wore constantly jammed down over her forehead now hid the upper part of her face, including those amber-colored eyes fringed with thick brown lashes.

And her hair. That beautiful thick mass of golden red hair had been cut down to a curly cap. What a crime. After he had gone to her hotel room to deliver the general's plea, Daniel had imagined that hair swirling loose around her naked white shoulders.

She showed spirit, if not sense, in going along with the general's plan. Daniel couldn't figure out why she would willingly put herself in such danger.

He scanned the deck and then returned to his study of Amanda. Her drawing took shape as she labored over the paper. The girl had artistic talent, that much was obvious, even to Daniel's untrained eye. The picture of the paddle wheel and the turbulence of the water came alive with detail as she labored over the drawing, the soft flesh of her bottom lip caught by her small white teeth in her concentration.

He wondered what she had done to flatten her breasts, unable to forget her feminine figure. Since he'd first seen her in camp, he'd been having lustful thoughts about her. Hell, he imagined every man in camp had had ideas of being alone with her. He shifted positions on the bench, drawing one knee up to hide the obvious strain against his trouser buttons, deciding it would be prudent to find a new train of thought.

Women were not cut out to do this kind of work. Too emotional. Daniel liked everything to fit in its proper place, and as pretty and appealing as this girl was, this was not her proper place. What rankled most was there wasn't anything he could do about it. He went back to reading the paper.

The steam whistle over the pilot house gave two sharp blasts. Amanda shifted position and peered over the rail. A deck hand yelled at her to move as he grabbed the rope she had used as a backrest, dumping her off the crate.

Daniel stifled a smile at the unladylike comment that sprang from her lips. Her comments were turning as rough as her clothing, he thought. At least everyone was treating her like a boy.

She closed her sketch book and faced him. "Where are we?"

Daniel pointed toward the dock and she followed the direction of his finger. "New Richmond."

As the paddlewheeler neared the mooring, Daniel found a deserted part of the deck and stood at the rail. He scanned the crowd, looking for a man resembling the one in the sketch, then glanced down at Amanda. She studied each of the individuals waiting to board.

He turned his gaze back to the people, lingering for a long time on two men standing off by themselves. They seemed to be looking for someone. He recognized them from a previous trip and had every reason to believe they were rebel agents.

When one of them turned to look up at where they stood, Daniel stepped back out of sight into the shadow of a passageway. It would be to his advantage to remain anonymous. He remained there for several moments before rejoining her at the rail. If the two were Confederate agents, it signaled the failure of Daniel and Amanda's mission. The contact wouldn't dare show his face with them on board.

Amanda gave him a questioning look but made no comment on his behavior. Good sign. Maybe she was learning to keep her tongue behind her teeth.

The paddlewheeler shuddered to a halt. Workers loaded luggage on the lowest deck as the passengers, including the two he had spotted, boarded.

Within minutes they were underway again. Daniel and Amanda watched the landscape in silence. She took a step closer to him.

"Who were those two men?" She jerked her head toward the dock.

He remained still, peering into the water. How much should he tell her? A thought occurred to him. The general had insisted he take her along, but if *she* got scared and left of her own accord, the general couldn't hold Daniel responsible. He could take the sketch and go on without her. He sensed she was about to repeat the question and he turned slightly toward her.

"I've seen them on this boat before. They do the same thing we do."

She thought for a moment, a little line of concentration furrowing the skin between her delicate arched brows. "But you don't know them? Are they from another camp?"

He shook her head at her naïveté. Scaring her away might be easier than he thought. "You could say that. They're not Federal agents."

She nodded and looked ill-at-ease. "Do you think they are looking for the same man we are?"

She was getting scared, and he could see it on her face. Now was his chance to get her off the boat and save his career at the same time.

"Without a doubt." He paused, looking behind him, then turning back to her. "They probably have orders to kill him." He put his forefinger under her chin and gently closed her gaping mouth. Let her chew on that bit of fiction for a while.

An hour later, just before the Foster stop, Daniel pulled Amanda away from the rail and guided her between two pallets of cargo. He spoke in low tones, forcing urgency into his voice, hoping he had sufficiently frightened her into wanting to leave.

"This situation has become too dangerous. We can get you off here at Maysville."

"Don't be silly." She bristled. "I owe it to Andrew's friend to warn him!"

Daniel wanted to shake her until her teeth rattled and she got some sense. "He's not a *friend*, he's a paid *informant*, and he can take care of himself!"

Her chin had that mulish set that he found had become all too familiar. "I don't care what you choose to call him, I'm not leaving without trying to warn him and get the information from him."

Daniel pointed to his chest with a gesture of exasperation. "I'll stay on board and warn him!"

She nodded, as if everything were settled to her satisfaction. "Good. We'll stick to the original plan. I'm staying with you!"

They stood and glared at one another, until Daniel finally gave up trying to intimidate her, turned and headed back to the rail, muttering under his breath. Damned headstrong female. She didn't have enough sense to be scared. He stood staring out at the riverbank until an old man came by, selling meat pies and cider.

While they ate a cold supper, word spread that a poker game was about to commence, and Daniel thought he should spend some time at the table. Men tended to wander in and out all night observing the play. It would be a good place to see and be seen.

"I'm going to get into that game."

She looked startled. "You're going to play poker? Tonight?"

He nodded, tired of explaining every move to her. "And you're going to stick close, listen, and be quiet. Go along with whatever I say and keep your mouth closed. If anyone sees through your disguise, our mission is over."

She got that belligerent look again. "What if someone talks to me?"

Exasperated, he scowled at her. "Don't answer. Are you worried about being impolite? Let the men think you're a mute."

Amanda was exhausted by the long day, and thoroughly annoyed at Daniel's sour attitude. She suspected he had been trying to scare her earlier to get her off the boat, but she wasn't taking any chances. She would be more than happy not to say a word. She followed him down the deck.

They entered a cabin similar to their own. Five chairs crowded a small table. Amanda recognized the two men already seated—a deckhand and a passenger who had come on board at the last stop.

Daniel motioned to her to sit on one of the lower bunks as he took a seat at the table. She scooted until her back was against the wall and sat in the deep shadows, where she could watch everyone and still be inconspicuous. Amanda paid close attention to details, figuring the scene would make a good sketch for her series. The men discussed the limits of the bets and waited for the last two chairs to fill.

Moments later she heard footsteps on the deck outside and glanced up to see the two men Daniel thought might be Confederate agents. Her breath caught in her chest. The rat and the slug, she thought as she watched them come in the room. Those were the creatures she had thought of the first time she had seen them down on the dock, and up close she could see she was right. The back of her neck tingled with an unpleasant sensation.

They took the last places at the table, and introduced themselves as Wardley and Bodin. Amanda shifted uncomfortably on the bunk as the rat-faced Bodin's eyes darted around the room, stopping when he got to her. Feeling his gaze on her made her skin crawl.

"Who's the kid?" He peered at her. "Ain't he kinda young to be here?"

"The boy's my brother." Daniel offered no other explanation. Bodin shifted his glance to study Daniel. Daniel returned the stare until Bodin looked away with a shrug.

The deckhand became impatient. "We gonna play or trace family histories?" He motioned to the man holding the cards to deal, and the game began.

With the men busy playing, she had the perfect opportunity to observe the players. Wardley, the slug, looked like something you might find under a rock. He didn't speak at all, and had a soft, repulsive appearance about him, except for his hands. Huge and square, his knuckles cracked as he flexed his fingers repeatedly.

The other one, Bodin, was his opposite, slight, dark, and nervous. He twitched in his seat and kept up a running conversation in a high-pitched voice, fiddling with his cards and chips, and telling crude stories that made her ears burn.

The game dragged on uneventfully for more than two hours. Amanda wasn't sure of the rules, but Daniel had a bigger pile of chips in front of him than any of the others, so she assumed he was winning.

Passengers wandered in and out to watch the game. Amanda studied each person who entered the room, hopeful of seeing someone who resembled the sketch she had done from Andrew's description of his contact, but not one man bore the slightest similarity.

The game continued until around midnight, when the deckhand announced he had to go to work, and gave up his seat. As far as she could tell, nothing of any benefit to her and Daniel had been said. She had listened to all the conversation. Most of it had been disgusting, all of it uninformative, as far as she could tell. She was beginning to wonder if Daniel had made up the story of Wardley and Bodin being agents to scare her.

The players decided to take a break, and Daniel approached Amanda.

"Time for bed." He pulled her off the bunk.

"Aw, do I have to? It's not that late." She mumbled, hoping her protest sounded convincing. No young boy she knew ever went to bed willingly.

"Sure do. Big day tomorrow." He pulled her jacket up around her shoulders more snugly and buttoned the top button. "I'll be there in a little while. Go on." He gave her a little push toward the door.

Grumbling to herself, she was secretly delighted to be leaving the smoky, noisy room. Let Daniel keep an eye on his enemy agents. She needed some sleep.

Bracing herself against her aversion to the small space, she paused at the doorway to their assigned accommodations. To her relief, the other bunks were empty. She and Daniel appeared to be the sole residents so far.

The only way she would be able to tolerate being inside the dank cabin would be to leave the door open. She crawled around her bag into the corner bunk, pulled off her boots, and curled up next to the wall. Closing her eyes, she imagined being in an open meadow, looking up at a wide, blue sky.

Thinking about open spaces always calmed her. Little by little Amanda relaxed. Water lapped against the side of the boat and the engines hummed. She welcomed the drowsiness. She had expected excitement, and instead the day had turned into one tiresome battle with the pigheaded Captain Daniel McGrath. At least she had some scenes for her sketches, she thought as she drifted off to sleep.

In the middle of a dream where she and Andrew chased fireflies into paper lanterns hanging from the antlers of motionless reindeer, voices intruded. She tried to shush them and tell them not to frighten the animals, but in her dream her own words were without sound.

Gradually she awakened and realized the whispering voices were not part of her dream. The murmuring drifted in through the door.

"Maysville." A pronounced southern drawl dominated a nasal voice.

"You sure?" Same drawl, different voice. Neither voice sounded like Bodin.

"Yup. Sent word. They'll give us a sample of the guns and the location."

She lay very still, not wanting to miss a thing.

"We give 'em the gold, just like before?"

"Yup. Same as before."

The more bits and pieces she heard, the more intrigued she became. Excitement vibrated in her like a living thing. At last, something thrilling was happening. This wasn't what they had come for, but she wasn't one to look a gift horse in the mouth.

The men stopped talking abruptly and she heard footsteps hurrying away. Something must have startled them. Amanda lay so still and tense her leg muscles cramped. Finally, sure they were gone, she crept out of the bunk, not stopping to put on her boots or hat. She needed to get to Daniel, to give him the information. She'd show him!

She tried to remember their itinerary as she crept to the door of their cabin. How much time did they have until they got to Higginsport? Quietly, she stood for several moments, listening. Cautiously, she stuck her head out, looking up and down the deserted deck.

Heart pounding with anticipation, she tiptoed toward the poker game. She couldn't wait to see the look on his face when she told him what she had heard.

Dampness from the deck soaked through her socks. She heard noisy laughter and saw light spilling out of the open doorway, and let out a sigh of relief. Not that she would ever admit to the mighty Captain McGrath that she had been nervous about running into the two men she had heard talking.

At that moment, someone grabbed her from behind and lifted her off the deck. One hand around her waist and the other clamped over her mouth, he pulled her backward into a dark passageway. Terrified, she fought and tore at the massive arm holding her, kicking back wildly with her feet. Her heels thudded harmlessly against the legs of her attacker. Frantically, she wished she had taken the time to put on her boots.

The hand covering her face cut off her breath, despite her frenzied struggles. The smell of smoke hung heavy in her nostrils. Just when she thought she might faint from lack of breath, she realized that the rumble of sound coming from the muscular chest behind her was the phrase ''friend to Daniel'' being whispered over and over. She calmed a little and the hand loosened just enough for her to gulp a breath of air. She forced herself to quiet a bit more and again the hand relaxed a fraction. Amanda focused on the voice whispering in her ear.

''If you promises not to yell, I lets you down. I has a message for Dan'l.''

She nodded her head as best she could, and the vise-like grip relaxed around her waist. She slid down his body until her feet hit the floor. Her knees buckled and she gasped for breath.

Two giant hands held her and turned her around. She stared at Tobias, the Negro from the furnace room. His white teeth flashed in the dark passageway.

"You sure got a heap of fight in you for such a skinny little one," he murmured quietly.

Amanda stood staring at him, her chest heaving for breath, her knees wobbly as a new calf's. "What did you do that for?" She wheezed at him, shaken.

"I gots to get a message to Dan'l, and I cain't takes the chance of bein' seen." Tobias let go of her and she braced herself against the wall.

"Well, what is it?" she squeaked, not fully recovered from the fright.

He motioned her to be quiet. "You all got to leave this here boat at Portsmouth. You cain't stay on t' Higginsport. Some men making plans to make yo' trip to Virginia less than hospitable. Can you get to Dan'l right away?"

Amanda nodded. She figured Tobias had to be talking about the same men she had overheard. "Are there two of them?"

Tobias shrugged his giant shoulders. "Don't knows how many." He started at a scraping noise. "Gots to go."

She nodded and watched Tobias melt away into the darkness. Braced against the wall, she remained in the passageway for a few moments trying to calm her frazzled nerves, then, unwilling to waste any time, moved down to the poker cabin. She stood in the door, staring at Daniel, willing him to look up. She didn't trust the steadiness of her voice to call to him.

Sleeves rolled up, Daniel concentrated on his cards. He hadn't had a run of luck like this in years. Feeling someone watching him, he glanced up from another winning hand and saw Amanda. Wearing her rumpled clothes and no boots, only filthy socks, the girl stood in the doorway looking like she'd seen a ghost.

"I'm out." He stood and folded his cards, crossing immediately to where she waited, unmindful of the grumbling from the other players. He put his hands on her shoulders and felt her trembling. "What's the matter?"

She backed out into the passageway. "Bad dream. I need to tell you about it right now." He saw her chin quiver and heard one of the men at the table mutter something about a sissy.

Daniel went back to the table to scoop up his winnings. "That's all for me tonight, gentlemen." He ignored a howl of protest from the other players as he led her back to their cabin.

Lighting the lantern, he checked to make sure they were alone before closing the door. "Now, you want to tell me what this is about?"

Amanda looked as if she might cry. She told him about a warning from Tobias, and how he had grabbed her from behind and scared her.

Daniel watched her intently as she spoke. She got a hold of herself and relayed everything she had heard and what Tobias had told her. Daniel was impressed. She might have just saved their lives.

"Well, you surely earned your keep tonight. The two you heard talking couldn't have been Wardley and Bodin. They never left the game."

"I know, their voices were different. I was afraid if I moved to get a look at them they'd see me." She ran trembling hands through her short curly hair.

"You did fine." Now he had some work to do. What was he going to do with her to keep her out of harm's way? "We'll find a safe place for you to hide."

She made a face at his statement and shook her head. "Oh, no. I'm going with you. I don't want to miss this."

Daniel watched as she pulled her boots on over her sodden socks and found her hat, ready to follow him out the door. She had more gumption than any woman he had ever met.

He hated to put her in jeopardy, but he did need her help to find the men who were after them. He eyed her closely, trying to determine if she would hold up under the strain of the evening. Reassured she was all right, he had to hand it to her. Amanda definitely had courage.

Resigned to taking her along, he motioned to her to follow him. "We'll walk around and see if you recognize any voices. Maybe we can find our men and then get off this boat." At least if she was with him he could keep an eye on her.

She took a deep breath and pulled herself together as they ventured back out. How hard could it be to find the two men? The boat wasn't all that large. Many people remained on deck despite the late hour, enjoying the warm evening air. No wonder, she thought, considering what the cabins smelled like.

For almost an hour they wandered around the deck, stopping near any group they found. She strained so much to overhear conversations, she gave herself a headache. No one sounded like the two men she had overheard. Exhausted by the strain, Amanda sat on a barrel and leaned against a crate. Daniel squatted at her feet on the stretch of deserted deck.

"Maybe we'll have some luck in the . . ." His whisper stopped abruptly at the sound of shuffling on the other side of the crate. He put his finger to his lips and they both stayed motionless, listening.

Amanda heard the voice. It was him. Her eyes widened and nodded silently at Daniel.

"Higginsport coming up." The sound of a match being struck and the smell of tobacco smoke filled the air.

"What about the Yankee? Found him yet?"

"No."

"You sure he knows?"

"Can't take the chance."

"We better kill him *before* we make the exchange."

Amanda felt her stomach turn over. Were they were talking about Daniel? Her nerves twitched. She prayed she wouldn't vomit.

"And the kid?"

"Him too."

Chapter 3

Just like that, the disembodied voice of the man they had been searching for announced that Amanda and Daniel were going to be murdered. No sound of emotion or hesitation flavored the statement.

Amanda took shallow little breaths through her mouth, trying to calm her stomach. The meat pie she had eaten for supper threatened to resurface as the conversation continued.

"When?"

"As soon as we find them. They aren't in their cabin."

"How?"

"You got your knife?"

"Yup."

"Quiet like. Then throw them overboard. No one will ever know."

Her rate of breathing increased.

"I'll meet you back here in a half an hour." Footsteps moved away, in opposite directions.

Daniel loomed up beside her and grasped her arm to pull her close while he whispered in her ear. "Stay put. I mean it. I'll be back."

He shoved her back between two huge crates and left before she could complain about being left behind. She should have followed him, but now she didn't know which way he had gone.

He left her here and those men were coming back. What if they got here before he did? What if they hurt him? Amanda had no weapon, and no watch to judge the passage of time. How was she supposed to defend herself if she needed to?

She imagined she could still feel his warm breath on her cheek as she wedged herself back as far behind the crate as she could get. There was nothing to do but sit and wait. She rested her chin on her knees and tried to count the minutes but found her thoughts jumped around too much to keep track of the time.

As silently as he left, Daniel reappeared in the small space between the cargo and loomed over her.

"Now we wait for the other one. Hold this."

Amanda gave a great sigh of relief at the sound of his whisper. Thank goodness, he was safe. He pressed a key into her hand and she slipped it into the pocket of her jacket. As curious as she was, she didn't risk speaking to ask him what had happened.

He hunched down in the narrow space in front of her, his back leaning against her knees. She welcomed the solid wall of warmth he presented, a formidable barrier between her and the bad men.

They waited in silence. Again they heard the sound of a match striking and caught the acrid smell of burning tobacco. Daniel rose and moved noiselessly around the crate. Amanda's heart thudded painfully. She resisted an urge to reach out and pull him back. *Let him be all right,* she chanted to herself over and over until she heard the sound of flesh hitting flesh.

She heard a grunt and a scuffle; then curses rang out in the quiet. Surely the noise the men made could be heard above the steady pulse of the engines. How could she stay where she was if Daniel might need her help not ten feet away?

Amanda wriggled from her hiding place. Someone rushed past her, knocking her down.

It was Bodin.

She saw his profile as he climbed the rail and paused for a moment. He turned his head and stared at her with his beady little eyes, then jumped over the side. She'd remember the evil look he gave her if she lived to be a hundred. With a shudder she watched him disappear into the churning black water.

More sounds of fighting came from the other side of the stack of crates. Daniel couldn't fight several of them at once. Frantically Amanda looked for something she might use as a weapon. She grabbed a small keg. Then she heard a familiar soft voice and realized Tobias had arrived to help Daniel.

Abruptly the noise of the fighting stopped and the huge Negro man appeared with a body slung over his shoulder, moving soundlessly out of sight.

Amanda stood frozen to the spot, wondering what had happened to Daniel. She jumped violently when she felt a hand close on her shoulder. Daniel pried the keg out of her hands.

"It's over. We got three of them." Daniel's voice sounded normal.

He acted so calm as he set the cask down on the deck. No excitement, no strain showed in his tone. He'd killed a man, or men, just like that.

The aftermath of all the excitement hit her. Amanda fought down a wave of nausea.

"There were four. I saw Bodin go over the rail." To her dismay, her voice quavered as she spoke.

Daniel peered into the dark water, his expression unreadable. "Are you all right?"

"I'm fine." She attempted a smile. Bile rose in her throat and she made it to the rail before she vomited.

When she had finished disgracing herself, Daniel didn't say a word, to her relief. He led her to the first-class deck and knocked quietly on a cabin door. When he got no response, he used the key he had given her to unlock the door.

He drew curtains over the small windows and lit the lantern. Amanda looked around. What a switch from their mean little room with smelly bunks. Nicely furnished, this cabin even had its own bathroom. Amanda went in and rinsed out her mouth, then splashed cold water on her face. She felt drained, like a bucket with a hole punched in the bottom.

She sank down on a chair and watched him. "Whose cabin is this?"

Daniel shrugged. "Not sure. Found the key in Wardley's pocket."

He began to look through drawers, showing no sign of feeling any emotions over killing the men who had attacked him. She wondered, *If you do it enough do you get used to it?*

Exhausted, Amanda watched as he methodically searched the room. Nothing but clothes in the closet. Two large leather cases sat in the corner between a desk and a bed. They looked like the sample cases she had seen shoe salesmen open up when they came to the door. Daniel dragged one to the center of the room. The muscles in his arms bulged with the effort. If these contained shoes, they certainly were heavy ones.

He took a tool from his pocket that looked like a metal shank and pried open the latches on the case. Absently she wondered if he always carried the tool. She felt strangely detached, as if she were a spectator at a play.

When he raised the lid she saw more clothing. He lifted the garments out and dumped them on the floor. There was an obvious false bottom fitted into the luggage. When he pried it up, the soft gleam of gold glowed in the lamplight. The small bars of metal seemed to give off light of their own.

"Holy Moses," she exclaimed.

He turned and glanced at her. "Yeah. Holy Moses."

"How much?"

"More than I care to carry." Lowering the lid, he tried the other case. They were identical.

She stared with fascination. "How much is it worth?"

"Enough to buy a hell of a lot of guns and ammunition." He replaced the garments on top of the flap hiding the treasure.

Amanda, her fatigue forgotten in the excitement of the moment, scooted to the edge of her chair. "Where did they get it?"

He tucked the clothes in and lowered the lid. "England, probably."

How could that be? "But England is in sympathy with the Union."

He gave her a look that made her feel silly for asking. "Politics and business are two very different things. Ever read an author named James? *Smuggler II*? He said it pretty well. 'All's fair in love and war.' "

Was "All fair?" she thought. Even the way those men had planned to murder them? Before this, Amanda had thought of war in vague terms of brave men on a field of valor. How naive she had been.

Searching through clothes laid out on the bed, Daniel found some papers in a coat pocket. After glancing at them, he put them in one of the cases.

"We get off at the next stop. I'll go get our things and come back here. It'll be safer to stay here than to move the gold. Lock yourself in."

Safer? Amanda shuddered, remembering the look of pure hatred Bodin had given her just before he jumped over the side. She would feel safer if she knew for sure he had gotten what he deserved and drowned like a rat.

Chapter 4

Daniel sat in the late afternoon shade in front of his tent, flicking sharply against his thigh the canteen strap that he had been mending. Only two legs of his chair rested on the ground as he leaned back against one of the giant hickory trees that sheltered the encampment, thinking up various ways to get rid of Amanda Giles. If he leaned just a little to his right he would be able to see her, sitting in her tent.

No one in camp had seen past her disguise because he had kept her confined to her tent since they had returned at dawn. He was not about to let her out among the other men. If anyone with half a brain paid the least bit of attention to her, they would be able to tell she was a woman.

Their mission to find Andrew's contact yesterday had been a dismal failure, but at least they hadn't come away empty-handed. Losing all that gold had to be a blow to the rebels.

His attention wandered back to Amanda. The girl was a puzzle. Daniel would have bet a month's wages she'd leave today after the scare she took on the boat, but here she was, stuck in a smelly little tent, willfully enduring the hardship of life in camp.

She refused to go until she saw General Allen. She kept saying she had made him a promise, and only he could release her.

The problem was that no one seemed to have any idea when the general would return. Daniel wanted Amanda gone now. Out of his sight. Then maybe he could get her out of his mind.

The memories of how she had looked on the boat after they had taken care of the Confederate agents haunted his thoughts. Scared silly, she had stood there with a keg of nails clutched in her small hands, ready to save him from men who were planning to kill both of them.

He had told her to stay where she was, had made sure she had a safe hiding place. Did she listen to him? No. The idiotic woman had decided she needed to defend him, armed only with a drum of penny nails.

When it was over, he had wanted to kiss her and turn her over his knee at the same time. Fortunately he hadn't been able to do either because she had been too busy losing her supper over the rail. He smiled, remembering how embarassed she had been.

He was becoming very familiar with the mulish set of her little chin. Silly female. He slapped the leather strap across his pant leg, raising a small cloud of dust. Why couldn't Andrew's sister have been one of those simpering females given to the vapors? Any normal woman would have fled camp after one night in a tent. Hell, any normal female would never have agreed to be part of this preposterous situation in the first place.

She'd spent hours confined to her tent, hunched over her paper, pencil flying. The afternoon had turned unseasonably warm, and by now she must be roasting with the heat, but she had yet to complain.

Every once in a while he'd lean forward and watch her. Those golden eyes of hers didn't miss anything, and her sketches captured scenes with incredible realism. Even with his untrained eye he could tell she had a rare artistic talent.

Daniel suspected that Andrew's contact would never resurface. If the general were here, Daniel could talk him into releasing Amanda from her commitment.

After one last stinging slap of leather, Daniel brought the front two legs of his chair back on the ground with a thud. He needed a distraction. He pushed himself to his feet, dropped the strap on his seat and headed toward the building housing the infirmary.

Daniel stood just inside the door, squinting into the semi-darkness of the empty room. The smell of lye and carbolic acid hung in the still air.

"Michael, are you in here?" Daniel heard a rustling sound and waited as his friend emerged from behind the curtain.

Dr. Michael Jervis motioned Daniel to join him at the back of the building. "I have coffee. Care to join me?"

"Sure." Daniel followed him past the curtain into his living area. Books, big heavy medical texts, were spread out all over the cot. Michael stacked them to one side to make room, and motioned Daniel to sit in the chair.

"What are you trying to do here, Michael, learn how to become a doctor?" He smiled as he kidded his oldest friend.

"No, just trying to sort out a baffling problem I keep running into when I'm treating a certain type of dysentery." Michael poured two cups of thick-looking black coffee from a pot sitting on a little stove in the corner.

He handed a cup to Daniel. "Thought I might find some answers among all these books. I certainly have plenty of time to read."

Daniel nodded in agreement and took a sip of the disagreeable brew. The beds in the infirmary were empty. "I guess we should all be grateful when you don't have much to do." He sat down and rested his elbows on his knees, staring at the rough flooring.

Michael handed him a tin mug. "Tell me about your trip. Did you find what you were after?"

"Yes, and no. I had to cut the trip a little short, but I got something I hadn't bargained for." Actually, they got a whole lot more than they bargained for.

It bothered Daniel that Bodin had gotten away. He had sent a description of him and an order for his arrest on sight to all the Union Army encampments along the Ohio River, even though chances were good the man had drowned before he made it to shore.

Placing the mug on the floor, Daniel stood and paced restlessly around the small area. He needed to talk about Amanda, but he couldn't. He had promised the general not to reveal her identity. Besides, how could he discuss the feelings he had for this girl when he couldn't clearly define them himself? He massaged the back of his neck.

Michael broke the long silence. "How about the young man you took along. How did he work out?"

Daniel glanced at his friend with surprise. "How did you know I took someone along?"

Michael laughed. "This camp is like a small town. Word gets around."

Daniel clenched and flexed his hands, trying to relieve the tension he felt. "We worked well together." His admission surprised him. They hadn't accomplished what they had set out to do and she hadn't followed his directions.

Michael pointed to Daniel's fists. "What's bothering you?"

Daniel lowered his big frame back into the chair. Pausing, he tried to find the right words to question Michael without raising his suspicions. Maybe her disguise wasn't as effective as he had hoped. "What did you hear about him?"

Michael shrugged. "Why? Didn't things go well?"

Daniel was slow to answer, picking his words carefully. "No, no, that's not it. I don't really think it's him at all. I think it's me."

"You want my opinion?" Michael asked.

Daniel nodded.

"Maybe you've been at this job too long. Placing yourself in danger. Perhaps it's time to get out." Michael paused to rub his hands over his face. "It's already been a year, and no one thought the war would last this long."

"Maybe you're right." They hadn't even touched on what

was really bothering Daniel. Oh, he thought about his safety. Every time he went out he took a risk. But he had never had the urge to kiss a fellow agent before. That kind of distraction could have gotten them both killed. He had to make sure there would not be a second opportunity.

"I've got to get back." He didn't want to leave her alone in camp for too long. "Thanks for the coffee."

"Anytime." Michael shook his hand.

Daniel headed back to his tent, thinking about what Michael had said. Whistling to himself, he decided it wasn't the work that was the problem, it was the boredom. He just had too much time to think. He passed by the back side of Amanda's tent and strode over to the camp kitchen.

Daniel greeted the cook. "Hey, Jeddy, you old dogrobber. How about a trip into town tonight after supper? What do you say?" He leaned against the heavy wooden table, sampling one of the old Indian fighter's famous biscuits.

"Sure, Captain. I think I could be talked into a little female entertainment. I'll get a couple of the boys to clean up for me here, and we can leave directly after everybody's fed."

The old cook wiped his hands on the towel tied around his waist, and shoved another pan of biscuits over the fire. Jeddy wanted a woman. Daniel had been thinking more in terms of a card game and a couple of beers.

"We going to take that kid you got hid out in the tent along?" He gestured in Amanda's direction.

Daniel choked a little. He cleared his throat and turned to Jeddy. "I don't think that's a good idea."

Jeddy took a fork and shoved the pan into position. " 'Course it is. The boy can't stay in that tent forever."

"Not tonight." Appetite gone, he tossed the last of the biscuit to a waiting squirrel.

Although, he thought sourly, it might be a way to be rid of her. He wondered if a trip to a whorehouse would shock her into leaving for New York, or if she would just drag out her sketch pad and start doing portraits of all the soiled doves.

Daniel pulled a handkerchief from his pocket and mopped

his face. He should get her out for some fresh air before she had heatstroke. He headed for her tent and found her where he had seen her last, sitting just inside, sketchbook on her knees.

Amanda looked up at Daniel with her big, whiskey-colored eyes and smiled. He felt like someone had punched him in the gut. His voice was more harsh than he had intended. "You staying out of trouble?"

"Yes sir." Face flushed, Amanda winked at him, then ducked her head and quickly went back to her task. "Where *aren't* you taking me tonight?"

She had overheard his conversation with Jeddy.

"None of your business," he snapped.

Her head whipped up at his harsh reply, and he bit back an apology. Why should he apologize to her? She was a big part of the problem.

The effect she had on him made him want to do something reckless. When she'd winked at him, he had almost grabbed her and hauled her up so he could kiss her.

Maybe if he was so easily aroused he *should* go into town and find a woman. He didn't like the way she made him feel, didn't like it one bit.

Amanda wondered what was eating at Daniel now as she watched him stomp away from her tent. Perhaps he suffered from a lack of sleep. It had taken them all night to get back to camp.

Tired herself, she worked for another hour until she finished her drawing, then set her sketch pad aside. She had hoped that being confined in her tent would help her get over her distress of small places, but unless she sat in the doorway she became uncomfortable. As the temperature rose, her skin felt too tight and she had to concentrate on taking deep breaths.

Restless and edgy, she wanted to get out, to go for a walk. There were still several hours of daylight left, and the heat inside the tent had become unbearable. She stood at the opening and looked around. The camp was quiet, so quiet she could hear a gentle snore coming from Daniel's tent.

If she lowered the flap of canvas covering her doorway and headed for the trees directly behind her, no one would know she was gone. She could be back before Daniel woke from his nap. She stuck her head out and took another look around. Seeing no one, she untied the canvas and let the flap fall into place, then moved quietly into the trees.

Amanda walked for a few minutes, taking deep breaths of cool, fresh air, feeling herself calm down. The woods were beautiful. A light wind ruffled new leaves, and sunlight shimmered down through the sparse foliage. She wandered until she came to a stream that emptied into a small pond.

The water looked so tranquil and inviting, she longed to strip off her clothes and feel the coolness against her skin. Lacking the courage to swim naked so close to camp, she'd settle for getting her feet wet. She sat on a log and stripped off her boots and socks, rolled up her pant legs and waded in, loving the feeling of the mud between her toes.

Absorbed by the sensation of the slick, wet silt, she finally registered the sound of men's voices. Scrambling out of the water, she grabbed her boots and socks. She raced a short distance up a slight incline and hunched down behind two large boulders and some brush.

Several men, fishing poles over their shoulders, walked along the stream. They stopped about twenty feet from where she crouched, at a small dam of rocks and fallen logs that created the pool. She recognized the camp cook, Jeddy Sawyer, and a few of the other men.

If she tried to sneak away, they were bound to see her. Carefully she eased herself into a more comfortable position to wait them out, praying their fishing skills were good, or their patience poor. Either way, it was doubtful she'd make it back before Daniel discovered her gone. She closed her eyes and leaned her head against the rock. This would just be one more thing to make him angry. She seemed to have a real talent when it came to annoying Captain McGrath.

Amanda adjusted her position so that she could see the fishermen through the brush, but still stay hidden by the rocks. As long as she was stuck here, she might as well get some ideas for sketches.

Within minutes they finished their preparations and had their hooks in the water. A companionable quiet settled over the fishermen as they lazed on the banks waiting for a bite.

Someone's line bobbed in the water, creating ripples. The man crowed triumphantly and pulled in the first fish, a small cat, and set about working the hook out of the fish's ugly, whiskered mouth.

"That the best you can do?" Jeddy kidded him about the size of the fish.

"I hope not. I don't want more of your beans for dinner." Several of the others hooted at his comment.

After an hour, the piece of string they were using to thread their catch through the gills held almost three dozen fish, most of them large. At this rate maybe Amanda might make it back before Daniel awoke.

Jeddy slapped at a bug on his arm. "Hell, there ain't no sport in this. They practically jump out onto the bank for ya' here. Now, out in the rivers in the West, they got catfish as big as this." He made an exaggerated motion with his two hands, holding the pole between his knees. "Them fish ya' have to fight for hours. 'Course only a couple of them would feed the whole camp."

Several of the men laughed at the story. From what she had overheard from her tent, Jeddy's tales were legendary in camp. He didn't seem the least bit perturbed that his account was not totally accepted.

Amanda leaned back and closed her eyes, listening to the conversation drift up from the pond. What a wonderful way to spend a warm spring afternoon.

If she had stayed at home in Philadelphia she would be sitting in a stuffy room doing needlework, or taking tea with her mother's friends, listening to some dreadfully boring conversation on putting up pickles. It amazed her that most women never seemed to realize there were more interesting things they could be doing with their time.

How could it happen that ladies could live their whole dull lives getting left out and never do anything about it? If that was what it took to be a dutiful wife, Amanda knew she would not be very good at it.

"Having any luck?" Daniel's voice carrying from the pond interrupted her daydreams, causing her to sit up so fast she banged her elbow on the rock and had to bite down to keep from crying out. She rubbed at the offended joint and peered through the brush.

Jeddy set down his pole and motioned to the pile of uncleaned fish. "I suppose we have enough here, but I sure do hate to leave such a pretty place."

One of the men stood up and unbuttoned his shirt. "If we're done fishing I can't pass up the chance for a little swim."

He shucked his clothes and headed into the water before it occurred to Amanda what was happening. She went still, fascinated by the change of activities. One by one all the others except Jeddy and Daniel peeled off their clothes.

Jeddy got busy cleaning the catch. As he pulled the skin off a fish, she heard him grumble. "Ain't healthy to get all over wet like that. Catch your death."

Amanda peered through the brush, her eyes locked on the men as they frolicked in the water.

One of the men had left his long underwear on. The flap at the back of his long johns floated out behind him like a flag. Their nakedness fascinated her, and seeing them left her with more questions than it answered. She found the male to be a very peculiar-looking creature.

The men played in the water like a group of overgrown boys. She wondered briefly what Daniel, standing on the shore beside Jeddy, would look like naked. Quickly she pushed the thought away.

Amanda had never been swimming in anything but a heavy bathing costume and thought it must feel heavenly to glide through the water and feel it flow over bare skin. She added swimming naked to the list of things she intended to do in her new life as a bohemian.

The soldiers splashed, skimming hands across the surface of the pond, throwing arcs of sparkling water over each other, shouting friendly taunts and jeers. Brown arms and faces contrasted greatly with the whiteness of their bodies. They did not seem the least bit self-conscious of their nakedness.

Jeddy broke the mood. "Time I got back to get supper." He turned to Daniel. "You gonna come with me, or wait here for the boys?" Jeddy got stiffly to his feet and dusted the leaves off his clothes. He hoisted the dripping flour sack, now filled with cleaned fish.

Daniel, his profile to her, looked out at the men cavorting in the water, then back at Jeddy, a smile playing on his lips. "I think I'll stay and go for a swim."

Jeddy shook his head and started toward the camp. "Suit yourself."

Daniel unbuckled his belt. Amanda's mouth went dry. Transfixed, she watched him unbutton his shirt and shrug the garment off his broad, tanned shoulders. Then he reached for his boots, one at a time, hopping a little to maintain his balance. With each movement his muscles rippled and flexed under his smooth brown skin. The boots dropped onto the ground next to his shirt.

With one fluid movement, he slid his trousers and drawers down his legs and left them in a heap beside his shirt and boots, straightening up in naked splendor. Museum statues of Greek gods suffered in comparison to his glorious nude form. In a perfection of proportion, every plane of his body exuded strength and power.

She came alive with sensation as she watched him. Her nipples drew into hard buds and a delicious tingling started deep in her body.

Eyes riveted, Amanda brought her hands up to cover her burning cheeks. The statues in museums weren't made of muscle and skin, weren't covered in places with hair. And they always had those fig leaves. She doubted she could have looked away from the scene unfolding before her if her life had depended on it.

He turned his back to her and walked toward the water, the muscles of his pale buttocks tensing with each step. With a cry like a wild Indian, he started to run, then threw himself into the midst of the other bathers, sending up huge waves of water. All the others hollered and shouted, igniting a splashing battle of historic proportions.

Now, with all the men in the water, she had a chance to get back to her tent undetected. With shaking hands, she pulled on her socks and boots. Using the rocks for cover, she darted into the woods and made her way back to camp. She ducked under the flap of her tent and dropped down on her cot.

How could she look at him now and not think of his splendid nakedness? She wondered if she could be in Daniel's company again and not have her face give away her thoughts.

Chapter 5

Amanda sat in her tent and finished up drawings of the men she had seen in the pond that afternoon. The smell of frying fish made her stomach rumble as she kept up a running argument with herself. The feelings of attraction she had for Daniel had no future. Shortly, she would leave this place and never see him again. She'd only known him for a few days, so her silly fascination with the man would fade in no time, as soon as she didn't have to see him every day.

Damn him anyway. Why did he have to be so good-looking, so big and strong? She had left no room in her plans for a lover. Her hand went still and her pencil dropped from nerveless fingers. A lover. Would she want to take a lover when she got to New York? A true bohemian believed in free love.

She could imagine wanting to invite Daniel into her bed.

She shivered at her wicked thoughts. Lust without marriage, seeking forbidden fruit. Amanda suspected that her mother's worst fear might just come true. Her daughter had grown up to be a wanton woman.

"Amanda?" Daniel's low voice came from just outside her tent.

She jumped at his presence, then slammed the cover of her sketchbook closed on her drawing of Daniel naked.

"Yes?" Her answer came out like the croak of a frog, and she had to clear her throat and try again. "Yes?"

Daniel pulled the flap to her tent aside. "Are you all right?"

His wet hair had dripped onto his shoulders, leaving damp patches, reminding her with vivid recall what he had looked like as he had undressed to swim. Her mouth went dry.

"I'm fine." This time her voice sounded a little better, but she couldn't imagine why.

"You look flushed." He rolled the canvas flap back and tied it to the tent. "As long as you're awake, might as well get some air in here."

She put her sketchbook on the cot. As she had intended, he had assumed she had taken a nap earlier when she let the flap down and snuck out for a walk.

"The general's back. He'd like to talk to you." He seemed preoccupied as he stood aside and let her pass, then walked her the short distance to the general's tent.

"Miss Giles, good to see you again." General Allen met her at the door of his tent and took her hand, drawing her inside.

Daniel followed her in and stood behind her. She imagined she could feel his warmth at her back, then realized it was probably just her own heightened awareness of him, rather than any physical sensation.

"I understand you had quite an escapade." He finally let go of her hand and stood beaming at her.

For a moment she thought he was talking about the pond that afternoon, and she resisted the urge to turn around and look at Daniel. Then it dawned on her that he was referring to the trip she and Daniel had taken on the paddlewheeler.

"Yes sir. A true adventure." And she had the sketches to prove it.

"On behalf of the army, I want to thank you. You deserve a medal for bravery, but as you might have suspected, those in the field of intelligence cannot afford open recognition."

"Thank you General Allen." Amanda thought his statement sounded rather final.

"I will have someone drive you into town tomorrow."

"Tomorrow?" This would be her last night? The last time she would see Daniel?

"I'm afraid you'll have to stay one last night. The roads are unsafe for travel after dark." The general threw Daniel a look she didn't understand.

General Allen had misinterpreted her question and assumed she wanted to leave tonight.

She had told herself all along she would be leaving, but she wasn't ready to go. She wasn't prepared to say good-bye to Daniel. "But what about Andrew's contact? And the information?"

"We received information he has been transferred out of this area. We can't ask you to stay any longer, under the circumstances. I know what an imposition this has been for you."

"I see." She spoke around a lump that had formed in her throat.

He took her hand once more and gave it a little shake. "If you will excuse us, I have some business with Captain McGrath."

"Of course. Good-bye." General Allen tipped his hat as she left the tent.

She resisted the urge to look at Daniel, afraid her emotions showed on her face. He might see her melancholy mood in her expression, and her pride couldn't allow that. He had told her from the beginning this whole endeavor was a mistake, and now it looked as if he had been correct. She didn't want to leave him and have his look of righteous satisfaction be the last thing she remembered of him.

Amanda had been back in her tent for less than half an hour when the camp seemed to come alive. She stuck her head out the flap and saw men hurrying back and forth, carrying lanterns and weapons. She paused in the doorway, holding the canvas aside, and watched the commotion with a rising sense of excitement. Wranglers held horses as a half dozen men mounted up. Something was up!

Daniel came barreling around the side of her tent, pushed her inside and followed her in. He loomed over her in the crowded space, gripping her by the forearms.

Breathless at his intrusion and his touch, she said, "What is it? What's happening?"

Excitement showed plainly on his face. "A scout came in and reported raiders crossing the river. We're going after them."

An enemy raid. She had to go with him. This would be her chance to see some action, to get some material for her sketches. The editor had said—

Daniel shook her. "I know what you're thinking, and you can just put it right out of your pretty little head!"

"But—"

"But nothing!" He turned his head when a voice from outside called his name.

She studied his profile, agitation clear in the tension of his features.

He turned back to her. "You'll stay here, in this tent, until tomorrow morning. Jeddy and a few of the others will be in camp. You'll be safe."

She wasn't the least worried about her safety. A nonsensical thought crossed her mind. He'd said she was pretty. "But—"

The voice called for McGrath again, more insistent this time.

"Amanda!" He gave a look filled with warning. "If I'm not back, someone will drive you into Cincinnati in the morning."

He might not be here, to say good-bye? "Daniel—"

"No time. Got to go." He let go of her and pivoted abruptly.

Then, just as she was formulating another protest, he swung back and grabbed her shoulders.

"Oh, hell! I've been wanting to do this for days."

Pulling her against his chest, he wrapped her in his arms and lowered his mouth over hers, cutting off her breath, and her thoughts.

All of the sudden there was no noise from outside, no sound at all, except the beating of her heart in her ears as he kissed

her. His tongue invaded her mouth and what little breath she
held left her lungs in a whoosh.

His mustache tickled her nose and his teeth worked against
her bottom lip with a ferocious fervor. All the physical sensations that had plagued her earlier in the day as she had watched
him undress at the pond rushed back tenfold. She changed the
angle of her head to give him better access to her mouth, and
he groaned, a sound she felt as well as heard from deep in his
chest.

Just as she was getting the hang of kissing him, he pulled
back and looked down at her, his eyes gleaming, his breathing
heavy, grinning like a wolf.

"Take care, Amanda Giles." He turned and left.

She couldn't believe he'd left her standing there alone, panting and wanting. She blinked at the tent flap for a moment
while she caught her breath and tried to get her spinning emotions under control. She had been kissed before, but never had
she lost her wits over it.

Amanda bolted out of the tent, frantically searching for Daniel. There were things she wanted to tell him. He needed to
promise her he would be careful.

She spotted him, already mounted, in a group of riders. Taller
than all the rest, he stood out as he shouted an order. They
wheeled as a group and left together in a thunder of hooves,
headed east. A cloud of dust hung over the camp.

Disappointment washed over her as she watched the riders
until they were out of sight. He was gone. She might never see
him again. And she was missing a perfect opportunity to see
some action.

A loud voice broke into her thoughts. "Second party forming
to leave for Covington!"

She had no idea where Covington might be, but she intended
to go along. Daniel would be furious with her, she thought as
she ducked back into her tent and grabbed her jacket and hat.
He had told her specifically to stay in her tent, but that little
daredevil born in her over the past few days craved adventure
and demanded to be fed.

What did it matter if he was angry with her? she reasoned. She would be leaving in the morning. Having a last adventure might make him easier to forget. She touched her fingers to her lips, swollen from his kiss. And pigs might grow wings and fly, said a little voice in her head. She ignored the taunt and headed toward a group of about a dozen men assembled near the horses.

Standing just behind the gathering, she watched for her opportunity. General Allen must have known about the raiders. She remembered the look that had passed between him and Daniel. That was why he said the roads were unsafe and she would have to wait until morning to leave. If her luck held, neither General Allen nor Daniel would even know she had left her tent for the second time that day. A shiver of excitement traveled up her spine. Today was her lucky day.

No one paid any attention to her in all the commotion. A thin, distinguished-looking man in uniform spoke as wranglers brought a string of horses into the clearing. The man gave the assembled men instructions.

"We'll follow McGrath's group to the river. Then we turn east and ride to Covington. Keep your eyes open and look for signs of riders. The report is the raiding party is small."

One by one the wranglers handed off mounts and the men saddled up. Amanda held back and waited for her turn, took the reins of a small bay from one of the wranglers and felt a thrill as she swung up into her saddle.

No one challanged her in the confusion. This was almost too easy. Raiders. The rebel attackers came across the river and struck at night, burning and looting homes and businesses of people known to be loyal to the Union. Traveling fast, they usually got back across the river before they could be caught.

A full moon bathed the countryside with a silvery glow, making riding easy. Amanda stayed at the edge of the group and rode in silence for two hours, watchful for signs. When they got to a crossroad, their leader instructed three of the men to stay and keep watch.

One of the three spoke up. "And if they come this way,

Lieutenant Martin? What are we supposed to do?'' The man sounded reluctant to stay.

Martin stroked the neck of his horse, calming the spirited animal. ''Fire three shots. We'll hear you. If they get past us, McGrath's men are covering the crossing at Silver Grove. Keep your ears open. His men will do the same.''

At the mention of Daniel's name Amanda's heart beat hard against her chest, and she pressed her hand to her breast, up underneath her jacket. Please, keep him safe, she prayed, gripped by a bizarre premonition. She felt no fear for herself, but was struck by a strange awareness that Daniel might be in danger.

Amanda's attention snapped back as the groups split up. She rode with the men toward the crossing. Restless and jumpy, she listened for gunfire and wondered if Daniel's men had any better luck finding the raiders.

Martin pulled up his horse and spoke in a low voice. ''The crossing is a few miles ahead.'' He motioned with his hand toward the faint glow of lights on the other side of the river. ''We'll move on until we find better cover for the horses.''

They passed a few scattered houses close to the road, and one in particular caught Amanda's eye. Two-storied and clapboard, a single candle burned in one of the upstairs windows. The well-kept residence reminded her of her grandparents' home, where she had spent many holidays as a child.

Flower beds lined the path to the front porch, the blooms all silvery in the moonlight. She could smell their fragrance. Her nostalgia disappeared when she noticed the small Confederate flag pinned to the curtain in the lighted window.

A couple of miles down the road Martin waved them to a stop. They were on a slight rise that gave them a good view of the river crossing and the approach. Tying the horses out of sight in the trees, they made themselves comfortable on the hillside up from the road.

Amanda sat cross-legged in the grass, away from the group. She could see the others in profile, silhouetted against the moonlight reflecting off the river. She studied them. If she could capture the feeling of the moonlight, this would be a good sketch. She would entitle it *Night Watch.*

They spoke in low voices, accompanied by a chorus of frogs. The warm night held the scent of honeysuckle, not the heavy, overpowering perfume of late summer, but just a hint of fragrance.

It was hard to believe anything could be wrong on such a perfect night. The premonition of danger still dogged her. It was like waking up from a dream you hardly remembered, feeling slightly bothered, unable to go back to sleep. Amanda's legs started to tingle from sitting on the hard ground and she flopped over onto her stomach and cupped her chin in her hands.

The sound of horses approaching sent them all ducking back to the trees. They waited for a tense few moments until the riders appeared. Amanda recognized Daniel immediately, and felt a surge of relief to see him safe.

Even in the darkness his tall form on the big horse was distinctive. She hung back when Martin ordered them to mount up and hailed the approaching riders.

Daniel and his group reined in their mounts at the sight of the men riding out of the trees. Daniel and Martin spoke quietly. Amanda watched the two men, then swung up onto her horse, but stayed at the back of the group, hoping Daniel wouldn't notice her.

"Did you spot anything?" Daniel stared toward the crossing of Covington, visible in the moonlight.

Martin shook his head. "Naw. Didn't even meet any locals on the road. Damned quiet night."

"We might as well go back. I left three men at the crossing at Silver Grove. I'll leave three here, just in case, but it looks like we missed them. Your men can go ahead and take the south road back."

Daniel looked weary as he scanned her companions. His gaze stopped on her and his expression changed to a scowl. He dismounted quickly and handed his horse off to a startled Martin, then stalked toward her.

Roughly, he grabbed her horse's reins and pulled her farther away from the others, back into the trees.

Daniel looked up at her, moonlight illuminating his angry features. He spoke in a low, menacing tone, biting off each word. "What the hell do you think you're doing here?"

Amanda swallowed hard and leaned down to him, not wanting the other men she had been riding with to overhear him chastising her.

"I . . . I wanted to come." Her excuse sounded lame.

Furiously, he reached up and took hold of her arm, shaking her. "You haven't got a lick of sense." His voice hissed in her ear.

"Sorry." Chastised, she glanced at the others. They watched the exchange with frankly curious stares. "Everyone's looking. Could we discuss this later?"

He made a disgusted noise in his throat and let go of her arm. She rubbed at the spot, sure she would have a bruise come morning.

"Bet on it. You're coming with me." His tone made her shiver. He turned and stomped off.

Thankful for the darkness that hid her flaming cheeks, Amanda moved toward the other riders. No one said a word to her as the groups separated to take their different ways back to camp. She wished she was going with Martin instead of with Daniel.

She trailed along at the back of the group. Daniel kept glancing back as if he wanted to make sure she was still there. Where did he think she would go?

In spite of what she had told Daniel, Amanda wasn't sorry she had come, but she did regret that when they parted tomorrow he would be angry with her.

They passed the white house that had reminded her of home. All the windows were dark, even the one sporting the Confederate flag. She looked around, feeling the tiny hairs on her neck rise in the cool evening air. Something wasn't right.

Then she spotted the source of her discomfort. The flower beds were trampled flat. She stopped in the middle of the road.

"Captain McGrath, wait." She called to him hesitantly in the darkness.

He pulled up. "What is it?" he said, sounding impatient and annoyed that she had spoken to him.

She motioned hesitantly toward the flower bed. "All the plants have been trampled since we came by."

His eyes followed to where she pointed. "Are you sure?"

Of course she was sure, or she wouldn't have said anything. "The hollyhocks were two feet high. And there was a small Confederate flag pinned to the curtain in a lighted window upstairs."

Daniel sat motionless for a moment. He rubbed the back of his neck and contemplated the house.

He pointed at Amanda. "You stay here." He began giving orders to his men. "Vance, Eddie, ride on about a quarter mile and keep a watch. If you see or hear anyone coming, fire a shot. Charlie, check around the back."

Daniel was so mad at her that he wanted to discount what she said, but he coudn't ignore the signs. He rode up the long front walk, peering down at the flower beds. The mashed flowers hadn't even wilted yet.

When he got to the porch, Daniel dismounted. He pounded on the door and waited. No sounds came from within. He pounded again and he could hear a muffled voice. One of the upstairs windows opened and a woman appeared like an apparition, the moonlight glowing eerily on her white dressing gown.

"Who is there?"

Daniel winced as the woman's shrill voice cut through the still night. He stepped off the porch onto the steps so he could see her better. "United States Army, ma'am. I need to speak with you. Will you come downstairs?"

"My husband, Mr. Bennett, is not at home." She sounded impatient as she began to draw back and close the window.

"That's all right Mrs. Bennett, I'll talk to you. I just need a minute of your time.'' He wasn't looking forward to a confrontation with an agitated woman. Daniel figured he had had enough of crazed females for one night.

"It's the middle of the night!" The woman's voice became even shriller.

Daniel tried to sound patient. "Yes, ma'am, I know, but I need to speak with you. Will you please come downstairs?"

The slamming of the window drowned out her reply. Within seconds the front door opened. Surprised the woman could get down the stairs that quickly, he rested his hand on his revolver. Perhaps someone else had opened the door.

In the light from the moon, Daniel realized a different woman had stepped out the door onto the front porch. This woman, a Negro, stood very tall and slender. He couldn't tell how old she might be.

Daniel removed his hat. "Evening, ma'am. Sorry to disturb you. How large a group of riders came through here tonight?"

The woman looked over her shoulder and shifted her weight from foot to foot. She seemed to consider the question for a very long time. "You say you're with the army?"

She asked a legitimate question. None of them wore uniforms. "That's right. We're from the camp about five miles down the road." He sensed her uncertainty.

The Negro woman looked over her shoulder again. She spoke in a low voice. "Yes, sir, we did have some riders tonight. 'Bout ten of them, I thinks. They stopped here a bit ago to water their horses. Headed up that way." She pointed away from the river, down the road.

The woman from the upstairs window came charging through the open door onto the porch, wearing a billowing white night dress and carrying an old musket.

"Lubirda, you stupid nigger, get in the house. Now, or I'll beat you till you can't stand up." The black woman scurried around into the house, standing just inside the door.

Like an apparition, Mrs. Bennett stood screaming at them from the front porch, waving the gun in the air. "Get away from here. You have no right, barging into my home in the middle of the night.''

Daniel unsnapped the strap holding his revolver in the holster. Her handling of that gun made him nervous.

He spoke firmly to the irate woman. ''There are some questions that need to be answered, ma'am. We can either do it here, or you can come along with us to camp.'' He was tired of her nonsense.

Faced with this choice, Mrs. Bennett made an obvious effort to calm herself. ''Well, what is it you need to know?'' she snapped, the gun clutched in her hands.

''Did you have any riders by here this evening Mrs. Bennett?''

She turned and glared at the Negro woman. ''No, no one. I've been here all evening.''

''Begging your pardon again, ma'm, but the other lady says you had a large group stop by. Perhaps you didn't hear them.'' Daniel baited the already furious woman, hoping in her rage she might let slip some of the truth, and back up what the Negro woman had already told him.

Mrs. Bennett turned back to the doorway and for a moment he thought she might shoot the Negro woman. Instead, she swung the stock of the weapon, catching the Negro on the legs with the heavy gun. She went down like a felled tree.

Daniel leapt up the steps, wresting the weapon from her hands. He had never wanted to hit someone more than he did just then.

Mrs. Bennett's screaming became incoherent. She collapsed in a rocking chair by the door, as if she had been the one struck. Daniel saw Charlie in the shadows by the porch, his revolver in his hand. He must have come all the way around the back of the house.

Satisfied Mrs. Bennett would keep with Charlie watching her, Daniel offered his hand to the Negro woman. ''What's your name?''

She flinched at his outstretched arm and eyed him warily. ''Lubirda.''

He held steady, and hesitantly she put her rough hand in his and he helped her as she rose and limped out onto the porch.

"Where is your room?" He spoke to her reassuringly, placing himself between her and the hysterical woman in the chair.

"Back of the kitchen, sir." She looked at him, her eyes frightened in her thin face.

Easing her down the stairs, he led her around to the side of the house. "Go get all your things. I'll take care of Mrs. Bennett." She nodded and headed around the back of the house

Daniel tossed Mrs. Bennett's gun to Charlie and motioned to him to follow Lubirda.

Amanda, still on her horse, had moved up to the front of the house and watched the entire exchange. Not many men had the patience to put up with someone like Mrs. Bennett. Why did he always have to come off looking like a hero? She wished he would show her some flaws, so she wouldn't have to like him so much.

"What's going to happen now?" Amanda couldn't figure where Charlie and the woman had gone.

He shot her an irritated glance. "The Negro woman went to get her things. We are going to take her with us. Charlie is keeping an eye on her."

Why did he have Charlie watching her? "Do you think she'll try to run away?"

Daniel shook his head. "No, it's for her own protection. She'll be a lot safer with us. And I want the chance to ask her some more questions."

Mrs. Bennett continued to howl from her chair on the porch.

"Where will she stay?" Amanda could take her into the city when she left camp tomorrow.

He took off his hat and wiped his sleeve across his forehead. "We'll put her in the infirmary tonight. She'll be better off almost anywhere than she is here."

Charlie and Lubirda returned. She carried a small bundle of possessions in one hand.

Daniel nodded toward Amanda. "Charlie, Miss Lubirda can ride double with the kid."

Amanda realized he was talking about her. Charlie gave Lubirda a hand up on the horse behind Amanda.

The howling stopped and Mrs. Bennett lurched to her feet. "Just where do you think you're going with my nigger?" She charged across the porch, her nightdress billowing out behind her.

Daniel faced Mrs. Bennett. "We're on free soil. This is Ohio, and if Miss Lubirda wants to go, I'd say that's up to her." He swung up into his saddle and wheeled his mount around, his tone ending his part of the conversation.

As she followed Daniel out to the road where the other men waited, Amanda could hear Mrs. Bennett's shrill screaming carrying in the still night. Lubirda wrapped one lean arm around Amanda's waist.

Feeling very uncomfortable at the closeness of the unfamiliar woman and at a loss for conversation, Amanda turned her head over her shoulder and asked the first thing that came into her head. "Have you worked here long?"

The woman peered at her, the moonlight shadowing hollows under her high cheekbones. "We been here a few months. Tell me child, what is a slip of a girl like you doin' dressed up in boys' clothes and running around the countryside with Army men in the middle of the night?"

Amanda twisted around and looked at the woman in horror. "Shhh!" she hissed. "They'll hear you." Her heart thudded in her chest.

Lubirda shot her an incredulous look. "You means they don't knows?" she hissed back.

"No! Well, he does." She nodded toward Daniel. "But not the others. Please don't say anything." Amanda glanced around to make sure no one could overhear their conversation.

Lubirda sighed and shook her head. "Most men is fools."

Amanda didn't have an answer for that as they rode to meet the men Daniel had sent ahead to stand watch.

Daniel spoke to the assembled group. "Vance, you and the

kid take Miss Lubirda back to camp. Make her comfortable for the night in the infirmary.''

Vance nodded to Lubirda and then to Daniel. His openly curious gaze came to rest on Amanda. She squirmed in the saddle and heard Lubirda mutter the word ''fool'' under her breath.

Daniel turned to the woman, tipping his hat. ''Sorry for the inconvenience, ma'am, but it's for your own protection. What time did the riders come through?''

Lubirda looked thoughtful for a moment. ''I thinks it was after ten. I heard the big clock in the parlor.''

He nodded, his expression serious. ''Which direction did they come from?''

She shifted on the back of Amanda's mount. The horse danced a little, resentful of the added weight. ''I don't knows. I was sleepin' and didn't hear them until they was at the house. Miz Bennett spoke with them for a spell while they watered their horses, and then they took off down the road. I couldn't hear what they said.''

Daniel took off his hat and wiped his brow with his sleeve. ''I have a feeling Mrs. Bennett saw us go by earlier and tipped the raiders. They wouldn't cross at Silver Grove or Covington if they knew a patrol rode that way.''

Daniel turned and spoke to Vance. ''You go ahead and take them back to camp.'' He jerked his head in Amanda's direction. ''Keep your ears open, and if you hear someone coming, get off the road. Take the track that cuts off the main road in about a half mile. It's slower going, but it will take a few miles off your way back.''

Amanda watched Vance nod in agreement, hoping Lubirda wouldn't say anything to give her away on the way back. They split from the main group and started off at a fast clip. When they had gone less than a quarter mile around a curve in the road, they saw a structure engulfed in fire.

Vance signaled for them to pull up. ''Do you remember any houses along this stretch?'' Amanda shook her head.

He pointed in the direction of the fire. "I'm not sure, but I think there was a shack just along there."

Amanda had only been on this road once. It was hard to tell exactly where they were because heavy smoke obscured the area.

By the time they got close, the flames were leaping high into the night sky, illuminating the area directly around the blaze, making the surrounding trees seem even darker. Amanda watched, feeling the heat on her face, fascinated as the flames danced against the darkness. The fire had an almost hypnotic effect, drawing them.

Completely devoured by fire, the structure was unrecognizable. The horses became agitated and Amanda struggled to control her mount. They needed to make their way past in order to return to camp.

Sudden shouting close by and the explosion of gunfire broke the spell. She saw figures materialize out of the darkness.

"It's a trap," Vance yelled.

The horses pranced and snorted, fearful of the fire and gunshots. Amanda held tight to the reins and caught sight of Vance, dismounted, firing from behind his horse. He was having as much trouble controlling his animal as she was.

Amanda, figuring they made too good a target mounted, slid out of the saddle, pulling the whimpering Lubirda with her. Smoke blinded her and burned her throat. She tried to stay close to Vance, but the horses shied and bumped her, knocking her away. Struggling to keep hold of the horse and Lubirda's skirt, she fervently wished she had a pistol too.

They needed to get into the cover of the trees across the road, away from the flames. Lubirda screamed and fought her, breaking loose. Amanda lost her in the confusion.

Gunfire seemed to come at them from all directions. She could hear the thud of bullets hitting trees and kicking up dirt.

Above the commotion, Amanda heard the pounding hooves of approaching horses. She yelled at Vance, but couldn't see him in the dust and smoke. Frantic to get to cover, Amanda let go of her horse's reins and decided to make for the trees alone.

Halfway across the road she thought she heard Daniel's voice calling her name. Suddenly he burst through the smoke, the others just behind him. Thank God, she thought, and some of her panic subsided.

Like an avenging angel, Daniel remained on his rearing horse, took aim at one of the figures outlined by the flames and pulled the trigger. The man dropped his gun and folded over at the waist. Amanda had the oddest feeling that time passed at half speed as she watched the battle.

A brisk breeze came up and blew away some of the smoke. She heard more gunfire and noticed two other men crumpled on the ground. Charlie drew up beside Daniel, a revolver in each hand, firing away at figures fleeing into the darkness. She heard Daniel yell to some of his men to follow them.

Lubirda had disappeared. Amanda looked around for Vance and saw him sitting against the trunk of a huge oak, a branch above his head in flames. She turned in a daze to find that Daniel had maneuvered himself until he was beside her. She looked past him and saw a man wearing a rebel cap taking aim at his broad back.

Amanda screamed a warning to Daniel, hoping he could hear her over all the noise. In the next moment, she felt something hit her, knocking her back into the flank of Daniel's horse. The terrified animal kicked at her with his hoof, catching her on the hip and knocking her face first to the ground. When she raised her head up she could see Vance, his eyes staring vacantly into the darkness, a small hole in his temple. His mouth hung open and he looked as if he was going to laugh.

She spit out a mouthful of dirt and screamed.

Daniel's horse pranced nervously and as she rolled to get away from his hooves, she heard Daniel yelling at her.

"Amanda, get up. We've got to get out of here."

Amanda tried to raise herself off the ground, but her left arm collapsed under her. *How strange,* she thought. *It doesn't seem to work.* She rolled to her right side and pushed her way to her feet, spitting out more dirt. Daniel calmed his skittish horse.

Frantically she looked around but could see no sign of Lubirda, her horse, or the horse Vance had been riding. *She must have let go of him,* she thought vaguely. "What about Vance?"

"We'll come back and get him when it's light. Come on, you'll have to ride with me. Charlie's got Lubirda. Hurry up."

The night began to look misty. It must be all the smoke, she thought, shaking her head, trying to clear her thoughts. She nodded to him and took a step in his direction, but the ground felt mushy.

"Daniel?"

He looked down at her. "Oh Jesus, why didn't you say something? He leaned out of the saddle and caught her by the arm just as her legs buckled. He hauled her up in front of him, and she felt him stuff his bandanna against her shoulder.

"Say something about what?" she whispered as the light from the dancing flames faded and the darkness closed in.

Chapter 6

Daniel pulled Amanda back against his chest as he rode. He grasped her body up high, around her shoulders, trying to stem the flow from her wound.

"Damn it, Amanda." He shouted into the unconscious girl's ear, trying to vent some of his fury. "I told you to stay in your tent!"

He pushed his tired horse hard and fast, frantic to reach camp. He could feel her blood, warm and slick against the flesh of his hand. Her chin bounced against the muscle of his forearm. A knot of anger formed in his stomach as he thought of the way Amanda, Vance and Lubirda had been ambushed.

Vance was dead. The Negro woman had disappeared into the woods with Charlie. Hopefully the rest of his men had all made it to safety.

The familiar curve of the road gave way to the lights of the few campfires still burning. "Thank God," he muttered.

"Halt." The sentry challenged.

Daniel shouted the password without slowing and heard the guard cough in the dust thrown up by his horse.

He saw Martin and the others huddled around the kitchen

campfire. Jeddy was pouring coffee. They looked up as they heard Daniel's approach.

He wheeled his horse and yelled. "I'm going to Doc's. Martin, meet me at the infirmary."

Daniel shifted Amanda's weight and got a better grip on her. He reined in his winded mount and took off toward the wooden building. Light shone through the doorway, outlining two men. He pulled the horse to a walk and halted at the entrance to the building. With relief he recognized Michael and his self-appointed assistant, Arthur.

"Michael, help me." He let her limp body slide down the side of the animal and into their waiting hands. Daniel dismounted, and flexed his aching arm. For such a little thing, she'd taken a lot of strength to hold.

The doctor grunted under the weight he carried. "What happened?" He asked as he angled their burden to get her through the door.

"Ambush. Rebel raiders." Furious with her, he spit out the words. What the hell did she think she was doing, riding out like that?

He led his horse to a trough by the door and dropped the reins, then followed Michael and Arthur, his eyes on Amanda, so still in their arms.

"Michael, I need—"

"Not now Daniel." His friend, intent on his patient, cut Daniel off.

Michael jerked his head toward the table by the wall. "We'll put him there." Arthur grunted and nodded. Together they hoisted Amanda onto the flat surface.

"But—"

The sounds of men crowding in the doorway calling his name drowned out his plea. The last thing he wanted in this room was more men. He pushed them out the door and hushed their questions. As soon as he turned his back, they started to surge forward. He yelled at them to be quiet and stay outside, then closed the door in their faces.

After a quick examination, Michael said, "Help me roll him

onto his stomach. The bullet went clean through. There'll be more damage at the back wound.''

"Michael, wait. There's something I need to tell you.'' Daniel reached out and laid his hand on the doctor's arm.

Michael shook his hand off. "Later, Daniel. We need to stop this bleeding.'' He slid her bulky jacket down her arms. The back of her shirt was soaked with blood.

"Well I'll be damned.'' Daniel heard Michael's whispered words.

He couldn't remember ever hearing Michael curse. He moved around the doctor, who stood motionless, Arthur beside him.

The front of Amanda's shirt was open, exposing her chest.

"I'll be damned,'' Arthur repeated Michael's words. The three of them stood staring at her. "I'll be damned,'' Arthur said again.

For a moment Daniel watched with fascination as Amanda's smooth round breasts with their small pink nipples rose and fell with each shallow breath. Arthur made a choking sound, breaking the spell.

Seeing the torn, discolored flesh, the terrible damage the bullet had done to her beautiful young body, Daniel felt anger well up inside of him. The force of the emotion took him by surprise, making him tremble.

"Arthur, go get the Negro woman. Bring her over here.''

Arthur didn't take his eyes off Amanda. "What Negro woman?''

"Go ask Jeddy. Now,'' Daniel roared. Arthur jumped at the tone of his voice and headed out the door.

"And close that door. See that someone takes care of my horse,'' Daniel called after him, then turned his attention back to Amanda.

She looks so young, Daniel thought as he watched Michael try to stop the blood seeping from her wound. *Damn her, anyway.* Why did she come along tonight? He had told her to stay in her tent. He should have put a guard on her.

Michael looked over his shoulder and interrupted Daniel's

thoughts. "Are you all right?" His eyes traveled from Daniel's face to his chest.

Daniel glanced down. The front of his shirt was covered with blood. Her blood.

"I'm fine. I wasn't hit." Guilt ate at him. He ran his hand tiredly over his eyes. "This is my—"

Michael shook his head and spoke in a voice full of exasperation. "Save it for another time. Time is of the essence here, and I need some assistance."

Michael bent over Amanda, taking her pulse. Daniel felt helpless. "What should I do?"

Michael glanced over his shoulder. "Cut off the rest of this shirt."

Daniel gently pulled the shirttails out of her trousers and stripped the remaining fabric away. The pale, unblemished skin of her breasts and belly glowed in the dim lantern light.

As Michael gathered his supplies, Daniel stepped out of his way holding a handful of tattered cloth. He discarded the remains of the bloody shirt and grabbed a blanket off the nearest cot, covering her gently.

"Come over here, Dan. You get her by her hips. I need to turn her over again, toward us. Ready? Now, gently." Her limp little body rolled easily.

Daniel tucked the blanket firmly around her.

Michael examined the ragged hole in her back. "The bleeding has almost stopped. Hand me that bottle." He indicated a brown glass container. Daniel took out the stopper and placed it within his reach. Michael poured a generous amount of the liquid over the wound. Amanda moaned and twitched. The doctor continued to examine her shoulder.

"Look in that box over there and find me the longest tweezers." As Michael spoke he blocked Amanda from Daniel's line of sight.

"You knew, didn't you?" There was no censure in Michael's statement.

"Yes. It was the general's idea, the old fool. I told him

something would happen." But ultimately it was his own fault, he thought. He held himself responsible.

He should have escorted her back to camp himself the moment he found her out with the men.

Michael turned back to his patient. "Hand me another blanket off that cot."

"I can't believe I couldn't talk the general out of it." He passed the bedding to Michael.

Allen was a stubborn man, but Daniel should have tried harder. He never should have let her come back to camp. He should have insisted she leave the minute he got her off the boat.

Michael shook open the blanket, ignoring his comment. "Daniel, take off her boots." He covered the trembling girl from armpits to toes with another layer.

"What's the matter with me? I should have gone back with her. They rode right into that ambush." He grasped her legs one at a time and pulled gently on her boots. His hand fit all the way around her slender ankle.

"Tuck the blanket under her feet and around her other shoulder. She's shaking." Michael worked methodically on the wound.

Daniel's face felt flushed and he fought to control the quiver in his hands as he covered her. He felt like smashing something.

Michael, totally absorbed in what he was doing, bent over the girl. He used the tweezers to methodically pick tiny threads of cloth out of the bullet hole.

Daniel paced up and down in back of Michael, slamming one fist into the palm of his other hand. "How did the general think she could pull it off?"

"You're repeating yourself. And she did pull it off." Michael glanced at his friend and went back to his task. "Hold this lantern up closer for me."

He jerked the lantern off the hook and stood next to Michael. As his friend worked, Daniel studied Amanda's face. How could anyone have missed recognizing her femininity? The delicate bone structure of her face and the full lips? Smooth skin without a trace of beard? He'd made her stay in her tent, but some of the men had seen her.

"Daniel?" Michael measured a length of thread.

"What?" He answered his friend without taking his eyes off Amanda.

"Now I understand." Michael passed the thread through the eye of a long needle.

"What?" Daniel smoothed the hair away from Amanda's forehead.

"Why you were troubled." He pinched the edges of the wound together and pushed the needle through the ragged skin.

"Oh." Daniel flinched as he watched the needle pierce her skin.

"Dan?" Pulling the thread up, he tied it off, then brought the needle down for another stitch.

"What?" Daniel took Amanda's limp hand, cradling it in his, chafing her cold skin.

"I think she's going to be all right."

"Thank you, Michael." Daniel, swamped by a feeling a relief, was quiet for a long time.

His thoughts were interrupted by another commotion outside. Without letting go of Amanda's hand, Daniel hung the lantern back on the hook. The door opened. Arthur walked in, followed by Lubirda. Daniel looked past them and saw half the camp on their heels. Arthur apparently had wasted no time spreading the news about a woman in camp.

"Shut that door!" Daniel snarled, and Arthur jumped to do his bidding. "With you on the other side!"

Arthur hurried out and slammed the door behind him. Lubirda hovered by the door.

Daniel could hear excited voices outside as he made the introductions. "Lubirda, come here. This is Dr. Jervis."

Michael nodded at the woman as he continued to work.

Daniel dragged his gaze away from Amanda and looked at the woman standing so still behind them. "Would you be willing to help him out here as a nurse?"

The woman hesitated, looking unsure. "I do what I can."

She moved around to the head of the table and stared down at the girl's face. "I wondered what this girl was doing, riding with Army men, but when I asks her she tells me it be a secret."

Daniel stared at the tall thin woman. She had only been with Amanda for minutes before the ambush. When he finally spoke his voice sounded strained. "You knew?"

She looked indignant. "Yessir." She began to hand supplies to Michael as he asked for them.

The commotion outside became unbearable. Michael glanced at Daniel. "This is going to take a while. Could you settle them down, and bring me a cup of coffee?"

Daniel didn't want to leave. Finally, when the noise increased again, he nodded and placed Amanda's hand at her side, then turned and stomped toward the door, opening it quickly and stepping through.

A group of expectant faces and a barrage of questions, all shouting at once, greeted him. The anger caused by all that had happened that night exploded inside his head.

"Shut up, all of you, and go back to camp. There's nothing to see here."

The harshness of his tone stunned them into silence. The group broke up and headed toward the tents, muttering to one another. It was plain on their faces they thought there was a great deal to see.

Daniel stood glaring into the darkness until they were gone; then he made his way back to camp. He wasn't going to answer any questions tonight. He needed to face his own guilt and confusion first.

Jeddy appeared out of the darkness with two tin cups. He pushed one of them into Daniel's hands. Daniel smelled the whiskey in the coffee.

"Thanks, Jeddy. I need a cup for Michael, too."

Jeddy nodded and threw some wood on the fire. When he spoke, the old cook's voice was quiet and low. "Well now I guess I seen it all. How'd she get by us, Daniel?"

Daniel rubbed at his temples with his free hand. " I knew,

Jeddy." He stared into the growing flames while he drank his coffee.

Jeddy let out a low whistle, but asked no questions.

"Thanks, friend." Daniel drained the mug, traded it with the cook for a full one, and walked off into the darkness.

Amanda awoke slowly, trying to remember what happened and where she was. Her strange dreams and fragmented visions seemed unreal, but she knew something terrible had happened. Her arm seemed caught somehow, and the effort to move made her head throb. About to give up and sink back into that effortless world of slumber, she heard a voice.

"Good morning."

Opening her eyes, she squinted against the light. Her mouth felt dry as cotton.

Confused, she looked around. "Where am I?"

"In the camp hospital. I'm Dr. Jervis."

Amanda tried to sit up. A shooting pain stabbed at her shoulder. Her head reeled and she groaned.

The doctor's gentle hands eased her back down on the cot. "Don't try to move. I don't want the bleeding to start again."

"Bleeding?" Still dizzy, she tried to focus on his face.

"Do you remember what happened last night?" Dr. Jervis pulled his chair closer to the bed.

"Last night?" She sounded like an idiot, she thought, parroting his words, but her mind was so muddled.

Amanda closed her eyes and tried to think. She remembered riding out of camp and waiting by the river. Then Daniel came and got very angry at her. They stopped at a big white house. After that, it seemed like bits and pieces of a nightmare, none of it real. There was a fire, and people running and shouting. Daniel had yelled at her over and over; then the pain hit, and finally darkness. She couldn't remember what was true and what she had dreamed.

For moment she forgot her discomfort. "Is Daniel all right?"

Michael reassured her. "He's fine. What do you remember?"

"I don't know." Head throbbing, she seemed unable to stop the tears that welled up in her eyes and slid down her cheeks. The doctor wiped her face with a damp cloth and folded the blankets in around her, making her feel like a sick child.

"Don't worry about it now. The important thing is, you need rest. As soon as Lubirda has a nap, she'll be back to sit with you."

Lubirda? Then Amanda remembered. The Negro woman they had rescued. She closed her eyes. Being tucked in felt good. Years had passed since anyone had done that for her. She fell asleep wishing Daniel would come and help her put the puzzle of last night together.

Michael sat by the bed, watching the girl. He rubbed his fingers over his gritty eyes. It had been a long night, but he felt a sense of fulfillment, knowing he had done his best and his patient would survive.

She looked childlike lying there, but he guessed she must be older than she appeared. He suspected from his friend's behavior last night that Dan's feelings ran deeper for her than he was willing to admit at present, even to himself.

Michael heard voices outside and went to investigate. Lubirda was sound asleep on one of the cots. She had proved to be a good nurse.

Dan was speaking to the guard he had ordered put on the infirmary. Through the open door Michael could see the rim of the sun showing above the horizon, breaking through the gray dawn.

When he spotted Michael, Daniel turned abruptly. "How is she?"

Michael could see the tension in Dan's large body. He had changed clothes, but from his appearance it was obvious he hadn't gotten any sleep.

Michael motioned him inside and spoke quietly as he closed the door. "She's still very weak."

Daniel ran his hands through his hair and paced the floor,

pausing briefly to glare in the direction of the curtain partitioning off the end of the room.

With an obvious effort, Dan spoke in a low voice. "The general wanted a full report. I couldn't get back until now. Will she be all right?"

"I think so. She was awake for a few minutes. Lost a lot of blood, but the bullet went clean through and didn't hit any bones. Unless the wound putrefies, she should heal just fine." Michael noted the relief on his friend's face. He was right, his friend's feelings for the girl went deep.

Dan turned toward the end of the infirmary where she slept. "When can I talk to her?"

Michael put a staying hand on Dan's sleeve. "I hope she'll sleep for a few hours, but I'll send for you as soon as she wakes."

"Thanks Michael." Dan turned to leave.

"Wait, Dan. What's her name?"

He nodded. "Her name is Amanda Giles. She's the sister of a dead agent. It's a long story."

"You can tell me later." Daniel looked as if he'd not slept for days.

Daniel glanced at his best friend. "I should have been there to protect her." His voice cracked.

Michael squeezed his shoulder. "I don't know why she was out there, but you can't take all the responsibility, Dan. We're at war. These are the things that happen. You need to get some rest. I'll send Lubirda to you when Amanda can talk."

Dan threw his friend a grateful look. "Thanks."

Michael knew Dan well enough to know he would take on the responsibility of what had happened if God himself were to give him absolution. That was the kind of man Dan was.

Lubirda took a final swipe with the hair brush, and stood back, a critical expression on her face. "You sure you all feelin' up to this? You only had three days of healing."

Amanda nodded, unwilling to admit how tired she really

felt. "Yes, Lubirda, for the fourth time." Gingerly she lay back against the pillows.

"Don't go gettin' sassy, missy. I is here to takes care of you." Lubirda pointed the brush at her as she spoke.

Obviously the woman took her duties very seriously. Amanda had not been allowed to do a thing for herself for days. She could manage to answer a few questions, for heaven's sake. Besides, she wanted very much to see Daniel.

Lubirda went to answer a knock on the outer door of the infirmary.

Amanda heard a male voice she did not immediately recognize ask to see Miss Giles. It was not Daniel. Deflated, she closed her eyes. She had not seen him since the raid.

A clearly embarrassed Lieutenant Martin peeked around the curtained partition. "Miss Giles?"

"Hello, Lieutenant Martin. Come in," she said, resigned.

He entered and stood next to the bed, holding his hat and looking uncomfortable.

"Please sit down." Amanda motioned to the chair.

"Thank you, but this shouldn't take that long. I've come to ask you some questions about the night of the raid. Miss Lubirda, too. I need to finish my report for the general." He waved a tablet in her direction but didn't look at her.

"We'll tell you what we can." Amanda raised an eyebrow in question at Lubirda, and received an affirmative nod in reply.

Amanda had a few questions of her own, but she dared not ask them for fear of the gossip they might create. Where was Daniel and why had he not come to see her these past three days?

Martin cleared his throat. "What happened when you left the main party?"

"We were riding back to camp and we saw a fire. When we went to investigate, it was a trap. Someone started shooting at us." Amanda shivered at the memory.

Mr. Martin made a note. "How many of the enemy attacked you?"

Amanda had no idea. She looked at Lubirda, who shrugged.

"I couldn't say. It was dark and they stayed in the trees. It seemed like they were all around us." Amanda made a one-armed gesture of helplessness. "I don't know."

"How long did you fight with them until Captain McGrath arrived?"

Her white knight, arriving in time to save a damsel in distress. "It seemed like a long time, but probably it was just a few minutes." And where was he now, she wanted to ask. Amanda lay back and closed her eyes, unable to ignore the throbbing in her shoulder.

"That's all. She be too tired." Abruptly, Lubirda ended the interview.

Amanda opened her eyes and regarded the Negro woman with amusement. She certainly took her nursing duties to heart.

With a look of profound relief, Mr. Martin excused himself and hurried out.

"He be one uncomfortable man," Lubirda observed after he left.

Amanda laughed. "I suppose the men are embarrassed now that they know there was a woman in the camp. The conversations I overheard from my tent were very . . . explicit at times."

Lubirda chuckled. "That explains it. You slide down there and take a rest. I'm going to help Mr. Jeddy with some cookin'."

When Amanda awoke, she wondered what time it was. She slept so much, her days and nights got a little mixed up. Lubirda arrived with a tray of food, fussing over her until she managed to eat some of it.

From her bed she had heard mournful music. That would be Charlie, the man who had rescued Lubirda, playing his harmonica. A salute to Vance, dead in the ambush. Lubirda had brought her talk from the camp. It seemed that Charlie and Vance were best friends. Saddened by the plaintive dirge, she felt like crying.

The boredom of enforced bedrest was driving her crazy, but she no longer felt quite so dizzy when she sat up. Her shoulder still ached horribly, too much for her to be able to draw.

What she told Lubirda she wanted most was a chance to

wash her hair and have a bath. Lubirda promised to help, as
soon as Dr. Jervis thought it safe. What she really wanted was
to see Daniel. She feared he stayed away out of anger, and she
wanted to apologize for her impulsive behavior. Heaven help
her, but what she wanted most of all was to be kissed by him
again.

"Good evening!" At the sound of the doctor's voice, Lubirda
pulled the curtain aside.

Delighted to have company, Amanda welcomed him. Talking
with the doctor might help her forget some of the sadness.
"Come in!" She liked Dr. Jervis, and the coffee he brought
smelled wonderful.

"I thought you ladies might like some. It's fresh." He offered
tin cups.

Amanda awkwardly pushed herself to a sitting position. She
took the mug and held the coffee under her nose, inhaling the
fragrant steam.

Dr. Jervis pulled the chair closer to the bed and sat down.

"Have you eaten, doctor? Amanda motioned politely to the
napkin-covered tray on the small table beside her bed. "There's
too much food here, more than I can eat. Lubirda plans to fatten
me up."

Lubirda answered with an unladylike snort.

Michael shook his head. "I ate while you were asleep."

He had stayed and talked with her several times in the past
days, telling her of his wife and children, whom he missed so
much. She longed to ask him questions about Daniel, but didn't.
She spent a great many of her waking hours trying to convince
herself she did not miss him. Knowing more about him wouldn't
ease the situation.

"You haven't asked about him." Michael asked, as if he
had read her thoughts. He took the cup from her fingers and
placed it on the table.

"Who?" She stared at her hands.

"Dan."

"Is he well?" The question of his general health seemed

like a safe topic. Michael's long hesitation made Amanda feel a stab of panic. She looked at him, searching his face.

Michael studied her for a long time before he answered. "Yes. Physically he's fine. He feels guilty that you were hurt."

Why would Daniel feel guilty? She was the one responsible for what had happened. She wished he would visit so she could set him straight.

"Is that why he hasn't come to see me?"

"No. He's gone again. I don't know where."

She was glad to hear he wasn't in camp. That meant he wasn't intentionally avoiding her.

He patted her hand, then released it. "Well, what do you think?"

Amanda realized Michael had asked her a question and she had no idea what it was. "I'm sorry. What did you say?"

"I have found you a place to stay while you recover. A woman who lives just down the road towards town is willing to take you in. Her husband and sons are in the Army and she has plenty of room. Lubirda will come along and help care for you." He paused, waiting for her reaction.

Amanda's heart skipped a little. She didn't want to leave without seeing Daniel once more. She needed to thank him for saving her life, and convince him he was not responsible for what had happened.

"I'm very comfortable here, really," she said, trying to reassure Dr. Jervis. Her chances of talking to Daniel were much better if she stayed in camp.

Dr. Jervis shook his head. "This really isn't suitable, I'm afraid, for you or Lubirda. The men are curious. It has become too difficult to maintain your privacy."

Clearly she would not be allowed to stay here. Amanda turned to Lubirda. The Negro woman made an excellent nurse, and she was becoming a friend, but she didn't want her pressured into something she didn't want to do.

"Lubirda, are you willing to come along with me?"

"Yessum," Lubirda answered with a look of relief.

Dr. Jervis addressed Lubirda. "Mrs. Bennett has been

arrested for consorting with the enemy." He turned back to Amanda. "In any case, staying with you will be a much better situation for Lubirda. Fact is, the army isn't sure what to do with her."

No wonder Lubirda had looked relieved. She had nowhere to go. Amanda felt selfish for not thinking of Lubirda's welfare.

Dr. Jervis helped her scoot down under the blankets. "Enough conversation. You rest. I will make the final arrangements tomorrow." He disappeared around the curtain.

Lubirda fussed with Amanda's covers and the pillows until she was satisfied. There was no sense in telling her not to bother. It only brought on a scolding.

Exhausted, Amanda lay thinking for a long time about her future, feeling very bleak. Just a week ago she had known exactly what she wanted and where she was going. Now she felt confused and uncertain. So much had changed since she had left home.

When Amanda awoke from her nap, darkness had settled and it was very quiet inside the building, but she could hear music in the distance. She remembered the recent conversation with Dr. Jervis. She was going to be sent away and she might never see Daniel again. She had to find him and change his mind.

"Lubirda? Are you here?" Not a sound in reply. She tried again, louder. "Lubirda?" Still nothing.

Amanda sat up and swung her legs over the side of the bed, tugging to pull down the borrowed nightshirt that had ridden up over her knees. She stood up slowly, testing her strength. She realized with relief that the worst of the dizziness was gone.

Moving to the curtain, she peered around into the darkness. Deserted. Not even anyone in any of the cots. She crossed back to the bed and awkwardly pulled the blanket around her shoulders, her arm still stiff and sore.

To Amanda's surprise, when she opened the outside door, there was no one there either. She found that odd. A twenty-four-hour guard had been posted for her protection and privacy.

She rested for a moment against the door frame, gathering her strength. Her wound ached, but it felt so good to be out of bed that she ignored it.

A huge campfire near her old tent drew her attention. Rousing banjo music and men singing drifted to her on the breeze. It sounded as if someone was beating on a wash tub in time to the tune. A string of firecrackers popped and sparked in the dark. Then Amanda realized the date. The men were celebrating Independence Day. It was the Fourth of July.

Tired of being cooped up, she longed to be outside in the soft fresh air of the summer evening. Uproarious sounds of celebration drew her. Carefully she closed the door behind her.

When the guard returned, he wouldn't know she wasn't inside. She picked her way through the dark, wishing she had stopped long enough to find her boots. Small rocks and twigs bit into her bare feet.

She stumbled and a jolt of pain shot down her arm. She cradled the limb with her good hand and rested a moment, breathing deeply until the worst passed.

Not wanting anyone to see her wearing only a nightshirt and a blanket, Amanda stopped when she got to Jeddy's deserted cooking fire. The coals still burned, and she was close enough to the large campfire to hear the words to the songs. She felt comfortable here, safely hidden from the others by the darkness.

Exhausted by the walk from the infirmary, she lowered herself onto a stump beside the dying fire. As soon as she rested, she would head back. She was weaker than she cared to admit. Once again she had been too impulsive.

She sat quietly and watched the men, bathed in the glow of the crackling, blazing fire. She recalled events from the past few days, and knew she would never forget her adventures, in spite of the discomforts. After this, New York City might seem tame.

A few of the men left the fire and headed for their tents. So very weary herself, she decided to return to her bed.

Hearing footsteps approaching from behind her, she huddled in her blanket and turned to see who it was. With a leap in her pulse rate, she recognized Daniel. Even in the darkness his broad shoulders and his height allowed her to identify him before she could see his face. Her heart pounded. She wanted to see him, but she had hoped to have time to make herself more presentable.

Nervous, Amanda tried to compose herself as she stood to greet him. The blanket slipped off her shoulders as she straightened up. She grasped awkwardly for it, but with one arm useless, the blanket slipped to the ground and settled in a heap around her feet.

Feeling naked in just a nightshirt, she bent to pick up the bedding. A sharp stab of pain stilled her movements. Amanda gave up trying to retrieve the blanket and looked up just as Daniel came close enough so that she could see his features.

He appeared tired and trail-worn and absolutely wonderful. Stubble covered his chin and his clothes were stained. She couldn't take her eyes off him.

Suddenly his expression changed and his face contorted with anger. The greeting she had been about to give him stuck in her throat.

"What the hell are you doing here?" he hollered at her. "I went to the infirmary and you were gone." He stopped in front of her, his hands clenched in fists at his sides. "There was supposed to be a guard on your door."

Amanda shrank back from him. Even the night she had been shot he hadn't yelled at her like this. She tried to speak and instead made a small squeaking sound.

She cleared her throat and tried again. "When I woke up there was no one there. I just came out this far to sit and listen."

He stood glaring at her, saying nothing.

Why was he in such a rage? Perhaps if she took the initiative, she could smooth things over. "I . . . I'm glad you're here. I've wanted to talk—"

He cut her off. "Do you have any idea what it is like for these men to be in camp for weeks on end, without ever seeing a woman?"

Amanda felt herself blush. Did he truly think she had come out here to entice the men? He was being absurd.

She drew herself up to her full height. "No one has seen me. That's why I'm sitting over here, alone in the dark."

His eyes traveled up and down her body in a way that frightened and excited her at the same time.

"Do you know what it would do to them to see you, uncovered like this? And it's not dark." The fury in his voice was evident as he gestured to the glowing coals.

Acutely embarrassed to be standing in front of him with her feet and ankles bared by the nightshirt, Amanda reacted to his retort with aggravation. She glanced over her shoulder at the main campfire, then turned back to him. "If you would keep your voice down, no one would even know I'm here!"

She resisted the urge to try again to scoop up the blanket and hold it in front of her. Why couldn't he be civilized about this and let her explain?

Surprised at how steady she sounded, she used her most haughty voice on him. "I don't think you should assume *all* men are plagued with certain baser feelings."

She glared at him, her good right hand cradling her left arm across her chest. Her healing wound throbbed like the devil. She didn't think she could stay upright much longer, but he had made her so angry she wasn't going to show him any weakness and give him the opportunity to offer up another lecture on why she, as a woman, didn't belong there.

He looked ready to explode. "Do you think no one will notice you sneaking around here in your nightclothes?" He raised his hands and took a step toward her, his voice harsh.

His sudden angry movement startled her, and she took a step backwards. Her foot caught in the blanket, throwing her off balance. She felt herself falling, falling back into the hot coals. Flailing her good arm, she tried desperately to regain her balance and twist away. She caught a glimpse of Daniel's face and saw his expression of anger turn to horror. He lunged at her and caught her by her damaged shoulder just before she fell, dragging her forward.

A searing pain shot down her arm as her partially healed wound tore open. Amanda heard her own scream fade as she slumped, giving in to the blessed blackness where nothing hurt.

Her piercing scream brought the men around the fire to their feet. They arrived in time to see Daniel holding Amanda's limp body in his arms. A dark stain spread across the shoulder of her nightshirt.

They all began to talk at once. Daniel shouted them into silence. "Jeddy, where's Dr. Jervis?"

"He went over to the main camp 'bout an hour ago, to have dinner with Captain Russell." Jeddy looked as curious as all the others.

Daniel didn't like the way they were all staring at Amanda. The nightshirt she wore had hiked up, leaving her legs bare from the thighs down.

"Jeddy, throw that blanket over her. Arthur, go get the doctor." The younger man didn't seem to hear him and stood staring at the girl who had been the first topic of conversation in camp for three days. "Now!" He bellowed at him and Arthur jumped and began running all in one movement.

Jeddy bent and picked up the blanket, dipping a smoldering corner in a bucket of water before wrapping it around the still form in Daniel's arms. "Come on, let's get her back to the infirmary."

Jeddy lit a lantern on his table and turned to the babbling crowd still gathered around them. "Don't you have nothing better to do? Get to bed, all of you." They stared at the old cook for a moment and then turned and left as Daniel and Jeddy headed for the infirmary.

Exhausted, wet to the skin after riding in the rain, and hounded by nagging memories, Daniel returned to camp. Wearily he turned his mount over to a waiting wrangler.

It had only been three days since he had confronted Amanda

in front of the campfire on the Fourth of July, but it felt like weeks. If he hadn't lost his temper, she wouldn't have been hurt again. Every time he got near her, bad things happened. He wondered if she had left camp yet.

Reports of more raids had come in just after Michael had begun to restitch Amanda's wound, and Daniel had had to leave. He and his men had ridden hard, intent on tracking down the raiders, finding the outlaws who had killed Vance and wounded Amanda.

What little sleep he had gotten in the rotten weather had been haunted by dreams of Amanda screaming in pain as he pulled her away from the hot coals. All his thoughts were of Amanda. He needed to apologize for what had happened, settle things with her so he could get her off his mind.

Memories of how she had looked wearing nothing but a short, thin nightshirt, her body outlined by the glowing coals of the dying fire, haunted him. His physical response when he had seen her silhouetted in front of the fire that night had surprised and angered him, and he had reacted badly, taking it out on her. He didn't need or want the feelings she awakened in him.

Daniel held himself responsible for Amanda's safety. She was under his protection and she had been injured twice, both times his fault. He wanted Amanda out of camp, in a secure place. If she hadn't left in his absence, he meant to see her gone as soon as possible, even if he had to personally drive her into Cincinnati.

Daniel sought out the general's tent in the fading light. The general's young aide greeted him with a smart salute. "General wants to see you. He can be found at the infirmary."

"Damn." Daniel muttered to himself as he acknowledged the salute.

Wanting nothing but dry clothes and his cot, he had hoped the general might have retired for the evening, and he could put his report off until morning.

Daniel slogged through the mud to the infirmary. A small group stood outside the building, bathed in a dim glow from the open door, listening to the general. General Allen nodded briefly at Daniel and continued to speak. Michael raised his hand in a silent greeting, and moved to make room for him in the circle of men. Martin, Billy and J. T. ignored him.

Their behavior struck him as odd since they were old friends, but he didn't stop to dwell on it, distracted by how ill Michael looked. Daniel hoped it was just the poor light that made his friend appear unwell. He turned his attention to what the general was saying.

". . . so the plan will continue as is. The Negro woman, Lubirda, has already been moved to the Wilson place. She has agreed to help us if we still need her. About Amanda, we'll just have to wait and see. It's up to her now."

Angry, Daniel couldn't believe what he was hearing. "General, you can't be thinking of using her further in our operations! This is no safe place for a woman. Why she—"

General Allen cut him off. "Had it not been for the wound she received, the men in camp still wouldn't know she's a female. She acquitted herself well, in spite of her lack of training. However, at this point in time, the question appears to be moot." He glared at Daniel, turned on his heel and strode off into the darkness.

The other men left too, without any further conversation. Daniel, stung by the general's comments, turned to Michael. "What did he mean? Doesn't she want to leave?"

Michael laid his hand on Daniel's arm. "Come inside Dan, I need to speak to you."

Weariness weighed heavily in Michael's low voice. Purple smudges marked the skin under his eyes and he'd lost weight. He looked more like a patient than a doctor. At least he looked Daniel in the face, unlike the others.

Daniel followed Michael into the infirmary and surveyed the mostly empty room. Two of the cots in the room were occupied and Arthur sat between them.

Since arriving back in camp, nothing seemed to add up for Daniel. Everyone had acted tense, reacting strangely to his presence. Now his best friend looked like he carried the whole world on his back.

Perspiration broke out on Daniel's skin. Something was wrong here. "What is it, Michael?"

"It's Amanda, Dan. She's taken a bad turn. Her wound is septic and I think she might have lung fever."

"Amanda." Emotions ripped through Daniel's stomach. "It's my fault."

"You can't hold yourself responsible, Dan."

"Why shouldn't I blame myself? I was the one who should have kept her safe. Where's Lubirda?"

"She's staying in Cincinnati. Those two cots are measles. I didn't want to take the chance that she might sicken." Michael rubbed his temples and swayed.

Daniel took another look at his friend and saw that Michael suffered from more than fatigue.

"My God, Michael, sit down before you fall down."

"I've got to get back to her." Michael cut him off and nodded toward the curtain.

Daniel steered Michael to an empty cot. "You go to bed. I'll sit with Amanda."

Michael folded up like a rag doll when the back of his legs hit the edge of the cot.

Daniel spoke to Arthur. "Take care of Dr. Jervis. Don't let him get out of this bed."

Arthur nodded.

Ready to drop himself, Daniel stood over Michael's cot and gathered his thoughts. What would he say to Amanda to express how sorry he felt? And how responsible. Confused, he needed a little time to think.

"I'll get cleaned up and come back."

Michael looked up at him, his expression full of pain. "Dan, go see her now. I don't expect she'll last long."

Chapter 7

Daniel moved into the small, curtained-off room and fixed his attention on the motionless figure on the narrow bed.

Amanda slept in a half-sitting position, propped up on several pillows, her face waxy and gaunt against the white linens. Her hands lay on top of the blanket, still and lifeless, blue veins shadowing her skin.

She struggled for each shallow, rasping breath. The smell of camphor mixed with an unpleasant odor in the room, making Daniel's stomach uneasy. Except for the rapid rise and fall of her chest, she didn't move. Gone was the vibrant young woman who had come into his life so recently.

Daniel pulled up the chair beside the bed and picked up one of her hands, cradling her hot dry flesh against his palm.

Feeling helpless, he needed to do something, anything that might make her more comfortable. Wringing out a cloth in a wash bowl on the small table beside the bed, he talked to her as he wiped her face.

"Amanda, I'm so sorry."

She stirred and began to wheeze. Choking coughs racked

her body. She clawed at the blanket in a panic, unable to catch her breath.

Daniel tamped down his panic and resisted the urge to yell for Michael.

"Sit up. Come on, sweetheart. Here we go." He slid an arm behind her shoulders and pulled her upright, hoping the new position might make her breathing easier. The spasms passed and he lowered her until she lay back against the pillows, gasping. Her eyes opened and she stared, unblinking, past Daniel.

Her voice weak, a mere whisper, made Daniel lean forward to hear her. "Andy, I'm sorry. I tried."

Glancing over his shoulder, he knew before he looked they were alone. He turned back to Amanda, distressed that she was talking to her dead brother. She closed her eyes and tears streamed down her cheeks.

He stroked her arm as he spoke to her in a low voice. "There's nothing to be sorry for. You did just fine. Andy would be proud of you."

Amanda sighed and fell back into a fitful sleep. He pulled the blanket up to her chin. "You rest."

Daniel turned down the lamp and sat in the half-light listening to Amanda's labored breathing, loud and frightening in the still night.

Alone with her, thoughts that had hounded him since the night she took a bullet crowded back.

He smoothed the damp hair from her forehead. "I'm the one who's sorry. I should have been able to protect you".

He had been so angry to see her out on the road, riding with the men, that he hadn't made rational decisions. Now she might die.

He wrung out one of the cloths in the bowl on the table beside the bed and wiped the hot dry skin on her face.

"You didn't have the faintest idea what you were getting yourself into, did you?"

He lifted her hand off the blanket, pushed up her sleeve, and wiped her arm. The blue veins stood out under her pale skin like the tiny lines that marked the rivers on his maps.

Resting his forefinger against the largest artery on her wrist, he felt the pulse of her blood.

"I'm not going to let you give up, Amanda. I want you to fight." He squeezed her hand, wanting desperately to feel some response.

Frustration welled in him. He wanted to give her some of his own strength, to help her fight this illness that had such a fierce grip on her.

As he continued to hold her hand, so small and hot in his, memories crowded back. How beautiful she had looked the first time he had seen her in General Allen's tent. The way she had looked, dressed as a boy, when she returned to camp. The lantern light shining on her tousled curls as she fell asleep sitting on his cot that first night. The way she had looked on the steamer, ready to defend his life with a keg a nails.

He wrung out another cloth. Over and over he thought of how she had felt in his arms that night just before the raid, of how he wanted more from her, of her.

Damn the war.

He had met her because of it, and now it threatened to take her as a casualty.

He looked down at her small white hand, dwarfed against his palm. And damn her talent. Even if she lived, he knew what she wanted, and it wasn't him.

Anger grew in his chest like a live thing, clawing to get out. He ran the cloth over her skin again, alarmed at how quickly the heat returned.

No matter what Michael said, this was his fault. Ignoring his orders, he had returned to camp three days ago before his mission was over to check on her. And then what had he done? Become as enraged as a jealous suitor when he found her sitting outside alone in her nightshirt. He had reacted like a stag in rut, then took his frustrations out on her.

If he lived to be ninety he'd always remember the fearful

look on her face when she had tried to back away from him just before she fell.

He had failed her, more than once, and this time it might cost her her life. How could he live with that?

General Allen had chewed him out and sent him back to his men like an errant schoolboy. He could have had him demoted for dereliction of duty. The general should have put him in front of a firing squad.

Fatigue caught up with Daniel and his head nodded against his chest. He was jolted awake by another round of Amanda's choking and gasping. Daniel pulled her into a sitting position again and sat down beside her on the cot, twisting around so he could hold her against his chest.

"Come on, sweetheart. Relax and breathe. Don't fight it." He rubbed her heaving back.

This time her spell lasted longer, and when it was over and she lay weakly against him, her lips were tinged with blue.

Helpless panic swept Daniel as he held Amanda, unable to do more to help her. The unnatural heat of her body reached him through her thin nightshirt as he lowered her back onto the pillows.

Daniel watched her closely as she moved restlessly on the bed, her head turning from side to side. Her pillow was soaked with sweat. He couldn't do much to help her breathe, but maybe he could make her more comfortable.

Unbuttoning her nightshirt part way, he pulled it down to expose her damaged shoulder. The thick dressing reeked. He peeled the bandage away until he could see underneath. The exit wound, on her back near her shoulder, had opened and yellow matter from the infection had seeped through the bandage, soaking through her nightshirt to the bedding.

Carefully he pulled the bandage clear of her skin, exposing the ugly purple wound. He cleaned the area as best he could with the carbolic solution on her bedside table. She flinched and moaned.

Guilt swamped him. He hated to hurt her, but the wound needed to be cleaned. He wished he could bear the pain for

her, to take it on and suffer on her behalf. After applying a
fresh dressing, he found a clean nightshirt in Michael's trunk.

Slowly, he finished unbuttoning the soiled garment, and eased
it off her body. Her skin looked all pearly with an unhealthy
translucence in the low lamp light. Sweat beaded on his upper
lip. Ill as she was, he found her beautiful. Her slender waist
and rounded breasts and thighs had been well-hidden under her
bulky clothing.

Her firm flesh and unblemished skin, marred only by the
ugly bandage on her shoulder, still felt much too warm to the
touch. He wiped her body down quickly, smeared her chest
with camphor to ease her breathing, then gently worked her
into the clean shirt, needing to cover her. He didn't want anyone
else to see her, not even Michael.

This feeling of possessiveness made him bitter. Amanda
would never belong to him. He didn't deserve her. Because of
him, she would never belong to anyone.

Daniel changed her bedding, gingerly rolling her to one side
as he eased the old linens off and the new on. He threw the
soiled linens outside, and the room smelled fresher. Through
the entire procedure, she had given him no resistance, only
moaning when he moved her.

Wearily, Daniel lowered himself onto the chair. Amanda's
sketchbook lay on the table, next to the pan of water and the
rags he used to wipe her down. He picked the book up to move
it out of the way of the puddle he had created, then opened to
the first page to look at her work. As he turned the pages,
scene after scene appeared, revealing an astonishingly accurate
portrayal of life in an army camp.

He came to a picture of Jeddy, cleaning fish down by the
pond, and frowned. When had she been there? The next page
showed several of the men swimming.

Had she been there? He glanced at Amanda. How else could
she have drawn this picture? He remembered heading down to
the pond the afternoon of the raid. The flap to her tent had
been down, and he thought she had been taking a nap.

He guessed what he would find on the next page. He turned

to the next drawing. A full-page sketch of him, a back view, as naked as the day he'd been born. Every muscle and tendon carefully detailed, every line skillfully drawn, down to the small crescent-shaped scar he carried on his left shoulder.

This picture looked as if she had spent much more time on it than any of the others. Or was that only his imagination?

Daniel stared at the drawing, emotions building in his chest, until he felt as if he might explode. Anger at the unfairness of her being so ill. Fury that she had defied him in the first place and accepted General Allen's absurd offer. Bitterness that they had no future. Rage congealed inside him like a living thing, and he lost his temper, at her, at himself and at God for allowing such a thing to happen.

He stood up and moved to sit on the side of her cot, raising her up against his chest where his feelings roiled like a nest of snakes.

"Damn it, Amanda, I'm not going to let you lie there and just slip away." He snatched up a wet cloth and wiped down her face and neck.

"You know what I'm going to do? I'm going to send your sketch book to New York." After he removed one page. "By the time you're better, they are going to want you to do a hundred more drawings. You'll be the most sought-after artist in the publishing business."

He shifted her higher against his chest and smoothed the hair back from her damp forehead. "Can you hear me? I want you to promise me you'll get better," he demanded as he talked loudly into her ear. "Where is that feisty, unreasonable female?"

She sighed and tried to nestle against him. He shifted her again and continued to talk. "You're going to get better. I know you can. You have courage, more than is good for you. Amanda, open your eyes!"

Then Amanda seemed to struggle with consciousness, mumbling softly. Daniel leaned close to catch her words, and her hands clutched at the front of his shirt. The strength he felt in them startled him. Her eyelids flickered, then opened wide. She stared back at him. Those eyes fascinated him, but he wondered if she even knew who he was.

"I'm glad you came back. I've missed you so." He heard her words and a glimmer of hope made him pray fervently that Michael was wrong, that she would live.

Even though she had spoken, he couldn't be sure she even knew he was there. Earlier she had been talking to her dead brother. He listened carefully to her labored breathing. She seemed less restless, but was it more from weakness than an improvement in her condition?

Feeling helpless, Daniel lowered her back down on the cot. He folded another blanket and gently pushed it behind the pillows, bringing her more upright to help ease her breathing.

His anger deflated like a downed observation balloon. In spite of all his efforts, a fearsome heat still emanated from her. Carefully he rubbed another layer of fragrant camphor ointment on her chest.

"You keep fighting, Amanda. Remember your plans to go to New York? You need to get better so you can go." With a sigh, he rested his elbows on his knees, holding her hand. He needed to feel connected to her, as if his touch could keep her from slipping away. The lantern wick burned low, finally sputtered and went out.

Distant thunder brought Daniel awake with a jerk in the first gray light of dawn. At first he couldn't remember where he was, or why he dozed sitting all cramped up on a hard wooden chair, his face on the rough wood of the table. He felt something was wrong, and sat very still, his senses alert. Then it hit him. The quiet. No raspy moans or gasping breath.

Sometime during the night he had fallen asleep and let go of her hand.

Squinting into the dimness, he could barely make out her still form on the bed. A knot of fear tightened his stomach as he stood and turned away, fumbling for a match to light the lantern. The flame blinded him momentarily, and he blinked to adjust to the light. Dreading what he would find, Daniel forced himself to turn back to the bed.

She blinked against the sudden brightness. Light reflected off her wide golden eyes. Daniel felt a rush of relief that left him weak at the knees. He eased himself back in the chair, staring at her.

Amanda watched him solemnly for a few moments, then reached out a shaky hand and laid it on his knee.

"Are you still angry with me?" Her voice sounded small and weak, but coherent.

His first impulse was to grab her and hug her. Instead, he covered her hand with one of his, using the other to brush the damp hair from her forehead.

His fingers touched blessedly cool skin. "No, Amanda, I'm not angry."

She smiled and closed her eyes. The effort to speak just the few words seemed to have exhausted her. He realized how very lovely she was, and how dreadfully worried he had been. His feelings bordered on an emotion he had no wish to explore. Closing his eyes, he sighed, letting his chin drop to his chest.

Chapter 8

Amanda moved restlessly around the small area in the infirmary that she had called home since the raid almost a month ago. Today she would be moving to a hotel in Cincinnati. The thoughts of privacy, clean sheets and a feather bed did not cheer her, but the time had come to leave Camp Dennison.

Still shaky and a little weak, she was determined to start doing things for herself, to get on with her life. Another week of recovery and she should be strong enough to head for New York.

She missed Lubirda, kept away from camp by the ongoing measles outbreak. General Allen had promised Amanda the Negro woman would meet her at the hotel and stay with her until she was able to travel. Amanda had decided that if Lubirda had not already found employment, she would ask her to accompany her to New York.

She went through her things one more time, futilely searching for her sketchbook. Dismayed, she couldn't imagine where it might have disappeared to. She could do all the drawings again, but that would certainly slow down her plans. By now she had hoped to have finished her series of camp drawings and shipped them off to New York.

The drooping bunch of wildflowers Billy Savage had brought on his last visit made her smile. No one from the camp was supposed to call on her, but Billy could charm the paint off a wall, and he had managed to get permission.

He said he had been along the night of the raid, but she didn't remember him, or much else from that night. He had been so kind to come and keep her company every few days, bringing stories of what went on in camp, or reading to her from the newspaper. She always hoped he would say something about Daniel. Once in a while the captain was mentioned, but never enough for Amanda.

It had been more than three weeks since she had seen him. She missed his smile and the sound of his voice. Even though they were usually at odds, she always felt vibrant and alive when she was in his company. Life seemed dull without him.

Amanda knew he felt guilty because of what had happened to her, but he shouldn't. She was the one who had made the decision to go on the raid. No matter what she said, he held himself responsible. She wouldn't have been surprised if he had shown up wearing a hair shirt. He acted as if he had to make up for something that was her fault.

Michael tried to spare her feelings by telling her Daniel's duties kept him away. Amanda suspected from all the doctor's excuses that she might be wearing her heart on her sleeve.

The possibility that he volunteered for assignments and willfully put himself in danger to avoid her frightened her.

Weary, Amanda sat down on the bed. After she left today, she would never see Daniel again. Twice she had tried to write him a letter, to say good-bye, but she couldn't seem to find the right words to express how she felt. Perhaps that was because she wasn't sure what she felt. She wiped away the tears on her cheeks.

From beyond the thin fabric partition, Amanda heard General Allen speaking to the measles patients. He had come to bid her good-bye. She decided she would prevail on General Allen to give Daniel a message from her telling him farewell.

Quickly she ran a brush over her hair and smoothed her skirt.

She was thankful Arthur had been sent into town to retrieve her trunk. At least she would look presentable when they sent her on her way.

"Miss Giles? May I come in?" The general hesitated, then pulled the curtain aside as she greeted him.

"Good morning, sir."

"Good morning to you, Miss Giles. You're looking better." He waved his hand vaguely in the direction of the cot.

"Thank you, sir," she said, a lump forming in her throat. All these good-byes were so hard.

He pulled a piece of yellow paper out of his coat pocket. "This telegram came for you a short time ago."

She reached for the folded message. Who would be sending her a telegram? she wondered as she read the terse message. Her newspaper editor in New York had bought five of her sketches on camp life and she could expect payment within the week. The telegram closed with a request for additional studies.

She frowned as she read the message a second time, trying to understand how the editor could have bought sketches she had never sent. Then she remembered her missing sketchbook. Daniel was the only one who knew about her plans. Could he have sent the book to New York? Was Daniel responsible for her success?

Before she could decide how she felt about Daniel taking such liberties with her sketches, the general interrupted her thoughts.

"Miss Giles, may I call you Amanda?"

She nodded, still thinking about the telegram.

"Good. Amanda, I know this has been a very difficult time for you, and I will certainly understand if you feel my request is beyond you now, but I will ask anyway."

The general paced in the small space, making her dizzy as she watched him. "Would you consider staying with us?"

Perhaps she hadn't been paying enough attention to what he was saying. His request confused Amanda, reminding her of the day she had met him, the day she had come to Camp Dennison to deliver Andrew's papers. It seemed like years had passed instead of weeks since that fateful meeting.

"Stay, sir? You mean not go to Cincinnati?"

The general stopped his pacing and faced her. "Oh, no, no. I didn't express myself very clearly. You must go and continue your recovery. I would like you to come back and work for me when you feel you are able."

He was giving her a chance to stay! She fought to maintain a calm demeanor. "What kind of work?"

"Why as a spy, my dear."

Considering what had happened on the boat and during the raid, Amanda didn't think she had shown much potential up to now, but the general definitely had her attention. She couldn't say what made the offer more appealing, the opportunity to do more sketches, or the chance to see Daniel.

The general's eyes twinkled. "You could be one of the finest spies I have ever trained. And your country needs you."

She stared at him, flabbergasted by his offer. "I . . . I don't know what to say."

Heaven help her, she welcomed the general's proposal. After what she had been through, she was surprised at herself for even entertaining the thought of returning, but she did. The prospect of working again as a spy intrigued her. The thought of the risks thrilled her.

A voice hailed the general from outside the infirmary.

"Will you excuse me for a moment? I'm expecting someone." He turned abruptly.

"Of course," she said to his back as he disappeared through the curtain.

Amanda was staring the telegram, thinking about the general's proposal when she heard him return. She glanced up, and instead saw Daniel standing just inside the curtain. Her heart did a strange little flip at the sight of him.

"Hello, Daniel. Come in." She felt her mood lighten, as if the sun had broken through a cloudy day.

He hesitated for a moment, as if he wasn't sure he should be there. "You're looking well, Amanda."

She looked terrible and she knew it. Why would he try to flatter her?

Puzzled, she responded, "Thank you."

The exchange was stiffly polite and uncomfortable. Immediately she missed the sparks of contention that dominated most of the exchanges between them.

She held up the telegram. "This just came from New York. Did you send my sketches to the newspaper?"

For the first time he seemed to really look at her. "Yes. They were too good not to see publication."

Finally she saw a glimmer of the old Daniel. As he spoke, he squared his shoulders and met her gaze with a look that challenged her to dispute his decision.

She wasn't about to disappoint him. "I was going to send them myself, you know."

"I wasn't sure you would live long enough to do that."

His blunt comment took her aback for a moment. She knew she had been ill, but she didn't realize that he had had doubts about her recovery.

"I see." She shifted on the cot, uncomfortable with the thought of her own mortality. His frank statement explained why he had been so apologetic earlier, when she had still been sick.

"I came to say good-bye and Godspeed." He gestured to her trunk, packed and ready to be loaded for the trip to Cincinnati.

"But I'm coming back. I just need a week or two to rest."

He took two steps forward and leaned down until he was eye-to-eye with her. His face darkened with the scowling expression that had become so familiar. "You can't be entertaining the general's suggestion that you continue to work for him?"

"Of course I am. *He* seems to think I will do a fine job." She folded her hands in her lap. Until that moment she had been undecided about accepting the general's offer.

"Have you lost your mind!" Daniel, obviously furious, waved his hand in front of her face and yelled.

Amanda grinned at him and nodded her head, delighted with his outburst. It certainly felt good to have her life return to its normal state.

Chapter 9

"Lubirda?" Amanda toyed with the edge of a laced, trimmed petticoat.

Her voice was muffled as she leaned into the wardrobe. "Hmmm?"

Amanda handed her another stack of undergarments. They had been shopping all morning.

"Do you have a nickname?"

"Mama called me Birdie." Lubirda took the clothes from Amanda, her hands very dark against the white fabric.

Feeling very alone, Amanda yearned for the familiarity of a personal relationship. She had grown very close to Lubirda in the week they had stayed in Cincinnati while she finished her recuperation.

"May I? Call you Birdie?"

The Negro woman gave her a startled look. "If you wants."

Now Amanda asked her what was really on her mind. "Birdie, are you scared?" After all, they were going into Southern territory.

"No." Her answer came back, quick and positive.

Amanda wondered why she hadn't taken any time before she answered. "Are you sure?"

"I'm not scared." Lubirda added an emphatic nod to her answer.

Amanda wished she could feel so sure herself. She wasn't scared, but she'd have felt safer if they were traveling with Daniel. She had been bitterly disappointed when the general had visited a few days ago and informed her that Billy Savage was going to pose as her husband. But she had committed herself to the general, and she had no intention of backing out.

Daniel had been so furious with her the day she left camp, he walked out and she hadn't seen him since. She imagined that he had refused to work with her, and she couldn't really blame him. Things had not gone well when they had worked together.

Missing him had become a persistent ache that had competed with her healing wound to make her miserable for the past week.

She pulled her thoughts away from Daniel. Pining for him did her no good at all. She needed to concentrate on the future. She and Billy were going to gather sensitive military information. The wealthy planters would think they were looking for investors in English ships to carry their crops of cotton to English textile mills.

Lubirda's voice brought Amanda back to the conversation. "I already been a slave. They couldn't do no worse to me."

Now Amanda understood. "Birdie, do you know what? I don't even know your last name."

Lubirda eyed her with a steady gaze. "I guess I doesn't have one now." She shrugged her slim shoulders and scooped up an armload of petticoats.

"What do you mean, now?" The remark puzzled Amanda.

"When I lived in New Orleans, I took the name of the family what owned me. But I is free now, so I don't have no name to claim." She shook the garments and laid them over a chair, plucking one from the pile to fold.

"What was your father's name?" Amanda felt she was prying, but couldn't seem to leave the subject alone.

Birdie hesitated. "Don't know who my daddy was. Me and Mama was sold off when I was a baby. She never said." Lubirda closed the trunk. "We finish putting these fine things away when we get back. Come on, time to go. We cain't keep the general waiting."

While Amanda followed Birdie down the stairs, she turned the conversation over and over in her thoughts. Amanda found it very curious that Lubirda didn't seem to feel any lack in not having a last name.

Their carriage waited just outside the hotel. During the pleasant drive to Camp Dennison, Lubirda told Amanda all about living in New Orleans. Amanda sat back and enjoyed being out in the fresh air. When they entered the camp, she found she listened with only half an ear, her attention diverted to the activity in camp. She couldn't deny she hoped to spot Daniel among the men.

General Allen helped her down from the carriage. "My dear, you look wonderful. A week's rest in the hotel was just the thing." General Allen grasped Amanda by her elbow and propelled her into his tent.

"Thank you, sir," she said, a little embarrassed at his effusive greeting. Lubirda followed them in.

"Now, let's get right down to business. Do you have any second thoughts?" He spoke in a low voice and paced back and forth in front of her chair, stopping abruptly to listen to her reply. "Any questions?"

She'd had a dozen questions, but her pride would not allow her to ask any of them. Where was Daniel? Had he refused to work with her? Would she see him again? She sat very straight, her hands folded primly in her lap.

"No, sir. No questions. I am still willing to go, and so is Lubirda." She gestured to her friend, who had taken a seat in the corner of the tent.

"Wonderful! Wonderful!" The general went back to his

pacing. "I had every confidence in you so I went ahead with the arrangements." He beamed down at her.

Heart pounding, Amanda nodded her head, struggling to contain a growing feeling of anticipation. She was going behind enemy lines. The very words rang with excitement.

Part of the plan puzzled Amanda. "General, why would an English couple have Negro servants?"

"What a good question, my dear. You will tell people, should anyone inquire, that your English servants took ill. I'm hoping Tobias and Lubirda will be able to collect information from the slaves on the plantations. White servants would not mix with the slaves."

For the better part of an hour the general talked with both women, and filled in more details about what he wanted them to accomplish. Amanda's head began to pound and she was so tired she had trouble paying attention. Thankful for Lubirda's presence, she was afraid she might miss something important. Much to Amanda's surprise, Lubirda abruptly ended the session.

"S'cuse me, sir, but I gots to get this child home. She still need her rest." She rose to her feet and stood gazing down at the general, being the taller of the two.

Amanda expected the general might take offense at Lubirda's forwardness, but he was immediately apologetic. "Of course. I'm so sorry, Amanda. It was thoughtless of me to keep you so long your first day out."

He turned to Lubirda and clasped her hand. "Well, I can see you are the right one for this job!" Lubirda nodded to the man who beamed with satisfaction.

They spoke briefly of their next meeting before leaving to go back to their hotel in Cincinnati.

"Stand up straight and stop daydreamin'." Lubirda, a hard taskmaster, adjusted the bodice of a green silk dress.

"I am. Don't be so bossy." Amanda heard the woman mum-

ble an unintelligible reply as she tugged a silk flower into place
on the shoulder of the dress.

A few of the ball gowns had needed extra alterations to cover
the scar on her shoulder. Lubirda did a lot of the sewing herself.
Amanda had tried to help, but the second time she sewed the
garment she was working on to her own skirt, Lubirda had
taken over the entire task.

Amanda watched Lubirda as she concentrated on her task.
The days were filled with a flurry of preparations for Amanda
and Lubirda. Fittings at the dressmaker to alter clothes, strategy
meetings run by General Allen and study sessions occurred
every day.

Amanda read everything she could find in the Cincinnati
lending library about England, studying maps of London and
the countryside to arm herself with background information
she might need.

Not once did she see Daniel. Her series of sketches on camp
life had been appearing for the past week. Every day she went
out and bought the New York paper. Thrilled to see her work
in print, she decided to forgive Daniel for doubting her recovery
and interfering by submitting her sketches while she was ill.

She still missed him terribly, and her feelings were beginning
to annoy her. He had taken himself out of her life and she
wanted him out of her head. She had hoped the memory of
him would fade as time went by.

Each time Daniel stole into her thoughts, she tried to carefully
put him aside, scolding herself for being so foolish. Her ploy
worked well enough during the days, but just before she went
to sleep, the memory of him came back to haunt her. She
wanted desperately to experience the rush of pleasurable sensations being with him caused. She couldn't forget how she had
felt when he kissed her the night of the raid. She feared Daniel
was the only man who would ever make her feel that way.

Amanda was delighted that her friendship with Lubirda had
bloomed these past days. The Negro woman had become invaluable, sewing, making suggestions about the wardrobe, and taking over the details of packing. Her help left Amanda with

more time to sketch, but the personal side of their relationship
was what Amanda treasured.

Amanda looked at the clothes spread over the coverlet on
the bed. Best of all were the nightgowns and undergarments
made especially for her of sheer, silky fabrics and laces and
ribbons, some embroidered with tiny flowers and hearts.

All her life she had worn plain thick cotton drawers and
chemises. Her mother had called them "practical." Amanda
hated that word. The only items in her new wardrobe that she
disliked were the heavy stays. If she never saw a whalebone
corset again, it would be all right with her.

A guidebook of the British Isles sat on the bedside table.
Amanda was sure she knew more about England than the people
who lived there.

"There." Lubirda stood back and eyed Amanda's dress with
a critical look. "This be the last bit of sewing. Step on outta
that gown."

Amanda waited for Lubirda to unfasten the garment, then
slipped on a wrapper.

For the hundredth time, she took the ragged copies of the
New York paper and turned to her sketches. She wouldn't be
able to take them along.

The sketches reminded her of Daniel. She vowed once more
to forget about him and concentrate on her purpose for her trip
to the South. Sketching and, of course, gathering information
for General Allen.

As much as she tried to quell thoughts of Daniel, they snuck
in to haunt her. Was Billy the general's first choice for this
mission, or had he asked Daniel to go? And had the captain
declined because of her? Such thinking made her feel miserable,
and she resolved once again to stop it. She wished someone
could tell her how to do that as she put the papers aside and
forced herself to get on with her final preparations.

Two trunks and several pieces of luggage bearing the Ashton
family crest, an impressive thing with lions and serpents entwin-
ing the letter A, stood in the middle of the room.

Amanda felt her pulse leap.

Tomorrow they would leave for Baltimore. It was a good jumping-off spot, a Southern city controlled by the North. There was no blockade, and foreign-registered boats were allowed to come and go from the docks.

Billy and Tobias would be there to meet them, and then they would catch a ferry south to Norfolk. Another ferry would take them as far as Williamsburg, and then they would go by carriage to Richmond.

Amanda studied her handwritten notes of background material gathered during meetings at camp. She knew every fact forward and backward. She got up and placed the pages, along with the newspapers, in the fireplace. She stared into the flames as they curled and turned into black ash.

At last it was time to retire. Amanda lay in bed and tried to picture meeting Billy in Baltimore, but the image of Daniel kept getting in the way. Finally she drifted off to sleep. In her dreams she wore one of her new ball gowns and danced the night away with Lord Ashton. He bore a striking resemblance to Daniel.

Chapter 10

Amanda shifted sideways in her seat, her hands clasping the sill of the railcar window, forehead pressed against the dirty glass in the first-class compartment. Open countryside gave way to the city as they sped by.

"Bal-t-imore! Next stop Baltimore!"

Amanda whispered to Lubirda, excitement welling up inside her. "Are you ready? This is it, Birdie. This is where we start."

"Ready as I'll ever be, missy." The Negro woman leaned over and wiped a smudge off Amanda's forehead. "You gots soot all over your face."

Amanda glanced toward the compartment door. "Stop calling me missy," she chided. "You have to remember, my given name is Charlotte. You have to call me Lady Ashton. You have to act like my maid, not my nanny."

"Don't worry, child. I'll remember." Calmly Lubirda finished wiping Amanda's forehead and tucked the handkerchief in her sleeve.

Amanda watched Lubirda, wondering how she could be so serene. She had as much to lose as anyone if they were caught. No, she wouldn't think about that. If she acted nervous, she'd give their secret plans away. Amanda was still talking to herself when the train ground to a lurching halt in the station.

She stood and peered out at the platform through the dirty glass, searching for Billy. The plan was that he would meet them at the train, and they would go directly to the docks. The boat taking them to Norfolk would leave with the tide that evening. She shook the wrinkles out of the skirt of her green traveling suit and a puff of soot rose from the fabric.

"I can't see him." Amanda struggled to open the window. She stuck her head out and looked up and down the platform. There were a few people standing around, but she didn't see Billy. As her gaze swept the area a second time, she saw a man who looked vaguely familiar. He resembled Bodin, from the steamboat, but his back was to her and he disappeared behind a pillar before she could get a good look at him.

She had convinced herself Bodin must have drowned in the Ohio. Could it have been him? She must be more nervous than she thought to imagine something like that.

Lubirda stood behind her, grumbling. "Don't matter what I calls you if you don't act like no lady."

She stripped off Amanda's soiled gloves one at a time while Amanda hung out the window hoping for another look at the man who resembled Bodin. Lubirda pressed a fresh pair into her hand.

Chagrined at Birdie's words, Amanda pulled her head back in. If it had been the rat-faced little man, she shouldn't draw attention to herself by hanging out the window.

"Come, let's get off and make arrangements for the baggage." Amanda spoke in the flawless English accent she had practiced endlessly. "Perhaps Billy's waiting inside the station."

The two women made their way out of the train, bidding good-bye to the conductor as he helped them down the steps. Amanda glanced up and spotted Tobias standing by the baggage car. She sighed with relief. He would have seen and recognized Bodin if the man had indeed been on the platform.

"There, Lubirda, in the blue jacket, by the baggage car.

That's Tobias." Amanda pointed at the huge, dark-skinned man who hoisted a trunk as if it were empty.

Behind her, Lubirda whistled softly. "Lordy, dat one big man."

Amanda smiled to herself at the woman's reaction. "That means Billy must be around here somewhere." Amanda tugged on her fresh gloves and offered up her wrists so Lubirda could fasten the tiny rows of buttons.

Daniel leaned against a pillar and watched the two women descend from the train. He emitted a low whistle between his teeth, aware of an increase in his heartbeat and an enormous sense of relief that she had arrived safely. Her track record for staying out of trouble was not good.

He had thought about her constantly since they had been apart. Staying away from her had been the hardest thing he had ever had to to. When he learned of the general's plans for her to travel into enemy territory, he had given up the hopeless task of trying to forget her and made his decision to take Billy's place.

His gaze ran up and down her figure. Amanda was a little thinner than she had been, but she looked marvelous.

The green of her outfit and bonnet complimented her red hair and delicate complexion. She looked the very image of a lady, more mature than she had that day he had met her for the first time in General Allen's tent.

She had been so weak the last time he had seen her. Michael Jervis had kept him informed of her recovery, but now that he saw her he felt reassured she had indeed regained her health.

Tobias glanced in his direction, and Daniel nodded. The man smiled, his teeth flashing white against his dark skin, and he shouldered a trunk, moving toward the outside door where the cabs awaited. Attuned to each other, the two men needed no words to communicate.

Daniel pushed away from his pillar and walked toward the two women. Amanda had her back to him. He noticed a start of recognition on Lubirda's face and the small smile that played on her lips. He shook his head slightly and nodded at Amanda. Lubirda's smile widened.

He leaned down and spoke quietly into Amanda's ear. "I wondered how long it would take you to get off the train. I started to think maybe you had come to your senses and decided not to come."

Amanda stiffened. She whirled to face him. Feeling foolishly pleased that she recognized the sound of his voice, even altered by the addition of an English accent, he studied her. Her charming face showed genuine surprise. Her mouth opened and closed several times, but no sound came out.

Lubirda looked from Amanda to Daniel, and then back to Amanda, and finally cleared her throat. "I'll go and see about them bags." She headed off down the platform, after Tobias.

Daniel took a step forward and they stood toe to toe. Her skirt brushed against his pant legs. He tipped his head to one side and studied Amanda for a long moment.

"Well, well. You cleaned up pretty good." He could feel her breath coming in choppy little bursts on his face.

Amanda found her voice. "Where's Billy? He's all right, isn't he?"

Annoyed her first words to him were of another man, he gave her a curt reply. "He's fine. Just a change of plans, that's all. Now, since it is possible we are being watched, don't you think you ought to give your husband a proper greeting?"

Before she had time to react, he pulled her into his arms and kissed her fully on the mouth. Her lips were soft and his body responded to her warmth. The force of his reaction to her startled him for a moment as he released her. He fought an impulse to reach out and pull her back up against him. She looked stunned.

"That's better, Lady Ashton." He covered his discomfit at his feelings with a little bow and offered her his arm.

He stood staring down at her for a moment before he spoke. "Now, I want to buy you and Lubirda a ticket to New York."

"What?" Her face clouded with a puzzled expression.

"This mission is too dangerous. I can do what I have to do without you." He knew from the furious expression on her face the exact moment she understood what he was saying.

Her eyes narrowed and she stiffened and turned slightly toward him. "I'm not backing out. I made a commitment to General Allen." She fairly spit the words at him.

Daniel leaned forward and used his forefinger to push back a curl that had escaped from under her bonnet. "We both know how ludicrous the general's ideas can be, don't we?" This mission was far more dangerous than their trip on the Ohio River.

She started to sputter, and he could tell she was winding up for a tirade, so he kissed her again.

Amanda pulled away and hissed at him. "Will you stop doing that!"

He smiled at her reaction, resigned to the fact that he would not be able to talk her out of going along. "Probably not. I figure Lord Ashton is hopelessly enamored with Lady Ashton."

She gaped at him for a moment, and he cupped her chin and gently closed her mouth. She certainly was a stubborn little thing. He resisted the urge to kiss her a third time. Lady or no, she'd probably kick him in the shins.

He hadn't really expected any other response from her when he proposed canceling her part in the mission. After all, when had she ever been reasonable?

He drew her hand through the crook of his elbow, pleased to feel her gloved fingers tremble at his touch. At least he was having an effect on her. If he could hold the upper hand and keep her in line by throwing her off balance, perhaps they could both come through this alive.

"I see Tobias and Lubirda have taken care of the trunks. Shall we go?"

Still looking a little dazed, Amanda nodded and let him lead her out of the station. He helped her up into a hansom cab, gave the driver directions, then climbed in behind her. The cab rocked as the driver clambered to his seat on top.

By the time Daniel joined her in the cab, Amanda had composed herself. She pulled her skirts aside to give him room on the narrow seat, but she didn't meet his eye.

"Where are Lubirda and Tobias?" Her voice sounded a tiny bit husky.

He made a motion with his hand. "Following us in another cab with the baggage."

She glanced up toward the front of the cab. "Can the driver hear us?"

He looked at her approvingly. Her caution pleased him. "Perhaps. But it doesn't matter. I hired him."

She questioned him about his substituting for Billy.

"It was necessary." His abrupt answer made her blink. He had no intention of telling her that he couldn't tolerate the thought of her traveling with another man.

"Nothing else about the plan has changed. Our boat leaves on schedule at six. This cab will take us directly to the dock. We'll take the steamer to Richmond, drive out to the Shipley plantation, charm the planters and gather military information. If we're lucky, we can get them to invest large sums of cash into our fake shipping venture, too."

His arm brushed against her shoulder as he pulled a pocket watch from his brocade vest and checked the time. He watched a flush creep into her cheeks. His touch seemed to unsettle her. He liked that. He wanted her to stay on her toes.

"What about our identities?" she asked. "Do you know everything? Is it to be the same story Billy and I were going to use?"

He smiled to hear how rattled she sounded. Apparently he wasn't the only one who had feelings he found difficult to deal with. The hard part would be getting her to admit to them. He remembered her statement about believing in free love. He intended to make sure he was the only one she would ever love.

"Have you got cold feet? It's not too late to go back to the train station." He stared at her, wanting very much for her to say yes, so he could send her away from the dangers.

She stared at him for a moment. "No. It's just that we expect these people we will be visiting to believe so much . . ." Her voice trailed off.

Since she wouldn't listen to reason and go back, he felt he needed to make the best of the situation and reassure her.

"Remember this, Amanda. The big lies people believe. The little ones will sound questionable, but you can get away with the big ones. At least for a while."

She nodded, then changed the subject. "I think I saw someone who knows us in the station."

Alarmed, he questioned her. "Were you followed on the train?"

"No, I didn't see him on the train. But in the station, just as we pulled in, I saw a man who reminded me of the man named Bodin, from the boat."

"Why didn't you say something right away?"

She folded her hands primly in her lap and glared at him. "I was a little distracted, remember? Besides, I didn't get a good look at him."

"Well, even if it was him, he wouldn't recognize you. You look very different now than you did on the boat." Still, he'd keep his eyes open for the little weasel.

"Perhaps not, but he'd be sure to spot you." Her voice quavered.

Daniel reached over and patted her had. "He couldn't know where we're headed."

She shook her head and sighed. "I guess I'm a little nervous."

"I think we were pretty convincing as a husband and wife greeting each other at the station." He watched her blush, assuming she thought about his kiss.

He knew he had taken her off guard, but even so, her response to his kiss had seemed naive. He liked that more than anything. Everything about her pleased him, except that she was here.

He shook himself from his reverie. Amanda had turned her attention to the city streets, bustling with activity in the late afternoon. Then she turned back to him.

"Did you see my sketches in the paper?"

"Yes. I saved them all." She had captured the essence of camp life.

She smiled and laid a hand on his arm. "Thank you for doing that for me."

He covered her hand with his. "I did take one out before I sent the packet."

She looked at him, one eyebrow raised in question. "Why?"

"I wasn't eager to have my naked butt pictured in the largest paper in the Union."

"Oh." Furious color flooded her cheeks. She pulled her hand away and stared out the window.

He figured she had forgotten about that one.

"There is one thing I forgot." Daniel reached for her hand in among the folds of her skirt in her lap.

He grasped her left wrist and turned her hand palm up. Slowly he unbuttoned her glove. Her pulse beat a furious pace in a small blue vein just under the skin he exposed. He remembered how those vessels looked all over her body. She would do more than kick him in the shins if she knew how much of her he had seen.

He thought again of the sketch she had done of him. They both had more knowledge of the other than was decent. He smiled at the thought.

Tugging at the fingers of her glove one at a time, he took much longer than necessary to slide the kidskin over her hand. The action had an unsettling intimacy to it, as if he removed a piece of clothing far more personal.

He glanced up at her face and saw she held her breath. When he ran his thumb over her bare palm, she gasped, and tried to draw her hand away.

"Wait. I'm not finished." He fished a plain heavy gold band out of his vest pocket and slid it onto her finger. "There, now we look official."

Amanda stared at the band. The ring fit her finger perfectly. The worn surface glowed with a satiny patina in the dim cab. She seemed afraid to meet his eye.

"Thank you," her voice squeaked. Cheeks flushed, she

grabbed her glove from him and pulled it on over the ring, then jammed her hands back in her lap.

He should stop teasing her like that. It made him doubly aware of her. But, he conceded, it was a lot of fun.

The cab rocked and swayed as it moved through the heavy traffic, and their knees and shoulders bumped gently together. Out of the corner of his eye he saw her watch him.

Amanda shifted again in her seat. "How much further?" she asked, her voice sounding strained.

"Not much. Why? Are you uncomfortable?" He was holding the strap that hung from the roof, but made no attempt to brace himself. His thigh brushed against her leg.

Her golden eyes glared at him, and her cheeks flared with new color. "No. I'm fine," she snapped.

He chuckled under his breath. "Good, so am I."

He loved to see her rattled. It reassured him that she cared for him, even though he knew she wouldn't admit it. He intended to keep her off balance until he could convince her to give up her daft ideas of working for General Allen and living alone in New York. Then he would convince her to marry him.

She remained silent for the rest of the trip to the docks.

Amanda couldn't decide if she was more furious at Daniel for taunting her, or at herself for responding. She tossed her gloves on the bed and scanned their accommodations.

The first-class cabin consisted of a suite of three rooms, far superior to the cabin Amanda and Daniel had shared on the steamboat. Amanda and Lubirda would take the largest, which also doubled as a sitting room, and Tobias and Daniel would use the smaller ones on either side. All rooms connected by interior doors, allowing the four of them to move between compartments without using the passageway.

The ship, French in registry and flying the French flag, was classed as a passenger vessel. It had been chosen because it was less likely to be harassed by Union ships enforcing the blockade along the Southern coast.

Disappointed by the lack of a proper bath, Amanda would have to make do with a basin of lukewarm water. Feeling grimy after the train trip, she would feel much better after a wash and a change of clothes. Lubirda was just beginning to unfasten her dress when a knock sounded on the outside door.

"Who is it?" Amanda took a step forward, holding the bodice in place. Lubirda jerked her back by holding tight to her dress. Startled, Amanda asked, "What are you doing?"

"You stay put. *I* the maid, *I* gets the door." Lubirda put a finger to her lips and brushed past her. "Who's there?"

"Captain's mate, madame. I have a message for Lord Ashton." The voice sounded young and carried an accent similar to the one she and Daniel used.

"One moment, please." Lubirda opened the door a crack.

As Amanda watched Lubirda, she heard the inside door behind her open. Before she could turn around, Daniel stood at her back, taking Lubirda's place. As his large hands fumbled with the tiny pearl buttons, his fingers brushed up against the bare skin on her nape. She tingled at his touch.

Lubirda took a folded slip of paper from the young man and closed the door.

Amanda tried to pull away from Daniel. "You can stop now. He's gone." Her voice sounded strained.

Daniel ignored her. "No, stay here. I'm just starting to get the hang of this."

He finished with the buttons. She flattened her palms against the front of her dress. He removed his hands from her nape, but stayed where he was, close behind her.

"You're going to have to alert me when someone is at the door. It won't look very good to have me coming out of the servant's room." His breath ruffled her hair and smelled slightly spicy.

She found she couldn't think clearly when he stood close to her. Amanda felt as if her whole body blushed. She bolted across the cabin and grabbed the note, ignoring a knowing look on Lubirda's face.

Damn Birdie, it's as if she could read minds sometimes.

Amanda felt like such a ninny for reacting to Daniel the way she did. After all, he was doing these things just to unnerve her. Amanda unfolded the message and stared at the paper, her thoughts jumbled.

She glanced up to see Daniel holding out his hand. Needing to keep her distance, she passed the note back to Lubirda, who handed it off to Daniel.

He read it, then addressed Lubirda. "Will you please go and inform the captain we would be pleased to dine with him tonight? Thank you."

The outside passage door closed behind the Negro woman and Amanda turned her back on Daniel, trying to ignore him as she busily picked up her fresh clothes. She waited to hear him return to his room, and was startled when he grabbed her by the arm and swung her around to face him.

Tension showed in his features, and his voice sounded coldly quiet. "If you can't handle the role you agreed to play here, tell me now. We are to appear as husband and wife, and if your behavior raises suspicions, you put us all in danger. Someone will notice how jumpy you are."

Her anger flared. "Then stop teasing me! Married people don't have to touch each other all the time."

His grip on her arm tightened as he stared at her without speaking. She twisted and tried to step away. The newly healed wound in her shoulder began to throb. She gave up struggling and took a step toward him, trying to alleviate the pressure.

"I want you to let go." She needed to stand up to him. She didn't know why he was acting this way, teasing her, and she wanted it to stop. It was far too disconcerting when she couldn't read his expression.

He finally spoke, his tone low and even. "I'm not going to risk this mission and our lives because you think you want a little adventure. Understand? You'd better be sure you're up to this." His grip tightened on her arm and he gave her a little shake.

Amanda nodded, tears springing to her eyes. Her voice choked on a whisper. "Daniel, you're hurting me."

He immediately let go of her, his expression contrite. "Sorry." He turned abruptly and left the room.

Daniel closed the door between their rooms and leaned heavily against the frame. He rubbed his temples slowly, as if the motion could improve his ability to reason. He hadn't meant to hurt her.

He thought he could keep the upper hand with her, but he was beginning to doubt himself. Whenever he got close to her, he acted like a schoolboy with his first crush. This wasn't the time to tell her how he felt. He was afraid she would reject him, thinking he only wanted her out of harm's way. So he covered his feelings, by teasing and taunting her, loving her reaction to him.

He had to admit that if he wasn't careful, he could be more of a threat to the mission than she was. His feelings got the better of him when he was around her. That was why he had insisted on kissing her earlier in the station.

What surprised him most about that kiss was not her naive reaction, but the force of his. He immediately remembered the night he had found her in a nightshirt, in front of the fire, and again his body responded to the memory. Angry with himself, he pushed the thought away. He had to get control of himself and call a truce with Amanda.

He blamed his dilemma on General Allen. Up until the time Amanda had come into camp, the general had made sound decisions, even under extreme pressure. Daniel no longer trusted General Allen's judgment. Or his own. At best this was a risky mission and his feelings weren't helping any.

When the general had decided to send Amanda and Savage, Daniel insisted they find a substitute for Amanda, but no suitable woman was available. He then convinced General Allen to change the orders, substituting himself for Savage.

He didn't trust the charming Billy Savage to act like a gentleman. He had wangled permission from the general to visit

Amanda while she recuperated. Daniel had seen him in action in town and knew how he behaved around women.

And what if it had been Bodin she had seen at the station? Chances were good he drowned when he went over the side of the steamboat that night on the Ohio, but it was possible he got away. One more danger for him to worry about.

Daniel pushed himself away from the door frame and wandered over to the porthole. He stood staring absently at the water. It was too late now to send her back, even if he had been able to convince her. He would just have to keep his eyes open.

At least he was sure of Tobias, and Lubirda could probably be trusted to do what she was told to do. Between the three of them they should be able to watch out for Amanda and keep her out of harm's way.

Amanda sank down on the edge of her bed, rubbing her shoulder to ease the ache, wishing she could do the same for the pain around her heart. Tears threatened, but she blinked them back.

"Cretin!" she muttered to the empty room. But she knew he was right.

She did forget the role she played when he was with her. Could she explain that to him? Hardly! Not when she couldn't explain it to herself.

Could she successfully carry out the mission? Yes, but at what cost to her emotions? It would have been so much easier if Billy had come. She never had any reaction to being close to him. All Daniel had to do was walk into the room and she felt as if she might turn inside out.

It shouldn't be so hard to act like a wife. Surely she could do that and not become irrational. After all, she would just treat it like a game of pretend. That's all it was, really. There was no need to feel as if she might fly into pieces every time he touched her.

She'd start at dinner tonight. She'd show him she could do

it. She just wished she could think of a way to convince him to keep his hands to himself. When he touched her she turned to mush.

Lubirda returned to the cabin while Amanda still sat on the bed, talking herself into the role of Lady to Daniel's Lord.

"You all take a little rest. It been a long day, and probably be a late night." Lubirda loosened Amanda's stays and made her lie down, then covered her with a blanket.

Amanda felt better when she awoke. She washed her face, and quickly changed into her dinner gown before allowing Lubirda to brush her hair. The Negro woman fussed at her, insisting the hair should come before the dress, but Amanda ignored her.

She would act like a wife, but there was no point in putting herself into any uncomfortable situations when she didn't have to. She would not sit around in a thin wrapper any longer than necessary, not when Daniel had free access to her room. Lubirda finished her hair and muttered to herself. They heard a knock at the connecting door. Lubirda let Daniel in.

Amanda rose from the chair and turned to him. "Daniel—"

He interrupted her by scowling and holding up a hand, motioning her to stop. "Try the name again. Who am I?"

"Oh. Edmund." The name felt strange. She needed to settle what had passed between them earlier. "About this afternoon . . ."

Again the hand went up. "Do you still insist on going through with the mission?"

She raised her chin and looked him in the eye. "Yes." Did he really think she might back out now? He should know her better than that.

"That's all I need to know." Daniel turned to Lubirda. "You and Tobias can eat in the crew's mess. If you're ready, he's waiting for you outside."

Lubirda nodded to him, made a minor adjustment of the sleeve of Amanda's gown, and left the cabin.

She had her back to him, relieved he had stopped her from babbling an explanation. Amanda chided herself. What was she going to tell him? That the reason she jumped away from his touch was because it made her tingle? Or maybe that when he's standing close, she felt light-headed because she forgot to breathe? That should reassure him she was ready to play the part of Lady Ashton.

His voice interrupted her thoughts. "Are you ready?"

She turned to face him. He looked wonderful in his dark evening dress clothes. The close-fitting coat and trousers of fine, navy blue wool suited him. Amanda tried to imagine Tobias laying out his clothes and taking care of them the way Lubirda did for her, and could not. She could not picture Tobias as a valet.

"I'm ready." She waited for him to lead the way.

"Good. We're a little early. Let's take a minute and go over some of the background information together." He fired several questions at her about England.

She answered every one without pause. Her stomach fluttered. Dinner tonight would be the first true test of how well they could impress people as Lord and Lady Ashton.

"I don't know if I can pull this off and manage to eat, too," Amanda muttered as she rubbed her hand over her midriff.

Daniel smiled down at her. "You'll be fine. I'm sorry if I was hard on you this afternoon. If you can do Lady Charlotte half as well as you did Andrew, you'll be all right."

Oh, Lordy, she thought to herself. Just don't smile at me like that and I'll have half a chance. "Thank you," she said sweetly, hoping she looked more confident than she felt.

"Tell you what, if you feel cornered, just swoon. Loudly. I'll catch you. We can tell people you have heart trouble." He grinned at her again.

I do have heart trouble, she thought. *You, my dear Captain McGrath, trouble my heart.* She picked up her wrap.

"Shall we go, Lady Charlotte?" He offered his arm.

"But of course, Edmund." She curtsied low, head bowed, not missing his appreciative glance at her low-cut gown. Amanda took his arm and they left the cabin.

The French captain and his two officers spoke excellent

English and proved to be charming and witty company. The *brandade de mortue* was very good, and the wine excellent. After a dessert of chocolate soufflé with raspberry sauce, Amanda grew weary and was amazed to hear Daniel say that it was after midnight and time for them to retire.

She daydreamed as they walked back to their cabin. Daniel had acted attentive and affectionate towards her. She couldn't remember when she had spent a more pleasant evening. The thought had occurred to her repeatedly during the evening how perfect it would be if they didn't stop pretending, and in the privacy of the cabin he would hold her in his arms and . . .

"Charlotte!" He sounded annoyed and she came abruptly out of her musings.

She was amazed to see they were standing in the cabin. She really had to stop drinking wine. It led her to flights of fancy.

His words echoed her thoughts. "You're going to have to pay attention."

"What is it?" Flushing, she laid her shawl over the chair.

"Nothing that can't wait until tomorrow." He studied her for a long moment. "You must be tired."

She nodded and turned away, hoping her expression of longing for him had not shown on her face in the dim light.

"Tonight went just fine." He stood quietly in the center of the darkened room. "We make a pretty good team."

"I hope so, Daniel. I really want this mission to be successful. It's very important to me." Amanda could feel the steady throb of the engine through the floorboards.

She thought about his kiss at the train station, and how it felt to be in his arms. The way she felt drawn to him frightened her. She was more nervous and uncertain about her feelings for Daniel than about having their identities discovered.

"I hope so, too. Your life may depend on it, as well as Lubirda and Tobias." He looked at her with his head cocked to one side, and she knew his face, even though she couldn't see him well in the dim light. She was getting to know him, to anticipate his moods, his expressions.

"Good night." Her voice was soft, almost a whisper.

He hesitated for a moment and then turned and knocked softly on the door to the smaller chamber as he pushed it open. He spoke quietly and Amanda could hear Lubirda's sleepy voice mumbling a reply. She was there in moments, trading places with Daniel.

Daniel disappeared into the small room, where he would sleep in the maid's bed. Lubirda helped Amanda undress. The two women spoke little, Lubirda still groggy with sleep, and Amanda preoccupied with thoughts of the past evening. She crawled into the big bed and fell asleep as Lubirda fixed herself a pallet on the floor.

Lubirda awoke to the sound of water slapping at the side of the ship, and for the briefest moment wondered where she was. Rolling to her side, she stood and, in the light of early morning, watched the young woman asleep on the bed.

She's so young, a babe, thought Lubirda. She laughed to herself. By the time she was Amanda's age she had borne two children and lost any illusions about what life might have in store for her.

She could never have anticipated the direction her life had taken, and viewed the whole turn of events with a bemused detachment.

Firmly believing her future, as well as her past, was God's will, and whatever happened was meant to be, Lubirda had protected herself against the cruel truths of her existence with her faith, making promises to herself about the kingdom of heaven when the incidents in her life on earth had become unbearable.

Her attention shifted back to the bed. Amanda made a small purring noise and rolled to her side, burrowing into the covers. The sunlight coming through the porthole burnished her short curly hair to a rich copper and tinged her lips and skin with hues of apricot.

Lubirda had a hard time believing this girl could have lived in an army camp for any time at all and passed as a young man. Even the first night she had seen her, she guessed almost immediately. *Well,* she thought, *most people just don't see what they look at.* It wasn't any different with white folks.

She smiled again as she remembered the exchanges yesterday between Amanda and the handsome captain. It was as clear as the nose on your face that the girl was in love with him. The poor child didn't even know what to do with the feelings.

Lubirda was as sure about how the captain felt about the girl. For some reason he held himself back, and seemed angry with Amanda because of his own feelings. She wondered why. It was very entertaining to watch the two of them together. Sparks did fly!

The girl stirred again and opened her eyes. She looked blankly at Lubirda for a moment, and then gave her a little smile.

"Good morning." Amanda rolled onto her back, stretching like a lazy cat.

Lubirda smiled to herself, enjoying the indulgent feeling she had for this girl. "How was yo' dinner?"

"Oh, Birdie, it was wonderful." Amanda proceeded to name several dishes they had enjoyed.

Lubirda, familiar with French food, from living in New Orleans for so long, corrected Amanda's pronunciation, emphasizing the roll of the R sound.

"I think perhaps I drank too much of the wine though." She rubbed her temples with her fingertips. "How was your dinner with the crew?"

The simple question surprised Lubirda. Rarely did anyone concern themselves with her comfort.

"Jes' fine." She ran her hand down the sleeve of her nightgown, enjoying the feel of the smooth, fine cotton. How her life had changed in the last few months.

"Did you get to know Tobias?"

Lubirda nodded in response to Amanda's question.

"To tell you the truth, he scares me a little." Amanda said. "He's so strong and, well, big."

Her observation amused Lubirda. "I don't think you have

to worry 'bout Tobias. He ain't a hurting kinda man, when it come to women, that is. And he very 'tached to the captain.''

"What do you mean, 'a hurting kind of man'?" The girl appeared puzzled.

"You knows, the kind of man what would ..." Lubirda turned to look Amanda in the face and studied her for a long moment. "You don't know, do you, about any kind of man?" A deep flush darkened the girl's cheeks.

"No," she whispered the reply. "No, I'm afraid I am sorely lacking in any information in that area. Tell me what you mean."

"Didn't your mama ever teach you anything?" Lubirda was amazed that a white woman could reach this girl's age and still be so unknowing.

"I think she was waiting until I married."

"Child, that too long to wait for most folks." Lubirda sighed and shrugged. "You going to need answers." And soon, too, if she wasn't mistaken.

"You tell me." Amanda sat upright and faced Lubirda, closely studying her face.

The girl's earnestness made Lubirda uncomfortable. She was pretty sure white folks saw the things that went on between men and women a little different than colored folks.

"You best ask someone else."

"I haven't got anyone else, and I think I'd like some answers now." Her face flushed a becoming pink.

Lubirda had no argument for that. Lordy, the child needed educating. Lubirda felt old and wise as she settled in to answer Amanda's questions.

Chapter 11

Amanda jerked upright on the carriage seat when she felt Daniel gently shake her arm.

"Are we there?" She blinked and rubbed her eyes, then turned to see past Lubirda out the window.

"Almost. According to the map, it's around this curve." He leaned into the plush seat to give her better access to his window.

She and Daniel had established a kind of unspoken truce on the ship. She wondered how long it would last.

"Holy Moses! Is that it?" Amanda asked the question without looking away from the magnificent Shipley mansion.

Lubirda sat forward on the seat and struggled to straighten and retie the ribbon bow on Amanda's bonnet.

Daniel grimaced at her choice of words. "Really, Lady Ashton. Such language from a duchess. Remember, our own Bedford Hall is much finer than this house."

Amanda had become so accustomed to Daniel's accent she hardly noticed it anymore.

"Oh, but look. It's beautiful, isn't it?" The house, Italian Renaissance in design, drew Amanda's full attention.

Surrounded by graceful weeping willow trees and formal

lawns, the house had an exotic, foreign quality. The drive curved across the front in a large half circle. The structure itself seemed to exude warmth as it glowed pink in the late afternoon sun, and light reflected off the west facing windows. The James River glinted silver in the background.

She leaned back against the seat with a sigh. "Nervous as I am, I do believe I am going to enjoy this. You know, I never asked. I don't really understand what made these particular people so anxious for us to visit."

The invitation to stay in Richmond with the Shipleys had come through the Ashton's New York bank, and the tone of it practically begged them to stay for as long as they wished.

"Well my dear, a rumor was started at a brokerage house in New York that an English Duke was so anxious for cotton, he would be willing to pay well over the market price. His family has been heavily invested in the textile industry for ever so many years."

Daniel paused to pick a piece of lint from his sleeve. "The invitations began to pour in. This looked like the most promising, given Shipley's connections, and the proximity of the Tredegar Iron Works to his property. If we can't get the information we seek here, we'll find a reason to move on."

Amanda smiled at him mischievously. "Had I known how much these Southerners craved important guests, I might have decided to come sooner! It looks more comfortable than camp, don't you think?"

Lubirda groaned and rolled her eyes. "We done created a situation here."

"Oh for heaven's sake, Birdie, I'm only fooling, and you know it. Look. Is that Mr. Shipley, do you think?"

Daniel and Lubirda followed her gaze to the front of the house as they pulled to a stop in the circular drive. A short, rotund man dressed in a garish green and yellow waistcoat that accentuated his generous girth stood on the front steps of the graceful mansion. Before the carriage pulled to a stop, a tall handsome woman wearing a stern expression joined him.

"Well, ladies, I would venture to say that is our host, Desmond Shipley, and his wife Blythe.'' Daniel spoke in an undertone as Tobias jumped down from the driver's seat to open the door. The huge black-skinned man dressed in purple velvet livery was a sight to behold.

Amanda studied their hosts from the dark corner where she sat. They looked humorous together simply because they were such opposites. Mr. Shipley, short, round, and bald, wore a big grin of welcome. Mrs. Shipley, tall, stately, with beautiful thick blond hair, looked none too happy at the prospect of their arrival.

Blythe, Amanda thought. *The name does not fit her. It should be something like . . . Catherine.* In that instant, Amanda realized how much this woman's bearing reminded her of her father's sister. A stiff, proper, unbending cold sort of person.

Amanda's opinion was amended almost immediately when Daniel descended from the carriage. Amanda saw the expression on Mrs. Shipley's face go from stern to interested. Amanda pushed away the stab of jealousy and extended her hand to Daniel, who had turned back to assist her from the carriage.

Amanda smoothed the full skirt of her dove gray traveling costume. Daniel took her by the arm and led her up the steps to greet their host and hostess. Lubirda stayed behind to supervise the unloading of the trunks.

''Welcome to Villa Anona! I am Desmond Shipley and this is my wife, Blythe. We are so pleased you will be staying with us, Lord and Lady Ashton. Come in, come in.'' Shipley gestured and shook hands with such vigor, a sheen of perspiration appeared on his forehead.

During the introductions, Amanda studied Mrs. Shipley and realized she was much younger than she had first thought. The woman turned and bestowed a beautiful smile on Daniel as she took his arm to lead him into the house. Again, Amanda pushed away the twinge of emotion.

Mr. Shipley, immediately at her side to escort her, inquired about their trip, then didn't give her time to reply before he said, ''You must be tired, Lady Ashton. You have been traveling for such a long time. Ophelia will show you to your rooms.''

He motioned to a huge Negro woman who stood off to one side of the entry. "After you rest, we will serve tea, and get better acquainted."

Amanda untied the ribbons on her bonnet and handed the hat to Birdie. "Oh, that sounds lovely, Mr. Shipley. Thank you." She felt like a child when he patted her arm and turned his attention to Daniel.

"My Lord, perhaps you would care to see a part of the farm before we lose the light. I have an excellent stable, and you both are invited to ride whenever you wish. We'll leave the ladies to chat and become acquainted."

It amused her to hear him refer to his lands as a farm, thinking briefly of the small modest frame houses and barns that sat in the middle of the fields of crops in the countryside around Philadelphia.

Daniel gave her a light kiss on the cheek. "You rest, my dear, and I'll see you at tea." He turned and followed Mr. Shipley out the door.

Amanda watched him until he disappeared from sight. She felt Blythe Shipley's eyes studying her intently.

An abrupt change occurred in the woman's demeanor the minute the men left the house. "Is such short hair the style now in London?" she said with a sniff.

Amanda thought the question held more malice than curiosity. Her hand flew to the nape of her neck. When she opened her mouth to reply, Mrs. Shipley cut her off.

"I will leave you to your rest and see you at tea at five. We serve a proper high tea at Villa Anona." Blythe Shipley became the stern, cold woman Amanda had glimpsed on the front steps as she turned and swept out of the entryway before Amanda could say anything.

Amazed by the woman's rudeness, Amanda motioned to Birdie, who had stood off to the side during the introductions. Together they followed Ophelia's wide swaying hips up the beautiful curved staircase. The slave moved with a quick grace incongruous with her size, surprising Amanda as she hurried to keep up.

They stopped in the middle of the hallway that ran the length of the house. "This be the one the master wants you all to have."

Ophelia pushed the heavy wooden door open. It was the first time Amanda had heard her speak. Her voice had a lovely sing-song quality to it.

A huge ornate bed with gauzy lace hangings dominated the beautiful pink and green bedchamber. French-style doors opened onto a balcony overlooking the gardens. Ophelia eyed her, waiting for a reaction. Careful, Amanda thought, act unimpressed. I'm supposed to be used to living this way.

"Thank you, Ophelia, this should do." Amanda crossed the chamber to the far wall, where there were two doors. "Where do these lead?"

"This one be the bathing room, and the other is for your maid."

Amanda opened the second door. The small room contained nothing but a bed and chest.

Perfect, she thought. The possibility of having difficult sleeping arrangements had bothered her ever since Daniel showed up in Billy's place. The thought occurred to her that sharing a room hadn't bothered her before the change in husbands. Daniel could sleep in the small room, and Lubirda could stay with her.

Ophelia nodded and left the room. Amanda turned to Lubirda, who shook her head and put her finger to her lips.

"Don't go exploding," she whispered, reading Amanda's pent-up feelings over their hostess's parting remark. "These walls has ears."

In her best English accent, Amanda proclaimed in a low voice, "Our hostess is a nasty twit."

"Be careful of her, missy. She be on your tail."

"Why? I don't even know her." Blythe's rude behavior puzzled Amanda.

Lubirda shrugged. "Some women don't like any kinda competition."

Within moments the trunks arrived and then the bath water,

ending their conversation. It appeared the Shipleys had a good many house slaves.

Amanda soaked in a tub full of steaming, scented water while Lubirda unpacked. The small bathing room containing the bathtub also held a dressing table and mirrors. High on the wall a stained glass window flooded the room with a beautiful pattern of colored sunlight. *Yes,* Amanda thought as she sank a little deeper into the water, *I could get used to this.*

Lubirda interrupted her thoughts. "You gonna be all wrinkled for tea time if you doesn't get outta that water." She held the huge fluffy towel and wrapped Amanda as she stepped from the tub. After finishing with the towel, Lubirda was behind her holding a robe. Someone had trained this woman well.

"Birdie, where did you learn how to be a maid?" Amanda wrapped the robe around her body and tied the belt at her waist.

"Why, I jes' growed up watching my mama, I guess. I laid out the gold silk. That all right?"

"I guess so." It seemed too dressy to her for an afternoon affair, but Birdie would know better than she. "Is that the type of gown I can wear for this evening?"

Amanda moved into the bedroom and studied the dress on the bed. She was not used to making these decisions. Life at home had never been so formal, and on most occasions she had been treated more like a child than an adult.

"Lordy no. You wears the gold to tea and then you comes back up and rests for a while before you changes for dinner." Lubirda went to the dresser to find a chemise for Amanda.

"Good heavens, Birdie, do southern women have time to do anything but change their clothes and eat?" Amanda was amazed that three changes of clothing would be required between now and bedtime.

"Well, you gots to set time aside to rest. Don't be forgetting that. It most tiring, changing and eating." Amanda caught the gleam of amusement in Birdie's eye.

"Please, do let me know if I appear to have too much energy. I might give myself away!" Both women gave in to a fit of laughter.

It felt good, and helped to ease some of the tension they both felt. They could not forget General Allen's comments about how important the information they might gain on this visit would be to the Union army.

Lubirda brushed out Amanda's hair, trimmed and shaped into a flattering cap of curls. After helping her to dress, she consulted a small clock on the mantel. "You all done." She studied her with a critical eye. Amanda felt like child being inspected before leaving for church.

Lubirda nodded her approval and announced, "Time to go down to tea."

"Do I go down by myself, or do I wait for Daniel?" It seemed they had talked endlessly about details, but Amanda realized there were a great many small decisions she would have to make herself on the spur of the moment. These were the little things that could trip her up and cause big problems.

"You best wait. I sees if I can find him." Lubirda left the room, leaving the door slightly ajar.

Amanda stood watching herself in the reflection of the full-length mirror that stood in the corner. She studied the young woman who stared back at her, and was reminded vaguely of her mother. Amanda spoke aloud to her reflection.

"Just what makes you think you can fool all these people?" She felt a little shiver when she remembered Blythe Shipley's coldness and her parting comment. A proper high tea. Did that require some behavior different than a regular tea?

She puckered up her face in a stern expression and mimicked Blythe Shipley's hard tones. "Well, Lady Ashton?" Perhaps if she just acted shy, she thought to herself, and let Daniel do the talking. "Well, I can always swoon, I suppose."

"You don't have time just now, my lady. Tea awaits." Amanda jumped at the sound of Daniel's voice and turned to face him. He looked every bit the lord of the manor, leaning against the door frame, smiling at her. Her heartbeat did a little skip as she realized he had been watching her.

"How long have you been standing there?" Amanda demanded as she flushed with embarrassment.

"Long enough to notice how lovely you look. Ready?" He pushed away from the wall and started toward her in one fluid movement.

For such a large man, he moved with grace. He paused before her and looked around the room, his eyes resting for a long moment on the magnificent bed.

Amanda gulped as the words began to tumble from her mouth as if she had no control over them. "There is another chamber . . . that is, another bed . . . I mean we don't . . . you don't . . ." She stopped abruptly, biting her tongue. What had gotten into her? The arrangement was the same as it had been on the steamer.

Daniel offered her his arm, chuckling. "Shall we go downstairs? Tea awaits."

Amanda averted her face. He was laughing at her. All he had to do was look at the bed and she made a fool of herself.

She wanted to tell him what had happened after he left with Shipley, but decided not to, not wanting him to think she couldn't handle herself with Blythe Shipley.

They paused at the top of the staircase. She tugged at his arm and whispered. "Wait. What is high tea? Do I do anything differently?"

He patted her hand where it rested on his arm. "According to what Shipley said, Blythe is very eager to impress us. It is just a little more formal than a regular tea, but as hostess she will be in charge and pour."

She nodded. Blythe? Already it was Blythe and not Mrs. Shipley? Amanda had a sneaking suspicion this woman was always in charge. She remembered the look their hostess had given Daniel when they descended from the carriage. Appraising and . . . predatory. Talk about trouble.

Daniel led her into a beautiful formal parlor. Floor-to-ceiling windows along the west side of the house let in the last of the day's golden sunlight. Beautiful furnishings were bathed in the soft glow of sunset. A huge carved pink marble fireplace dominated one end of the large room. A portrait of a woman holding a baby and surrounded by three young children hung over the mantel. She had a fragile, gentle appearance, almost Madonna-like. Her face reminded Amanda of an old Italian painting hanging in the art museum in Philadelphia.

"That was Laveda, my first wife." Desmond Shipley stood at Amanda's side, his look wistful. "She was a beautiful woman."

"Yes, she was. Where are your children?" Amanda had seen no sign of young ones around the house.

Shipley laughed. "That is a rather old portrait. The baby you see in my late wife's arms lives in Atlanta with her husband and her own two children. I am a grandfather several times over." He gestured to the wall beside them where seven paintings of children hung in identical gilt oval frames. "As each grandchild turns five they come here for a visit and I commission their portrait."

"Why Mr. Shipley, I had no idea you were old enough to be a grandfather." Amanda moved to study the paintings. She glanced back at Shipley and saw Daniel wink at her from behind their host's back. "They are all beautiful children."

"I hate to interrupt, but the tea is getting cold." Blythe Shipley's icy tone broke into their conversation. Amanda had not noticed her sitting in a high-backed chair in the far corner of the room.

"Of course, my dear, I'm so sorry." Shipley immediately guided Amanda to a chair opposite his wife, indicating a seat for Daniel between the two women.

Amanda stole a glance at Daniel, who studied Blythe Shipley with an amused look. She turned her attention to the spread before them. The food, beautifully prepared and served on fine china and silver, looked delicious. Small cakes, iced and decorated with flowers, and tiny sandwiches cut into fancy shapes filled several trays. There was enough food on the tea table to feed four times their number.

During the entire time they had tea, two young Negro women waited in the doorway, their attention riveted on their mistress.

My goodness, Amanda thought to herself as she sipped from her fragile china cup and surveyed the room, *this woman cer-*

tainly knows how to run things. She could teach a few of our officers a thing or two. . . .

"How does that sound?" Amanda realized Mr. Shipley was speaking to her, and the others waited for her reply.

"I'm sorry. I didn't hear you." Amanda shrugged helplessly and looked at Daniel, wondering if a swoon would be in order after all.

"I think I can speak for my wife. Your plans sound just fine. Are you all right, my dear?" He scowled at her.

Amanda didn't miss the smug look on Blythe's face, and had no wish to spend any more time with the woman. "Yes, I'm just tired after our long journey. If it's not too much trouble, perhaps I might have a tray this evening in our room."

Daniel stood and helped Amanda to her feet, then addressed their host and hostess. "I will see you at eight."

Mrs. Shipley simpered as Daniel bowed over her hand, then addressed her comments to Amanda. "Of course. I hope you feel better in the morning."

Amanda felt instinctively that Blythe Shipley hoped no such thing. She looked like a cat with cream. The fact that Amanda would not dine downstairs seemed to please their hostess a great deal.

"Thank you. Good evening." Amanda's good-bye was stiff and forced. She would never be able to relax around that woman.

They didn't speak until Daniel closed the door to their room. Lubirda wasn't there. She turned on him, letting out her anger. "That woman is insufferable. Did you notice how she treated me? She was being nice compared to how she acted earlier, after you left."

"It was perfect! You were perfect." At the sight of his warm grin, her anger evaporated.

"I was?" Amanda studied him, puzzled by his pleased attitude.

"Of course. You played them just right."

She shrugged and shook her head.

"Don't you see? If you allow her to play the bitch, and make her believe you are a weak little ninny, people will be more likely to relax around you, be less guarded.''

Did he think she acted like a ninny? Amanda felt she needed to offer an excuse. ''Blythe Shipley makes me nervous.'' Amanda removed her earrings and dropped them on the dresser.

''Makes you nervous! Did you see the way Shipley jumps to her call? That is a formidable woman, but I'll bet in the long run she is as valuable to us as Shipley.''

Amanda shrugged. ''I suppose I can manage to keep my mouth shut. If you want a ninny, I'll be a ninny.''

Daniel took off his jacket and rolled up his shirt sleeves.

The growing intimacy of their situation also made her nervous. ''Ah, what exactly are the plans for tomorrow?''

Daniel stopped smiling. ''You really weren't paying attention, were you? So help me—''

''All right, I'm sorry! But I *am* tired and Blythe Shipley *does* make me feel like a ninny!'' Before she knew what was happening, Daniel grabbed her and hugged her, planting a kiss on her forehead. Just as quickly, he let her go.

''Amanda, you are priceless.'' He strolled across the room and seated himself on the settee, picked a Richmond paper off the table and settled back to read.

How could he do that, she thought to herself? Even when he treats me like a child, he makes me feel like I want to be a woman more than I ever have before.

When he glanced up from his paper, she still stood in the center of the room where he had left her, staring into space.

''The plan for tomorrow is a formal tour of the farm, as Shipley so humbly refers to it, and a party in our honor tomorrow night at a neighbor's home. Their name is Hunt. Shipley seems anxious for me to meet Mr. Hunt. Now, if you're very good all day, Mrs. Shipley and I will let you stay up and go to the party.'' He grinned at her and ducked in time so that her well-aimed slipper missed his head.

''For heaven's sake, will you just leave it alone?'' Amanda, exasperated by the teasing, wanted the subject dropped. It prod-

ded at a sore spot, reminding her of the difference in their ages
and experience.

"All right, I will. But seriously, why don't you change and
make yourself comfortable, and relax until your tray arrives?"

How could he act so nonchalant? Where did he expect her
to change?

As if he read her mind, he waved his hand toward the two
doors at the end of the chamber. "Go in my room. If you need
help, call me." At once he was back to reading his paper.

He is thinking of me as a child, Amanda thought. She was
tempted to change right here in front of him to see if he would
notice. She moved to the armoire and found her robe and
nightgown just as Lubirda hurried into the room.

"I thought you all would be taking longer with your tea."
She returned Daniel's nod and took the clothes from Amanda,
herding her toward the door of the bathing chamber as if she
were a goose.

Once the door closed behind them, Amanda turned to face
her. "No questions? You don't seem surprised it's to be a
nightgown instead of an evening gown."

"No, I ain't surprised. You gots to remember, the darkies
in a house like this knows what's happening as soon as it
happens. I was in the kitchen. There ain't no secrets. And
the house slaves sticks together more than most 'cause of the
missus." She quickly undid the buttons on the gown.

"What do you mean?" She hopped a little on one foot,
trying to step out of her petticoats and keep her balance. She
heaved a sigh of relief when Lubirda loosened the corset laces.

Lubirda looked at her with curiosity. "You has met her. You
think she be easy to please? Darkies gots to step lively 'round
here lest they ends up in the fields, or worse." She gathered
up the nightgown and drew the garment over Amanda's head.

Amanda poked her arms into the full sleeves and wondered
what would be worse than field work. "I see what you mean."

The gown settled around her feet. Lubirda handed her her
robe, then carried the discarded clothes to the other room.

Amanda followed and seated herself at the dressing table. Daniel didn't look up from his paper.

Lubirda picked up a brush and began to work on Amanda's hair with firm, even strokes. She continued the conversation. "You best be careful of her."

Amanda watched the Negro woman in the mirror with a mischievous look. "Oh, I will, Birdie. I would be of no use in the fields. I don't know how to pick cotton."

Lubirda shook her head with mock dismay and went to pull back the quilt on the bed for her. Daniel cleared his throat and they both giggled at his puzzled look, but there was no time for an explanation. Her tray had arrived.

Daniel left for dinner and by the time he returned, Amanda was asleep. He stood next to the bed where she slept. Thin shafts of moonlight glowed across the white linens, touching on the smooth skin of her face. She lay curled on her side, one hand tucked up under her chin, the other flung out over the brocade bed cover.

He watched the even, gentle rise and fall of her breasts under her modest gown. He wanted to reach out and untie the thin ribbons that held the front of the gown closed and expose the beauty hidden there, bare it to his eyes and hands and mouth. Prudently, he kept his hands at his sides, and cursed the way his own body responded to his thoughts.

She stretched and turned onto her stomach. He smiled, thinking how beautiful she looked, and how fiercely he wanted to protect her.

He could not let her know how he felt. The complications of wanting her made this mission too dangerous for all of them. He must not let her know, because he guessed that, in her own naive way, she wanted him too. He didn't trust his own self-restraint. It would be too easy for things between them to get out of control. Plenty of time for that kind of involvement after the mission ended.

He was in love with her. Totally, hopelessly in love.

Since he had met her he had begun to yearn for a home, a loving wife and children. At first he tried to tell himself it was because of the war. Now he knew it was because of Amanda.

Amanda had made clear what her plans for the future held. Her determination to build a career as an artist seemed so much a part of her. She observed everything and everyone around her with the eyes of an artist. Could they ever reconcile their wants?

He drew a ragged breath. There might not be any real hope for them. Perhaps the best he could do would be to keep her safe. The future was not something anyone could predict, not in times like these. Drained and frustrated, he crossed the room and passed into the small chamber to spend another night on a cramped little bed, dreaming of her, waking in the dark with his body yearning to touch her as only a lover could.

The day dawned bright and promised perfect summer weather. Shipley took them both on a tour of his property. Amanda had been relieved when Mrs. Shipley failed to join them.

Her husband explained her absence by commenting that she rarely emerged from her rooms before noon. Amanda wondered what in the world would keep her behind a closed bedroom door until the middle of the day.

The countryside, lush and green in the heat of summer, captivated her. She made several sketches of workers in the fertile fields as they drove in the open carriage. The tour brought them close enough to see several military encampments, and she committed them to memory, to be drawn later.

Amanda asked innocent-sounding questions. She confided in Shipley with a brainless giggle that she was fascinated by the military after hearing stories on her grandfather's knee about his participation in the battle of Waterloo. After this Shipley went out of his way to point out sights he felt might interest her, all the while making sure Daniel was fully informed about the productivity of his plantation.

COME WHAT MAY   143

They stopped for a picnic lunch on the banks of the James River overlooking the Tredegar Iron Works. It seemed a strange choice. The river ran murky from the outflow of the factory. Dead fish floated at the shoreline, and the air stank of sulphur. The reason he chose this spot became clear when Shipley spoke of the advantage he felt he had having lands located close to such a strategic military property.

"I don't think I understand, Mr. Shipley." Amanda turned to him wide-eyed, with what she hoped would pass for an innocent look.

"Please, my dear Lady Ashton, call me Desmond." He patted her hand, and explained his feelings to her as if she were a young child. "These buildings you see across the river are very important to our war effort, and so the army guards it well and will never let the Yankees into Richmond, making my lands safer. My crop is guaranteed." He waited to see if she understood.

"Oh, I see. How clever of you, Desmond." He smiled at her vacant reply and then glanced around at Daniel, who shrugged. From behind Shipley's back Amanda could see Daniel's mustache twitch with suppressed amusement. He gave her a wink that threatened her composure.

Soon the time would be right to wangle a tour of the Tredegar Iron Works from Shipley. This whole charade was really too easy, she thought, but strangely that did not offer her any comfort. Rather it had much the opposite effect. When things were too easy, she always knew the situation could change in a moment.

Blythe Shipley's severe visage drifted through her mind.

Chapter 12

Amanda stood in the center of the bedroom while Lubirda fussed with the sleeves of her ball gown. "Are you almost finished?" Anxious to be ready, Amanda knew Daniel would be back shortly to escort her downstairs.

"Dis here sleeve gots to come up higher." Lubirda jerked hard enough to cause Amanda to lose her balance.

"For heaven's sake, Birdie, it looks fine." Amanda fluffed the cluster of silk roses and leaves that sat atop each shoulder.

"No, I gots to do the other side too. Dat big scar of yours shows back here." Amanda had almost forgotten about the wound. "Here, holds onto the bedpost." She gave the dress one last jerk and stood back, apparently satisfied.

Amanda heard footsteps in the hallway outside the door, then the sound of Daniel clearing his throat. He always managed to make some noise to alert her when he was about to enter the room. She turned to face him as the door opened.

"My, my. Don't you look lovely tonight, Lady Ashton." He surveyed her from head to toe, his eyes lingering on her low neckline.

Amanda twirled, sending the full silk pongee skirt floating

out around her. The shimmering green color of the dress had made it one of her favorites as soon as she saw it. She glanced down, a little unnerved at the cut of the bodice.

"Do I look all right?" There was no vanity in her question. Like an actress, Amanda had dressed for a role, and wanted to make sure the costume was correct.

"You look wonderful. Are you ready? The carriage is out front and the Shipleys are waiting." Lubirda handed Daniel a deep green velvet cape and he draped it around Amanda's shoulders. They bid good-bye to Lubirda and went downstairs to the carriage.

During the short ride to the Hunts' plantation the two couples discussed the upcoming party the Shipleys were hosting in Lord and Lady Ashton's honor. All the guests tonight would also be present that night.

Amanda watched Mrs. Shipley. Her cultured voice and elegant hand gestures emphasized her words. She spoke to Daniel and Mr. Shipley, not addressing any conversation or making any eye contact with Amanda. Blythe Shipley treated Amanda as if she didn't exist.

Light spilled from the windows of the mansion as they approached, and they could hear music as they came up the drive. As soon as the carriage came to a stop, two Negro men in ornate red satin livery hurried off the wide front porch to hand the guests out. Another Negro, also in livery, met them at the front door and supervised the maid, who took their wraps. Their host and hostess for the evening, the Hunts, came forward and introductions were made.

With Amanda's hand tucked comfortably into the crook of Daniel's arm, the six of them moved as a group up the wide stairs and into the third floor ballroom.

The scene unfolded for Amanda like a dream. Chandeliers held hundreds of candles, each small flame of light reflected again and again by the mirrored panels between the many tall windows. Huge vases of flowers nestled in every nook and corner, perfuming the air. The gowns of the women made bright splashes of color, contrasting with the somber gray of the uniforms worn by so many of the men. Musicians in military garb sat on a raised platform at one end of the room. If it were not for the uniforms amid the gaiety, Amanda could have easily convinced herself there was no war going on.

The splendor took Amanda by surprise. *Careful,* she thought to herself. *You are supposed to be accustomed to this kind of thing.* She had assumed the party would be on a much smaller scale. Amanda wondered if the Shipleys would try to top this at their gala. She suspected that Blythe Shipley could not stand to be outdone.

Within moments, several men wanting an introduction to Lord Ashton approached. Mr. Hunt excused himself to the ladies and led the men out of the ballroom. As soon as they departed, Blythe Shipley turned her back on Amanda and disappeared into a group of women without a word. Amanda did not see where she had gone, nor did she care.

Mrs. Hunt paused and blinked, apparently taken aback by the woman's rudeness.

She made an attempt to smooth the situation. "Well, Lady Charlotte, let me introduce you to some dear friends."

She took Amanda by the arm and introduced her to several people nearby. Within moments, Amanda danced in the arms of the Hunts' son, Alexander, who looked to be about her own age.

"How nice you were able to come home for your mother's party," Amanda smiled up at the young lieutenant.

Alexander threw back his head and laughed. "You don't know my mother very well. It would be easier to desert my post and attend than to try and tell her no."

Amanda laughed. She instantly liked this young man. "And where is your post?" It wouldn't hurt to learn everything she could.

His expression became serious. "I'm waiting for orders now. I've been home on medical leave."

Not wanting to appear nosy and ask personal questions of a stranger, Amanda simply nodded and concentrated on her dancing.

As they circled the room, Amanda noticed a handsome, fair-haired man in a captain's uniform standing by one of the windows, staring at her. There was something vaguely familiar about him, but she was sure she had never met him before. When he caught her eye, instead of looking away, he smiled and winked. She pointedly ignored his far too familiar gesture.

As the music stopped, a young man in a naval uniform approached and begged an introduction from Alexander Hunt. After thanking her for the dance, he introduced her, and by the time the dinner dance was announced, she had been handed off so many times the names and faces of her partners became a blur. After hours of small talk, she did not have one shred of information that she thought would be of use to General Allen.

Amanda noticed that the man by the windows continued to watch her, but he made no effort to ask her to dance. The constant way he gazed at her unnerved her.

Finally, with relief, she saw Daniel return to the ballroom. Amanda excused herself from her partner and joined him. Daniel led her onto the floor. She smiled up into his face and spoke in a low voice. "Well, have you had an interesting evening so far, milord?"

Daniel laughed. "Interesting, but not very productive. These men seem much more interested in personal investments and markets for their cotton than in the war effort. How about you?"

"My feet hurt, and I'm starving. I thought I'd have better luck with the men, but I haven't spent enough time with any one man to really find out. Perhaps if I flutter my eyelashes and—"

Daniel's grip tightened on her hand and he cut off the rest of her sentence. "Don't forget your role as the loyal wife, my dear."

Her heart did a little jump. Was that a hint of jealousy in his voice, or was he worried about their image as a couple? She warmed to the idea that he didn't like the thought of her spending time with other men.

"Why sir, even the most loyal spouse sometimes engages in some harmless flirtation." He didn't return her smile. Just then the music ended and dinner was announced.

Daniel escorted Amanda downstairs and into the dining room. To her surprise, they were seated at different tables. He pulled the chair out for her and introduced her to the man on her left, an old friend of Shipley's he had already met. The chair to her right sat empty.

Amanda watched Daniel find his place. He was seated next to Blythe Shipley. She wondered with a scowl who had done the seating arrangements. Or rearrangements.

"Is something not to your liking, Lady Ashton?"

Startled from her thoughts, Amanda looked up into a pair of beautiful blue eyes. The same ones that had watched her from across the room all evening.

"You need only say the word and I will right the wrong." There was a definite twinkle in those eyes.

The slim man standing to her right smiled and showed white straight teeth under a well-trimmed mustache several shades darker than his blond hair.

"Please allow me to introduce myself. I am Captain J. Cash Walker, at your service." He clicked his heels and gave her a jaunty salute, befitting his well-tailored uniform.

"How do you do, Captain Walker?" she said, again thinking there was something familiar about him.

The man made an appropriate reply as he seated himself next to her. The liveried servants began to serve the first course.

Amanda turned to Captain Walker. "Such chivalry is refreshing, but there are no dragons to be slain."

She saw Captain Walker glance at Blythe Shipley's back. "I wouldn't be too sure, my lady." He made his comment in an undertone, almost to himself.

Amanda smiled. He was very good-looking, although not as handsome as Daniel, she thought. Or as tall, or quite as well built . . . she caught herself. Must she compare every man to him? She knew she had tonight, and none had yet come close.

Amanda chatted casually with Cash Walker all through din-

ner. She managed, wide-eyed, to fit in the story of her grandfather and the battle of Waterloo. During dessert she commented
on the insignia on his uniform.

"We are a part of the old Virginia State Militia." His back
straightened just a bit. "My troops guard the armory and the
iron works, as well as Libby Prison."

What luck, Amanda thought to herself. Finally. Information
on the Tredegar Iron Works was one of their top priorities.
Meeting Captain Walker was more than she could have hoped
for on her first night out. Daniel's warning about her role as a
loyal wife, little more than an hour old, came back to her. But
surely she had to take advantage of this situation, didn't she?
There was no time to check with Daniel, so she quickly made
her decision. *He'll understand,* she reassured herself.

"Oh, Captain Walker, you have such a large responsibility.
In my country it would be unusual for a man as young as
yourself to be in such a position." Amanda amazed herself
that the art of being coy and simpering came so easily. Unlike
most women her age, she had never practiced such behavior
before.

Captain Walker flushed a little and cleared his throat. "Well,
Lady Ashton, times of war create situations such as these."

Amanda leaned toward him ever so slightly and lowered her
voice. "Oh, I'm sure that is not the case, Captain Walker. You
look to be a very capable man."

His flush deepened. "Thank you, Lady Ashton."

"Please, when we're speaking alone like this, call me Charlotte." Amanda, taking advantage of his sense of chivalry,
made sure Walker was looking directly at her when she sent
a worried glance toward Daniel.

Deep in conversation with Blythe Shipley, Daniel hadn't
appeared to take any notice of her since dinner had begun.

"Charlotte." He hesitated for a moment. "Is anything
wrong?"

Amanda fluttered her eyes, and glanced again at Daniel.
"No, oh no." She made her voice breathy and uncertain.

Captain Walker looked puzzled. Amanda felt a little surge

of power. She wondered if most men were this easy to manipulate. It was a heady feeling, no doubt enhanced by the wine she had consumed with dinner.

After the seven-course meal was over, Captain Walker offered to escort her to the ballroom. Amanda accepted, placing her hand in the crook of his elbow. She loved to dance and was enjoying herself immensely as she bided her time in the arms of the Confederate Captain Walker and several other men who vied for her attention.

After two rather fast country dances, back to back, the musicians began the introduction to the Virginia reel. There was a stir, even among the guests who had not been dancing. Amanda excused herself from her partner and headed to a chair on the sidelines.

"Lady Ashton, you can't mean to sit out this, of all dances?" Captain Walker appeared at her side.

"I'm afraid the music is unfamiliar to me, sir." Amanda managed a wistful look at the dancers forming on the floor.

He held out his arm to her. "Come. We'll stand at the end of the line and I'll explain it to you. With your skill, by the time it is our turn, you should have no problem keeping up."

"Why thank you, Captain." Amanda again slid her hand into the crook of his elbow, squeezing ever so slightly.

He pulled her hand up close against his side and escorted her onto the floor. He was correct. She loved the dance, and had no trouble following him.

The dancers responded with such enthusiasm that the musicians played a second set. By the time it ended, Amanda fanned herself, flushed and out of breath. The ballroom seemed very warm.

"Captain, I think I need a little fresh air." She gazed up at him.

"Allow me to accompany you." He watched as she looked uneasily around the room.

It was difficult to act as if she was worried Daniel would see her with another man, when her "husband" had appeared to pay little attention to her since dinner, but Captain Walker didn't seem to notice Daniel's lack of concern, only her uneasiness.

They went downstairs and out through a set of French doors onto a long terrace. It did feel good to be out in the cool air.

"Tell me, Captain, are you required at your post every day?"

"Please, call me Cash." He stopped by a large pillar.

"All right. Cash. Is that a family name?"

He laughed. "Yes, my grandmother's maiden name. She was a Charleston Cash. You see, here in America we don't have formal classes, but we do have families." His soft drawl sounded more amused than proud.

For a moment, Amanda felt a little guilty using him the way she did. She actually had started to like this man.

"We had a picnic lunch with Mr. Shipley down by the river, overlooking your iron works."

Cash laughed. "Not a very pretty place for a picnic."

"Well, I think he was more interested in business than beauty. But I enjoyed it. It seemed to be a fascinating place. Too bad we won't be able to see more of it."

Amanda held her breath. She was sure she was being totally transparent trying to wangle an invitation, and he would see right through her.

"Would you really like to take a tour? I can arrange it, you know. As my guest." He sounded genuinely excited.

Amanda turned and took a small step toward him. "I would love to see it with you." She smiled up into his face.

He hesitated for a moment. "Do you suppose Lord Ashton would like to come?"

Amanda turned away from him and brought her hand to her face, poking her finger in the corner of her eye. When she turned back, her eyes burned with tears.

"I don't think so." She made her voice soft and sad. "He doesn't often choose to be with me." She wiped away a tear that threatened to fall with the tip of her gloved finger.

Cash had a stricken look on his face. He grabbed her hand and brought it to his mouth.

She could feel his warm breath against her glove as he spoke. "How could he not want to be with you?"

Amanda leaned toward him, absorbed with her performance. "Oh Cash, you must understand. It's not his fault. Our marriage was arranged because of our families and our, well, status. It is not Edmund's fault."

Her voice trembled and she whispered. "You see, he was in love with another woman." She sounded so loyal, so wifely.

"Well, he's a fool." Cash's voice, hard and flat, made her blink. He took the hand he held and pulled her to him.

He was going to kiss her, she thought, shaken by how quickly Cash had responded to her little drama. Now what was she going to do? His mouth was inches from her face when she heard Daniel's voice behind them.

"Excuse me, my dear, but it is time we leave."

Daniel's voice, low and angry, made Cash start. He dropped her hand and she quickly took a step back. Daniel turned back toward the house.

"I apologize, Charlotte. I had no right to put you in this situation." Cash looked distressed.

She whispered to him. "It's all right Cash, really. His tempers are usually short. Please, say you'll still come to Shipleys' party tomorrow. Please?"

Cash glanced nervously at the French door where Daniel stood stiffly with his back to them, waiting for her. "Go now. I'll try." He gave Amanda a little shove. She hurried across the terrace to Daniel.

Daniel took her by the arm and together they said good-bye to their host and hostess. He ignored her, but spoke politely to the Shipleys on the way home. Finally, tired of being overlooked, Amanda pleaded a headache and settled into the corner of the carriage, her eyes closed.

When they arrived at Villa Anona, Daniel dismissed her abruptly. "Go to bed, Charlotte. You're tired."

She had the strangest urge to stick her tongue out at him. She hated when he ordered her around.

"Good night, Mr. Shipley, Mrs. Shipley. I had a lovely evening." Like a dutiful child, she climbed the stairs alone.

She didn't know if he pretended to be angry, to go along with what she tried to do, or if her behavior had really angered him. She didn't know which way she wanted it to be. The whole situation had become very confusing.

She found the lamp lit in the bedroom, but Lubirda was not there. Wondering where she might be at this late hour, Amanda struggled alone with her gown and stays. Too tired to face Daniel tonight, she hurried to be in bed, at least pretending sleep, before he came upstairs.

After donning a nightgown, she turned down the lamp and crawled into the big bed, pulling the gauzy hangings closed. No sooner had she snuggled into the pillows than she heard the door open. Amanda could tell by the sound of the footsteps it was Daniel. She smiled to herself, eyes closed. In the morning they could talk.

In one swift motion he reached in and pulled down the covers. He grabbed her arm and dragged her off the bed. "Would you mind explaining to me exactly what you were trying to do this evening?" He looked furious.

Amanda straightened and took an involuntary step backward, indignant at the way he had yanked her out of bed. "Could this wait for morning?" She was very aware of standing in front of him in nothing but a thin nightgown.

"No! Now."

"All right!" Annoyed at his attitude, she shook off his hand. "I know I should have checked with you first, but there was no time. I couldn't pass up the opportunity."

"What opportunity? To be led astray on a dark terrace?" He was still growling.

"No! Captain Walker is in command of the guards at the armory and the iron works." She waited for him to congratulate her.

Daniel's expression didn't change. "And?"

She was puzzled. "What do you mean, 'and'?"

''Well, there must be a reason you had to hurry and seduce him tonight.''

Amanda couldn't believe what she was hearing. ''Seduce him! I was not!'' her voice squeaked.

''What would you call it?'' He arched an eyebrow and crossed his arms over his chest.

''I was just . . . I mean I wanted to . . . .'' Her voice trailed off. The word ''seduce'' seemed awfully strong, but in essence that was exactly what she had tried to do to Cash Walker.

Daniel turned his back on her and lit a lamp, then threw his hands up in the air. ''My God, Amanda, not only do you lack experience at seduction, you didn't even realize what you were doing!''

''I did too know what I was doing!'' Her hands were clenched into fists at her sides.

Daniel spun around to face her. ''I was on that porch too. The situation was getting out of control. What would you have done if he had decided not to act like a gentleman? If I hadn't been there to stop things? The man has twice your strength. You couldn't have fought him off.''

For a moment Amanda felt as if she were facing her father. Then a thought struck her. ''Wait a minute. Why are you angry?''

Daniel looked surprised. ''What do you mean, why?''

''The real reason you're angry is because I might have compromised myself as Amanda, not my role as Lady Ashton.''

Daniel was visibly taken aback. ''I'm responsible for you.''

That comment made her mad. Amanda moved toward him and this time it was Daniel who stepped back.

Her tone was low and measured. ''I'm responsible for myself. And it seems to me I remember discussing my reputation before. I haven't changed my mind about not needing it!''

''How would it look if the married Lady Ashton turned out to be a virgin?''

Amanda stammered, not knowing what to say. She wouldn't have let it go that far.

He leaned in close. ''You are, aren't you?

She felt her face turning red. "What has that got to do with this?"

He pointed his index finger at her and jabbed at the air in front of her nose, emphasizing each of his words. "Things like that can get you caught."

Furious, she put her hands on her hips. "Did you think that you would take all the chances? Assume all the risks?"

He shrugged. "That was *my* plan."

"Tell me Daniel, if they catch you here in Richmond, what will happen to you?"

"Most probably I'd be hanged. Why?" He sounded defensive.

"And what do you think they would do to me?" After a moment Daniel hadn't answered, so Amanda continued. "They would likely lock me up in a room somewhere and then find a way to send me back up north. The gentlemen here in the genteel South could hardly bring themselves to execute a woman, let alone imprison her for any length of time."

Daniel recovered himself. "Regardless of what you say—"

Amanda cut him off, furious. "I am in this for the same reasons you are and I plan to do whatever I need to. So don't ever again try to put your silly notions about my virtue and the value of your life on equal terms."

Now Daniel's anger matched hers. When she turned to walk away, he grabbed her by the arm again. "Don't make the mistake of dismissing this evening as just my concern about your virtue. Your inexperience puts us all at risk. How convincing could you be if Walker had managed to seduce you tonight, or any night? Could you respond like a married woman should? You don't even know how to kiss properly."

Amanda was so furious now she sputtered. He'd kissed her twice already and she thought she'd done a pretty good job.

She twisted, trying to get away from him. "Don't know how to kiss! How dare you!"

Daniel tightened his grip. "I mean kissed the way a husband would kiss you, the way a lover would kiss you."

Amanda glared at him. His eyes flashed back at her. In one

swift movement he pulled her up hard against his chest, his arm circling her waist. His other hand slid up her arm, across her shoulder, and he grabbed a handful of her hair. He held her stiff body pinned against the wool of his jacket for a moment and she didn't even breathe. The sound of her heart beating pounded in her ears.

He pulled her head back and slowly, ever so slowly lowered his lips to hers, staring directly into her eyes. His breath fanned against her cheek. She swallowed and tried to speak, but for the life of her she didn't know what she would say even if she could find her voice.

He touched his lips, warm and firm, to hers, and for a moment he held them quietly, without moving. Amanda closed her eyes and savored the feeling. His mustache barely brushed against her, tickling her nose. Her arms hung limp at her sides.

Daniel began to move against her mouth, ever so slightly, back and forth. After a moment, she relaxed a bit. His big warm hand shifted from her waist to the middle of her back. The thin fabric of her gown let the heat of his palm penetrate instantly to her skin.

His lips moved a little more. It felt so good she moved her lips, too. The pressure of his hand increased. She heard a small moan, but couldn't decide which of them had made the noise.

Amanda felt the strength leaving her tingling body, and leaned into him for support. He licked her upper lip with the tip of his tongue, and then gently nibbled on the lower one. She gasped at the sensation, and when her lips parted, he ran his tongue inside her mouth.

Amanda found she could not trust her legs, and she swayed. He pulled away from her and she opened her eyes, but for an instant had trouble focusing.

In a husky voice he said, "Good night, Amanda."

By the time she got her wits back and realized he meant to leave, the door had closed behind him. She brought her fingertips up to her lips, trying to recapture the sensation, so bereft at his parting.

"Good night, Daniel," she whispered to the closed door.

He was right, she thought. She had never really kissed anyone else before.

Daniel leaned against the closed door, struggling for control over his aroused body. He could hear the creak of the floorboards as Amanda moved across the room to her bed. Thinking of her climbing onto the feather mattress did nothing to decrease the ache in his groin.

"Damn her," he muttered aloud. But even as he spoke he knew the fault for what had just happened was his.

Jealousy had made him pull her from her bed; lust had provoked the kiss. For a moment, seeing her with another man out on that terrace, he had come close to losing control.

Daniel wanted her. He had never felt so vulnerable. It threatened him, this fragile self-control of his. It threatened both of them.

Be honest, he thought. His feelings had little to do with this mission. Her ability to flirt and charm at will had bothered him from the time they had arrived at the Hunts', partly because she had never tried it with him. She was always straightforward and businesslike with him, like a friend would be.

Dammit, he loved her. He didn't want her for a friend.

Chapter 13

Amanda awoke feeling tired and bleary-eyed. Sleep had been slow in coming after her run-in with Daniel last night. She brought a finger to her lips, remembering the way he had kissed her.

Lubirda hummed to herself as she laid out clothes on the settee.

Amanda watched her for a moment before she spoke. "Where were you last night? After I went to bed?"

Lubirda jumped. "Lordy, you startled me. I thought you was still asleep." She ignored Amanda's question.

Amanda dragged herself from the bed. "I think I'll go riding this morning. Would you get me my habit, the green one?"

Lubirda nodded and without another word efficiently laid out the clothes as Amanda washed her face. When she finished dressing she sent Lubirda downstairs to see who was in the dining room. She had no intention of spending time this morning with Daniel or Blythe Shipley.

The more she thought about last night the angrier she became. He kissed her and then just left her standing in the middle of the room.

In spite of the way she felt about him, she wanted to be responsible for herself. Amanda didn't even want to think about the way she had responded to him, and how her feelings could complicate what they needed to do in the coming days.

Lubirda returned and reported to her that the dining room was empty. The men had already gone into Richmond and Mrs. Shipley was still in her room.

"Riding a good thing to do today. This one crazy house, getting ready for the big party. Jes' be back in time for a bath and to dress."

"What are you going to do today?" Amanda said, still curious about where the woman had been the night before.

"Jes' be around, keeping my ears open. Some darkies comin' from other plantations to help out for tonight." Amanda remained puzzled by the woman's closed expression.

Amanda packed a bag with her sketch pad to tie to her saddle, bid Lubirda good-bye and headed to the dining room. A large breakfast had been laid on the buffet and two Negroes served her. Amanda felt a little silly sitting all alone in this huge room, being waited on by two people.

She was deeply engrossed in the Richmond paper when Blythe Shipley sailed into the room. Up until now Amanda had avoided being alone with her, but there was no way to make a graceful escape with her plate still full of food.

Blythe impatiently waved the servants away, seating herself next to Amanda. She stared at her guest for a long moment. Amanda smiled and waited for her to speak, willing herself not to fidget.

"I know what you are. A fraud. I know all about you, Lady Ashton." Blythe's voice was cool, measured, and calculating. She continued to stare, apparently waiting for a reaction.

Amanda felt numb. She knew? But how? Her heart pounded in her chest, and she didn't trust herself to speak. Did Shipley know too? Would he turn Daniel in when they got to Richmond today? A cold, clammy perspiration broke out across her forehead.

Blythe took advantage of her silence to continue her accusations. "You play the part of the devoted, loving wife well, but I suspected you from the start. Last night only confirmed my beliefs." Her face contorted in an ugly sneer.

Amanda tried to gather her wits. Her first instinct was to flee. Her glance darted to the doorway leading to the entry hall.

"I know who sleeps in your bed, and it's not your husband, it's your nigger woman. Is that your preference? Another woman? Or perhaps he requires more than a child like you to fulfill his needs. Perhaps he needs a woman, a real woman." She stood up and smoothed her skirts, giving Amanda a long, meaningful look before she turned and left the room.

Amanda sat where she was, trembling too much to get up from the chair. Blythe Shipley's final words sank in and Amanda covered her mouth to suppress the hysterical laugh that threatened to erupt.

Thank God she had not jumped in and said anything in her own defense, because the woman knew nothing of their real reason for being in Richmond.

Relief lasted just until Amanda had a moment to think about the implications of Mrs. Shipley's insinuations. Unless she was mistaken, the woman had accused her of being sexually unnatural!

"That busybody!" Amanda said the words under her breath. Who else might she tell her hateful thoughts to?

"S'cuse me, ma'am?" A voice startled Amanda. She had forgotten she was not alone. The young Negro maid moved closer to the table.

"Nothing, I was talking to myself." She mumbled and eyed the maid suspiciously.

Blythe Shipley was obviously getting detailed information on her personal life from the house slaves. Her hostess had just drawn the wrong conclusions.

Amanda ignored her breakfast and left the house. At the stables she requested a mount and twice tried in very firm tones to refuse the offer of a groom to accompany her. It became obvious she would not get a mount if she insisted on riding alone. She finally gave up, and ordered the man to stay far behind her when they rode. She wanted to be alone.

After several hours of riding, skirting the lush fields where slaves worked weeding the cotton, thirst drove her to the banks of the river. She chose a spot upstream from where she had picnicked with Daniel and Shipley. The water seemed clean enough here.

Amanda tied her mount so he could graze. The groom followed her like a silent shadow, hanging back. She probably had him scared to death after her demands in the stable.

She settled down on the bank in the cool shade of a tree and watched the smoke rising from the stacks of the iron works, her mind jumbled with thoughts of Daniel, Cash Walker, and Blythe Shipley.

The warmth of the sun as it filtered through the leaves gradually relaxed her. Amanda lay down in the grass, bunching up her jacket to use as a pillow. Insects hummed in the still, warm air. Tired from last night, she closed her eyes, welcoming sleep.

"Lady Ashton. Lady Ashton. Please, lady. We gots to go back." The groom called to her.

Amanda awoke stiff and sore from lying on the ground. With a start she realized how late it was. The sun already hung near the horizon.

"Oh, dear. I didn't mean to sleep." She apologized to the worried-looking man. "Show me the fastest way back to the house." With his help she mounted quickly and followed him.

Several horses stood saddled and ready outside the stables. Amanda wondered who would go riding so late, especially with the party about to start. The head groom greeted her and took her horse, helping her to dismount.

Shipley came barreling out of the stables. His full face flushed, he appeared very agitated. "Lady Ashton, are you all right? Thank goodness you're back! His Lordship has gone to the house to change into riding clothes. We were getting ready to go looking for you."

She could hear the head groom berating the man who had accompanied her. Wanting to intervene, she refrained, knowing it would be out of character for Lady Ashton to come to the aid of a slave.

Amanda remembered the part she was supposed to play and giggled. "I'm so silly, Mr. Shipley. I fell asleep." She giggled again and rolled her eyes.

Amanda had no intention of offering him more of an explanation. She figured Lady Ashton would not explain herself.

She glanced around, and gestured to one of the boys who worked in the stables.

"You, there. Run up to the house and inform Lord Ashton that I am back. Tell him I will be along shortly." The boy nodded solemnly and took off for the house at a dead run.

Amanda followed at a more sedate pace, not waiting for Shipley.

The house blazed with lights, and when she entered, Amanda could see the transformation for the party. Huge silver bowls of flowers, placed on gleaming waxed furniture perfumed the warm evening air. House servants bustled from room to room, their arms full of dishes and linens. Wonderful smells of cooking food drifted in the air, reminding Amanda she had not eaten since breakfast. Her stomach growled in response. She hurried up the main staircase and into her room.

Daniel stood in the middle of the floor, fumbling with the cufflinks on a ruffled shirt. The front hung open and she could see the hair covering his chest.

"Where have you been? I was changing to go and look for you." His tone sounded clipped and businesslike.

Amanda wished he would button up his shirt. "I went out riding."

"Alone? For seven hours?" She looked at him again and saw the tight little lines around his mouth. A muscle twitched along his jaw.

"No. I know enough to take a groom." She certainly wouldn't admit she had tried to leave the man behind. "I stopped to rest and fell asleep." She watched him closely. "I was tired. I didn't sleep very well last night."

She wanted to tell him what had really driven her from the

house, what Blythe Shipley had said to her this morning, but she sensed that now was not a good time for that particular conversation.

He didn't look at her but concentrated on his other cuff. The lines around his mouth deepened. "The party starts in one hour."

Daniel headed toward his little room. He spoke abruptly, without turning around. "You'd better hurry up. We are due downstairs to greet guests." He closed the door behind him.

She felt bad that she had made him so angry. Her gown lay spread across the bed, ready for her. Amanda glanced in the mirror and groaned as she took off her riding hat. Her hair, tangled and matted, had a leaf stuck to one side. A smudge of dirt streaked her cheek.

Lubirda bustled out of the bathing chamber. "I thought I heard you. Lordy, ain't you a mess! Where you been?"

Amanda stared at Daniel's door. "I went riding and stopped to rest. I fell asleep." She began to peel off her riding habit. "Birdie, I'm starving. Will you run down to the kitchen and get me something?"

"Child, you ain't got time. You're a mess and you needs to git ready and go downstairs and greets the guests."

Lubirda helped her with the rest of her clothes, and brushed up her hair before she climbed into the waiting bath water.

"Mister Daniel 'bout had a worry fit when he got back and you was still gone."

The remark surprised Amanda. "That's strange. He didn't seem too concerned just now when I came in. He was just afraid I wouldn't be ready when the party started."

Birdie picked up a sponge and scrubbed Amanda's back. "That's what you think. He calmed down considerable when that child come in here with the word you was back." Birdie handed Amanda the sponge and returned to the bedroom for fresh underclothes.

Amanda lay back and relaxed in the water. Daniel should understand that she could take care of herself.

Lubirda came back, holding a towel. "Come on and git outta

there. You ain't got time for daydreamin'.'' She waved the towel impatiently.

Amanda obediently stepped out of the tub and dried off. She put on her gown and sat at the dressing table, paying little attention to Lubirda as the woman fussed over her.

Amanda stood up from her seat and moved to the center of the room, where she could get a better view of herself in the mirror.

Lubirda had used a curling iron and done her hair up in a sophisticated style that flattered her face. The tight, low-cut bodice of her pale peach silk dress showed the soft swell of her breasts and made her skin look warm and creamy. She had good color in her cheeks from her day spent outdoors, and the gold of her necklace highlighted the color of her eyes.

Blythe Shipley's words came back to her. ''Maybe he needs a real woman.'' Tonight she looked like a woman, and she certainly felt like one. Until she had more information, she would be careful not to get herself into a situation that surpassed her knowledge. That lack bothered her, especially since both Daniel and Mrs. Shipley in their own way had made such a fuss about it.

Lubirda had answered some of her questions when they had sailed south on the steamer. As soon as she worked up her nerve, she would question her friend and expand her understanding on the subject of men and women.

The doorknob rattled, interrupting her thoughts, and after a brief pause Daniel opened the door. ''Ready? The guests are beginning to arrive.''

Amanda nodded. ''Good night, Lubirda. Please don't wait up, we will probably be very late.'' Amanda said, irritated that she sounded breathless. Lubirda must have pulled her stays too tight.

Daniel offered his arm without a word about how she looked. He must still be angry with her. Together they went downstairs and greeted guests along with the Shipleys until the musicians began to play.

Amanda danced first with Daniel, who held her stiffly and

acted aloof. At the end of the dance he handed her quickly off to Shipley without giving her a chance to suggest they find a quiet place where they might talk. After that came a quick succession of partners, some of whom she knew from the Hunts' party.

Cash Walker arrived, but carefully avoided being alone with her, even to dance. She searched the room several times for Daniel, but it appeared he planned to avoid her too.

The evening grew warm, even with the doors and windows open to the soft night air. There was no sign yet of dinner being served, but servants circulated among the guests, carrying silver trays filled with glasses of French champagne. Had they gotten enough wine for the party through the blockade, or were their cellars just very well-stocked?

Amanda accepted a glass from her partner and enjoyed the feeling of warmth the wine made in her empty stomach. After several more dances and as many glasses of champagne, she forgot all about the blockade, the cellar, and dinner.

The room swirled with lights and colors, and Amanda, feeling a strange, light-headed detachment, began to notice how much handsomer her partners seemed to be, and how witty. They all had such amusing stories to tell, such entertaining anecdotes. She couldn't remember when she had had a better time, she thought, reaching for another glass of champagne.

Daniel stood on the opposite side of the room, watching Amanda entertain a group of young officers. He noticed with little amusement that Cash Walker chose to keep his distance from both of them. As much as he hated to admit it, he knew her technique of flirting with the men could probably net them more military information in one evening than he could gather in a week.

Daniel moved across the dance floor to claim Amanda. Her face appeared flushed, and as he came near, he noticed with alarm that her high-born English accent had deteriorated to that of an Irish scullery maid. She carelessly held a full glass of wine that sloshed a little onto her dress when she laughed.

She had obviously had too much to drink, and was in danger of giving herself away. He had to admit to himself as he watched her though, that aside from the accent, even after drinking too much she played her part well.

Daniel looked around sharply at the young men surrounding Amanda, relieved to see they were even drunker than she was. He felt his anger lessen as he took her by the arm and excused her from the group, over several loudly voiced male protests.

Amanda looked up at him and gave him a wide, rather lopsided smile. "Is it time for supper?" She stumbled a little and he tightened the grip on her arm.

"I think you and I will wait to eat." He leaned close to her. "I want to speak to you alone." Daniel felt her shiver.

"All right. I'm not very hungry anymore, anyway." Amanda held up the wine glass and stared at it stupidly, as if she couldn't remember where it came from. Daniel smiled when he took it from her hand and handed it to a passing servant.

After the man took the glass Daniel asked the servant to inform his master that Lady Ashton was ill and would not join them for dinner. The man nodded and hurried away.

"Don't be silly. I feel wonderful!" Amanda had difficulty negotiating the stairs, and finally Daniel picked her up and carried her to the top, ignoring her protests.

By the time he set her down outside the bedroom door, she giggled so hard she gasped for breath. He had never seen her like this, and even though it was due to the amount of wine she had consumed, he took delight in her mood. She was soft and warm and smelled of lavender.

He found he no longer felt angry with her for disappearing earlier in the day. She had had him worried when she was gone so long.

Daniel opened the door and guided Amanda into the bedroom.

"Lubirda. Where are you?" He got no answer.

Thinking perhaps she was asleep in the little room he used,

Daniel left Amanda holding onto a bedpost and checked. It was empty.

"I wonder where she is?"

Amanda turned to face him, putting her fingers to her lips. "Ssh. It's a secret. Birdie won't tell where she goes." Amanda hiccuped loudly and dissolved in another fit of giggles, lurching away from the bedpost to collapse face down on the bed.

Daniel slipped an arm around her waist and hauled her off the bed, standing her up once again by the bedpost.

"Hold on. I'll help you." He braced himself for a protest but heard only a hiccup.

He unfastened the dress and helped her shrug it off her shoulders. It slithered into a pool of fabric around her feet. She fumbled with the ties of the petticoats and hoops, and they joined the dress. Next he unlaced her corset strings. She wiggled out of the constricting garment. She stood in her chemise, still clinging to the post for support.

Daniel bent and, grasping her ankle, lifted one of her feet, setting it down after he retrieved the various garments. Then he repeated the maneuver with her other foot. The feel of his hands on her skin unsettled him.

Pulling down the covers, he reached for her, anxious to cover her up. "All right, young lady. Time for sleep." He was surprised when she pulled away from him.

"Wait, Daniel. I need to talk to you." She let go of the bedpost.

He looked at her, amused. "What is it?" She looked so serious.

She braced a hand on his chest and lifted the other to his face, resting it briefly on his mustache. "You have nice lips."

He smiled. "Is that what you wanted to talk to me about? Lips?"

"No." She giggled again. "Daniel, are we friends?" She swayed a little, slurred her words, and dropped her hands to her sides.

He put his hands on her arms briefly to steady her. "Yes,

Amanda, we are friends." Her skin felt smooth as satin. He pulled away.

She considered his answer for a long time. "Will you do me a favor, as a friend? Help me? I have a problem."

He suppressed a smile. Her biggest problem would be the way she felt in the morning.

"Of course I will help you." She swayed a little more and he took a step forward again.

She reached out and grabbed the front of his shirt. "Daniel, this is serious. Stand still!" She lurched forward and buried her face in the linen ruffles for a moment.

He could feel her warm breath against his chest. She was so damn appealing. Filled with amusement at her tipsy state, Daniel could barely contain himself. "I'm sorry. I'll stand still. What can I do for you?"

She pushed him back a step and looked up into his face with eyes that did not quite focus.

"I want you to teach me about sex." She gestured toward the bed.

It was a simple statement, not at all coy or teasing.

At first Daniel didn't react. He thought he had not heard her correctly, or perhaps he had misunderstood her meaning.

When he didn't answer, she repeated herself. "Just show me. It's just too much trouble, not knowing, I mean. It would be so much easier. . . ." Her voice trailed away.

Daniel stood there as if he were an awkward fifteen-year-old. He felt a flush spread across his face. How could he answer? As tempting as she was, he certainly wouldn't dream of fulfilling her demand, not when she made it after drinking a large amount of champagne.

"Uh, Amanda, I . . . I just . . . ."

She stared at him, unblinking. "Think of it as part of my training. There is so much I don't know. Daniel? You promised. You said you'd teach me what I need to know."

Amanda made her request sound so reasonable, as if she were asking for a second helping of dessert.

Daniel couldn't think of anything to say. He had just

undressed a woman he desired, she was inviting him into her bed, and he stood there staring at her.

He knew he would never join her on that bed tonight, but his body responded to her, ready to oblige. Suddenly the question was moot, as Amanda gave one last little hiccup and closed her eyes, crumpling quietly back onto the bed.

Chapter 14

Lubirda hurried across the dark back lawns, anxious to be upstairs before the captain and Amanda returned. It would look strange to the household staff, and questions might be asked if she wasn't there when her mistress returned.

She heard music drifting out through the open windows and saw people dancing in the main salon. For a moment she wished she could sit outside in the cool evening and watch the party.

She went up the back stairs and down the narrow hallway. All the other house servants must be busy downstairs. She sighed with relief as she closed the door behind her and entered the little room where the captain slept.

Lubirda opened the door into the bedroom, prepared to light the lamp and pull down the bed covers. She stopped just inside the door. The lamp was already burning and clothes were scattered all over the floor. Her attention was pulled to the bed by a small moan.

"Missy, that you?" Lubirda approached the rumpled bed cautiously. She heard another moan.

The girl clawed at the bedclothes, trying to untangle herself. "Birdie? Hurry. I'm going to be sick."

Lubirda reached for the chamber pot and held it as the girl retched miserably. After helping her to lie back on the bed she stashed the pot in the other room, returning quickly to Amanda.

"When you start feeling bad?" Lubirda demanded, her hands balled up in fists rested on her hips.

Amanda sounded pathetic. "Just now, when I woke up." The girl, dazed, looked around the room, as if she wondered where she was.

"I'm gonna go find Mister Daniel." Lubirda turned toward the door.

"Wait!" Amanda sat up, sounding frantic. "Please don't. He knows I'm not feeling well. Let him enjoy the party."

Something here did not add up for Lubirda. She eyed Amanda closely and then shrugged. "All right, iffin' that's what you want."

She helped her off with her shift and into a nightgown. "You be fine for a minute while I takes care o' that pot?"

Amanda nodded weakly and sank back on the pillows. By the time Lubirda returned, the girl had fallen asleep. She picked up the dress and petticoats from the floor and caught the sour smell of wine. Suddenly she understood why the girl was ill.

She smiled. Amanda was still such a child in many ways. It amazed Lubirda that she managed to pull off the part of a lady so well.

After putting the room in order, Lubirda settled down in a chair and her thoughts drifted as she watched the girl sleep. She knew Amanda was in love with the captain, but the girl just wouldn't admit it yet. Anyone who spent any time around the two of them would notice. And Daniel was in love with her too, or close to it. For some reason they both held back, and they could not seem to give in to what was happening to them.

Amanda cried out in her sleep and Lubirda moved quickly to sit on the bed. She stroked her brow gently and soothed her, and she quieted, never really waking. Lubirda sat with her for several more moments. She missed the feel of having a child to care for.

Lubirda heard the rattle of the doorknob and knew it was Daniel. He entered the room with an expression of amusement on his handsome face. It turned instantly to concern when he saw Lubirda on the bed.

"What's wrong?" His long legs brought him swiftly to the side of the bed.

"Shush! Nothin' wrong. She had a bad dream, I'm guessin'." Lubirda was puzzled by the guilty look on Daniel's face. "She be fine until she wake up in the mornin'. Why you let her drink so much?"

Daniel sputtered, keeping his voice low. "Let her! What do you mean, let her?" He moved around the room, obviously agitated. "When did I ever have control over what she does?"

Amanda stirred again, groaning. Birdie glared at him. "Hush, you want to wake her?"

"Believe me, Birdie, the last thing in the world I want to do is wake her!" With that, Daniel retreated to his little room.

Birdie shivered at his belligerent tone.

Lubirda tucked a sheet around Amanda, then reluctantly followed Daniel. She told him what little she had heard from the slaves bringing guests from Richmond and the outlying plantations. Given his dark mood, she would have liked to leave it until morning, but she was afraid she would forget something if she waited.

He made some notations as she spoke and gruffly thanked her for her good work and loyalty. Lubirda was proud to do whatever she could. Not even the most dedicated white abolitionist could ever feel as deeply about slavery as she did.

Lubirda returned to the bedroom and readied herself for bed. She crawled into her pallet on the floor beside the snoring girl and sighed. There would be more fireworks between Amanda and Daniel before they get this thing settled, she thought as she drifted off to sleep.

* * *

Lubirda set the breakfast tray beside the bed with a clatter, and then tied back the drapes at the windows. Bright morning sun streamed into the room.

"Lubirda please, close the curtains." Amanda's voice croaked from under the quilt. The top of her head throbbed with a powerful ache.

"You come on outta there and eat." Lubirda pulled the covers out of her grasp, uncovering her face.

"Are you trying to kill me?" Amanda sat up and wailed, then immediately brought both hands up to cradle her head. "On second thought, go ahead," she mumbled into the front of her nightgown. "Dying would be a relief."

Callously, Lubirda ignored her. "When's the last time you ate?"

Amanda dropped her hands and half opened her eyes, considering the question. "Breakfast, yesterday. I had a piece of toast and then Mrs. Shipley joined me in the dining room and I lost my appetite."

"No wonder you got so sick last night. Didn't nobody ever tell you not to drink wine on an empty stomach?"

"The only thing anyone ever told me about drinking was not to do it." Amanda fell back against the pillows. "I wish to heaven now I had listened to them."

She closed her eyes and rubbed her temples, wondering if she would ever feel normal again. "Thank you for putting me to bed last night. I hope I wasn't too much trouble."

"Don't go thankin' me. You was in bed when I come in."

"How . . .? Don't answer that. I don't think I want to know."

Amanda knew she must look green around the edges, considering how awful she felt. The last thing she remembered about last night was Daniel carrying her up the stairs. She didn't want to think beyond that.

"Well, you eat something and you gonna feel better." Lubirda placed the tray across Amanda's lap.

She sat up slowly and eyed the food with suspicion. Amanda

couldn't believe tea and toast, stewed fruit and oatmeal could possibly make her feel better.

"Go on and eat, while it still hot." Lubirda stood over the bed, not moving until Amanda began to drink tea and take bites of the toast.

"Birdie, do you know where Captain McGrath is this morning?" She wondered how long she could avoid him.

Lubirda glanced at her. "He left with Mister Shipley 'bout an hour ago. He won't be back till supper."

"Oh." Good. That would give her some time to recover. "What time is it?"

" 'Bout ten, I'm guessin'. Why?"

"Ten! I should get up!" She had never slept this late in her life.

Lubirda put her hands on her hips. "Why? You got someplace to go?"

"No, but I can't lie in bed all day." Mrs. Shipley would think her lazy.

"Why not? You a lady, and you feelin' poorly. Stay in bed. Then you don't have to see Miz Shipley, or nobody you don't want to."

"Birdie, are you sure?" Amanda thought the idea of hiding in this room all day sounded wonderful.

Birdie nodded.

Amanda didn't have to ask twice. "All right, bed it is."

"Eat!" Lubirda pointed a long black finger at the tray.

"Yes, ma'am." She felt better already.

When Amanda finished, Lubirda took the tray and returned it to the kitchen, assuring Amanda she would make a few comments about her Ladyship's poor health this morning. Blythe Shipley would know everything within moments.

When Lubirda returned to the room, Amanda lay back, eyes closed. Birdie began to straighten the already tidy room.

"Birdie, stop fussing. The room is fine. Come and sit with me." Bits and pieces of last night were coming back to her.

"Iffin' you want." Amanda knew Lubirda still felt awkward when she treated her like a friend.

"I want." She scooted over. "Sit here, on the bed." She patted the quilt beside her.

"You feelin' better?" Lubirda perched gingerly on the edge of the bed.

"Yes, thank you. I was sure breakfast would kill me, but you were right, as usual." Amanda plucked nervously at the bedclothes. There was something she really wanted to know. "Birdie, remember when you said I could ask you questions?"

"Yup."

"Well, could I . . . I mean would you mind . . . Do you still feel that way?" She didn't want to impose on their friendship.

"Ain't nobody gonna interrupts us here. Good time to talk. Ask."

"Lubirda, have you ever been married?" Surely she would know the answer if she had been married.

"Well, no, not exactly."

"What do you mean, 'not exactly'?"

"Slaves, they don't get married legal, like white folks. We calls it jumpin' the broom together, but it mean the same thing."

"Jumping the broom? Did you really jump over a broom?" Intrigued, Amanda studied the bland expression on the Negro's face.

"Yup. Then we had a big party, with food and dancin'." Birdie gave a little sigh.

"Birdie? You've answered a lot of questions for me, but I need to know exactly what happens between a husband and wife. What is it like to be with a man?"

"Lordy, child!" said Lubirda, aghast.

Amanda rushed to apologize. "I'm sorry!" She reached for her hand. "I never should have asked such a question. Please forgive me."

Lubirda looked down at the pale hand that briefly held her very dark one. "No child, it ain't the question. Fact you been wondering and not asked is what bothers me. Why didn't you say something when we be talkin' like this before?"

Amanda sighed, unable to admit how much she had wanted to ask. "I guess I can only take in so much at one time."

"Well, it's high time you knew. It's sorta like music."

"Music?" Amanda did not expect that for an answer.

"Yeah. You ever have feelings for a man, physical feelings?"

Amanda flushed, remembering how she felt when Daniel kissed her. "Yes."

"Ever kiss him?"

"Yes." Amanda felt her flush deepen.

Lubirda seemed to be gauging her answers. "How'd it make you feel?"

Amanda thought about the last time Daniel had kissed her. "Strange."

"Funny? Kinda inside-out?"

"Yes, kind of weak and wobbly, I guess."

"That the beginning. I calls that the hummin' stage. Your body jest gettin' warmed up." She eyed Amanda. "What happened after that?"

"Nothing."

"Nothin'?"

"Well, I mean he left. Went away." He had just walked right out of the room. Her worst fear was she had been so inept, he hadn't been interested in staying. She couldn't confide that, even to Birdie.

"How you feel then?"

"Awful. Empty. Like I wanted something but I didn't know what."

"You wanted the song. The song come next, that is if he be a good lover, he make your body feel like it singin'."

"And if he's not?"

"Then he take what he want and don't care 'bout your pleasure. Just like the animals."

"Oh." Amanda's eyes were fastened on Lubirda, fascinated with the description she gave. What was the pleasure?

"This next part best if you take your clothes off. All your clothes. Touching warm skin, touching secret places real slow and easy make the body feel like it singin'."

"Oh." Amanda repeated, feeling incapable of any coherent

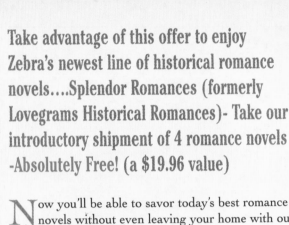

Take advantage of this offer to enjoy Zebra's newest line of historical romance novels....Splendor Romances (formerly Lovegrams Historical Romances)- Take our introductory shipment of 4 romance novels -Absolutely Free! (a $19.96 value)

Now you'll be able to savor today's best romance novels without even leaving your home with our convenient and inexpensive home subscription service. Here's what you get for joining:

- 4 BRAND NEW bestselling Splendor Romances delivered to your doorstep every month

- 20% off every title (or almost $4.00 off) with your home subscription

- A FREE monthly newsletter, *Zebra/Pinnacle Romance News* filled with author interviews, member benefits, book previews and more!

- No risks or obligations…you're free to cancel whenever you wish…no questions asked

To get started with your own home subscription, simply complete and return the card provided. You'll receive your FREE introductory shipment of 4 Splendor Romances and then you'll begin to receive monthly shipments of new Zebra Splendor titles. Each shipment will be yours to examine for 10 days and then if you decide to keep the books, you'll pay the preferred home subscriber's price of just $4.00 per title plus $1.50 shipping and handling. That's $16 for all 4 books plus $1.50 for home delivery! And if you want us to stop sending books, just say the word…it's that simple.

Check out our website at www.kensingtonbooks.com.

4 FREE books are waiting for you!
Just mail in the certificate below!

If the certificate is missing below, write to:
Splendor Romances, Zebra Home Subscription Service, Inc.,
P.O. Box 5214, Clifton, New Jersey 07015-5214
or call TOLL-FREE 1-888-345-BOOK

FREE BOOK CERTIFICATE

Yes! Please send me 4 Splendor Romances (formerly Zebra Lovegram Historical Romances), ABSOLUTELY FREE! After my introductory shipment, I will be able to preview 4 new Splendor Romances each month FREE for 10 days. Then if I decide to keep them, I will pay the money-saving preferred publisher's price of just $4.00 each… a total of $16.00 plus $1.50 shipping and handling. That's 20% off the regular publisher's price plus $1.50 for shipping and handling. I may return any shipment within 10 days and owe nothing, and I may cancel my subscription at any time. The 4 FREE books will be mine to keep in any case.

Name _____

Address _____ Apt. _____

City _____ State _____ Zip _____

Telephone ( ) _____

Signature _____
(If under 18, parent or guardian must sign.)

Terms and prices subject to change. Orders subject to acceptance by Zebra Home Subscription Service, Inc. .
Zebra Home Subscription Service, Inc. reserves the right to reject or cancel any subscription.
Offer valid in U.S. only.

SN030A

response, wondering if she would ever have the courage to disrobe in front of a man. Last night didn't count.

"Then when your body come together with his, it like a whole choir singing together on a Sunday morning, building up slow, louder and louder, but pretty, you know, till they get to the end, all at once. Then it be all still and quiet-like."

Amanda knew she was still staring, struggling to take in this new information. "How do they come together? The bodies, I mean, exactly what happens?"

"God made them to fit together. His manhood fit up inside you, in that soft dark place between your legs."

Amanda thought about the men at the pond that day in camp, how their naked bodies looked as they swam, and couldn't quite picture what Lubirda described. She reached for Lubirda's hand again.

"Thank you for telling me this." She had more questions, but this had been enough for one day.

Lubirda pulled the quilt up around the girl. "You take a nap. You looks tired."

Amanda smiled at her and obediently curled herself into a ball, closing her eyes. She doubted if she could sleep, knowing she had a lot to think about. She did fall asleep, and dreamed of Daniel. Strange, fervent dreams that left her wanting when she woke.

Chapter 15

Amanda heard Daniel moving around his tiny room next to hers. Late afternoon sun slanted into her bedchamber. She wiped her palms on the skirt of her dressing gown.

Because of all the wine, she didn't remember everything she had done the night before at the Shipleys' ball, but she was sure he deserved an apology. Maybe she hadn't behaved too badly—after all, he hadn't come in to yell at her yet. She moved to his door and knocked hesitantly.

"Daniel, do you have a minute?" Her voice cracked in the middle of the sentence.

"Of course." He opened the door with his shirt unbuttoned to his waist and his hair damp. She had interrupted him washing up.

He tossed the towel he held on the washstand and moved into her room. "How do you feel?"

She thought she saw his lips twitch ever so slightly at the corners, under his mustache. A small spot of shaving soap clung to the underside of his chin.

"Better, thank you," she said, surprised by his thinly veiled amusement. Amanda had expected him to be angry rather than to tease her. From what she could remember, she had made a fool of herself the night before.

"About last night . . . I wanted to apologize." Her head still ached. She kept her eyes fixed on his face, trying not to let her gaze drift down to his open shirt and bare chest.

He raised an eyebrow. "Well, it's good we left when we did, but no harm done. However, no more wine. You have no head for it."

Amanda rolled her eyes, then regretted the movement. "You needn't worry on that account. It no longer holds any appeal, believe me." She was relieved by his easy reaction, but didn't understand the amused expression on his face.

"What can you tell me about last night?" He eyed her attentively.

Amanda thought back. "There really wasn't much I learned. It's hard to have any kind of a conversation and learn anything in the time it takes to dance one dance." She hesitated for a moment. "Cash Walker did extend his invitation to the armory and the iron works again."

He looked relieved. "Good. When do you want to go? I'll hold my next message to Washington until after your visit, if it's going to be soon."

Daniel was due to send another of his coded letters in care of his "New York Bankers," who forwarded information they gathered to the War Department in Washington.

Amanda thought for a moment she had not heard him correctly. "You don't object to me going? The invitation does not include you."

"No, I don't object. I think you can learn more without me." He smiled at her.

She threw up her hands, exasperated. "What made you change your mind? You almost bit my head off the last time we talked about me being alone with Mr. Walker."

Daniel shrugged. "The circumstances are different. We have more control. You won't be out on a dark porch alone with the man after a couple of glasses of wine."

Again the amused smile. Why did he look at her like that?

She had a suspicion it had to do with something she had done last night that she didn't remember. She recalled Birdie's comment about not putting her to bed.

His voice drew her attention back to the present.

"Besides, you'll take Birdie with you. An English Lady wouldn't think of going without her maid. How soon can you contact Walker?" Daniel buttoned his shirt as he talked.

Amanda watched his hands, wondering if they had removed her clothes last night. Her voice sounded tight. "I'll send him a note in the morning."

"Send it tonight. Tell him you want to go tomorrow. Then we need to find a reason to move on. The planters are ready to invest their money." He turned and started back into his room. "I'll see you at dinner."

"I am going to have a tray in my room." She spoke to his retreating back. "I'll write a note and have Birdie take care of seeing it delivered to Walker."

Amanda felt as if she had spent very little time with Daniel in the past few days, and she missed being with him. "What are your plans?"

He turned toward her and leaned against the door frame. "Shipley wants me to meet two boat captains who have been running the blockade, so most of tomorrow I'll be at the docks in Richmond again."

"Hopefully I'll be at the iron works." She fought the urge to walk over and reach up to wipe the soap off his chin.

"You're very confident about Walker, aren't you?" He rolled down his sleeves and fastened the cuffs.

Amanda smiled coyly at him, exaggerating her accent and fluttering her eyelashes. "Good sir, never underestimate the power of a lady's charms."

Daniel studied her for a moment and then gave her a sly smile. "Having just recently viewed the lady's charms, I would never be inclined to underestimate them." He gave her a little bow and stepped through to the adjoining room and closed the door.

Amanda stood for a moment, staring, her mouth open. She

couldn't think of a response, but she no longer had any doubts as to who had helped her to bed the night before.

Damn his smug hide, she thought to herself, at the same time wondering just what his opinion of her charms might be.

Amanda composed her note to Cash Walker. Lubirda took it to the slave quarters to find someone to make the delivery. After supper Lubirda returned with a reply. Officer Walker had detained the man delivering the note until he could write a response.

He would be pleased to meet her at the main gate to the iron works the next morning. Amanda gave a whoop of delight and immediately began rummaging through her dresses looking for the perfect outfit. She decided on a russet serge riding habit, even though they would go by carriage. Wide skirts and hoops would get in the way, and she didn't want to be hindered during her tour. She wanted to see it all.

When her clothes were all laid out, she prepared for bed, listening all the while for Daniel to return, anxious to tell him of her plans for the morning. Lubirda left, saying only that she had someone to meet and she would be back late. Amanda wondered again about the Negro woman's mysterious evening rendezvous.

Daniel had mentioned to her that Birdie brought him information, but said nothing about where or how she got it, just that she was sure of its accuracy. Every time Amanda tried to ask questions, the woman deftly avoided answering.

Needing a good night's sleep, Amanda went to bed. She had difficulty getting to sleep, and woke several times. Annoyed with herself, she decided she must be excited about the day to come. Once more she awakened, and heard Daniel and Lubirda talking in Daniel's room.

She got up and found her dressing gown in the dark. Knocking quietly on the door, she waited for an invitation, then opened the door. Daniel was sprawled on the narrow bed in his shirtsleeves, a tablet propped against one knee.

He gave her a quick, distracted look, then concentrated on the figures he carefully recorded as Lubirda gave him information.

"Lubirda, you are doing a fine job." He spoke to the Negro woman without looking up.

Lubirda nodded, smiled and left the room. Amanda wished she could be so relaxed around Daniel.

He continued to put down figures on the tablet as Amanda spoke. "I'm going to the iron works tomorrow. It's all arranged."

At first she wasn't sure he had heard her. He appeared distracted and very tired. Finally he looked up and answered her.

"That's fine. I'll arrange for Tobias to take you in a carriage after breakfast. You'd better get some sleep." Absently he stood and reached over and slid a warm hand around the back of her neck.

Pulling her to him, he kissed her on the forehead. "Good night."

"Good night Daniel." She left the little room in a daze. He had touched her with his casual affection.

She stepped over Lubirda, already bedded down on her pallet, and climbed into the bed. Now that she knew he was safely in his own bed, she fell into a relaxed sleep.

The tour of the iron works was better than Amanda could have hoped. The collection of huge buildings sat on the edge of the James River. Acrid smoke billowed from tall smokestacks, tainting the air with noxious smells.

Captain Walker saw to it that Amanda had the grand tour. She viewed the smelters where they melted iron and formed it into projectiles for cannon, the molds for wheels and axles for railway cars, and the huge rollers used to form the plates for ironclad ships.

All during the tour she had the same nagging feeling she had had at the Hunts' ball and at Shipleys'. He looked familiar to her. She asked him if he had ever traveled in the North before the war, thinking she might have seen him in Philadelphia, but he said he had never left the South.

The director of the factory accompanied them, reeling off

facts and figures Amanda struggled to remember. Heat and noise overpowered much chance for conversation, and she bided her time, asking as many questions as she dared between buildings.

By the time the tour ended she knew the strengths, the weaknesses, output, and future production plans.

Captain Walker's troops guarded every part of the factory. It became apparent during her tour that any attempt to put the iron works out of commission would prove very difficult. Too bad, thought Amanda, for several times Captain Walker stressed the fact that this was the only factory in the South that could do this type of work.

Lubirda did her own listening and watching too, lingering to speak with the Negro workers as much as she could. On the way home they shared what they had seen, Amanda writing down all the information they could remember on paper she had hidden in the carriage.

Feeling grimy after the long day, Amanda bathed and readied herself for dinner. Lubirda went downstairs to eat in the kitchen, then came back and laid down on the bed for a nap. Apparently the late nights she had been keeping had finally caught up with her.

Amanda heard Daniel return and she slipped into his room to tell him what she had seen. He sat on the narrow bed pulling off his boots. He looked up at her as she entered, and smiled.

An impulse made her want to reach out to him, to tell him she missed him. Aghast at the ease with which this thought came to her, she silently chided herself.

Before she could speak, he held up his hand. "I want to hear everything, but it will have to wait until after dinner. I hardly have enough time to change." He glanced up at her. "You look happy. Good day?"

"We saw everything."

Amanda handed him the papers. "I made some notes and sketches. I was afraid I might forget something."

Scowling, he took the papers from her hand. "*Never* put anything in writing. It puts you in too much danger."

"The writing is all coded." Amanda wanted to lighten his mood.

"Anyone who knew where you were today would know what this is." He didn't seem impressed with her efforts.

He slid the papers into an inside pocket in his jacket and glanced at the closed doorway leading to the back hall. "Someone has been going through my things."

Amanda's stomach clenched. "Is anything missing?"

He shook his head. "As a matter of fact, they went to a great deal of trouble to put everything back exactly the way it was."

"That must be how she knew," Amanda muttered under her breath.

"Who knew? What?" He took her elbow and pulled her around to face him.

Amanda didn't look at him. "Blythe Shipley. She knows you sleep in the other room."

He sounded more curious than upset. "What did she say to you?"

Amanda stammered, unwilling to relate the whole ugly conversation. "Just, well, that I was a fraud. She scared me. At first I thought she knew the truth about what we were doing here. I wondered how she knew about where you slept." She still did not meet his eye. "She accused me of preferring another woman in my bed to a man."

"When?" His voice was deadly calm.

"Day before yesterday, the day of the party. She came into the dining room when I was eating breakfast."

"Why didn't you tell me then?" He loosened his grip on her arm, sliding his hand down to catch hers. His other hand cupped her chin, bringing her face up.

Amanda felt warm at his touch, making it hard to concentrate. "You had already left. Then there was so much going on. It didn't seem that important at the time." She had been embarrassed by the other woman's outlandish accusations.

"Be careful of her."

His warning was not necessary. Blythe Shipley reminded

her of a deadly, cunning snake. Amanda would not have been surprised to see a forked tongue slip out between her lips.

"Are you ready to go downstairs?"

Wanting to lighten the mood, she turned around slowly in front of him, stopped, and dropped a small curtsy. "All ready, sir."

When she looked up, his hands were on the waistband of his trousers, unbuttoning fasteners.

"I'll be ready in a moment." He grinned as she hurried from the little room.

Within minutes he joined her. Amanda held her fingers to her lips and motioned to Lubirda, curled up on the bed.

Daniel looked wonderful in a dark brown cutaway jacket and light gold satin vest.

Dinner went smoothly. Daniel and Shipley described their day, and Blythe spoke of a letter from her brother.

No one showed much interest in Amanda's activities after she announced rather vacantly how perfectly smelly and hot the iron works had been. After dinner, Shipley invited Daniel for brandy and a cigar, and Amanda excused herself and went upstairs to wait for him. She had no intention of being alone with her hostess.

Lubirda sat on the couch mending the flounce on one of Amanda's petticoats. She set her sewing on a small table. "Tobias say we goin' to leave."

Amanda faced Lubirda. "Did he say when?"

Lubirda shook her head and stood up. "Soon, I'm thinkin'. You done for the night?"

Amanda nodded. "Can't be too soon for me."

"That Miz Shipley, she one nasty woman. She best be careful or folks here be putting spells on her." Lubirda started on the fasteners on the back of Amanda's dress.

"Spells? What are spells?" She craned her head around to look at Lubirda, wondering what in the world the woman was talking about.

"You know, black magic. Voodoo. Spell to make all her hair fall out, or make her teeth go black."

"Have they got a spell that could improve her disposition?" If there was anything that would improve Blythe Shipley, it would be a better disposition.

Lubirda snickered as she helped Amanda step out of her gown. "Don't think they got magic strong enough to do that."

Amanda laughed at Lubirda's wit.

"They gots love potions."

"For Mrs. Shipley?" Somehow the notion of Blythe in love was hard to imagine.

"For you. And the captain." Lubirda gave Amanda one of her rare smiles. "It you I worried about mostly."

Startled, Amanda stared at Lubirda. Where had that comment come from? "I'm not going to fall in love. I can take care of myself, and I'll be going to live in New York after we finish our business."

"He loves you." Lubirda shook out the gown and laid it on the bed.

"No he doesn't. He's always annoyed with me. And he worries what people will think of me." Lubirda was wrong about Daniel. He teased her and kissed her, but he didn't love her.

Stubbornly Lubirda shook her head. " 'Cause he love you. He want you safe."

Then Lubirda startled Amanda by embracing her. "I is worried about your heart. Don't you pay no mind to what folks might think. You do what yo' heart tells you. This life too short to wait, 'specially now, with the war. Them who wait and wait for what other folks thinks is right end up with the 'if onlys'."

Amused by the woman's unusual fervor, Amanda pulled back and grasped Lubirda's hands. "And what are the 'if onlys'?"

"You know, folks who passes up their chances and spends the rest of their lives thinking 'if only' I done this or 'if only' I done that.' Thems the 'if onlys.' You do what your heart tells you about the captain. He a good man."

It was Amanda's turn to draw the other woman into an embrace. "Thank you, Birdie, but I have my own plans, and the captain isn't part of them." Why did saying that cause a little ache in the vicinity of her heart?

Birdie shook her head, her brown eyes sad. "Remember. No regrets, child, no regrets."

Lubirda tapped a finger on the bodice of Amanda's dress and whispered. "Remember, child, what's in here be most important."

"I will, Birdie. I will." Amanda felt big tears run down her cheeks as she watched Lubirda walk out of the room.

She washed her face and sat on the couch, trying to finish the current issue of the Richmond newspaper and a French fashion catalog. Neither held her interest.

Fitfully, she moved about the room, opening Daniel's door and stepping inside. The room smelled of him. She stood in the darkened doorway for a long time. Could Lubirda be right? Or was she so drawn to Daniel because they had been thrown together in dangerous situations?

Wondering what was taking him so long to return, Amanda wandered out onto the balcony. She leaned against the cool stone balustrade and gazed over the darkened landscape. Just as she was about to go back inside, she heard the murmur of voices from the garden below. As her eyes became more accustomed to the dark, she could see a couple walking in the garden, their bodies so close they threw only one shadow in the moonlight.

Amanda knew immediately it was Daniel and Blythe Shipley. She dropped quietly to her knees, so as not to be seen. *Damn that woman,* Amanda thought. *Damn him too.* A sudden spurt of jealousy engulfed her.

The couple came closer, stopping almost under where she crouched, and she could make out their words. With very little encouragement from Daniel, Blythe Shipley was relating the contents of her brother's letter. He was an aide to General Forrest, and his correspondance contained a detailed description of troop movements that included what sounded like half of the rebel army.

Amanda thought the tone of the letter sounded very impersonal, and wondered if the brother was as cold and rigid as Blythe. At least, she reassured herself, Daniel was after information. She wondered what Blythe was after.

As she listened to the voices below, a plan formed in Amanda's head. They needed a reasonable excuse to get them away from the Shipley plantation. At the same time she could get even with Daniel for his comments about her charms the night of the party. It was vindictive, she knew, but seeing Blythe Shipley so close to Daniel in the dark made her angry. She wanted to show the woman she could give as good as she got.

Everything depended on her timing. From Blythe's snide comments and behavior, Amanda had no doubts about the other woman's desire for Daniel.

Amanda made her way down the dark back stairs and out the kitchen door. Soundlessly she moved across the lawns and around the side of the house to the gardens. She hesitated by a low boxwood hedge to get her bearings, wondering briefly if her plan was really such a good idea. Amanda pushed second thoughts aside.

The lamp still burned in her room and she spotted her balcony, orienting herself. Peering into the darkness, she realized the couple, blocked now from her view by a screen of camellia bushes, had not moved.

Amanda made her way to a break in the hedge, keeping out of sight. Needing an excuse to be wandering in the gardens, she stopped to break off a few fragrant stems of mint. She could always say she needed to brew a tea to settle her stomach. They made a snapping sound as she picked them.

"What was that?" Blythe Shipley whispered, sounding alarmed.

"I didn't hear anything," Daniel soothed her.

"Well I did!" she hissed at him.

"You mustn't worry. Shipley's gone to bed on the other side of the house. With the amount of brandy he drank after dinner, we could be in the same room and he wouldn't hear us. Read the rest of the letter."

Amanda maneuvered herself around the bushes and into the deep shadows of a tree. She was quite close to the couple now.

"Come here, you're all tense. Tell me more about your brother." She saw Daniel draw Blythe into an embrace, massaging her shoulders and neck. Amanda could almost hear the woman purring.

Amanda held herself back. *Timing,* she repeated over and over in her brain. *I have to time this just right.*

Blythe Shipley pulled slightly out of the embrace to free her arms and wound them around Daniel's neck, then began to kiss him fervently.

Amanda was glad the time seemed right, because she didn't think she could watch for another second. She stepped out onto the path and moved toward the couple, stopping about fifteen feet in front of them.

"Edmund! Oh, my God. Edmund, what are you doing?" she screamed. "How could you, out here in the garden, where anyone might see." Amanda paused for dramatic effect.

She gasped convincingly, pretending only then to recognize Blythe Shipley when the startled couple separated. "It's you! A married woman! Oh, how could you!" Amanda struggled not to laugh at the expression of surprise on the other woman's face.

Blythe recovered her icy demeanor and slapped Amanda as she swept by her on her way into the house. "You stupid twit! I warned you this would happen. You'll never be enough of a woman for Edmund! You say one word about this and I'll . . . well, you'll be sorry!"

Amanda, unprepared for the physical attack, flinched away from Blythe and brought her hand to her stinging cheek.

Daniel waited until the woman had left, then grabbed Amanda by the arm and led her back around the side of the house to the kitchen door. They could hear people talking, disturbed by the scream and loud voices.

He leaned down and whispered in her ear. "Bravo. That was quite a performance." Hauling her up the stairs, he didn't speak to her again until they were back in their room. She couldn't tell if he was pleased or angry.

Amanda put both trembling hands over her mouth to stifle a hysterical laugh. Daniel left the door to the main hallway open a crack, and returned to her side. His voice was low.

"Nice timing, but we're not finished yet. A wife would hardly let the scene in the garden be her last word."

Relieved he did not seem to be annoyed by her impromptu performance, Amanda gathered her wits and took his cue. She turned away from him, toward the door, afraid if she looked him in the face she would not be able to finish. "You bloody bastard! How dare you treat me like this? I won't have it, do you understand?" Her voice, loud and shrill, carried into the hallway.

Daniel murmured some encouragement as he went into the bathing room and wrung out his handkerchief in the washbowl.

She continued her tirade. "I want to leave here as soon as possible! I will not stay in this house another night." Face flushed and breathing deeply from the effort, she gestured to him, giving him the cue to continue.

He pressed the cool cloth to her smarting cheek. "Oh, for heaven's sake, Charlotte. Don't you think you're over-reacting?"

"No! I'm leaving, with or without you! Is that clear?" Amanda opened the door to his room and slammed it hard.

The door hit the doorjamb and bounced back open, the knob knocking a chunk of plaster out of the wall. If there was anyone in the entire household that was not aware the Lord and Lady were doing battle, it was due to deafness.

"Perfectly. I'll take care of arrangements first thing in the morning. You *will* stay the night." He quietly closed the outer door and turned back to Amanda, giving her a hug and a kiss on the end of her nose.

"You were excellent. Such emotion! Perhaps you should consider a career on the stage." He smiled down into her face. "You do make life interesting."

Amanda wiggled out of his arms, smoothing her gown.

"Well, not all the emotion was forced." He arched an eyebrow at her. "I detest that woman."

Daniel laughed. "She's quite a predator, isn't she?"

"Speaking of that, what would you have done if I hadn't come into the garden when I did?" She watched his face closely.

He grinned at her. "Well, I don't know exactly. I was playing it minute to minute. I'm sure I would have thought of something."

"I bet you would." She sounded disgusted.

"Seriously, Amanda, thank you." He pulled her to him and kissed her lightly. "You were wonderful."

She stood quietly in his embrace, enjoying the warmth from his body. "We'll leave tomorrow?"

He nodded. "Can you be packed by noon?"

"Yes," she said, her cheek resting against the smooth linen of his shirt.

Releasing her, he pulled back the covers on her bed before he left the room. "Sleep well," he said as he closed his door.

"You too," she whispered into the dark, resisting the urge to go to him, and have him hold her, to help her interpret and define the sensations in her body whenever she thought about him. She yearned for him in a way she didn't yet understand. But that wasn't love. She was sure it wasn't.

Lubirda burst through the hallway door, then whispered fiercely to Amanda. "What been happening here? Talk is all the way to the quarters!"

Amanda stifled a laugh. The speed with which word traveled through the Villa Anona amazed her. She related the incident in the garden to Lubirda, who nodded her approval at every word. She had began to organize the packing before Amanda finished talking.

Chapter 16

Lubirda was filling the trunk with the last of their things as Daniel walked through the door, closing it carefully behind him. Amanda stood beside her, dressed in a yellow dress that looked as fresh as a spring morning.

"Are you ladies about ready?"

Amanda looked up at the sound of his voice. "Yes, just a few more minutes. What did you tell Shipley?"

"I used the excuse that I need to be in Charleston by the end of the week. Shipley knows something else is wrong, but he's too much of a gentleman to ask. Perhaps it would be best if you acted a bit formal with him and a little stiff toward me when we leave."

"All right, that sounds easy enough." She turned away and put the last few things she folded on top of the trunk.

"Birdie, thank you for all your efforts here. The contacts you established were very helpful." Daniel reached out and patted the Negro woman on the back.

Amanda turned to Lubirda. "Is there anyone you need to say good-bye to? I'll finish up here."

"No, no one special. I says what I wanted to say earlier.

'Sides, we most finished. I go get somebodies to carry these here things down to the carriage.'' Lubirda closed the last of the luggage and left.

"Who is going to drive?"

Tobias wasn't with them. Daniel had sent him ahead on an errand.

"I lined up a driver in Richmond, a man I can trust. I sent him a message last night. He's waiting downstairs with the carriage. We'll pick Tobias up in Norfolk." He stood quietly, watching her move nervously around the room, checking the straps and locks on the luggage. She wasn't going to like what he was going to say to her.

"Amanda, come here." She stopped for a moment, still as a doe sensing the air in a forest clearing, then moved across the room to face him.

"I'm sending you back, with Lubirda and Tobias." He kept his voice soft and gentle, hoping they could have a reasonable conversation and she would see things his way.

"No! I'm supposed to go with you!" He felt no surprise at her vehement reaction. He had expected her to argue.

"Keep your voice down! I have things to do alone. I don't need you."

A look of hurt flashed across her expressive features. He took a step toward her, and she moved back. He wanted her safe, as he had from the first moment he had met her. The longer they remained in enemy territory the more dangerous their position became.

"I want to go with you." She stuck her stubborn little chin out and looked him in the eye.

"No. I'm sending you north with Tobias and Lubirda. I can't guarantee your safety." He felt resigned, wondering why he had even bothered to talk to her. He was never going to convince her.

"I never asked for a guarantee. You're not sending me back. I need to do my sketches."

Her damn drawings. She would risk her safety for her sketches. He fought to keep his voice calm. "I don't need you anymore. I want to know you're safe, back in Washington with Lubirda.''

"No." Hands fisted at her sides, she faced him squarely. He'd seen that posture before. She wasn't going to give an inch.

With an effort, he kept his voice even, hoping to soothe her. "I know sometimes you get scared. I don't want you to have to live like that."

Her lower lip trembled. "I am scared, but not because of the work." She blurted the answer out, and then looked sorry she had spoken.

Puzzled, he watched her belligerent pose wilt. "Of what, then?"

She looked at a place on the wall behind him, unwilling to meet his eyes. She shook her head.

He persisted. "What? What scares you?" He moved slightly to the left, to catch her glance.

Her answer came too quickly. "Nothing. Nothing at all."

Hope kindled like a small flame inside him. Maybe she had feelings for him she wasn't willing to admit to. He decided to push her, not letting it go.

"I don't believe you." He pinned her with his gaze.

Suddenly her eyes filled with tears and she looked overwhelmed with feelings.

"Me. You. I'm scared of what I feel." Her voice was a whisper he had to strain to hear.

He took a step to cover the distance between them, needing to feel her in his arms.

"Lord, I know. I feel it too." He pulled her to him.

Was she finally going to admit she might be wrong about her plans for her future? He felt her stiffen, then shudder. With a sigh, she finally relaxed against his chest.

Daniel cursed to himself when he heard voices in the hallway, wondering if they would find the time alone to really talk about the future. He let go of her and stepped back.

"Daniel, I . . ."

Someone cleared a throat and a knock sounded at the door.

He put two fingers to her lips. "Ssh. Not now. We'll talk later."

The moment was lost when Lubirda entered the room, followed by two men who hoisted the heavy trunk on their shoulders and carried it down to the waiting coach.

"Ready to face the dragon lady?" Daniel offered his arm.

She didn't meet his eye. "I'm ready." Her quiet voice sounded resigned.

They moved together out the door. Lubirda stood staring at them with open curiosity. Shrugging, she followed.

The scene when they were leaving went more easily than Daniel had thought it might. Blythe did not appear to bid them farewell.

Shipley met them in the entry hall. Obviously upset by their hasty departure, he accepted Amanda's stiff good-bye. If he had heard of their argument the night before, he did not let on.

"Please, Lady Ashton, Lord Ashton, won't you reconsider and stay a few more days?" Shipley begged, a note of desperation in his voice. "I don't understand what has made you want to leave in such haste, but if you feel we have slighted you in some way. . . ." His voice trailed off and he grasped Amanda's hand while he made his plea.

Amanda pulled her hand away and coldly glared at him. "Why don't you ask your wife why we must leave, Mr. Shipley? She can provide the details for you." She swept down the stairs, ignoring Daniel's offered arm.

Lubirda helped her into the carriage. From inside the vehicle, Amanda listened to Daniel and Shipley's parting remarks. How anxious the planter appeared to be for the investment opportunities Daniel pretended to represent. Apparently the two men could do business in spite of any personal upheaval. Amanda felt sorry for the likable little man. All the voodoo in the world was not going to improve his wife.

Shipley seemed somewhat mollified when Daniel promised to try and stop by on his way north.

Poor man, Amanda thought to herself, studying their host.

He doesn't even know what's going on. She wondered how Shipley's children felt about his second wife.

Amanda glanced up at the house and saw Blythe staring down at her from an upstairs window with an expression of such hatred on her face Amanda shivered and looked away. That woman had the power to scare her with just a look.

When she glanced back up, the face was gone. Daniel took the seat opposite her and they left. Amanda felt relieved when the house was finally out of sight. "Poor Shipley."

Daniel nodded. "He's desperate to make the investment. His money, along with the other planters', will be in an account in New York by tomorrow."

Amanda nodded. "Where are we going?"

Daniel glanced over at Lubirda, then back at Amanda. "Amanda—"

"Don't start, Daniel. I'm going with you."

She watched his features harden.

"Not this time. I'm sending you away."

Chapter 17

Amanda and Daniel stood on the street overlooking the Norfolk docks and watched in the distance as Tobias picked up the last trunk, Lubirda right behind him, telling him exactly what to do as they walked up the gangplank. The two former slaves had developed the oddest relationship.

Heavy wagons, carts and carriages rumbled on the road behind them, kicking up clouds of dust. Drivers shouted to their teams and at each other, adding to the din.

The boat was due to sail in five minutes. She had argued with him all the way into Norfolk about sending her back, and couldn't get him to budge.

Amanda stared at the black cloud billowing from the smokestacks on the boat. She would have to turn and say good-bye to Daniel, then go down and join Tobias and Lubirda. She might never see him again.

Just before they had left Shipley's house he had said they would talk, but they hadn't had a minute alone on the trip to Norfolk. In a way she was relieved, because she was so confused she didn't know what she was going to say to him.

A few weeks ago she had had her life all planned. She knew

what she wanted to do and how she would do it. Then she had met Daniel and all kinds of bewildering feelings had left her in a muddle.

She still wanted to go to New York and be an artist, but the thought of never seeing Daniel again left an empty feeling inside her that she wasn't sure she could bear.

The steam whistle sounded their imminent departure. "Amanda. It's time for you to go."

She shaded her eyes and stared off at the horizon across the Atlantic. "I know."

There was no point in arguing anymore. Nothing she said was going to change his mind and let her stay with him, and the general wasn't here to issue an order.

"I'll miss you." His breath was warm against her cheek.

And she would miss him, more than she could ever say. She turned and looked up at him, wanting to memorize his face so that she might carry his image in her mind.

"Will you? Why? I've caused you nothing but problems."

His eyes sad, he smiled down at her and ran his finger down her cheek. "Some of the best problems I ever had."

If he kept talking like that she was going to cry. "Daniel—"

"Damn."

The expression on his face turned hard. He was looking over her shoulder at something.

She turned around and saw a dozen soldiers, about a block away, walking toward them. Her mouth felt dry. "Do you think they're looking for us?"

"I don't know. I want you to turn and walk slowly toward the gangplank."

Amanda looked back at him and from the corner of her eye saw another group approaching from the other direction. Bodin walked with the gray uniformed men.

She grabbed at Daniel's sleeve. "Daniel. Look behind you." Fear clawed at her throat, making her voice weak.

"Come on." He grabbed her hand and yanked her into the road between two wagons. They were so close to one team a horse stepped on the hem of her skirt. She stifled a scream as they darted around a carriage and into an alley that smelled of fish.

"Run." He took off, yanking her after him.

She couldn't keep up with his long strides as he pulled her along, stumbling and tripping over her skirts.

"Daniel." Terrified for him, she gasped out his name. "You go on ahead."

He slowed a bit. "No. Keep moving."

She tried to pull her hand from his grasp. She was slowing him down. If they caught him they'd hang him. He had such a grip on her she thought he would break the bones in her hand. He turned into a narrow walkway between two buildings. She couldn't catch her breath to ask him where they were going.

The passageway opened into another alley. After running for two more blocks she slipped on the cobblestones and fell to her knees.

He hauled her up and, breathless, she begged him again. "Please. Leave me and go ahead."

"In here." He shoved her through a wooden door into a warehouse filled with barrels.

The stench of whiskey hung in the air. They ran to the rear of the dark building and crouched down behind some huge casks. Amanda heard the sound of boots pounding on the pavement and men shouting, but they ran on, past the building where they hid.

Daniel pulled up her skirts and looked at her knees. Her stockings were shredded and her skin scraped raw. He pulled her skirts back down and gathered her into his arms.

He whispered against her cheek, "All I needed was five minutes and you would have been safe."

Amanda huddled in an overstuffed chair by the fireplace in the dank little room, wondering if she would ever get warm. They were hiding on the second floor of a tavern and she could hear giggles and thumps coming from the room next door.

Daniel had been standing by the window staring into the dark for the last hour.

He cleared his throat. "We need to discuss our plans. Are you up to it?"

She knew he felt terribly guilty that he had failed to get her on the boat. She wasn't going to add to the problem by letting him see how scared she was.

"First, what about Lubirda and Tobias?" She had been terribly worried about the pair traveling alone.

"Tobias knows what to do. He has the papers he needs for both of them."

Daniel sounded so sure of the pair's safety, Amanda felt a surge of relief that brought her to the verge of tears.

Reassured of her friends' security, she could concentrate on the two of them. "Where can we go?" Amanda took a swipe at her nose.

"Back to Richmond," he said, with no inflection in his voice.

She shot out of the chair. "Are you serious?" Her voice was filled with dismay. "Back to the Shipleys'?"

Daniel shook his head. "No, not back to Shipley's. I have a few places to go first. Then we'll pass through Richmond on our way home. At the first opportunity that seems safe, I'll send you north. We aren't that far from Washington."

She knew he was trying to reassure her. She also knew he was in much more danger than she was. "And you'll come with me. To Washington."

He shrugged. "I'm waiting for a message."

Amanda held her tongue. Perhaps when he stopped blaming himself for what had happened today she would be able to talk some sense into him. Until then she would do what he said and not argue.

"Where to first?" Amanda concentrated on Daniel, not wanting to think about what danger might lie outside the front door of the seedy tavern.

He crossed the room and knelt beside her on one knee. With a thin piece of kindling he drew a crude map in the soot on the hearth.

Amanda studied his thick wavy hair, enjoying how it lay curling against his neck just above the top of his collar. She wondered what it would feel like to let it curl around her fingers as they rested on his warm skin, very aware of the fact they were now alone.

"We're going to work our way north to Williamsburg." He didn't look up right away as he scratched out the outline and threw the wooden stick into the fireplace. "Amanda?"

She pulled her attention back to what he was saying, searching for an appropriate response. "How will we travel?"

"Horseback, mostly. There is some ferry service, but word is it's not very reliable. It's not going to be very comfortable." His voice held a note of apology. He brushed off his hands and stood up. He looked very tall standing beside her chair.

Amanda waved her hand. "Don't worry about me. I've been uncomfortable before."

She eyed the old carpetbag that held clothing. He had given the boy who swept out the bar a gold piece to bring them some old clothes.

"I assume we will be brothers again? Like we were on the paddle wheeler?" She glanced up at him.

"No, I think we'll go as father and son." His steady gaze unnerved her and her eyes drifted back to the bag.

She had a vision of him being questioned and arrested.

"Won't people wonder, I mean the fact that a man like you is traveling around and not fighting with the army?" She didn't want him to know how scared she was and tried to hide the tremor in her voice.

He shook his head. "They might question a healthy man, but I doubt they would object to a wounded soldier returning to his home."

He went back to looking out the window.

Dread ate at her like a living thing. "Daniel."

Concern showed in his face as he turned to her. "What is it?"

He asked the question as he moved across the room to her. Amanda wanted to be brave about this, she really did, but her fears got the better of her as she leaned toward him, whispering, "I'm so frightened for you."

Daniel gathered her into his arms, their noses almost touching. "Oh, sweetheart. I'm so sorry."

The terror loosened its grip as she felt his breath warm against her face. She nestled against him, fitting herself to the hard contours of his body, wanting to protect him and shield him. His arms tightened around her and her body began to hum. She recalled her conversation with Lubirda.

She leaned back and, reaching up, took his face between her hands. She moved her chin ever so slightly, reaching up on her toes, until her lips barely brushed against his.

He went perfectly still. Threading her fingers into his hair, she pulled, a tiny tug, gently bringing him closer. Eyes closed, she touched him with her lips again, enjoying the feel of his mustache against her face. He swayed forward and she bent back, keeping a distance between them. With a groan, he covered her wrists and drew her arms around his neck. His warm hands on her back pinned her against his body.

Daniel controlled the kiss now. Gone was the gentle searching. His lips were hard on hers, seeking, demanding response. Amanda met those demands eagerly, her whole being centered for that moment on lips and tongue and mustache. Like a blind person she tasted and explored, eagerly following his lead.

As the kisses deepened, she became aware of other sensations. A fiery, fluid feeling seeped into her limbs, making her feel curiously weak. Amanda perceived the arousal in Daniel's body too. She felt his hardness and pressed against him. He responded instantly by sliding his hands down over her bottom and holding her tightly against him. She marveled at the speed of the changes in them, and his response to her.

She pushed back against his chest with her hands, and after a moment's hesitation, he eased his hold on her. Amanda pulled away so she could see his face. His skin was flushed.

"Amanda, I'm sorry. . . ."

She put her fingers over his lips to silence him. Lubirda's words bounced around inside Amanda's head. She wanted to know what it was really like, to experience life, to relieve the terrible curiosity. She made her decision. "Lie with me tonight."

He pulled her hand away, massaging her knuckles. "Ah, I don't know. . . ."

"I want to be with you." She spoke with no hesitation in her voice, because she felt none.

He still looked unsure. "You've thought about this?"

"Oh, yes." She looked him in the eye. "I'm sure." She slid her hands up his chest and around his neck, pulling him back to her, wetting his lower lip with her tongue. "I'm so sure." She whispered against his mouth.

With a moan he crushed her to him. "I want you so much." His voice was hoarse with need.

Amanda felt a giddiness at his statement. She had feared if she asked him, he would say no. She trailed kisses across his cheek to his ear, enjoying the rough feel of his whiskers against her lips and tongue. "I don't know what to do," she whispered, feeling uncomfortably naive despite Lubirda's answers.

"Ssh. Don't worry about that." He moved his hands up her rib cage and massaged the sides of her breasts with his thumbs.

Amanda wanted to say something but pure sensation took over and she couldn't talk. Tiny vibrations seemed to come from his fingertips, and they pulsed across her skin causing her to shudder. Her breathing came in short pants.

His hands reached around her back and found the buttons of her dress as her fumbling fingers unfastened the front of his shirt. Amanda pulled back the fabric, exposing warm skin rough with hair. Burying her face against him, she delighted in the sensation. She had wanted to know what it would feel like to touch him.

He pushed her dress down over her shoulders, pinning her arms at her sides. Untying the ribbon at the neckline of her chemise, he pushed that down too. Daniel stepped back for a moment to look at her. The sudden movement away from his warmth jarred her.

''Daniel?'' He stared at her, making her uncomfortable. ''Turn out the lamp.''

''No. I want to look at you.'' His voice was quiet. ''You're beautiful.''

His scrutiny made her uncomfortable. She flushed. ''Please, hold me.'' She leaned toward him, struggling to free her arms from her dress.

''Stand still.'' His voice held a quiet command. She froze in place. Her heart pounded. He helped her free her arms from the dress, leaving it bunched around her waist. Then, without taking his eyes from hers, he removed his shirt.

Using both hands, he traced a line down the sides of her neck and across her shoulders, stopping to silently finger her scar, and then continued down to her breasts. When she began to quiver, he followed the same path with his lips. Amanda didn't even feel his hands once again at the buttons of her dress. Her whole being was centered on his mouth as it played over one nipple and then the other, back and forth until they stood in hard, wet peaks. She twined her fingers in the hair at the back of his neck. It felt as good as she had imagined it would earlier.

In one swift movement he slid her dress down over her hips and onto the floor. Daniel took her by the hand and she stepped out of the mound of fabric. Next he untied the petticoats at her waist and, along with her chemise, they joined the dress on the floor, leaving her in nothing but her pantaloons, stockings, and shoes. He led her to the side of the narrow bed and perched her on the edge, squatting in front of her. Taking hold of her ankle, he settled her foot against his groin, holding her firmly as he loosened her shoe. He slid it off her foot and put her stockinged foot back against him. Amanda could feel the hard heat of him through his trousers. She trembled as he dropped her foot and repeated the movements with her other shoe.

Standing up, he lifted her by the ankle and she sank back onto the bed. He ran his hand up her leg under her pantaloons and found the top of a stocking. Stroking the soft flesh on the inside of her thigh, he rolled the stocking down her leg. Amanda's body began to throb with a need she didn't understand. He removed the other stocking in the same manner and she groped for him, trying to bring him closer.

He pushed her back on the quilt. "Not yet."

"Please." She begged him, not yet knowing what her need was, desperate to find out.

"Soon." It was all he said as he unbuttoned the waistband of her only remaining garment. He teased it over her hips. Amanda saw that he too breathed in shallow gasps, a fine sheen of perspiration covering his body. She felt a thrill of power at his reaction to her.

Daniel straightened up and watched her lying naked on the bed. Amanda became self-conscious and tugged at a corner of the worn quilt in an effort to cover herself.

"No." Her hand fell still at his word. "Don't be ashamed. You're beautiful," he repeated as he unfastened his trousers and slid them off.

Amanda gasped at the sight of him. She had seen naked men before, but never in a state of arousal. She didn't take her eyes off him.

"Move over." She scooted across the bed to the wall.

He stretched out on the bed beside her and she rolled toward him, winding her arms around his neck, her lips seeking and finding his mouth. The delightful sensation of skin against skin overwhelmed her. Over her breasts, down ribs, across her stomach, it felt as if his hands were everywhere, lighting fires within her body. As he moved lower she clamped her thighs together in a protective movement.

He breathed in her ear. "Let me."

Her thighs relaxed a little and warm fingers played in her soft hair, seeking entrance to her. She heard a moan, but couldn't tell whether it came from her or him. Slowly he moved his hand. The throbbing increased tenfold. Lubirda was right. It was if he was making her body sing.

His fingers felt wet and wonderful as they caressed her, finding her. Her thighs fell open. Softly he stroked her. She begged again with unknowing need. "Please, please."

He swung himself over her, knees between her thighs, arms braced beside her head. He lowered his body slightly and the erect shaft of his cock took the place his fingers had just left. Ever so gently he swayed against her, rubbing gently, seeking entry. She stiffened at his probing.

Amanda opened her eyes and watched him. The muscles of his arms and shoulders bunched powerfully as they tensed above her, his face set in concentration as he fought for control.

She began to enjoy the feeling as he moved against her, the tip of his penis nestled in the opening of her body, and she relaxed a little.

"Good." He whispered down to her . "Move with me." He eased himself down on her, increasing the pressure.

Suddenly she felt the pushing increase, and she feared he was too large for her. Amanda tried to wiggle away. He stayed her with his voice.

"Don't. Don't move away from me. I want you."

In spite of her discomfort, she responded to him, wanting to please him. Rocking her hips to follow his lead, she heard him gasp. He became more insistent as her body continued to move with him, resisting his entry at the same time.

His breathing heavy, teeth gritted, he spoke low, into her ear. "Open up to me. I need you, now." He lost his fine edge of control and with a lunge pushed into her.

Amanda yelped, the tearing pain taking her by surprise. He murmured incoherent words of comfort, and kissed her. She stiffened and clutched at the quilt as he moved his hips, gently at first, thrusting in and out. After a few moments the pain subsided, and other sensations took over. Just as she started to move her body to match his, he shuddered and went slack, the weight of him forcing the air out of her lungs. She pushed at him and he rolled to the side, wrapping her in his arms and taking her with him.

Amanda lay very still, listening to his breathing return to normal. He stirred and shifted so he could see her face. "I hurt you."

"A little." She buried her face against his shoulder, feeling a strange mixture of embarrassment and agitation. Lubirda had been wrong about one thing. Amanda was fairly sure it was over and she didn't feel still and quiet.

His arms tightened as he cradled her against his chest. "I'm sorry. I didn't want to hurt you."

"I'm all right." She tried to pull away from him, confused at her feelings.

"No. Stay here with me." His voice was sleepy. He shifted his weight, nestling her more snugly against him. He rubbed the back of her neck until she forced herself to relax.

Amanda listened to his breathing become deep and regular. She wanted to get her chemise and put it on, but, afraid she might wake him, she stayed where she was. Her body was sore and tired, but her mind jumped from thought to thought, uncertain about how she really felt. Finally exhaustion took over and she slept.

Dreams she could not remember woke Amanda several times, leaving her feeling uneasy. Each time she tried to edge off the bed, she was stopped by Daniel's grasp, possessive even in sleep.

Amanda remembered the last dream to awaken her. It was a replay of what had happened between them. In her dream she felt his hands and his lips on her. When she awoke, panting and drenched in sweat, her body throbbed with wanting him. *What's the matter with me?* she thought.

Daniel lay sleeping on his side, with an arm thrown over her and one of his legs high between her thighs. Amanda, struck by an overwhelming desire for closeness, was startled by the strength of her need. She grasped his thigh between her legs and rubbed herself against him.

The motion awakened him. "What?" He sounded sleepy and confused.

Amanda tried not to tremble as she spoke, but it was beyond her. "I . . . I don't know." She was panting and clutching at him.

He came fully awake and raised himself on his elbow so he could see her face. He grasped her hips, holding her against

him. She could feel his erection against her stomach, surprised
at the quickness of his arousal. Perhaps he had been dreaming
too, she thought vaguely.

Without a word he rolled her to her back. Her legs opened
willingly to him and he moved between them, stroking the
inside of her thighs. Planting her feet, she lifted her hips up
off the bed, reaching for him.

In a single motion he lowered himself, filling her. This time
there was no pain, only a soreness overridden by the incredible
sensation of him inside her. Again he urged her to move with
him and she replied with her body. Gently at first, then more
and more until she arched to meet every thrust. She could feel
a tension building within her, and when she felt as if she might
burst, there was an explosion of millions of colored sparks
inside her head. She felt a white heat everywhere. Her body
quivered, and she called out his name. A moment later, as if
in reply, Daniel's body answered with a spasm.

Amanda's limbs felt as if her bones had dissolved. Once again
Daniel pulled her into his arms and this time she welcomed the
embrace. He stroked her hair as she drifted off to sleep.

Daniel awakened at dawn. Amanda's place on the bed beside
him was empty, but still held her warmth. He sat up and looked
around. In the early morning light he spotted her in the overstuffed chair by the fireplace.

''Amanda?''

''What?'' said a small voice, not looking at him. He crossed
the room and saw her cheeks were shiny with tears.

Self-reproach assaulted him. ''Tell me what's wrong. Are
you sorry?''

She shook her head.

It occurred to him he had been too rough with her. He knelt
down in front of the chair and laid his hand on her hip. ''Did
I hurt you?''

She shook her head and turned away, pulling the front edges
of her chemise closed.

"Sweetheart, tell me what's wrong."

"I can't." He could barely hear her whisper.

"Yes, you can and you must. Why did you leave me?"

"Oh, Daniel, I'm so embarrassed!" She surprised him with noisy sobbing.

He stood and picked her up, settling back in the chair with her in his lap. Daniel pulled her against his chest and rubbed her back. The crying subsided. "What happened last night was good, Amanda. We both wanted it."

"I know." She hiccuped. "It's not that."

"Then what is it?" Her bottom felt soft and warm against his lap, and he enjoyed the sensation as he shifted to find the most comfortable position.

"I think there's something wrong with me." She whispered into his collarbone. "When I woke you up and ..." She couldn't seem to find the words she needed.

He tipped her chin up and gave her a grin. "That was the nicest thing that could happen." He felt a tenderness for her, his heart full of love.

He could see the flush on her face and she was whispering again. "But it just happened again. I woke up and ..." Again words failed her. "Do you think I'm ... a ... a wanton?" Daniel could tell she was holding her breath.

"No, my darling, I think you are the most wonderful thing that has ever happened to me." And he proceeded to show her how extraordinary loving someone could be, right there in the overstuffed chair.

Chapter 18

Amanda studied herself in the cracked mirror over the dresser, looking for something new in her appearance. She felt so changed after last night it was hard to believe it didn't show. She turned away from her reflection, trying to reassure herself.

"That was last night and doesn't change anything today." She didn't think she sounded very convincing.

Despite her protests about his safety, Daniel had left the room early this morning after depositing her on her bed. He told her to get ready; then he kissed her and she had wanted to drag him back down onto the sheets.

Lubirda had failed to mention that finding out firsthand about the mystery of what went on between a man and a woman was only the beginning.

Thinking of him made her breasts ache under the bindings that flattened them against her chest. The old worn overalls and shirt fit loosely, further concealing her figure.

Satisfied with her clothes, she began to slick down her hair, still short enough to pass for a boy's. Thoughts of last night kept intruding into her concentration, and she found herself staring into the mirror.

Pull yourself together, she told herself sternly. Even though she was tired and sore, the intensity of wanting him had not subsided. Amanda was afraid her suspicions that she might have the makings of a woman of easy virtue were true, despite Daniel's reassurance.

As she jammed a felt cap on her head, she heard a tapping on the door. She hesitated, relieved he had returned but embarrassed to face him after what they had done last night. And this morning.

He didn't wait for her to answer and stepped into her room, quickly closing the door. Daniel reached out and caressed her cheek.

"How do you feel?"

"Fine." She stepped away from him, not meeting his eye. He reached out and grasped her hand.

"Amanda, marry me. Today. As soon as we can get you north I'll send you to my family. You'll be safe there."

His sudden proposal threw her. "I ... uh ... no!" She moved away from him, trying to gather her scattered feelings. A sense of panic urged her to turn him down. She didn't know what she wanted.

His hand on her arm caught and held her where she stood. "Why not?" His voice held an angry edge.

"Because! You didn't seduce me. I came to you of my own free will." She tried to jerk her arm away.

"What difference does that make?" His hand tightened.

She'd been afraid of the way he would react to last night, afraid that he would feel he had to be honorable.

She felt trapped and blurted the first thought that came to her mind. "You're asking because you feel guilty."

"I don't feel the least bit guilty. Do you?" His tone softened and he pulled her gently toward him.

"Yes! I mean no. Oh, I don't know. I'm confused." She stood still, cradling her head in her hands.

He slid his warm hand around the nape of her neck, and rubbed her tense muscles. "Last night was the normal thing to do when two people feel the way we do." He moved closer to her, so their bodies almost touched.

Amanda dropped her hands and looked at him. He wanted to marry her. Anger was overtaking the confusion caused by his sudden proposal. She didn't want anyone to take care of her. She could take care of herself.

"Last night was . . . lust. I can't give you the kind of love you need to make a good marriage."

But the hard thing was, she did love him. Enough to give up her dream and marry him? She wasn't sure, and she didn't want to be pressured into making a decision.

"Besides, I'm never getting married."

Daniel scowled at her. "It was more than lust and you know it."

She decided not to answer that one. "I can't get married. I can't turn my life over to someone else. There's so much I want to do. Places I want to go." Amanda looked at him. His face was closed and hard.

His voice had a harsh edge. "I don't want to control your life. I want to share it."

"You do want to control it! The first thing you think of is sending me away. That's an interesting definition of sharing." Amanda knew she had hurt him by refusing him, but she was angry he would push her when she had told him how she felt. No one was going to bully her out of her dream, even if that dream didn't seem as bright and shiny as it once had.

Wanting badly to end the conversation and heal the rift between them, she leaned toward him, taking his face in her hands. "Let's not speak of marriage." She kissed him.

He grabbed her shoulders, pinning her up against his long, hard body. He took control and his hard kiss contained no tenderness.

She realized she had wounded his pride, but his aggression frightened her. She was no match for him physically. Amanda struggled against him, trying to get away, and sensed, to her relief, when he regained control of himself.

She stepped back, watching the stricken emotions cross his

face. She understood why he had been rough with her, possibly far better than he did himself.

Her voice was soft. "I won't be forced into anything."

Daniel reached for her cheek. "I'm sorry," he whispered as he tucked a wisp of hair behind her ear.

Amanda trembled. "I know."

She straightened her clothes to give herself some time to regain her composure, then turned to him. "Daniel, you have to understand how I feel. I need some time. It's not right. Not now."

The look he gave her was intense and full of emotion. "Time?" He turned away, his voice quiet. "I hope to God we have some time."

Damn it, he thought to himself as they rode toward their next destination. He knew he should have kept away from her last night. She was right. He did want to protect her. He wanted to send her home to his family in Bridgeport, where he knew the war would never touch her. He looked over at her, riding beside him. They hadn't said two words to each other since they left Norfolk.

They were on a back road, headed east. The setting sun cast their shadows long on the road in front of them.

In a while, when he was sure they hadn't been followed, they would backtrack and turn toward Williamsburg. There had been no sign of Bodin since they had outrun him at the docks, but Daniel wasn't taking any chances.

No matter how much he wanted to silence it, a little voice in his head refused to leave the subject of Amanda alone. *What scares you,* the little voice kept on relentlessly, *is that she doesn't want you. Not only do you go and fall in love with her, and then take her to your bed, but when you try to do the right thing and ask her to marry you, she refuses.*

The voice had become so annoying, Daniel tried to turn it off without success.

"Oh, shut up!" Exasperated, he didn't realize he had spoken out loud.

The sound of his voice startled Amanda after the silence of the ride. "I beg your pardon?"

She was amused as she caught sight of the surprised look on his face and the blush that crept over his cheeks above the stubble of his beard. He had a patch over one eye, making him look like a pirate. He had tied a crutch to his saddle.

"Nothing." He mumbled and concentrated on the road ahead. "There's a ferry around the next bend. If it's operating, we'll cross there. It will save us some time. You let me do the talking."

Amanda nodded in agreement. The sun was setting and she would be more than happy to get off her horse. Her mount's uneven gait was doing nothing to help her already tender bottom.

She could make out a cluster of buildings and hear the soft lap of water against the land. From where they were she couldn't see a ferry.

"Where's the landing?"

He pointed to the southeast. "About five minutes or so down river. We can check here to see if it's running. The man who owns the roadhouse runs the ferry."

He adjusted his eyepatch and pulled up in front of a two-story building. A sign nailed to the second floor balcony read:

SMITHVILLE HOTEL
EFREM SMITH, PROP.

"This is it. Dining room in the front, bar in the back, and rooms upstairs."

"Looks fine to me." Amanda prayed silently for hot food and a clean bed. Beyond that she didn't much care. Her lack of sleep from the previous night was catching up with her.

They tied their mounts to the rail out front and Amanda waited on the porch while Daniel went inside. He was back in a moment. "Ferry made its last run half hour ago. How about a meal and a rest?" He grabbed both saddlebags off the horses.

Amanda lay sleeping on her back, like a child, her hands palm up beside her head. Daniel shook her gently.

"Come on, Amanda, wake up." She rolled toward him and reached out.

Her first coherent thought was that he was sitting on the side of the bed, fully dressed. His clothes smelled of tobacco smoke and his breath of beer. Then she remembered he had gone downstairs last night.

She sat up, rubbing her eyes, trying to see him in the dark. "Where were you?"

"Playing poker. Get dressed." He sounded excited.

"Why?" She wasn't fully awake, but she could see it was still dark outside.

"It's almost dawn. I'll explain later. Just get up and get dressed. I'll see to the horses and meet you out front." He disappeared into the dark hallway.

Amanda sat on the edge of the bed blinking in the darkness. Her eyes felt gritty. She had a strong urge to climb back under the covers, but forced herself to her feet. Why were they leaving in the middle of the night? What exactly had happened at that poker game?

She hurried into her clothes and found her bag in the dark. Tiptoeing along the hallway, she felt her way down the stairs. The only sound was a rattling snore coming from one of the rooms, and the faraway hum of conversation from the bar. Amanda bumped against tables and chairs in the dining room as she made her way to the front door. It was pitch black outside too, and cold. *This better be good, Daniel McGrath*, she thought.

He was waiting for her. One of the horses whickered softly. She tied on her pack and mounted up, following Daniel. They were headed back up the road they had used coming in.

"Would you mind telling me where we are going?"

"Ssh! Keep your voice down!" He was beside her, his voice

a whisper. "Yorktown. We need to get a message through to the ships blockading Charleston. Come on."

Amanda felt a quiver of excitement. "What happened last night?" She tried to lean closer to him.

His voice was very low. "I played poker with a gentleman whose conversation became very interesting as the evening went on. He kept winning and drinking and talking. Seems this fellow is part of a group of—"

"Wait. I can't hear you very well." His voice was pitched so low she could barely make out what he said.

Daniel took the reins from her hand and with one swift motion slid his arm around her waist and pulled her onto the saddle in front of him. She could feel his breath against her neck.

"Better?" His voice was a low rumble in her ear, his chest warm against her back.

Her laugh was low and breathy and she felt his arm tighten around her waist. "Now I can hear you, but I don't think I can concentrate on what you're saying."

"Neither can I. All I can think about is you. Do you have any idea how difficult it was to stay downstairs tonight knowing you were up in that room?" He kissed her neck as his hand wandered low over her stomach. He slipped his fingers inside the side opening of her overalls, and down over her belly. Her heartbeat went wild as he caressed the hair covering her mound through her drawers.

Daniel guided the horses off the road into a stand of trees. Amanda felt a warmth seep into her arms and legs, a curious, weak feeling. She relaxed against him with a sigh. Before she realized what he was doing, they were off the horse and he pulled her into his arms, kissing her hard.

Their hands fumbled with clothing until they were both half naked and on the ground, bodies quivering with need. Their joining was swift and hard, satisfying them both. The suddenness of it jolted her.

"Is it so different every time?" Amanda said, surprised her

voice sounded steady. She lay on her back, surrounded by the
smell of crushed grass.

Daniel leaned over her, pulling up her overalls, dressing her
like a child. She lay still and enjoyed the feel of his hands,
doing for her. He didn't answer her question, but gathered her
into his arms and held her. She shifted against him. Her healed
wound ached from laying on the hard, damp ground.

He reached up and massaged her shoulder, without a word
being said. They were in tune, she thought, a kind of harmony
existed between them. The thought was at once both satisfying
and disconcerting. They sat holding onto each other as the first
pink light of dawn broke in the east.

"The man in the poker game last night was an investor in
a ship being built in Liverpool. Officially it is being built for
the Italian government, but the gentlemen paying the bills are
all from South Carolina. According to him, as soon as it's
finished, and that might already have happened, it will sail for
Greenock, near Glasgow, and take on a cargo."

"What's the cargo?" Amanda savored the feel of his warm
hand rubbing her shoulder.

"He didn't say, but my bet is war materials. There is a
gunpowder factory in Greenock. Then the ship will sail to the
Bahamas. It's supposed to be a neutral port, but the arming of
ships there is common. Then it is a short trip to Charleston.
He said the whole deal is being arranged by a man named
Bodin."

Bodin. The bad penny that kept turning up "What are we
going to do?"

"We can get word to the Federal ships involved in the
blockade to be on the lookout. If the weather is good, the ship
could be off our coast in three weeks."

She wiggled out of his arms and headed to her horse, who
stood quietly munching grass. "You mean we left in the dark
of night and the ship isn't due for weeks?"

"I didn't want anyone to see us heading toward Yorktown."

She grinned at him. "I understand Charleston is beautiful
this time of the year."

''You're rushing things! Who says we're going to Charleston?'' He cupped his hand under her bottom and gave her a boost up onto her horse.

''Well, even if we don't, we do need to get to Yorktown.'' She turned her mount onto the road.

She thrilled at the possibility of sending sketches from Charleston, the most active port of the Confederacy. At the end of the war, if she built enough of a reputation, she would be able to tell the newspapers who she really was.

Chapter 19

Daniel and Amanda boarded the ferry for Charleston. His mission was to destroy the newly built armed ship if it managed to avoid the blockade. Her mission was to stay with him. So far, she was able to do just that because he hadn't been able to find a way to safely send her north.

Amanda stood leaning on the railing, facing into the wind, struggling to keep her sketch pad steady.

"We can sit inside out of the wind." Even though they were in the harbor, it was cool on the deck.

"No!" She turned to him. "I want to sketch the damage to Fort Sumter." She wasn't going to miss anything, in spite of any discomfort.

He looked dangerous with his eye patch and beard. Much too dashing an escort for her, she decided. Her sack-like dress of faded calico and her droopy sunbonnet made her look like a worn-out farm wife.

He nodded and kept by her side. Together they watched the damaged stone sentinel of the harbor fade into the distance. Then they turned their attention to the waterfront area of

Charleston that lay between the Ashley and the Cooper rivers. The charm of the old city was evident even at a distance.

She felt her accent was passable, and claiming she was from a small, sparsely populated inland area made her more believable. Daniel would do most of the talking anyway, but her presence would help lend him credibility as a wounded veteran traveling home with his wife.

Cupping a hand under her elbow, Daniel guided Amanda down the gangway onto the dock. A Negro boy carried their bags, one of the many children who leapt aboard even before the vessel tied up, anxious to make a few pennies helping the passengers with their belongings.

Daniel hailed one of the dockside cabs that met the ferry and directed the driver to a hotel on Calhoun Street.

Within minutes they entered an impressive structure of columns and marble and rich draperies. The subdued murmur of voices ceased and Amanda was aware of being watched as they crossed the lobby. It was obvious from their clothing that they didn't belong in a place so fine. She unconsciously smoothed the fabric of her skirt. Her grip tightened on Daniel's sleeve.

"Everyone is staring at us. We can't stay here. We're attracting too much attention," she whispered into his ear.

He patted her hand. "This is just what I have in mind. Trust me."

Daniel seemed to ignore the silent speculation that was going on around them. Approaching the reception desk, he quietly placed a gold coin on the counter, requesting a room near the stairs. The clerk glanced from Daniel to the coin and silently pushed the large register across the highly polished surface of the counter. Signing with a flourish, he turned to her again, offering his arm. The man had a flair for the dramatic, she thought. You'd think she was wearing a Worth gown and diamonds!

They followed a liveried bellman to the ornate elevator. Amanda watched through the iron scrollwork as the lobby disappeared below them. The doors slid open on the third floor and they made two turns down a hallway. Their room was at the end, next to the stairs, as Daniel had requested.

Daniel declined the offer to unpack for them, and the bellman accepted his tip and left. The room more than met their needs, being large and airy, complete with a basket of fruit, as well as access to the stairs.

Daniel checked the door and then turned to her. "I'll go look around."

"Couldn't I . . ."

Holding up a hand he cut her off. "I'd better go first. Alone."

Amanda knew when there was no point in arguing. He headed for the door, speaking to her over his shoulder. "As soon as I see what's up, I'll be back." With that he left.

Within the hour he was back. She heard the key in the door and was on her feet before he got it open.

"Well?" She waited in the middle of the room, leaning toward him in anticipation.

"There's an auction in the ballroom. Looks like whole households. Kind of sad, really. I guess these people are getting hard up for cash." He tossed aside his cane and peeled off the eyepatch.

"How about clothes?" She tried not to sound anxious, but she only had the dress she wore, along with the overalls in her bag.

"Plenty." He spoke around a mouthful of the peach he had selected from the basket on the table.

"Only one problem. Well, make that two problems. I don't know what to buy, but I can't take you down there. There isn't a woman in the place." He sprawled on the couch and chewed thoughtfully.

Without a word Amanda turned to her bag and drew out the overalls. "I can be ready in ten minutes."

He thought for a minute and then shrugged. " I don't want you overusing that disguise. It's not safe."

She didn't even take the time to ask him why. Hurrying into the clothes, she worked on her hair while he described the location of the ballroom where the sale was being held.

He took both her hands and held her at arm's length, studying her. ''We'll make this quick.''

Amanda nodded. She would be as agreeable as necessary as long as he would take her with him. She hated being left behind, waiting.

Daniel gave his final instructions. ''I'll take the main stairs to the first floor. You take the back stairs and follow the hall. That way you'll come to the ballroom without having to go through the lobby. I don't want you to be questioned by the clerks. Give me two minutes head start.''

He squeezed her hands and started to let go, then tightened his grip and jerked her up against him, giving her a long hard kiss that left her trembling. He knew her so well now he could have her breathless in moments. She wasn't sure she liked being at his mercy.

Amanda watched the door close behind him and stood transfixed, rubbing her lips with her fingers. She chided herself, realizing she was lost in thought and had no idea how much time had actually passed since he left.

''You ninny.'' She said the words aloud and decided to go.

He was waiting for her just inside the huge double doors. When he signaled her to come and stand beside him, he spoke to her under his breath.

''What took you so long?'' She could hear the teasing in his voice and detected a smirk. She wanted to poke him, but was afraid of drawing attention to herself.

''Later, McGrath,'' she hissed softly to him, scowling.

''Promise, Giles?'' he breathed back, making her go all shivery inside.

She averted her face and turned her attention to the open doors so he couldn't see her flushed cheeks.

The huge ballroom was bright with light streaming in through large fanlight windows. It wasn't a single auction, but many individual ones. Men stood in front of piles of goods, hawking their wares. Sun glinted off silver and sent shards of light beaming into the room. Fine furniture gleamed with years of careful polishing. Piles of white linen lay in mounds between trunks filled to overflowing with all types of clothing. Everything combined to cause an assault on her senses.

Amanda felt a pang of sadness at the display of cherished personal belongings being bartered for coin. To buy food? Is that why people were selling their personal belongings? She wondered if the population of Charleston was that needy.

Daniel was right, there were no ladies here, just men acting as agents for the owners of the goods, middlemen who would take a cut of the profits and didn't care what was being sold, only what price it might bring. She let their callous bartering grab her attention away from the melancholy situation.

Amanda noticed as they circled the room that several of the men greeted Daniel with a handshake or a nod and two even made casual introductions, patting him on the back. Strange, she thought to herself, he had spent very little time downstairs earlier. He couldn't have possibly met so many people, but there was no opportunity to question him about it now.

Daniel steered her to two likely looking clothing brokers and within an hour they found what they needed. The quality of the clothing was excellent, and several of the women's garments looked as if they had never been worn. It seemed curious for used clothing to be in such good condition.

"Sad, isn't it? People having to sell off their things because of the damn Yankees," she mused, out loud.

The broker raised an eyebrow. "This auction has been going on here for years, not just since the war. The only reason these people are selling is so they can buy more. The ships are running the blockade every night with luxury goods from Europe."

Amanda immediately lost any feelings of guilt over her new clothes.

Daniel was making the final arrangements to have the purchases delivered to their room. Amanda, relieved to be leaving, found the whole thing depressing. Besides, she was anxious to be alone with him, full of questions about her observations.

She wandered over to a raised platform at the end of the room, and sat down to wait for him. Her attention was pulled to a side door by a flurry of movement and raised voices.

She saw a group of people moving into the room. Two things struck her at the same time. The people were being herded toward her in a tight mass, and they were mostly Negro. Then she heard the unmistakable clink and rattle of shackles.

Amanda felt as if a fist had hit her in the belly. These people were going to be auctioned off, just like the furniture and the clothes and the silver.

She felt Daniel's fingers digging into her shoulder.

"Steady. Your thoughts are showing on your face." His voice was low and calm, bringing her back.

He pushed her a short distance, into an unoccupied corner of the room.

Staring at her boots, Amanda clenched her hands into fists until her short nails dug into her palms. It took a moment to outwardly compose herself.

"I've seen it several times and it still twists my gut." He gave her a sympathetic glance.

Amanda nodded, her eyes on the group of slaves. One woman in particular caught her attention. The graceful way she walked reminded her of Lubirda. Amanda felt a stab of pain, witnessing firsthand the degradation her friend had suffered.

The tall slave woman who had caught her attention had light skin. Amanda couldn't make out the color of her hair, because her head was wrapped in a cotton bandanna, but her eyes were a queer shade of light green. She carried a baby wrapped in a shawl, and a small child moved at her side, hidden by her skirts.

"Go, or stay?" Daniel's voice cut in on her thoughts.

She didn't want to watch, but she had to. For Lubirda, and for herself.

"Stay."

He nodded, seeming to know what she was thinking. "This is not a sale. Today is a preview. So buyers can see the group."

Amanda fought to keep her composure. *So they will have to stand up there twice,* she thought. When she turned her attention back to the platform, her eyes were again drawn to the woman. The shawl had fallen away from the baby, and the small child, a girl, had come out from behind the mother's skirt. The children both appeared to be white. Amanda could see no trace of Negro features. Their skin was as light as her own and their hair smooth and straight.

"Come on, let's go. I can't take any more." Daniel pulled her by the arm and headed for the door.

Amanda followed him with a sense of relief. "Daniel, where will they go? Until they're sold?" She had a hard time with that last word.

"My guess would be there are outbuildings nearby where they'll hold them." He continued to grip her arm firmly, urging her along.

They took the stairs and did not speak until after they were in their room. Overwhelmed, Amanda could feel a burning in her throat, and tears ran down her cheeks.

"Oh Daniel, how can anyone feel justified doing that to another human being?"

He took her in his arms and rocked gently side to side, cradling her.

"Ssh, it's alright. It will end, I promise." And he continued to hold her until she believed him.

Amanda pulled away to reach for a handkerchief, embarrassed by her tears. She blew her nose and wiped her eyes.

"You know, one time I asked Lubirda if she was scared of getting caught, and she said no, because they had already done the worst to her they could. I didn't really understand."

"Tobias once told me pretty much the same thing. Hard to think about what they've been through, isn't it?"

Amanda nodded. "Daniel, that one woman, with the two children, did you notice her?"

"Tall, with the blue bandanna around her head?"

"Yes. Those children with her. They were white."

Daniel sat on the edge of the bed and pulled her into his lap, absentmindedly rubbing her back.

"Their father was probably white, but under the laws of this state they are still considered colored. This time they'll most likely be sold with her because they're so young."

Amanda had not considered the possibility they might be separated. She stood up and paced around the room. Then she remembered what she wanted to ask Daniel downstairs.

"Why did so many people down in the ballroom seem to know you?"

Daniel watched her. "Well, I told two of them I was a spy, and I guess word got around."

Amanda was horrified. "You told them what?" Had he lost his mind?

"You heard me. I told them I was wounded at Bull Run and unable to fight, so I became a spy. For the Confederacy."

"Oh." She should know by now how much he liked to tease her and be ready for it.

"I said I'd been operating in Canada and was forced to leave in a hurry, and that's why we are here with nothing but the clothes on our backs." He seemed to enjoy her discomfort.

She leveled him a look that let him know she was in no mood for any of his teasing. It had been a long morning. "You only told two of them?"

"Word like that travels fast in a crowded room."

"I guess so! They were all greeting you like some kind of hero. They must have believed your story."

"Like I've said before, it's hard sometimes to get away with the little lies, but people never seem to doubt the big ones."

Amanda didn't say anything, but silently hoped he was right. No matter how confident he acted, she worried. What could she do if he got caught? The thought frightened her more than she would admit, even to herself.

By the time they returned to their room, the clothes they had purchased had been delivered. Daniel left and Amanda organized her new things while he went out to, as he put it, "prowl around."

This was the second wardrobe she had acquired and would probably leave behind, too. She sighed as she smoothed a beautiful cloak trimmed with fur.

Daniel returned and they went out for supper at a place around the corner from the hotel on King Street. Two of the tables near them were occupied by officers in Confederate uniforms. None of the conversations Amanda overheard sounded particularly helpful.

They returned to the hotel after dark. The lamps were lit and the bed turned back. Daniel announced he was heading down to the docks. Amanda hurriedly began to change.

He sat and watched her. "What are you doing?"

"Changing. I'm going with you."

"No you're not." He picked up a nightgown off the end of the bed, holding it out to her.

"Daniel!"

"Amanda, please. Do we have to fight every time I make a decision?"

She turned away from him, muttering to herself. That was what galled her. He made all the decisions!

"I can't hear you."

"Believe me, you don't want to hear me!"

He wrapped his arms around her waist and pulled her back against him. He whispered into her hair. "Why don't you change and get into bed and wait for me?"

Daniel rubbed her midriff and moved one hand to stroke the side of her breast. To her chagrin her body responded to his touch.

"You don't play fair, Daniel McGrath." And it was her fault. She was the one who had given him this power.

He laughed and caressed her again. "You're right."

The next thing she knew the door closed behind him and she was left standing half-dressed in the middle of the room.

"Damn him!" But this time she wasn't going to sit still. There was something she needed to see. Amanda finished changing into her overalls and jacket. She made her way down the back stairs and into the hallway without seeing anyone.

The huge deserted ballroom seemed dark and eerie. Moonlight poured in through the tall windows and turned piles of merchandise into ghostly heaps. She shivered as she made her way to the door the slavers had used earlier in the day. Forcing the bolt open, she went outside and found herself in a dark, empty carriage yard adjacent to the stables. Amanda crossed the yard and discovered what she was looking for.

Behind the stables was another building. Light shone weakly through the small, filthy windows. She stood on tiptoe and peeked in. There were iron beds lined up along the far wall. People slept on bare mattresses. Each one had a foot sticking out from under thin, tattered blankets. Irons circled ankles and locked to the foot of the beds. A couple of the beds were pushed together. She could see the two small children asleep beside their mother. The remainder of the room was piled with trunks, boxes, and crates.

Amanda turned away from the window and leaned against the side of the structure. She took deep breaths to calm herself against a mounting rage. She turned back for another look. As far as she could see there was just one guard inside, dozing in a chair in front of the door with a gun across his lap.

She heard horses approach, and, moving as quickly as she could, Amanda skirted the building. Sticking to the shadows, she rounded the corner of the stables. Riders entered the yard and blocked the way to the ballroom door.

Heart pounding, she ducked inside the stable entrance and slid into the back of a stall, burrowing into the hay as best she could. She heard men laughing and talking as they dismounted, leading their horses. They called for the stableboy.

Damn, Amanda thought to herself. Why didn't she think about the fact that there would be someone around to tend the horses?

"Go check the kitchen. He's probably in there." She heard one of them leave.

"Shakespeare, you stay." A dog whined.

"Why did you name that mangy hound Shakespeare?" The deep voice had a pronounced drawl.

" 'Cause he dotes on sonnets." A man snorted laughter. She could hear the jingle of the bridles.

How was she going to get out of there when the stableboy returned? She heard a rustling outside her stall, and the dog began to growl, deep in his throat. The stableboy became the lesser of her worries. She stiffened. The dog came closer. She could see his eyes gleaming in the darkness.

"Shake, come away from there."

"Leave him be. He probably just found a rat."

"The last time he cornered a critter, he lost half his nose. He don't know when to let go."

"Yeah, but he's a fair hunter. If we have a few more days before that ship shows up we can take fresh meat back to camp along with the arms." The dog continued to growl.

"If the weather holds. Rain will make the roads bad and those wagons will be mighty heavy when they're loaded." Amanda held her breath. It occurred to her that they were all waiting for the same ship. The dog crouched just outside the stall, still growling.

"Damn it, Shakespeare. I said come here." A man stepped to the stall and hauled the dog out, still growling.

Amanda could feel the sweat trickling down her ribs. She let out the breath she was holding as slowly and quietly as she could.

"Tie him up and let's go. I need a beer. We can come back later and see to the horses if Raney hasn't found the stableman." The other man grunted in agreement.

Amanda waited until they had been gone only a moment, then scooted out of the stall. The dog set up a terrible racket.

She returned the way she had come, remembering to bolt the outside door to the ballroom. She hurried up the back stairs to their room. The last thing she needed just now was for Daniel to return to the room before she did.

She bathed and changed, climbing into the bed to wait. She needed to talk to him, but she knew she must be very careful how she told him about the plan she was forming to free the slave woman and her children. Perhaps if she just hinted and let him think it was really his idea . . .

Amanda drifted off to sleep and had a dream that she was being chased by someone wearing a long hooded cloak. She tried to run, but she was carrying two babies and she felt as if her shoes were lined with lead. Waking up abruptly, she sensed someone standing in the shadows by the bed, watching her.

For a split second she froze, heart pounding, and wondered if she could roll to the far side of the bed and get away. Then she realized it was Daniel. The dream had really spooked her.

"For heaven's sake, you scared the life out of me!" She sat up as he lit the lamp.

"Sorry. I was trying not to disturb you." He began to prepare for bed.

"Well, what did you find out?"

"Word on the dock says one ship just made record time crossing the Atlantic and is holding off the coast. If the weather obliges, things may happen sooner than we figured." Daniel turned out the light and Amanda felt the mattress dip under his weight.

"Is it the one we're waiting for?" He smelled of tobacco and beer.

"I don't know for sure, but it's possible. This one made a stop in the Bahamas before coming here." Daniel lay on his back, his hands clasped behind his head.

"How will we know if the ship is caught in the blockade?" She stayed where she was, resisting the urge to snuggle up against his big body. She knew she should tell him about what she had overheard in the stables, but she knew he would be angry at her for getting trapped there. Besides, he already knew about the ship.

"There is an incredible amount of information available on the docks. I've made a few contacts and I'm sure we'll know when the time comes." He shifted his weight and drew her up against him, ignoring her stiffness.

Amanda raised up to peer at him in the darkness. "Can't we do something to signal the blockade?"

"No. I don't want to arouse any suspicions." He pulled her down against his chest again.

She lay still, refusing to respond to the hands stroking her.

He trailed his hand from her breast to her thigh and back up again. "What's the matter?"

She scooted away from him. "You make all the decisions and just leave me behind. I know you're in charge, and you know more than I do, but I don't like being left out! Besides, you smell like the inside of a tavern."

"I do?" He reached her and easily pulled her back. "Do you want me to order a bath?" His fingers found her nipple.

"Mmm." Bathing would take time, she thought to herself, and the combination of odors wasn't really so bad. Amanda lost the train of conversation.

"Stop that. You're distracting me." She pushed his hands away. She really did want to stay angry with him, so he would know she was serious.

His laugh was a low rumble. He pulled her nightgown up over her head and tossed it to the floor. "You want to be in charge for a change? Think you can handle it?" He wrapped his arms around her and pulled her on top of him, then let his arms drop.

Amanda stopped fighting him and gave herself over to the warm, sensual feel of skin against skin as she lay atop him. Putting her hands behind his neck and straddling him, she slid up his body until her mouth reached his, tasting a faint saltiness.

Daniel couldn't keep still and stroked her back and buttocks with his hands. "Oh Lord girl, do you have any idea what you do to me?"

Amanda laughed and reached down between them where she could feel him, hot and hard, resting against her belly. "I have a faint idea."

Daniel groaned, and as she shifted her weight onto her knees to gain better access to him, he grasped her hips and lifted her up, entering her with one swift stroke. Amanda clutched at his shoulders and gasped at the incredible sensations vibrating through her body.

His voice was low and husky. "I thought you would enjoy this." He moved his hips as he held her to him.

She experienced feelings so intense she could not answer him. Daniel coached her movements for a few moments, and when she caught the rhythm, his hands left her hips and began to stroke her breasts. She felt out of control as she rocked against him. Waves of sensation broke over her, leaving her weak and trembling.

He watched her face as she exploded in a frenzy of motion and then collapsed on his chest, gasping. He turned her on her back and, still buried in her warmth, in a few strokes gained his release.

Daniel pulled her tightly against his body and held her within the curve of his arms as they both slept.

Amanda and Daniel spent the next day touring Charleston. Preoccupied and tired, the short sleep she had managed the night before had been filled with dreams of the slaves that would be sold at auction. It was a relief for her to be out, away from the hotel.

Tired as she was, Amanda could not fail to note that Charleston was a beautiful old city with its church spires and tall narrow homes painted a rainbow of colors. The residential sections where they strolled had granite block sidewalks and cobblestone streets. Both of them were impressed by the armaments along the Laurens Street battery that fortified the harbor.

Daniel suggested a visit to the Charleston Museum, and the time spent proved to be very enlightening. A great deal of basic information about the natural history and geography of South Carolina might prove useful later if they needed to leave quickly overland.

Amanda was amused by the irony of a history display that proudly described the involvement of the "Patriots of South Carolina in the Fight for Independence during the American Revolution." Here it was less than a hundred years later and this city had been the scene of the beginning of the war to tear that same country apart.

They returned to the hotel, Daniel to nap and Amanda to sketch. She wanted to capture the flavor of the city while it was still fresh in her mind, and found the only thing she could manage to draw with any clarity was the Negro woman's face.

She put her sketchbook aside, and read the copy of the *Courier* they had picked up in the lobby on their way in. A notice for a slave auction to be held at their hotel appeared on the third page. It was too much for her.

"Daniel, wake up." Amanda sat on the edge of the bed, amazed at the instant alertness in him. There was no slow awakening here.

"What is it?" He pulled himself into a sitting position.

"I'm sorry to wake you, but, well I can't stop thinking about those people."

She showed him the advertisement in the paper. Then she told him what she had done the night before, and what she had heard in the stables.

"Amanda, our first and only priority is the shipload of arms that is due to come through the blockade any day now. We can't risk doing anything about those slaves." Angry, he spoke to her as if she were a child, which infuriated her.

The wakeful night and worrying caught up with her and she burst into tears. Amanda had come face to face with the realities of slavery and the exposure had left her desolate.

He lay with her on the bed until she cried herself into an exhausted sleep. She awoke disoriented. Her head felt as if it was stuffed with cotton and her eyes were gritty. The lamps were lit and Daniel sat eating from a tray.

Amanda studied him for a few moments; then she sat up and swung her feet over the side of the bed.

"Daniel, I'm sorry."

"There is nothing to be sorry about. If we could do it, I'd get those people out of here tonight. Come on. I had your dinner sent up." He gestured to the tray.

She caught sight of her reflection in the mirror and was glad she didn't have to go to the dining room. Amanda took a cloth and wrung it out in cold water, pressing it to her face as she lay back down on the bed.

"Amanda?" Daniel stood next to the bed.

Her voice was muffled by the cloth. "I'm not hungry. I'll

just rest for a while.'' He stroked the hair away from her forehead.

''I'll leave the tray in case you change your mind. I'm going out. I'll tell the desk you are not to be disturbed.'' He pushed the cloth aside to kiss her cheek. Amanda heard the door close.

In the short time they had been in Charleston, their days and nights had fallen into a predictable routine. Daniel would be out until late, prowling the docks, listening for useful information, waiting for their ship. He gave her only a vague account of his activities. He assured her it was not because he didn't trust her, but rather to keep her safe. Wishing she could be with him, Amanda placed a lower value on her own safety than he did. She drifted back to sleep.

Awakening to the sound of men shouting, she lay still for a moment and listened, but couldn't make out what they were saying. She made her way in the dark room to the window, and pulled back the drape. Figures hurried down the street and into an alley beside the hotel. A building at the rear of the hotel was on fire.

Oh dear God, she thought. All the slaves being held for auction would burn up if someone didn't let them out.

Chapter 20

Eyepatch in place, leaning heavily on his cane, Daniel limped along the docks, not betraying the excitement he felt. The ship, the one they had been waiting for, was coming through tonight.

Her name was the *Oralia*. Daniel smiled. He remembered enough schoolboy Latin to know it meant "The Golden One." Its owners had tagged it well. Successful blockade-running ships earned fortunes for their captains and owners.

Before long he would know. The timing surprised him. He never thought the captain would attempt to run the blockade on the night of a full moon. If the *Oralia* was not stopped and it reached the docks here in Charleston, then Daniel would have to take over.

He lowered himself to sit on a crate, his leg sticking stiffly out in front of him as if he couldn't bend at the knee. As he waited, his mind drifted back to earlier this evening. He had sat on the couch watching Amanda sleep. The sight of the slaves being previewed for the auction had upset her to the point of making her ill.

His fist clenched around his cane. *She shouldn't be here,* he thought, feeling a blaze of impotent anger at the series of misadventures that had brought them to Charleston. He should have been able to keep her safe, and here they were, getting deeper and deeper into danger. And she thought it was all a lark.

He had wanted to pick up her damn book of sketches this afternoon and chuck it into the fire. No ambition was worth getting killed over, and that was what was going to happen if he didn't get her out of harm's way.

The acid burn of jealousy ate at him. He resented her talent. If she wanted him as much as she wanted success as an artist, she would have listened to him weeks ago. He loved her but how could he compete with a dream?

The sound of approaching footsteps pulled him out of his black thoughts.

He nodded and tipped his hat to two men he had met the day before. Just then he heard a cheer go up from the end of the far dock. Moonlight shone on a full set of sails in the harbor.

He decided to leave. He didn't want anyone associating him too closely with the arrival this evening, considering what he now planned to do.

Daniel headed off the wharf toward their hotel. His attention diverted from the approaching ship, he noted the red-orange glow in the sky, and billowing smoke that obscured the moon. From where he stood, it looked very close to Calhoun Street.

Finding a cab, he gave the driver his destination. He eased himself aboard, feigning difficulty with a stiff leg.

The man peered down at Daniel. "I'll get you as close as I can. Big fire up there."

Daniel's heart pounded. He imagined Amanda asleep, unaware. "The Pinckney?"

"You got folks there?" Daniel nodded. " 'Bout half hour ago it was the stables out back. They had plenty of time to get out if it spread." The driver whipped the horse into a trot.

Daniel sat back. The hazards he faced every moment down on the docks caused him no fear, but the thought of Amanda in danger unnerved him. The short ride seemed to take an eternity.

During the trip back in the cab, the smoke billowing into the night sky had turned from black to white, and was even more visible against the nighttime sky. A huge crowd milled in front of the hotel. Daniel could see no fire damage to the building.

Eyes searching the people out front, Daniel recognized some of his fellow guests, but he did not see Amanda.

He paid the cabbie and went through the lobby. When he was sure no one was behind him, he took the stairs two at a time. If she's not there, he thought to himself, I'll leave a note and try to find her in the crowd.

The door was locked, so he used his key to get into the room. Daniel was greeted by two startled pairs of eyes set in soot-smeared faces.

"Daniel!" Amanda's voice was raspy.

"What the hell . . . ?" He closed the door behind him and leaned against it. Both women had tear tracks running down their dirty cheeks. There was a child curled up by their feet, asleep. He recognized the other woman. It was the slave they had seen in the ballroom with the blue bandanna around her head.

Amanda stood up. "Daniel, I'd like to introduce Sylvie . . ." Her voice trailed off.

She seemed to realize that this was not the time for a formal introduction.

The woman looked from Daniel to Amanda and back again, saying nothing. She sagged against the couch, pulling a blanket around an infant in her lap in a protective gesture.

Daniel ignored the introduction. "Amanda, that fire, did you—"

She interrupted him, irate. "Of course not! Do you think I would be so stupid?"

He could tell she was furious. "I'm sorry. I had to ask. The timing was quite a coincidence."

Sylvie understood the half-asked question. She spoke up in a timid voice. "Somebody name of Shakespeare start dat fire. I heared another man yelling that he upset the lantern by not minding a rope.'' Sylvie shrugged, looking puzzled that her own explaination did not make sense.

Amanda let out a yelp of laughter that ended in a fit of coughing. ''Shakespeare. It figures.''

Daniel was baffled. ''Shakespeare?''

Amanda nodded. ''That was the mangy old hound who almost got me in the stables last night. They had him tied up when I snuck out.''

Daniel stared at the slave. *Just what we need,* he thought to himself, *another complication.*

The two women sat looking expectant, on the couch. The next move was up to him. ''Amanda, I need to see you privately, please.''

Amanda stood up and scooped the slumbering child off the floor, placing her next to her mother. She crossed the room to join him in the far corner. He turned her so his back was to Sylvie. His voice was low and controlled, but his anger evident.

''Suppose you tell me what you think you're doing?''

Amanda shifted nervously, but didn't meet his eye. ''Well, I woke up and the stable was on fire, so I changed and went down to see what was going on. I was afraid the fire might spread to the storeroom.'' As she spoke, her words tumbled out faster and faster. ''When the guard unlocked the slaves to get them outside I figured I could get Sylvie and her children away, so I brought them here. I would have brought more, but I was afraid someone would notice.''

He stared at her, incredulous. ''You don't think they're going to notice she's gone?''

''Not right away! Everything was very confused because of the fire. Besides, when they discover she's gone, I don't think they'll look right here in the hotel. Do you?''

She was probably right, but he was not about to give her any encouragement. ''Just how do you think we are going to get them out of here?'' Daniel noticed she smiled when he used the word ''we.''

''I've been thinking about that. We can travel as husband and wife, with Sylvie as our maid.''

He thought about it. It sounded possible. No one would be looking for them to be traveling in a group.

"What about the children?"

"We can pass them off as ours. They look white. We can dress them up. What do you think?"

He thought Amanda looked like a ragged twelve-year-old. She took both of his hands as she pleaded with him. Daniel wondered if he was capable of denying her anything.

"Your timing stinks. The ship arrived tonight and ran the blockade, fully armed and filled with munitions. We have to take care of it now, before they put a heavy guard on, or unload. Then we'll have to leave Charleston right away. It'll be too dangerous to stay. Not a word of this to her."

Amanda nodded in agreement. *Lord,* he thought to himself, *where will we all be tomorrow?*

Oh, well, they could only hang him once.

Chapter 21

Amanda stared at him. "The ship? Tonight?" she repeated dumbly.

"Yes, tonight." He was irritated with her, but he didn't sound really angry. Maybe he was just keeping his emotions under control because of Sylvie.

"You're taking me?" She wanted to go so badly.

"I have no choice. I can't do this alone. Wash your face. We'll go as soon as I talk to the woman."

Poor Sylvie, Amanda thought. The woman looked terrified.

Daniel turned away from Amanda and crossed the room. Sylvie shrank back against the couch. To Amanda's relief, Daniel's voice was gentle.

"Sylvie, settle yourself as best you can. Don't open the door for anyone. If someone comes to the door, tell them you're sick. And for God's sake, don't let the children make any noise. There's food on that tray if you're hungry."

Sylvie just nodded, not saying a word. As he spoke, Daniel stripped off his eyepatch and leaned his cane in a corner. He rummaged in his bag, stuffing a few things in his pocket, then motioned to Amanda. She followed him to the door.

"I'll go see if the way is clear. You stay here by the door until I come for you."

Amanda nodded in agreement. He was back within a minute, motioning her out. She turned to wave silently to Sylvie, who still sat on the couch, looking bewildered. Then she closed the door behind her and followed Daniel out of the hotel.

Most of the guests were still out front, winding down after the excitement of the fire. Someone had brought out several bottles, and the guests were drinking champagne. Skirting the crowd, Daniel and Amanda headed for the docks. The streets were empty and they could talk freely for the first time that evening.

"If we're lucky, we can get this thing done before they have time to post a heavy guard."

Amanda trotted along to keep up with Daniel's long strides.

She had to talk to him about what had happened, to make him understand. "Daniel, about Sylvie . . ."

"What about them?" He sounded annoyed.

"I had to do it." She tried to see his expression in the darkness.

"I suppose you did." He sounded resigned. "But it sure isn't going to make things any easier. Let's discuss it later."

"What exactly are we going to do now?"

"Set her afire. Shame, too. She's a beautiful ship." He slowed slightly to allow her to catch her breath.

"What's wrong with burning the ship?" Amanda was puzzled. She had seen how destructive fire could be only an hour ago, and assumed that was their goal.

"Well, first it will attract a lot of attention, and it may make it hard for us to get off the docks. And second, the water is shallow and they may be able to recover some of the cargo."

"True, but it surely will slow them down." She grinned up at him.

He nodded in agreement. "That it will."

They were within sight of the docks. They could hear loud voices and singing. Someone was doing a drunken rendition of "Dixie." It was mercifully drowned out by a church bell tolling the hour. Daniel pressed a handful of matches into Amanda's palm.

"I think the celebrating has begun."

"Sounds that way." She slid the matches into her pocket and peered through the darkness in the direction of the noise.

A lantern sitting on one of the bales that lined the docks backlit the small group of revelers. There was a loud splash followed by laughing and cursing.

Avoiding the merrymakers, they approached the *Oralia* from the far end of the wharf. Making their way in the shadows, they got as close as they dared. They stopped about halfway between the ship and the entrance to the docks.

Daniel crouched beside a cotton bale and Amanda squeezed in beside him.

"What now?" She whispered in his ear.

"We wait." He drew her against his side.

"For what?" She snuggled against him, grateful for the contact.

"To see how many are on board. Watch the back of the ship and tell me if you see any movement."

Amanda shifted her position to get more comfortable. After several minutes of observation, she had seen no movement. "I haven't seen anything. How about you?"

"Nothing. We can't wait any longer. The fellows down the dock are making enough noise to cover us. I'm going on board now and look around."

Amanda got to her knees. "What about me?"

"I need you to stay here and watch the docks for me. I'll look around and come back for you. Signal me if you see anyone coming."

"All right." She would have rather gone with him. "How can I get your attention?"

He handed her a child's tin whistle. "Give me three blasts on this, then throw it in the water."

"Why?" She slid the whistle into her shirt pocket.

"So if they catch you, you won't have it on you. Now stop

asking questions!'' He sounded exasperated. She shivered at his answer.

"Sorry." She chided herself for annoying him.

He cupped his hand around the back of her neck and pulled her close for a quick kiss. "Keep your eyes open." He pushed away from her.

"I will. Daniel?" He knelt back down.

"What?" Now he really sounded aggravated.

"Be careful." She could see his white teeth in the darkness as he smiled. He kissed her again, harder, and left.

Amanda could barely see him moving down the wharf in the shadows of the cotton bales. He disappeared from sight completely as he neared the ship. She turned her attention to the docks.

She had lost track of time and was listening for the church bells when she spotted men gathering on the ridge of land beyond the docks. Amanda could tell by the silhouette they were in uniform and carried weapons. She counted twelve men. They must be the guards for The *Oralia*.

"Holy Moses."

She looked toward the ship and saw no sign of Daniel. Heart racing, she watched the men, silhouetted against the city, for any signs they were headed down to the dock. Daniel needed time and she didn't want to sound the alarm too soon. Some were standing, some sitting, waiting.

Waiting for what, she thought. More men? It was a possibility. As it was, there were enough of them to cut off any escape from the docks.

Leaning heavily against the cotton bale, she tried to think. The burlap covering, torn away in spots, bulged with huge tufts of the fiber. She poked at it and was reminded of something Daniel had told her earlier. It burned very well.

She began to pull off chunks of the cotton and stuff them inside her shirt. When the buttons were so strained her shirt would hold no more, she removed several matches from her pocket.

Ducking low, she moved along the dock toward the *Oralia*,

striking the matches one at a time, lighting the bales as she went. She paused between bales to watch the soldiers. They still gathered on the ridge. So far no one had noticed the fires. She lit two more bales before she heard the cry.

"Fire, fire! There's a fire on the docks."

Amanda put the rest of the matches back in her pocket and hunched over, moving as quickly as she could on the narrow portion of wharf between the cargo and the water. It was difficult to make herself small with her shirt padded the way it was.

She paused behind the last bale before moving out into the open. Everyone was shouting and running toward the burning load of cotton. They were trying to push the first one into the water. Amanda ran up the gangway and onto the ship, tripping over two bodies and sprawling face down on the deck. She picked herself up and hurried away from the gruesome sight, stomach churning.

Everything was so quiet on the ship.

"Daniel, where are you?" She whispered down the first hatch she came to.

No answer. Amanda moved to the next hatch and listened. She passed a cabin up top and peered in. It was the empty galley. She ducked in just long enough to grab a can of grease off the back of the stove. As she backed out of the doorway, an arm tightened round her throat and a hand covered her mouth.

"Amanda, what are you doing? What's going on?" Daniel's voice hissed in her ear. He let go of her. She could see his face clearly in the light of the fire coming from the docks.

"Come on, we have to hurry. The guard for the ship was gathering."

Daniel looked over her shoulder at the fire.

"I thought I told you to blow the whistle." He looked down at her. "What the hell do you have in your shirt?"

"Cotton. We can use it and the grease to set the fire. We still have time. Is there anyone left on board?"

He took the can out of her hand, shaking his head. "No.

Come with me. I found kegs of powder in the hold." He turned and disappeared down a hatch.

Amanda followed him down the ladder into pitch dark. Daniel called softly to her and she tried to follow his voice, swearing under her breath when she whacked her shin on a crate. She bumped into him before she saw him. He struck a match.

She used the feeble light to start placing the cotton she pulled from her shirt, stuffing it up against the kegs.

Daniel put his hand on her shoulder. "A little further away. Let's give ourselves time to get out of here."

She pushed the wadded stuff back and smeared it liberally with the grease. "There, that should do it." Amanda wiped her hands on a stack of folded canvas.

"Good. Amanda, start up the ladder. When you get to the hatch and tell me it's clear, I'll light this." She poked her head up and glanced nervously back at Daniel.

"Hurry up. Everybody is down by the fire, but they're moving this way."

"Go and wait for me by the gangway."

She heard him strike a match. Amanda crawled onto the deck and stopped dead when she spotted two soldiers, guns propped on their shoulders, standing at the bottom of the narrow planked walkway connecting the ship to the dock. They were watching the others push the burning bales into the water. The whole end of the wooden dock blazed, sending sparks into the night sky.

She tiptoed back to the hatch. Daniel was at the top of the ladder and she could see the fire behind him in the hold.

"Get down on the dock. This thing is going to blow any second." He shoved her ahead of him. She stopped and he plowed into her back, almost knocking her over.

"We can't go that way," she whispered, pointing to the soldiers who had moved halfway up the plank to get a better view of the dock.

Luckily their attention was focused on the burning dock. If they turned and came any farther onto the ship they would see the two bodies on the deck.

"Come on." He grabbed her arm and dragged her around to the opposite side of the ship. Without a word he picked her up. She opened her mouth to protest, but shut it quickly when he dropped her over the side. She hit the water, and two seconds later he landed about five feet from her. She hoped the confusion and noise on the dock covered the splash they made.

"Swim!" He pushed her in the direction of Battery Park.

They hadn't been in the water for more than a few moments when a huge explosion sent a fireball over their heads. Amanda turned to look and Daniel grabbed her shirt.

"Keep swimming!" He pulled on her and she shrugged him off, paddling furiously for shore. There were several more explosions before they made it to land. Pulling themselves out of the water, panting for breath, they collapsed on the damp ground and watched the dock burn and the ship smoke and hiss as the wrecked hull sank into the bay.

Chapter 22

Amanda's legs trembled so with fatigue, she wasn't sure how she made it back to the hotel. Slipping past the dozing night clerk, they finally made it to their room. She collapsed across the bed and moaned.

"Sh. You'll wake the children."

Amanda rolled her head toward the sound of Daniel's voice. The children, she thought vaguely to herself. In the excitement of blowing up the ship, she had forgotten all about Sylvie. The woman must have made herself a bed on the floor.

"Go back to sleep, Sylvie." Daniel sounded as tired as she felt.

Amanda struggled out of her stiff, salt-soaked clothes and into a nightgown without lighting a lamp. She crawled under the quilt and was asleep instantly.

With the morning light came the realization of the difficulty of their situation. After what they had done last night, they had to leave the city as soon as possible. Managing the escape was the problem.

Daniel explained to Sylvie that they would try to get her to freedom, without telling her anything else. The escaped slave made no comment about the previous night, their wet clothes, or the soot stains on the bedding from their hair and faces. She seemed less frightened than the day before, but she said very little.

Amanda wondered at her lack of curiosity. If the situation were reversed, she would be bursting with questions. Sylvie just moved quietly around the room, picking up after them.

Amanda and Daniel washed and dressed, then went down to eat breakfast in the hotel dining room. Daniel requested a paper with their coffee.

The front page was devoted to stories about the fire and explosion at the dock, as well as the hotel fire. Arson was suspected on the waterfront, and three slaves were missing from the vicinity of the hotel. The paper held a description of Sylvie. The ages of the children were listed as "unknown." Fortunately, no mention was made that they were light-skinned.

"Well, I guess we don't have to wonder if they know about Sylvie." Daniel handed the paper to Amanda.

The description was very accurate. Amanda knew this made it much more dangerous for them, but she wasn't sorry for what she had done.

The authorities would be looking for a slave woman and two children. If anyone had spotted Daniel and Amanda last night, they would also be looking for a tall man and a boy. The account in the newspaper of the dock fire did not give descriptions of any arson suspects, which was a relief.

If anyone had seen them and connected them to the fire, at least it was not common knowledge. Yet.

"What now?" Amanda's voice, raspy from the smoke, was quiet.

He covered her hand. "We don't have any alternatives. We get out of Charleston as soon as possible."

"Can we rent a carriage?" She turned her hand palm up and gripped his hand.

"Too risky. Probably watching the roads." Absently he sipped coffee and stroked the inside of her wrist.

"Train?"

"Hmm, yes, I think so." He dropped her hand. "We'll need clothes."

Amanda thought of all their recent purchases. "We have so much—"

"For the children. And we need widow's black for yourself and the woman."

Amanda nodded. "I think I have what we need for me and Sylvie."

"Come on." They were up and moving before Amanda finished her meal.

Amanda returned to the room with food wrapped in a napkin for Sylvie and the children. Daniel left to buy train tickets and clothing. There were several black dresses among the lot Daniel had purchased earlier, and Sylvie and Amanda spent time deciding on the best fit for each of them. Fortunately, the women were similar in size, Sylvie being taller. The children played quietly for a while, then curled up on the pallet in the corner and fell asleep, apparently still tired from the night before.

The dress that fit Amanda best in length was rather shapeless through the waist with an intricate series of ties up under a long over-bodice. She was puzzling over this when she heard Sylvie laugh.

"That be for a woman what is increasing." Sylvie moved to adjust the size.

"Increasing?" The meaning of the term eluded Amanda.

"You knows, carrying a babe." Sylvie tightened the tapes.

Amanda blushed. Even tied down as snugly as possible, the dress was too large around her slender waist.

"Oh, yes, of course." She began to unfasten the dress.

"Wait." With the first show of animation Amanda witnessed in the woman, Sylvie snatched a small pillow off the couch and lifted the hem of the dress. Stuffing the pillow into the waistband of Amanda's petticoat, she dropped the skirt and smoothed the dress over the bulge. Amanda glanced at her enhanced profile in the mirror. They both began to laugh.

Daniel returned, his arms loaded with packages. He stared at Amanda for several moments without speaking, dumping the boxes on the bed. She couldn't read the expression on his face. Embarrassed, Amanda turned from him and reached up under her skirt to retrieve the pillow.

"Leave it," he said. She hesitated for a moment, then dropped the fabric. He moved to her side and searched for the hidden ties. "Try another pillow."

"Daniel, really, I—"

He cut her off. "It's what we need to help explain our haste to leave the city. We need to get you home to Richmond before your confinement." He adjusted the petticoat to accommodate the second pillow.

"Oh, for Heaven's sake!" Amanda tried to squirm away, but he held fast to the dress.

She couldn't explain the feelings of longing that came over her. So silly, she thought, she didn't want children. She refused to look at her reflection.

Daniel took her gently by the elbow and turned her around, running his hand over the bulge. "There, does that feel secure?"

Already he was treating her differently, more gently. She didn't like it. How odd, it was only a couple of pillows.

"It's fine," she snapped at him. He shrugged at her and opened the packages of children's things.

"Walk across the room." Amanda glared at him and strode to the far wall, then wheeled around to face him.

"No." He shook his head. "Not right. Sylvie, show her how to walk."

For the next few minutes Sylvie coached Amanda on how to thrust her hips forward and sway as she moved.

It doesn't make any difference, it's only a disguise, Amanda told herself. She felt more comfortable masquerading as a boy than as a pregnant woman.

They dressed and finished packing, putting the bags outside the door. Looking at Sylvie's two children, it was hard to believe they carried any Negro blood. They were both as fair as any white children.

Daniel put on his eyepatch, took his cane and went downstairs to settle the bill and arrange for a coach. He would pay the driver to load the luggage and then check out, waiting downstairs for them. The women and children could go directly to the carriage from their room, without lingering in the lobby.

Everything went smoothly until Sylvie put on her bonnet with the heavy black veil. Face obscured, she bent to scoop the baby off the floor where he played.

The child, terrified, began to push away from her and scream. It took both women several moments to convince him it really was his mother under the hat.

In the meantime, his sister began to wail too, more in sympathy it seemed than for any other reason. By the time Amanda and Sylvie descended the main stairs, Daniel had been waiting for several minutes. The baby was still tearful and stared suspiciously at his mother.

"What took you so long?" He scooped up the little girl and carried her easily on his hip.

He looked so comfortable with the child. Amanda felt awkward when she handled either of the children.

"I'll tell you in the coach." She slipped her hand into the crook of his arm. She glanced at the perplexed desk clerk. The same one who had checked she and Daniel into the hotel. Obviously he didn't recognize them.

The trip to the station was uneventful, except that the baby insisted on crawling into Daniel's lap. Hiccuping and sniffling, he refused to look at his mother, as if she wore the veil to purposely scare him.

The three adults laughed at his behavior. The girl sat in her mother's lap and stared out the window, enthralled by her first carriage ride.

The train station was crowded. Daniel had warned them it would be. Travel schedules were unsure, and people had to wait hours and sometimes days to make connecting trains to some destinations.

To avoid any delay in leaving Charleston, they were willing to take any train just to get out of the city. Hopefully they could make connections to Richmond when they put some distance between themselves and Charleston.

Amanda held onto Daniel's arm as they moved through the crowd. They paused to wait so the porter with their luggage could catch up. Daniel consulted the huge board behind the ticket sellers' windows to find their track number and time of departure. Amanda noticed men in uniform standing beside each window, questioning those buying tickets. She squeezed his arm.

He nodded. "Police. They weren't here earlier when I bought our tickets." The porter arrived with a cart full of their bags. "Come on. We're on track seven."

They walked down a long tunnel and up a ramp to their train. There was another group of uniformed men at trackside, scrutinizing the people as they passed. Amanda reminded herself to walk with a sway, the way Sylvie had shown her. She smiled and nodded to the soldiers, her hand resting on her distended stomach.

Conductors were busy helping passengers board, checking each ticket. Daniel stopped to tip the porter, and he directed them to a car about halfway down the train. The two women and little girl were handed up first; then Daniel followed holding the baby.

The interior of the train car, which at one time must have been beautiful, was shabby and in need of a good cleaning. Finding four seats together at the end of the car, Daniel put Sylvie and the two children just in front of them.

Amanda shifted in her seat. The pillows dug into her stomach and made breathing an effort when she was sitting down.

"Wouldn't a compartment have been a better idea?" Amanda whispered. She could have removed the pillows if they had had a little privacy.

"There weren't any available on this train." Daniel had put his hand on the back of her neck and pulled her close to whisper in her ear. "Besides, it looks less like we're trying to hide out here."

Amanda glanced around. Although most of the passengers were in uniform, the three of them did blend in. Several of the men were using canes or crutches. One was missing an arm. All of the women were dressed in black.

Glancing idly out the window, Amanda noticed three of the armed men who had been asking questions at the ticket windows join up with some soldiers on the platform. They were talking to two conductors. She put her hand on Daniel's sleeve and nodded at the window. He covered her hand with his.

"Just keep calm and stay in your seat." He got up and leaned over to whisper something to Sylvie and lift the baby out of her arms before sitting back beside Amanda.

He settled the baby in his lap. When she looked out at the platform again the men were gone. Her relief proved to be short-lived. Within moments two of them were at the far end of their car, pausing to question people in each seat. One, a tall thin man, looked bored. The other one was short and scruffy. He put her in mind of an aggressive little dog.

"They must have split up to cover the cars more quickly. We're already a half-hour late leaving." Daniel consulted his watch. The baby immediately made a grab for the shiny metal case. Daniel held the timepiece to his little ear so that he could hear the ticking sound.

How can he be so calm? Amanda thought to herself, looking down at her gloved hands, knotted in her lap. She was thankful for her heavy veil that hid the perspiration beading on her forehead and upper lip. When she looked up, the men were there, just in front of her, staring at Sylvie.

"Excuse me, ma'am." The man touched the brim of his hat. "Sorry to bother you, but we have to ask some questions."

Amanda froze, knowing the moment the two armed men heard Sylvie speak in her soft drawl they would know she was a Negro under her heavy veil.

Daniel thrust the baby into Amanda's arms and got to his feet. "Pardon me, gentlemen, but what authority do you have to bother us?"

The rough-looking little man glanced briefly at Daniel's eye-patch and cane, ignoring his question. "You kin to this woman?'' Amanda could see Sylvie tremble. Her own heartbeat thudded in her ears.

''Yes, sir. She is my sister-in-law. She has just lost her husband and her brother. I'm afraid she is not up to conversation.''

''Well, I'm sorry to hear that, ma'am.'' He turned his back on Daniel. ''But I have my orders. Could you stand up, please?'' He voice was no longer cordial.

Sylvie clutched Beatrice and cringed in her seat. The little girl must have sensed her mother's fear and began to wail.

''Really, I must protest!'' Daniel moved a step closer to the two men.

Amanda saw both of them shift their hands toward the revolvers holstered on their hips.

Amanda stood up and placed the baby on her seat. He joined in his sister's crying. Amanda squeezed around behind Daniel and into the aisle.

''Please, sir.''

The tall man ignored her.

The other one tipped his hat and rudely stared down at her belly, then turned away, repeating himself. ''I need to talk to the lady.''

It was obvious to Amanda the men weren't going to back down.

Amanda pushed forward into the two men and clutched at the pillows at her waist with one hand, and one of their sleeves with the other. She moaned and fell heavily against them, knocking them off balance.

''Oh, Lordy, what's the matter?'' The tall man pushed her and backed away. Amanda dropped to her knees, still clutching at the short man's sleeve.

Daniel took his cue from her and yelled, ''See what you've done. You should be ashamed of yourself!''

Sylvie started to cry harder and both children wailed. People all around them were on their feet, trying to see what was going on. Amanda moaned again, louder.

The tall man took off his hat and began to fan Amanda with

it, speaking for the first time. "Gee, Mister, I'm sorry. Is there anything we can do to help?"

"You've done quite enough." Daniel shouldered him aside. "Just get out of our way. I must get my wife off this train."

He scooped Amanda up in his arms and motioned to Sylvie. One of the men put out his hand to stop them and Amanda let out a loud shriek. He quickly backed away.

"You both are responsible for this! I intend to speak to your captain!" Daniel stood aside for Sylvie, waiting for her to get out of her seat.

She collected both children and bolted down the car and out the door. Amanda continued to moan, hiding her face against Daniel's chest.

As soon as they were out of sight in the tunnel, Daniel put her down and took the children.

"What now?" Amanda asked Daniel as she put her arm around Sylvie, who was quaking so badly she could hardly stand.

"Follow me." He started up a ramp on the other side of the tunnel, and when they reached the track, they were at the front of the train.

"We're going to get back on?" Amanda couldn't believe he meant to reboard the train.

"If they started at the front they've already been through this car." He stood back to let them board, as if what he said made perfect sense.

Sylvie turned to Amanda in disbelief. " 'Dis man crazy." She managed to whisper.

"Daniel . . ." Amanda hesitated. She looked down the track and saw the two men who had questioned them disappear down the same tunnel they had just used.

"All aboard!" The cry came from one of the conductors.

"Hurry up, or we'll miss it. Besides, our bags are on this train." Daniel gave her a shove.

He really is crazy, thought Amanda, and she pushed Sylvie ahead of her onto the train.

* * *

The remainder of the trip was blessedly uneventful. They changed trains twice, sat on a siding for hours, and spent an uncomfortable night on the train.

The children never lacked for a lap to sit on or an adult to play with. Many of the soldiers who traveled with them on the train missed their own children and were always ready to entertain Sylvie's son and daughter.

Finally, travel-worn and weary, they got off the train in Richmond. It was as far as they could go by rail. For a good part of the trip they had traveled at no more speed than they could have gotten out of an old mule.

The tracks needed mending in some places, and the railroad had neither the men nor materials to do satisfactory repairs, so the engineer had to crawl along, often times sending the fireman out to walk in front of the engine and declare the roadbed safe.

Amanda was delighted to finally be off the train, but being anywhere near Richmond made her uneasy. She would be relieved to be headed north across the Potomac River to Washington. Sylvie could take the children on to Canada, where they would be safe.

Amanda didn't know where she and Daniel would end up, but anywhere was better than here. The last thing they needed now was to see someone who might recognize them. She had not spent time near the railroad station or downtown, but there were many people in Richmond who knew Daniel as Lord Ashton.

In spite of his disguise, Amanda knew how vulnerable he was, and that, more than anything else, frightened her. All the way out of town, she searched the faces of passers-by, holding her breath that they wouldn't run into anyone they had met.

Chapter 23

"Tired?" Daniel held her loosely in one arm, using his free hand to smooth the hair off her forehead.

"Yes. And dirty. It amazes me that just sitting on a train could wear me out." Amanda leaned against him, loving the feel of his strength.

It seemed so long since they had been alone, and she craved his touch. She flushed as she recalled the dreams that had interrupted her sleep the past few nights. Her wanton thoughts still disturbed her.

He brushed his knuckles against her burning cheek. "What is it?"

She curved herself along his side and whispered. "I'll tell you later."

He groaned and crushed her against him, echoing her thoughts. "It's been too long." His breath was warm against her hair.

Before Amanda could speak, Sylvie's voice interrupted them. " 'Scuse me." Daniel sighed and let her go.

"What is it, Sylvie?" Amanda had forgotten for a moment the woman was there in the hotel room with them.

"Is we at de star place?"

Amanda didn't understand the question. Feeling unsafe in the city, they had hired a driver and gone as far as the first small town with a hotel, somewhere north of Richmond. Amanda recalled the name being Glen something. She looked to Daniel for help. He shrugged.

Sylvie seemed to be close to tears, at a loss to explain herself. The strain of the journey showed on her face. Amanda found herself wondering how old this woman was. Strange, she thought, she'd never thought to ask her.

" 'Dis place of de north star. 'Dis de freedom place?"

Then Amanda understood. Sylvie had told her the first night, the night of the fire, that she had heard talk of following the North Star to freedom, but the slave woman didn't really know what it meant.

Amanda felt guilty, remembering she had told Sylvie not to worry, they would take care of everything. She should have explained.

"Not yet. We're still in Virginia, but we're close. It won't be long." Amanda didn't think it wise to mention that the most dangerous part of the journey was still to come.

It was hard to tell Sylvie where they were going when the woman didn't even know where she had come from. Amanda had asked her where she lived before coming to Charleston, and her reply was "More south, by de river." She couldn't name the river.

What would it be like not to know where you were from? she thought.

"It won't be long. I know people near here who will help us on our way," Daniel assured her.

Sylvie appeared relieved as she busied herself with her children.

"How long has it been since you've seen these friends?" Amanda was concerned that the war might have changed things since Daniel was through here last.

"Almost three years." He seemed to understand her reason

for asking. "They're Quakers, so the men should still be at home. They will not fight in any war."

"How can they just refuse? What about the draft?" Amanda knew there were a lot of men who would rather not go, and the government took a dim view of their feelings.

Daniel's reply was quiet and full of conviction. "Fighting is against their religion. I know John Martin. He would go to prison before he would go to war."

Their converstion ended with the crying and fussing of the children. The baby twisted and wriggled in his mother's arms, while the little girl stood defiantly, hands clenched, stomping one tiny foot.

Daniel turned and eased the baby from his mother, then scooped up the little girl. "I think I know what these children need. How about we explore a little outside and see if we can't find a place to play?"

Sylvie nodded in weary agreement as they disappeared through the door.

"You all got one fine man, Miss Amanda." She moved to the window to catch a glance of them as they left.

"He's not mine, Sylvie. For now maybe ..." Amanda's voice trailed off.

"Why for only now? He be belongin' to some other body?" It was the first personal question Sylvie had asked Amanda.

"No, but I have things to do with my life. Things that don't include him." The words sounded hollow and selfish, and somehow, she thought, dishonest.

"Then you a fool." Amanda was startled as much by her flat tone as by what she said. "You be free. He be free. He a good man. You all could have babies and raise 'em up to be anythin' you all want."

Amanda knew that from Sylvie's point of view, she was a fool. She was beginning to have real doubts herself.

Sylvie, looking horrified by her outburst, retreated several steps. "I sorry. Never should be saying dat." She trembled and bowed her head.

My God, thought Amanda, *she thinks I'm going to hit her.* She was quick to reassure.

"Don't be silly. We're friends, aren't we?" Amanda could tell by her surprised look Sylvie had expected a much different reaction.

"Friends? Yessum, I guesses we is." The Negro woman looked much relieved.

"And friends tell each other the truth, even when they don't want to hear it."

"Yessum."

"Alright, then, let's get this place tidied before they come back." The two women set to organizing the room in companionable silence. Amanda recalled the conversation in her head, trying to sort out her feelings.

When Daniel arrived back with the children, the little girl's hands were full of treasures. A rock, some leaves, and a twig with a cocoon attached to it. She hurried across the room to show her mother. Both the little ones were in a much better mood. The baby clutched at a peppermint stick. From the looks of him, he had more on his face than in his mouth. Daniel gave him over to Sylvie.

"The children have eaten. This is for you." Daniel apologized. "I wish we could get you a hot meal, but it's too risky."

Sylvie shook her head. "No, dis be fine. Thank you, suh."

Sylvie appeared touched by his care of herself and her children, and threw Amanda a telling glance.

"Sylvie, I'm going to take Amanda out. We'll be back in a few hours. Will you be all right?"

"Yesuh."

Amanda found her veil, stuffed a pillow under her skirt, and within moments she walked out the door on Daniel's arm. They were on the street waiting for a wagon and a carriage to pass before he spoke.

"I wanted to be able to talk without upsetting Sylvie."

Daniel's comment alarmed Amanda. "Why, what's wrong?"

He patted her hand where it rested on his arm. "She's not out of danger yet. I just don't want to frighten her."

Traffic had cleared and he guided her across the dusty street. "Just glance to your left."

Amanda did so without turning her head. Her veil obscured her vision.

"See the man on the corner, leaning against the building?"

Amanda took note of him. An average-looking fellow in a brown suit, a hat pulled low over his face. "I see him. Why?"

"He was at the train station when we got off in Richmond." Amanda didn't remember him at all. When she glanced back to get a second look, all she saw was the back of the man as he walked away.

"Do you think he was watching us?" Her heart was pounding.

"I don't know, but I sure don't like the coincidence."

They entered a small cafe and chose a corner table, away from the other diners. Several people turned their way, eyeing them curiously. They made small talk until their meal arrived.

Daniel glanced around and spoke in a low voice. "I asked at the general store. John Martin is still working his farm. It's only about twenty miles north of here. There is a mail wagon from Richmond that goes through here early tomorrow and we can get a ride almost to his house."

That was good news. "And then what? Will they take us all north?"

Daniel shook his head. "I think it will be safer to split up and let John decide how he is going to get Sylvie and her children away."

"Do you know how they do it? How they go?"

Daniel shrugged. "I know a little. The Quakers have been doing this for many years. I never asked too much."

Amanda was intrigued by these people who would risk so much to help runaway slaves. In years past the penalties had been harsh.

"The Quakers, why do they do this?"

"They cannot abide slavery, just as they would risk prison

to not fight in a war. I once saw a Quaker in Philadelphia attacked by a drunk, and he wouldn't even defend himself.''

Uneasily, Amanda imagined a group of religious fanatics.

It seemed that Sylvie's future was decided. Amanda wondered about herself and Daniel. "What about us? If we don't go with John Martin, how will we go?"

"I think we should stay at his farm for a time and rest up. Then we can head for Washington. It's only about eighty miles from John's place."

"Fine. I could use a rest." Amanda didn't like the thought of staying with the Quakers, but because they were friends of Daniel's, she didn't say anything. They stopped speaking while the waiter cleared the table.

As they were having coffee, a man of about fifty stopped by their table. He had an enormous belly and wore a badge on his coat. He removed his hat and nodded to Amanda.

"Evening, folks. Sorry to interrupt your supper, but I make it a point to greet new folks in town. Name's Duffy. Sheriff Erastus Duffy."

Daniel stood and shook his hand. "No interruption, sir. My name is John Davis and this is my wife Frances. We are lately from Richmond. Will you join us for coffee?"

"Thank you, no. My wife is waiting supper for me. You folks traveling alone?" He leveled a look at Daniel that made Amanda think he knew the answers to his questions before he ever asked them.

"As a matter of fact, no. My wife's sister and her children are with us. She's not well enough to come out. Just lost her husband at Antietam. He rode with General Lee. We're taking her home to her folks outside of Fredericksburg.

"Sorry to hear that. You going to be with us for a while?" Amanda bet herself he had already checked with their hotel. Daniel had told the clerk they might be there for as long as a week.

"Seems like we might have to. At least several days, until Mrs. Ellsworth is able to travel."

The sheriff put his hat back on and nodded to them. "You

all have a nice stay and if you need anything, my offices are just down the street here.'' He motioned with his big beefy hand.

"Thank you, sir. I shall remember that.'' They watched him greet some of the diners on his way out.

Amanda shivered. "Do you think he knows?"

"No. If he knew he wouldn't be nosing around like that. I think he likes to know what goes on in his town.''

"We still leave tomorrow?'' Amanda held her veil out of the way to drink her coffee.

"Yup. No reason to stay here.''

"Daniel?''

"What?''

"Don't ever tell anyone my name is Frances again.''

He grinned at her. "Had a dog by that name once. She was a good hound.'' Amanda kicked him under the table. He grunted when she connected with his shin.

The five of them set out very early the next morning, before anyone was astir at the hotel. Daniel didn't check out, but left money in their room to cover the bill. The mail cart proved to be a cramped, dusty way to travel, but it was good to be on their way. They didn't see the sheriff or the man in the brown suit when they left.

By late afternoon they bid good-bye to their driver. John Martin's farm lay just over a rise of land off the main road. They paused at the top of the hill for a moment to take in the idyllic scene. The farmhouse, nestled in among huge shade trees, was almost hidden.

White buildings glistened in the late afternoon sun. Huge fenced areas for animals surrounded the barn. Amanda could hear the soft lowing of cows waiting to be led into the milking shed.

Fields stretched all around the house. Everything appeared to be well-tended, giving the place a look of prosperity. Smoke curled from the chimney and the muted glow of a lamp at the

window seemed to invite them in. The tranquil scene made
Amanda feel better about staying at the farm.

Daniel touched her shoulder, startling Amanda out of her
reverie. "Let's go on down."

The only thing missing from the scene was people. There
was no one in sight.

As they approached the house, Amanda could see it had been
added on to several times. Rooms jutted out from every side.
The original dwelling was two stories high, but the additions
sprawled all around the first floor. It gave the house an unstruc-
tured appearance, at odds with the symmetry of the fields.

As they got closer, Amanda could see a group of adults and
children in the front room. They sat listening to a man read.
Daniel motioned Sylvie and Amanda to a wooden bench on
the porch. John Martin and his family were at their evening
prayers.

They sat and watched the sunset, and again Amanda was
struck by the tranquility of the place. The strain she had felt
for days melted away.

People inside the house stirred. The door opened and the
porch filled with members of the Quaker family. Introductions
were made and Amanda was immediately struck by the resemblance between John Martin and his wife Hannah. They were
almost the same height, had the same stocky build, dark hair
streaked with gray, and skin brown from long hours in the sun.

Upon meeting them, Amanda's remaining uneasy feelings
were put to rest. They were open and friendly. The rest of the
family consisted of their twelve children, along with the wives
of the two eldest sons. The Martins' youngest child looked
little older than Sylvie's girl. That explained all the additions
to the house, Amanda thought.

The Martins welcomed them warmly. Hannah hustled everyone into the kitchen and served them supper. Through the
window Amanda could see the cows being herded into the barn
for milking.

Two of the children dragged milk cans from what she guessed

was the spring house. The intricate workings of the farm intrigued Amanda.

Hannah served them all a simple meal and then took Sylvie and her children to a hidden room in the attic. Daniel left to talk to John Martin. Two of the daughters cleared the table and started the dishes, waving Amanda off when she tried to help. She felt useless, and wandered onto the porch.

The farm glowed in the twilight. Soft light poured from the windows of the house and outbuildings as everyone went about their evening chores. Faintly she could hear Sylvie singing to her children. At this moment it was hard to believe a war raged. Hannah came out and stood beside her.

"Thou must be tired after thy long trip. I fired up the stove in the wash house if thou wants to bathe." Amanda gave the woman a grateful look, smiling inwardly at her quaint manner of speech.

"Thank you. A bath sounds wonderful."

Hannah patted her arm. "Just get thy things and meet me over there."

Hannah gestured to a small structure just beside the kitchen. "Have the older girls show thee where thy room is. I put thee in with them."

Amanda went back into the kitchen and one of the daughters, who appeared to be about eighteen, showed her to a large room on the second floor. Her bag was on one of the beds. She gathered the things she would need and headed for the wash house.

The building held a pleasant smell of soap and starch. A fire crackled in the old stove and water hissed as it dripped from the spout of one of the huge kettles. Hannah was busy pouring steaming water into a large tin bath.

Amanda felt guilty having Hannah wait on her. She knew the woman had probably been working since before sunup. "Here, let me do that."

"No bother, child. I have it almost ready."

Amanda added a bucket of cold water into the tub, testing the temperature with her hand.

"Hannah, I really appreciate what you all are doing for Sylvie and her children. I got Daniel into a spot and now I have put everyone in danger."

Hannah finished pouring the kettle and then hung it on the pump to refill it. "Helping these people to freedom is something we have been doing for many years, and John's father did before us when John was a boy on this land. Thou has not brought us any danger we have not already chosen for ourselves." She gave Amanda a quick hug. "I'm just pleased that God put the courage in thy heart to do what thou did."

"I'm not sure it was courage at all. I didn't have any choice."

Hannah crossed her arms over her ample middle and smiled. "My dear, thou art wrong. Thou always has a choice, no matter what thou does. Now hurry with your bath before the water gets cold. Doest thou need anything else before I go?"

Amanda shook her head and Hannah hurried away.

The hot bath felt heavenly. Amanda lingered until the water grew cold, then quickly scrubbed her hair and rinsed it as best she could with the last bucket of water. She dressed in a clean nightgown and tidied the room.

Pulling a shawl around her shoulders, she opened the door, hoping to see Daniel. He was nowhere in sight as she hurried to the house.

Inside the house it was dark and quiet. Amanda found the stairs and was on her way up when she heard a murmur of voices and smelled the sweet, pungent smoke of a pipe. John Martin and Daniel must be on the porch. She couldn't go out to him in her night things. She continued up the stairs, disappointed she would not see him until the morning.

When Amanda got to her room, she found the three sisters still awake. Shyly at first, but with obvious interest, they asked her questions. They wanted to know about Philadelphia and Richmond, about her schooling and her drawings.

It became evident these girls led a sheltered life with little contact outside their close-knit community. They had never been to a city or ridden on a train or a boat.

A brisk knock on the door caused the giggling and laughing

conversation to halt abruptly, with the girls giving each other guilty looks. Hannah Martin called good night to them, nothing more. By their behavior, Amanda knew the evening was over. She had not enjoyed the fun of a bedtime chat with young women her own age for a long time.

Getting off the bed to hang her shawl over the back of a chair, Amanda saw Daniel in the moonlight, headed for the barn, with a quilt draped over one arm.

After whispered good nights, Amanda curled up and went to sleep, wondering why he had not been invited to sleep in the house.

Amanda woke with a start. It was dark outside and she had no idea of the time. She turned her head to look at the person sharing her bed. In her dream it had been Daniel. Instead she saw a fifteen-year-old Quaker girl.

Amanda wished desperately that it was Daniel in the bed. *That damn dream again,* she thought. It was always the same, wonderful and wicked. She lay naked in Daniel's arms, his large warm hands stroking her body. Then she woke, bathed in perspiration, the throbbing between her legs a painful need.

She clasped her hands tightly between her thighs and waited for her breathing to return to normal, willing herself to go back to sleep.

It didn't work. The longer she lay there, the more awake she felt. Finally, restless as a cat, Amanda could stand it no longer. She crept out of bed and grabbed her shawl, letting herself quietly out the bedroom door. She felt her way along the hall and down the stairs, the only sounds in the house that of gentle snoring coming from several rooms and the tick of a clock in the parlor.

The kitchen still held a faint hint of warmth and the pleasant odors of last night's meal. Amanda went out the back door and headed for the barn. Two of the farm dogs were tied to the fence. They wagged their tails in greeting but did not stir. The moon shone silvery on the huge building. She shoved at the large sliding door, and it hesitated, then slid quietly on runners. She pushed it open just enough to squeeze through.

The warm air of the barn smelled of hay and animals. She stopped and listened. There was the shuffle and snorting sounds from the cattle, but nothing else. Amanda peered into the darkness, trying to discover where Daniel might be sleeping. The animal stalls were all occupied by horses and cows. She didn't want to call out and wake him. She just needed to look at him, to be close.

Moonlight shone in through the hay doors and down through the cracks in the loft floor. That must be where he was sleeping. Feeling her way along the feed passage, she came to a ladder. Hiking up her nightgown and securing it against her body with her elbows, she began to climb.

As her head cleared the floor of the loft, she saw it in the moonlight. A long, bare, well-muscled arm held a revolver, pointed directly at her head. The rest of him was in the shadows.

"Daniel?" Amanda's voice cracked.

"You're lucky I didn't blow your head off! What the hell are you doing, sneaking around in the middle of the night? Is something wrong?" He lowered the gun and she heard the click of the hammer as he released it from its cocked position.

"Nothing. Why are you sleeping up here instead of in the house?" Ignoring his brusque words, she cleared the top of the ladder and stepped onto the floor.

Straw poked her bare feet. He leaned up against a bale of hay, bare-chested. A quilt covered him to the waist.

He laid the revolver on a pile of clothes beside him. "I can see the road from here." He motioned toward the open hay doors.

Then she remembered the dogs tied outside. They would alert him if any stranger came near the barn.

"What are you doing here?"

Amanda moved across the floor and sank down beside him. Her nightgown mushroomed out around her and the straw scratched her bare legs. He hadn't moved.

What could she say to him? That she ached for him, that

dreams of him caused her to wake and want him so badly she didn't sleep for the rest of the night?

Too embarrassed by the truth, she couldn't say the words. "I just wanted to see you, make sure you were comfortable."

His face told her he knew. He grinned that grin that never failed to quicken her pulse.

"Liar," he whispered.

He reached over and slid his hand under her night dress, caressing the bare skin of her thigh. Hooking her behind the knee, he lifted her leg and pulled her over until she straddled his waist. He kicked the quilt away. She shuddered at the feel of his naked warmth beneath her.

Amanda wanted to feel him against her bare breasts. She pulled her nightgown off and tossed it aside and leaned into him, rubbing her nipples against his chest.

His hands now lay still at his sides. "Tell me what you want, Amanda." His voice neutral, he made no move to touch her.

She lay against him, wanting his hands on her. This was a frustrating game he was playing. If it weren't for his hard erection against her thigh, she might almost believe he was as uninvolved as he sounded.

"I want you," she whispered into the hair on his chest.

"I can't hear you. Tell me again." Daniel still made no move to touch her.

Frustration sparked her. She leaned back so she could see his face. He was grinning at her.

She whispered, "I want you. I want you inside me."

She was ready for him, as she always was when she woke from her dreams of him. Amanda reared back until she could reach his sex, and felt a great deal of satisfaction when he groaned as her hand closed around him. In one swift motion she thrust him inside her.

She heard him suck in his breath as she settled on him.

"You asked what I wanted," she purred smugly, and she made a little move with her hips.

He groaned and thrust his hips up under her.

She savored the feel of him filling her as she shifted her

weight forward and raised up on her knees just a tiny bit. Daniel ducked his head and took one of her nipples in his mouth.

At that moment her mind ceased to function and her greedy body took over. She rocked atop him with a growing frenzy until she was aware of nothing, except the spot where their bodies joined.

He matched his movements to hers, thrusting up to meet her. She quickly built to a shattering climax that left her gasping for breath. Limply, she collapsed against him, aware only that he had ceased to move too.

Hands that had been holding her loosely at her waist slid up to wrap around her as their breathing returned to normal.

He rolled her to her side and curled his big body around her, pulling the quilt over both of them.

"I'm so glad you came to check on me," he whispered in her ear as she drifted off to a dreamless, satisfied sleep.

Chapter 24

Amanda awoke at the crow of the rooster. The faint glow of sunrise colored the horizon as she pulled away from Daniel's warmth and sat up to look out the hay doors.

She watched with dismay as the sky turn glorious shades of gold and crimson. She had fallen asleep instead of sneaking back into the house while it was still dark.

Embarrassed anyone might see her leaving the barn, Amanda scooted out from beneath the quilt and found her gown and shawl.

Daniel reached out and tried to pull her back against his sleep-warmed body.

"Let go. I have to leave." She pushed at his arm.

He nuzzled the back of her neck. "Why?" His voice was muffled by her hair.

"I have to go before anyone gets up." She pulled away and scooted to the ladder, not looking back, afraid she might not be able to resist him.

After descending the ladder, she moved quickly through rows of expectant-looking cows. As she pushed the barn door open, the yard was empty, but she could see a lamp in the kitchen.

Hannah was already up.

Well, the only thing she could do was pretend she had gone out to use the privy. She skirted the barn, and stopped by the outbuilding, then approached the house.

Hannah looked startled when Amanda opened the back door. "Goodness child, I thought I was the only one up. Thou art the early bird." Hannah placed strips of fatback into a huge iron skillet on the stove, then wiped her hands on her apron.

"I woke up and it was such a beautiful morning, I couldn't stay abed." She smiled nervously at Hannah and walked through the kitchen. "I'll just get dressed and come down and help you with breakfast."

As she passed by the stove, Hannah stayed her with a hand on her arm. The older woman reached up and pulled a piece of hay from Amanda's hair.

"No need to hurry. John and the children have yet to do the milking. Wake the girls for me, please." There was no censure in her look or voice, but Amanda blushed furiously and hurried on up the stairs.

She dressed as the sisters rose from their beds. They all had chores to do, and Amanda followed them into the barn after Hannah insisted she needed no help in the kitchen.

The girls set about showing Amanda how to milk. Seated on a low milking stool, she was surprised to find the chore was much harder than it looked. Finally the sisters decided Amanda had had enough of their instructions and moved off to other animals.

The cow Amanda attempted to milk kept turning her head to watch the fumbling attempts. The big animal gave little sounds of what Amanda took to be bovine displeasure. Her hands ached and she had made very little progress filling the bucket at her feet when she heard Daniel chuckle.

She raised her forehead from where it rested against the side of the huge cow and glared at him. "What are you laughing at?"

He was so handsome in the early morning light, hair damp, shirt unbuttoned, leaning on a stanchion.

"I just figured with those talented hands of yours you could go a little faster than that."

"Shush! Someone will hear you." She flushed and turned back to concentrate on her task. She had attracted two of the barn cats with her awkward efforts. They licked at the milk running down the outside of the bucket.

He placed his hands on her shoulders and ran them down her body, stopping his downward motion for a moment to caress the sides of her breasts.

"Daniel, please." Her voice sounded slightly breathless.

He whispered in her ear. "Please what?" He was doing it again, that infernal teasing of his.

Just then, they heard John Martin's voice. "Daniel, is thou awake?"

"Over here, John. I was just giving Amanda a lesson." He smirked at her glare.

John tipped his hat to her in greeting. "I need help with the wagon."

"Of course. Amanda, just stroke and squeeze with that firm grip of yours and you'll do fine."

She was tempted to throw the contents of the bucket at him, but the milk barely covered the bottom and she couldn't bear to waste it, it had been so hard to come by.

Within minutes the shout came from the house that breakfast was ready. One of the daughters took over from her to finish milking. Amanda was glad for the assistance. She was sure that if she kept up the milking she wouldn't be able to hold a fork in her cramped fingers. She suspected the sigh the cow gave off when she got up from the stool was one of relief.

Sylvie was not at breakfast. "Where are Sylvie and the children?" Amanda asked the question around a mouthful of flapjacks. She was starving.

"For her own safety, she must remain were she is for a short while, until it is time to leave." John Martin's voice invited no argument.

"I took her breakfast. She and the little ones are fine," Hannah hastened to add.

Amanda felt sorry for Sylvie, cooped up with the two children. She remembered how cranky they could get. Yet, she had not heard any crying.

After breakfast the men worked on the wagon and Amanda climbed the hill above the farm with her sketchbook. She did one drawing of the farm as a gift for Hannah and John, and in a second one she altered the look of the farm just enough so that if it were published it would not be recognized. She would like the Quakers' heroic story to be told, but not at the expense of their safety or privacy.

When Amanda saw John Martin bring the wagon around to the front of the barn, she hurried down the hill. She wanted to say good-bye to Sylvie.

Amanda climbed two flights of stairs and found the woman in the tiny, windowless cubbyhole she and the children occupied. When Sylvie answered her knock and invited her in, Amanda was amazed to find the children dressed but asleep on the narrow bed.

Whispering, Amanda motioned to the two children. "Goodness, Sylvie, I didn't think they'd sleep much past sunup."

"Oh, miss they was up early. Nappin' now." Sylvie finished packing their things into a single bag.

Hannah bustled into the room and took the bag from Sylvie's hands. There was barely room for the three of them to stand. "It's time now. Is thou ready?"

"Yessum." Sylvie looked more rested than she had in days. She turned to Amanda. "I wants to thank you for all you done. 'Specially for my babies." Tears ran down the woman's cheeks.

Amanda took Sylvie by the shoulders and held her at arm's length. "Promise me one thing, Sylvie." The woman nodded. "You'll send your children to school so they can get an education."

"Yessum, I promises."

Amanda pulled her close in a hug and felt Sylvie stiffen. Physical contact was not something the woman seemed comfortable with.

Amanda whispered in her ear. "And when they are learning

their lessons, you learn with them. Then you can be really free.'' She released her, and Sylvie nodded.

John Martin called from outside, and Hannah motioned to them. Sylvie picked up her daughter, who did not stir in her arms. Hannah scooped up the baby with the practiced ease of motherhood and he continued his quiet snoring.

Picking up the bag, Amanda followed them out. ''Hannah, what makes them sleep so?''

Hannah answered over her shoulder. ''Ah, just a small dose of laudanum. This wagon ride frightens most children.''

When they got downstairs, Amanda understood the need for a sedative for the children. The very thought of crawling into the space made her breath come fast and her palms sweat.

There was a low wooden box, six feet long and about four feet wide, set on the bed of the wagon. Even with the cracks between the boards, it looked like an oddly shaped coffin. The end of the box, angled toward the rear of the wagon bed, had a door that flipped up to reveal a quilt. The men directed Sylvie to crawl in and then they slid the sleeping children in to her, one at a time. She took them with trembling hands and settled them beside her.

Hannah made a trip to the kitchen for a sack of food and a jar of water. She also handed over a tiny bottle of the laudanum and repeated detailed instructions on the amount to give each child.

Sylvie's bag was stowed at her feet and she waved a final good-bye before John Martin closed and latched the little door. With John's signal, two of the boys in the loft of the barn forked hay into the bed of the wagon, covering the box. Within minutes it was impossible to tell there were three human beings under the load.

Daniel came out of the barn and approached John. ''I want you to take Amanda with you.''

She started to protest and was stayed by Hannah's hand on her arm.

John gave Daniel a sad look. ''I cannot do that Daniel. It be too unsafe for her.''

"It's not safe for her to be with me." Amanda could hear the frustration in Daniel's voice.

"Yes, but if I'm stopped by the slave catchers, they ask no questions if they find contraband. There is no trial, Daniel. It wouldn't matter that Amanda's a woman." John shook his head and climbed onto the wagon seat.

Daniel turned and disappeared into the barn, the tension in his shoulders and the way he held his head warned her not to follow.

Amanda shuddered at the Quaker's words. She watched until the vehicle disappeared from view, thinking about the risks John Martin took and the future Sylvie had to face. She prayed that the gentle man would return safely and hoped she had truly done the woman a favor.

Curiously, Amanda felt a tremendous letdown. Returning to the hill where she had left her sketch pad, she sat with her back against a tree. The next thing she knew, Daniel was gently shaking her shoulder. She had fallen asleep in the warm sun. He settled down beside her.

"Oh, dear. I'm a mess." She ran her fingers through her hair and tugged at her dress.

"You're beautiful." Daniel grasped her hands to still them and kissed her gently. "Do you understand why I wanted you to go with John?"

"Yes. And I understand why you didn't talk to me about it first." Amanda scooted up against him.

It seemed like the only place she wanted to be. She glanced over at her sketches. Even they didn't seem very important anymore.

Daniel flipped a penny into her lap. She glanced up at him. "What's this for?"

He kissed the end of her nose. "Your thoughts. What else?"

Amanda still wasn't ready to admit she loved him, to say the words out loud. She hadn't yet come to grips with her confused feelings.

Besides, she thought as she slipped the penny into the pocket of her skirt, he hadn't said anything for a while about getting married. Now that she had given herself to him, and the newness of being lovers was over, maybe he didn't feel the same way anymore. She remembered something her grandmother used to say when she was a child. ''Why would a man buy a cow when he could get the milk for free?'' She hadn't understood the saying then, but she did now.

''Well?'' Daniel was looking at her intently.

''Just wondering where we go from here.'' Her comment held a double meaning.

''How about we head north to Washington? It's only about eighty miles. We can be there in a few days.''

Amanda brightened. ''Sounds fine to me.'' And it did. It would be a relief to be back where she could feel safe and not have to be looking over her shoulder all the time.

Daniel stood up and dusted off the seat of his pants. Extending his hand, he pulled her to her feet and scooped up the sketch pad.

''I spoke to John's son. He'll let us have horses.''

''When?'' She wanted at least one more bath in that big tub before they left.

''Tomorrow.''

Amanda nodded in agreement and together they headed back to the farmhouse.

Sitting on the porch, Amanda watched Daniel talking to two of John Martin's older sons. She was idly wondering if she dare risk sneaking out to the barn again tonight when she spotted the wagon on the road. It was then she realized how tense she had been waiting for the farmer's return.

''Daniel, look.'' She pointed. She hurried along with the three men as they headed to the barn.

John Martin heaved his bulky frame out of the wagon and landed on his feet with a grunt. He appeared agitated and Amanda feared something had happened to Sylvie.

''John?'' She stepped forward and laid a hand on his arm. He patted her hand reassuringly.

"They are safe." It was apparently all he was willing to say, but she could tell something was wrong.

Turning to Daniel he spoke. "I need to speak with thee alone. Milo, take care of the wagon for me."

John's son nodded and moved to do his bidding. Amanda took note that the farm seemed to run with such ease because everyone minded what John Martin and Hannah said, without any discussion.

He had said he wanted to talk to Daniel alone, and Amanda made no attempt to follow. She clasped her hands together over her stomach and prayed the Quaker did not have bad news about Sylvie and the children.

Amanda wandered back to the kitchen and was helping Hannah shell peas when Daniel stuck his head through the back door.

"May I steal your helper for a few minutes?" He winked at Hannah. She nodded and smiled, taking the bowl from Amanda's lap.

Untying her apron, Amanda hung it over the back of her chair.

Daniel stood outside the back door, lost in thought. When he heard her come down the steps, he smiled at her and caught her hand. "Let's take a walk." He said no more as they climbed through a fence and headed across a pasture toward a stand of trees.

A small creek ran through the trees. Amanda took her shoes off and sat at the very edge of the cool water, letting it run over her bare toes, waiting for Daniel to speak.

She turned at the sound of his hesitant voice. "John Martin has heard a rumor I think needs to be checked out. There are some people gathering for what could be an interesting meeting near Richmond . . ."

Richmond. Again. Amanda couldn't think of a place she would less like to go. She would always associate that beautiful city with that witch of a woman, Blythe Shipley. Amanda realized she wasn't paying attention to what Daniel was saying.

". . . so you can stay here with Hannah and John until I get back."

She got the distinct impression from the hesitation in his voice there was more.

"I don't want to stay here." Amanda stood up and moved closer to him.

"Well you can't very well start for Washington by yourself." He purposely seemed to misunderstand her.

She was getting tired of always arguing with him. "I want to go with you."

"It's not safe." He hesitated again.

"What aren't you telling me?"

He looked off into the distance. "Someone has been asking about us."

"Who?" She held her breath.

"A man that fits Bodin's description."

Her sigh hissed out between her teeth. "People saw us take the mail coach and get off here. What makes you think he won't find me if you leave me here?"

"You will stay hidden in the room Sylvie and the children used."

She listened to his words and felt a wave of panic as she thought about the tiny, windowless room. "I can't. I can't stay in there. Please."

"It won't be so bad. You can do it." He patted her on the shoulder and looked impatient. "I can move faster and get out quicker alone."

"No, please. You don't understand." She was having trouble catching her breath.

"Amanda . . ."

She sensed his hesitation and grabbed his sleeve. "I'll go crazy."

Frantically she thought of ways to get him to take her. "You can have more of a cover story if you bring me."

Amanda slipped her hand around the back of his neck and pulled his head down until she could reach his lips. While she kissed him she ran her hand inside the waistband of his trousers.

His arms tightened around her, pinning her hand between them. He groaned. "You don't play fair," he said, his voice husky.

"I know. I learned it from you." She felt him stir and pushed her hand lower. "I want to go with you." She breathed the words in his ear, then pulled her head back so she could look him in the eye, her hand still searching.

Daniel cupped the back of her head and kissed her deeply, then sighed his words against her lips. "Don't stop."

"Will you take me with you?" She moved her hand back and forth over him, marveling at the completeness of his response.

"This is blackmail." His breathing was getting heavier.

"Yup." Her hand closed around him. She felt her excitement rise with his.

"Oh, geez, Amanda." Daniel sank to his knees and took her with him. He toppled her back onto the soft grass and ran his hand up under her skirt, finding her warm and wet.

They took no time to remove clothes, only pushing aside what was necessary in their frenzy. It was over in a few sweet, delicious moments. They lay side by side as their breathing returned to normal.

Daniel reached down to adjust his trousers and smooth down her skirt. He clasped his hands behind his head and stared up into the trees that shaded them. Amanda rolled on her side to watch his face.

"You are going to take me, aren't you?" It wasn't a question, it was a statement.

"Yes, against my better judgment. But you'd better be careful, because if anything happens to you, I'll write in my report the exact reason I brought you along."

Amanda felt the heat in her face and knew she was blushing.

Chapter 25

Hannah gave Amanda a pair of trousers and a shirt to pack and another set of clothes to wear. They took only what they would need for a few days and left the rest at the farm to pick up on their way back.

Riding for most of the day, they took shelter in an old abandoned barn in the late afternoon. Daniel figured they were about ten miles outside of Richmond.

"Well, this will be the third time I've been to Richmond. Once as a Lady, once as a pregnant wife, and now as a boy." Amanda tried to cover with conversation her own misgivings about the city.

"Amanda, I have to go meet someone. Alone." She could tell by his tone there was no point in arguing about going with him.

"How long will you be gone?" He didn't seem to notice she wasn't fighting his decision.

"Only a few hours."

"I'll be here." She kissed his cheek.

He smiled. "Get some rest while you can, we may have to travel fast when I get back." Daniel reached out and brushed her cheek with his fingertips. He turned and grasped the reins of his horse and led him from the barn.

Amanda watched him walk out the door, enjoying the sensation his touch always brought. She unsaddled her horse and led him to a stall. Looking around, she found the cleanest pile of straw in the deserted structure.

After spreading a blanket from her saddle pack, she brushed the dust from her jacket and trousers and lay down. It felt good to be off the horse. The sour smell of the decaying hay filled her nostrils as small slits of sunshine filtered through the cracks between the boards of the old barn.

She felt drowsy and after a few moments her eyelids closed and she slid into sleep. Her dreams filled with scenes from childhood, carefree summer days on grassy slopes and evenings alive with fireflies and the smell of lilacs.

A scraping noise brought Amanda out of her dreamy sleep. She opened her eyes without moving and saw within inches of her face a pair of boots. Groggy with sleep, but anxious to hear Daniel's news, she rolled over into a sitting position. Without warning she was smashed back into her bedroll by a foot in the middle of her back.

"What the—" She looked around and saw a second pair of boots.

Instantly Amanda came fully awake. There were at least three men in the barn. Her stomach knotted in fear. She spoke with a bravado she didn't feel.

"What the hell do you think you're doing? Leave me alone!"

The man who had pinned her to the bedroll leaned forward and grabbed her roughly by the upper arms and hauled her to her feet.

There were four of them. Two were dressed in filthy remnants of Confederate uniforms. One of the civilians stood off to the side in the shadows. She tried to wrench away from the one who held her, but he tightened his grip and twisted her arms until she yelped in pain.

The man in front of her was the first to speak. "Well, what do we have here, boys?"

His voice was a soft drawl and she caught a whiff of whiskey. "Traveling all alone, kid?"

He was a big man, at least as tall as Daniel, and heavier. What was left of his jacket showed the markings of sergeant, and he smelled as bad as the other three looked.

"Got any food?"

"In my pack." Trying not to tremble, Amanda nodded toward the saddlebags hanging over the open gate to a stall.

He handed her off to one of the other men.

She could see it was dark outside and that meant at least two hours had passed since Daniel left. Frantic that Daniel might walk into the barn unaware of the situation, she began to talk, hoping her voice would alert him to the fact she was not alone. She knew these men wouldn't hesitate to kill Daniel if he got in their way.

"Who are you?" She directed her question to the large man who appeared to be in charge of the sorry-looking group.

He was holding a lantern over the saddlebags to get a better view of the contents.

"Why little man, two of us are the brave troops of Jefferson Davis. Don't you recognize us by our fine uniforms?" The last part of what he said was hard to understand because it was spoken through a mouthful of food.

For the first time the man who held her arms spoke. "Hey, save some for me. What do you want me to do with this kid?"

The man in the shadows spoke for the first time. "Where is it?"

Amanda recognized his voice. A shaft of pure, cold fear shot through her chest. It was Bodin.

Her mouth felt so dry she didn't know if she could speak. "Where is what?"

"The gold. Where is it?"

"It's gone."

He didn't know who she really was. Had he been following them all this time?

"We sent it north." Did he really think they would carry all that money with them?

He walked over to her and calmly raised his hand, slapping her hard on her face.

"Where is it?" He acted as if he hadn't heard her the first time.

Amanda could taste blood in her mouth, and her cheek stung fiercely, bringing tears to her eyes.

"It was all sent to Washington." She struggled against the man who held her, desperate to get away.

He made a disgusted sound. "Cut some straps off that old harness over there and tie him up. Jake, help him out."

The one named Jake began to whine about the order and Bodin made a fist and slammed him between the shoulder blades. "Move!"

The man lurched foward, choking on a mouthful of food.

Bodin rummaged through her saddlebags, then threw them aside with a curse.

Amanda had no illusions about his ruthlessness. The fact she was a woman would gain her no mercy from this man. The knot in her stomach turned to a lump of fear. She lowered her head and tried desperately to get her thoughts together enough to come up with a sensible plan.

Fear clouded her thinking, numbing her brain. As she stared down at her boots, Amanda glanced at the front of her jacket and saw it gaping open. She could feel her breasts pushing against the fabric of her shirt.

Panic seized her, and when the man holding her let up slightly on his grip, she slid her arms out of the jacket and made a lunge for the barn door. He made a grab for her and caught a piece of her shirttail.

Jake, who had a length of leather strap ready to tie her, threw himself against her, knocking her face first onto the dusty floor of the barn. The force of the blow stunned her as she slid across the dirt floor on her chin. Instinctively, she curled up on her side, arms over her head, trying to protect herself.

The commotion in the dimly lit barn brought Bodin to his feet. "You idiots! Can't two grown men handle one stupid kid?"

He made a fist and was about to strike the man closest to him when he saw the dumbfounded look on the man's face. He followed his gaze, and his mouth dropped open.

Amanda lay gasping for breath on the floor of the barn, the entire front of her shirt torn away, revealing the thin fabric of her chemise. The four men stared at her for several seconds, and then a leer spread across Bodin's face.

"We are in Confederate territory here, and you are definitely out of uniform." He laughed the ugliest laugh Amanda had ever heard.

A look of recognition spread across his face. "I've been following McGrath for weeks. You're that woman who met him at the station in Baltimore, *and* the kid on the boat."

Her mind lurched about, trying desperately to think of a way out. Rolling to her hands and knees, she scooted toward the door. A heavy boot stomped down on her ankle. She screamed in pain.

Hands gripped her legs and flipped her on her back. Her chin was bleeding and sore, but her first move was to cover herself. She pulled at the torn shirt and turned away. Hot tears of embarrassment stung her eyes.

As Bodin took a step toward her, he grabbed the leather thong from Jake's hand. He reached down and grasped one of Amanda's wrists and jerked it up in the air, quickly wrapping the strap around it several times. Then he lashed her hands together.

"You know boys, as I was saying, we have ourselves a little Yankee here, and out of uniform to boot."

One of the men snickered.

"Usually I would recommend shooting a spy, but these are special circumstances, wouldn't you say?" He looked around at the other men, his rat-like face made even uglier by his smirk.

As Amanda stared up at them, they all nodded in unison. For one crazy second they looked like giant marionettes whose strings were all being pulled at the same time.

Bodin yanked the thong, pulling her wrists up and back over

her head. Tugging on the painfully tight straps, he dragged her across the floor, tying the loose end of the thong around the bottom of one of the stall gateposts. As he stood over her she kicked out with her foot and caught him in the shin. He grunted in pain as his knee buckled under him.

Bodin reared up cursing, and gave Amanda another backhanded slap across the cheek. He leaned toward her from his half-kneeling position, until his face was only inches from hers.

She could smell his fetid breath as he whispered the words into her face. "You're going to be real sorry for that, you stupid little bi—"

As he spoke Amanda heard the tremendous roar of gunfire at close range. Bodin fell on her, his unmoving body trapping her, pinning her to the floor of the barn.

She couldn't breathe under his weight. Her panic turned into a live thing, clawing at her. She tried to buck him off, but he was too heavy. She tried to scream, but she couldn't draw in enough breath.

Amanda had the curious feeling she was growing smaller and smaller. Everything around her faded away, the sounds and smells became fainter and the weight pinning her to the floor didn't seem to matter anymore.

Daniel grasped Bodin's body by the collar of his jacket as he held his revolver to the back of his head. He jerked him away from Amanda. Bodin's lifeless eyes stared back at him.

Daniel shifted his attention to Amanda, and for a moment he thought he was too late to save her. She did not move, and her eyes were open and vacant, as empty as the eyes of the dead man. He detected a small movement of her chest as she took a breath, and he felt relief wash over him.

Quickly he untied her hands, cursing himself for leaving her here alone. He assessed her physical wounds, but he knew these were not all she had suffered. Her shirt was ripped from her back and her chin was scraped raw and bleeding. She had bruises on her cheek and jaw.

Still she did not move or speak, and he tried to rouse her from her stupor. "Amanda, sweetheart. It's over. You're safe."

She blinked at him, then closed her eyes. He couldn't be sure she even knew he was there.

He had never felt such a killing urge in his life. He wanted to shoot Bodin and his pack of deserters all over again.

He loosened the leather straps that bound her wrists. "Amanda, we are going to get you someplace safe. I'll get the horses and we'll go."

She began to tremble, her whole body shivering, but still she did not move or respond.

Daniel left her for a moment to get her bag. He found a shirt and came back and dressed her. It was like dressing a doll. She did not resist him, but neither did she do anything to help. Her trembling lessened, and he wrapped her in the blanket and carried her to a pile of straw.

Daniel worked to drag the bodies of the dead men out of sight, into the back of one of the horse stalls. The whole time he worked, Amanda lay unmoving, curled up on her side like a small child.

Daniel held the reins of both horses with one hand, and with his other he held Amanda on the saddle in front of him.

She had not responded to anything he said or did since he had found her in the barn.

They were riding through a small town. The lights shining through the windows cast yellow patches on the dirt road. Daniel pulled the horses to a stop in front of a wooden building with a sign that announced rooms were for rent.

Amanda did not stir in his arms, and he thought for a moment she was asleep. Gently Daniel eased her away from the spot where her head rested on his chest, and he could see her eyes were open.

"Amanda." No response. He shook her gently. "Amanda, can you hear me?"

He thought he saw her nod her head. He turned her and in

the dim light the empty look in her eyes made him feel cold and clammy.

Daniel dismounted, keeping a hold on her arm. He wasn't even sure if she could stay in the saddle without his help. For the tenth time that night he cursed himself for leaving her alone.

"Amanda, listen to me. I want you to do as I say. I'm going to take you inside and try to get a room. I don't want you to move or talk. Do you understand?"

She looked down at him and her head bobbed. He pulled her down off the saddle, still wrapped in the blanket and hefted her across his shoulder like a sack of grain. She uttered a small moan, but offered no resistance.

He stood for a moment in the shadows by the horses, waiting to see if she would struggle, unnerved by her lack of response. When she remained still, limp on his shoulder, he walked up the wooden steps into the hotel.

The sound of his approach awakened the grizzled little man behind the desk. He eyed with suspicion Daniel and the bundle he carried.

The old man wheezed and came unsteadily to his feet. "What do you want, mister?"

"Why, I want a room." Daniel forced a cheerful heartiness into his voice. "That's what the sign out front there says, don't it? Rooms to rent?" Daniel shifted the load on his shoulder.

"That all depends. What's the matter with the kid? He sick or something? This ain't no nursing hospital, you know." The clerk kept his bloodshot eyes trained on Amanda.

Daniel threw back his head and laughed. "Sick! No, he ain't sick, just all wore out. Had his first woman and his first whiskey all in one night."

With those words, Daniel took a twenty-dollar gold piece out of his pocket and flipped it onto the counter. It rolled until it hit the edge of the ledger and settled on the scarred surface of the desk. The old man's hand shot out and captured the coin.

"That should take care of the room and our horses. I'll be needing our bags and some hot water, too. Oh, and some whiskey. For me. Think you can arrange it?'' Daniel was not a drinking man but he felt the need tonight.

The old man studied the coin and his face lit up. He grinned and nodded. ''Right away!''

He tossed Daniel a key. ''Number five at the end of the hall.'' He scurried through a door behind the desk and Daniel could hear him waking someone in the back.

Daniel found the room and groped in the darkness for the bed. He laid Amanda, still wrapped in the blanket, down gently and covered her with a quilt.

After lighting the lamp he returned to the bed and rolled her over so her back was to the room. He didn't want anyone coming to the door to be able to see her face.

There was a knock at the door. When he opened it he found a sleepy-looking young girl struggling under the weight of a bucket of steaming water. He took the bucket from her and she left the room, only to return in minutes with their saddle packs and a bottle. She managed an awkward little curtsy when he tipped her.

Daniel locked the door and took a drink straight from the bottle. The scalding liquor jolted him. He poured some of the hot water into a basin and took towels from the dresser. Sitting on the side of the bed, he reached across to Amanda, rolling her toward him. She stared at him for a moment, then tried to push his hands away.

Keeping his voice low and even, he talked to her. ''Amanda, we need to get these clothes off you and get you cleaned up. I'm going to help you. Let me know if I hurt you.''

With these words she blinked and he thought he saw a flicker of fear in her eyes. He wished she would fight him. A reaction, any reaction, would be better than this.

Daniel unbuttoned her shirt, pushing the garment down off one arm. He rolled her on her side to free her other arm. He saw scrapes low on her back that had oozed and dried, gluing torn fabric to her skin. Wetting the towel, he laid it across her skin.

He used another towel to wash her face. There was a swelling,

purple bruise on her jaw, and another on her cheek. Her chin
was scraped raw. He turned his attention to the cuts on her
wrists caused by the leather thongs they had used to tie her.

Daniel felt fury rise in him like bile. "They deserved worse
than killing," he muttered to himself.

It didn't take much imagination to figure out how much she
had struggled, but he puzzled about what had made her give
up now and retreat, now that the danger was over. It scared
him.

He knew he had to do something to get through to her.
Soothing her hadn't worked.

"Did they hurt you, Amanda?" She twitched at his words,
making Daniel feel like a heel, but he was afraid she might
draw further and further into herself, hiding from what had
happened.

Daniel rolled her onto her stomach and pulled at the fabric
that clung to her back. It came away leaving raw patches crusted
with dirt and bits of straw. She groaned and tried to scoot away.
He grasped her shoulders and pulled her back. She stiffened
at his touch.

"Did you try to get away, Amanda? Did you try to run
before Bodin caught you?"

He continued to work on her back, pulling out slivers of
straw and washing away the dirt, using the whiskey as he
finished each spot. He asked her more questions, each time
gauging her reaction. She struggled more, but he was unable
to tell if it was due to the pain he caused her or his words.

Daniel turned her over. "Did you fight him? Did you make
him angry?"

He had to hold her by the shoulder with one hand as he
wiped away the dried blood underneath her chin. She tried
harder and harder to get away from him, but he pinned her
easily to the bed. Her eyes darted around the room, looking
for an escape. Her vacant stare was replaced by a look of terror.

Daniel gripped her upper arms. Amanda twisted against his
strength, becoming more and more agitated. He didn't know
what he would do if she started to scream.

"Amanda, listen to me." He leaned close to her face, speaking harshly, shaking her.

For the first time since he had found her, there was a sign of recognition in her eyes. She stopped twisting in his grasp and began to quiver. Her lips moved almost soundlessly. He strained to hear.

"Daniel, he hurt me. They all wanted to hurt me." Her eyes filled with tears and she started to cry.

Daniel gathered her into his arms and held her against his chest as she was consumed by great gulping sobs.

Daniel felt such relief at the sound of her voice using his name that he felt like crying too.

"I'm sorry darling. I'm so sorry." He held her against his chest, gently rocking her and stroking her hair, thanking God he had gotten there in time.

He should have forced her to marry him, should have tied her up and shipped her home that night he saw her in front of the campfire at Camp Dennison. Knowing his thoughts were irrational didn't help. He loved her so much.

Daniel sat on the bed, holding her, even after she had cried herself into an exhausted slumber. Throughout the night he soothed her when she moaned and reassured her when she stirred.

In the middle of the night she had a bad dream that caused her to cry out, and he rocked her in his arms and told her she would be all right.

He waited for the dawn, unable to sleep himself because the thought of how close he had come to losing her terrified him.

Chapter 26

Amanda awoke in a cold sweat. She had been in the midst of a terrifying dream.

She lay without moving in the unfamiliar bed, trying to determine where she was. The first light of dawn showed through the dingy curtain covering the one window in the room.

Daniel lay beside her, snoring gently. The events of the previous day came rushing back, and her dream took on an awful reality.

She rolled gingerly to the edge of the bed, not wanting to wake Daniel. Every muscle in her body ached. She pushed herself to a sitting position, feet dangling over the edge of the mattress.

Raising her hands to smooth her hair, she found it crusted with dirt and straw, a terrible reminder of what had happened on the barn floor. Sitting quietly, Amanda pushed the thoughts away and folded her hands in her lap. She heard Daniel stir behind her.

"Amanda, sweetheart, are you all right?" His big warm hand stroked her back.

"A little sore, but I'm fine, really." The mattress dipped as he moved toward her and she came stiffly to her feet, wanting to be out of his reach.

She didn't want him to touch her when she felt so dirty. She probably smelled bad, too.

Daniel stepped around her and she realized he was fully dressed. He hadn't even taken off his boots. She smiled at the look of concern on his face.

"Thank you for coming in time."

Her eyes filled with tears. She couldn't bear to think what might have happened if he hadn't gotten there when he did.

He cupped her face in his hands, stroking her tears away with his thumbs. "I never should have left you alone. I'm so sorry."

She could see the pain in his face, and she put her hands over his, wanting to reassure him. "It's over, and we're both all right."

And it really was all right. Just knowing he was here with her made her feel secure.

He put his arms around her and she leaned into his warmth, welcoming his embrace. Then she stiffened and pulled away when she remembered how filthy she was. She didn't want him to get too close. "I really need to bathe."

Amanda busied herself with her saddlebag, finding her brush. She had difficulty pulling the bristles through her matted tangle of hair, but she worked at it, very slowly and methodically.

He stood quietly behind her, his hands on her shoulders, watching her struggle with her hair. "Are you hungry?"

Amanda considered his question. She answered him without looking at him. "Yes, but I'd really like a bath first." She continued to brush her hair.

Daniel turned and stood with his back to her, looking out the window. "How about we go out and have a bath and then find us a decent meal? I'm tired of cold food."

She was surprised when she felt an edge of panic. "Go out? Can't we just stay here and have some water sent up?"

She felt safe here in the room with Daniel.

He was still looking out the window. He spoke gently. "All

you're going to get here is a bucket of lukewarm water. There's a place down the street advertising hot baths. I can see it from here.''

His voice was coaxing. ''You can't wash your hair in a bucket. Come on. If you can't have privacy, we'll come back here.''

Amanda agreed, because she was too tired to argue and she wanted a hot bath more than anything else. She dressed in trousers and a shirt with her back to him and then stood mutely by the door, waiting.

They didn't speak as they walked down the street. Amanda could feel Daniel watching her, and it made her uncomfortable. What did he want, she thought? But she deep down she knew. He needed reassurance that she was all right. If she hadn't been dressed like a boy she would have taken his hand.

The bathhouse was a lean-to in a muddy yard behind a tavern. It smelled of damp wood and was steamy and warm inside.

Daniel negotiated with the proprietress, a thin, tired-looking woman, for extra towels and soap. A curtain that didn't quite reach the floor separated two tubs inside the structure.

Amanda longed for four solid walls and a door with a lock, but this would have to do. She felt better knowing Daniel was just a few feet away. She shed her clothes and scrubbed herself as quickly as she could, avoiding the tender bruises that covered her body.

She struggled back into her clothes before she had taken the time to dry off. Amanda could hear Daniel splashing on the other side of the curtain.

She spoke to him without pushing the fabric aside. ''I'm done. I'll wait for you outside.''

''Already? I'll be there in a minute.'' He sounded surprised.

She jammed her hat down over her wet hair and hurried into the yard in back of the tavern.

Daniel stood at the door of the wash house and watched the small figure crouched against the tree across the yard.

Dressed as she was, she resembled a twelve-year-old boy. Something in the way she held herself today made her look weak and helpless. Yesterday, she had looked feisty.

He didn't know what to do or say to her to make her feel better. She was keeping her distance, but at least she was not withdrawn the way she had been last night.

Amanda was staring at a spot on the ground, and Daniel had to walk across the yard to get her attention. She started when his shadow crossed her line of vision.

"Come on, let's get breakfast." She nodded. "Feel better?"

She looked up and gave him a quick smile. "Oh, yes." He saw a flash of the old Amanda.

They found a little cafe just up the street that advertised breakfast, and went inside. There were several other people eating breakfast and the cloths on the tables looked clean enough. A middle-aged woman in a white apron motioned them to a spot in the corner.

"What can I get you fellows? The special is ham and eggs, johnnycakes on the side." She stood with her hands folded over her ample stomach.

"Sounds good to me." He glanced inquiringly at Amanda, only to see her shrug. Daniel ordered the special for both of them.

He glanced around at the other diners, then reached under the table for her hand and gave it a squeeze. "You all right?"

She nodded. "I'm fine, really."

When the plates arrived, Daniel ate with great appetite. Amanda pushed her food around, concentrating on the task.

"Amanda." She started again, just as she had done outside a few minutes before. "If you can't finish all that, could I have that piece of ham?"

He doubted if she had eaten more than a few bites.

"Of course." She put down her fork and leaned back in the chair, letting him reach across the table and help himself. He was torn with indecision. What should he say to her? Should he push her to talk or leave her alone? Perhaps she was just tired.

Yesterday had certainly been an ordeal, and he knew she had slept very fitfully last night. He watched her as she picked idly at a loose thread on the tablecloth. Physically she looked battered, but the marks on her face would fade.

Her spark was gone, her readiness to constantly question every decision he made, even down to the ordering of breakfast, was gone. Two days ago she would have glared at him if he hadn't asked her what she wanted. This morning she didn't bat an eye. It was so much easier, having her this way. He hated every minute of it.

They finished breakfast and went outside, standing for a moment in the sunlight, looking up and down the main street of the dreary little town.

In spite of his worry about Amanda, he still had work to do. "I want a newspaper. Come on."

She fell into step beside him. She felt sorry for him. He was trying so hard to make her feel better, but the aftermath of yesterday's terror had left her numb. She needed some time to come to grips with her feelings, but she didn't have the energy to try.

They stopped at a small newspaper office. Daniel went inside while Amanda stood and read the front page of the weekly tacked to the outside wall. The list of battle dead brought tears to her eyes. So many names. The township's population on the masthead was listed at a little over five thousand people and there must have been almost two dozen names.

Was that for this week? This month?

Overwhelmed by the thought of so many young men dying, she leaned her head against the side of the building.

Daniel came out with several newspapers and she pushed herself away from the rough wooden siding. In silence they headed down the street.

She didn't ask to see the papers. She didn't want to read anymore. Breakfast, what little she had eaten, had not settled well and she felt a fatigue more draining than she had ever felt before. All she wanted to do was sleep.

Back in the room she crawled onto the bed, pausing only to

pull off her boots. Amanda didn't ask what Daniel's plans were. She didn't care. She just wanted to sleep.

He flipped the edge of the quilt over her and squatted down so he was eye level with her.

"You sleep while I read these papers. I'll wake you when I decide what we do next."

She nodded and closed her eyes. Sleep came quickly.

Daniel sat beside her on the bed and propped himself up against the headboard. He smoothed the Richmond paper out on his lap, glancing at her. Amanda lay on her side, curled up tightly, knees to chest, arms crossed over her belly.

He turned the page and saw it. Set in a different type face, the cryptic message sat in its little border of black ink. Finally, Amanda's brother Andrew's elusive contact had resurfaced.

Damn, he thought to himself, the whole thing was happening faster than he had expected, sooner than they had told him yesterday. This meant he had to be in Richmond the day after tomorrow.

He wouldn't have enough time to take Amanda back to John Martin's farm. That was where she needed to be, with Hannah, to rest in a home with a family, surrounded by safety and love.

Well, he thought, trying to decide what would be best. He had two choices. He could leave her here or take her to Richmond. He didn't like either alternative. As he considered the possibilities, Amanda began to whimper in her sleep. She stretched out and thrashed about, kicking off the quilt.

She was having another bad dream. He wanted to comfort her before her nightmare could escalate into terror.

Daniel shook her gently, then gathered her into his arms, holding her tightly.

He shook her gently and spoke to awaken her, wiping her tears away with his fingers. "Amanda, wake up."

She opened her eyes and looked up into his face. Tears rolled down her pale cheeks and she clung to him like a frightened child.

He pulled her into his lap and enfolded her in his arms. In between sobs she managed to tell him the whole story of what

had happened yesterday in the barn. Daniel cursed himself
again for leaving her alone.

She turned her tear-stained face up to him. "It wasn't your
fault."

He knew she was wrong, but he didn't say so. His answer
was to brush her lips lightly. She startled him by sliding her
hands up around his neck and deepening the kiss. Never breaking the contact with his mouth, she twisted in his arms until
she straddled him, rocking her body into his.

His body reacted immediately. She took his tongue into her
mouth and sucked gently as she moved her hips in an echo of
the deep kiss.

Her fingers unfastened the buttons on his shirt, stroking the
skin as she worked her way down to the waistband of his
trousers.

Thoroughly aroused, he returned the favor with her clothes.
They parted only long enough to discard the garments; then he
rolled her to her back and poised himself between her knees
as her thighs fell open in invitation, and she reached to guide
him home.

He held her in his arms for a long time after. She became
very still and he could tell from her even breathing against his
chest that she had fallen back to sleep. He eased her down onto
the mattress and covered her with the quilt.

Around noon she began to stir. He watched her come awake.
"Hello, sleepyhead. Feeling better?"

She blinked owlishly at him a few times, then rubbed her
eyes with her fists. "I think so. What time is it?" She swung
her legs over the side of the bed.

He noticed how stiffly she moved. "Noon. Hungry?"

She considered his question for a moment, then smiled at
him. "Famished."

He breathed a sigh of relief. She looked more like her old
self.

Before they left to get something to eat, he wanted to tell
her what they needed to do. He folded the newspaper back to
the item he had been waiting for and showed it to her.

He would have liked to be able to put this business off, and let her rest for a few days, but he couldn't. "I need to meet someone, in Richmond, day after tomorrow. I wanted to take you back to John and Hannah, but I haven't got time. That just leaves us two choices."

He didn't want to leave her here, but if she couldn't face Richmond, he wouldn't force her to go. She studied him, without expression.

"You could stay here." She shook her head. "Or you could come with me."

She turned her head and stared out the window. "To Richmond." Her voice was flat.

Daniel laid the newspaper aside. "It would only be for a few hours. We can ride in and I'll meet with this contact and then we can ride straight out again. We don't even need to spend the night in the city."

"Then can we go home?" She was still turned away from him.

"Of course," he answered, relieved she seemed so much better, but not knowing exactly what she meant by the word home.

As they packed their few belongings, Daniel explained why he needed to go back to Richmond. Amanda thought it was dangerous to return to the city where someone might recognize them, but Daniel insisted the information he could obtain would be valuable, worth the risk.

He reassured her they would be in disguise, and no one would link them to Lord and Lady Ashton. With Bodin dead, they were safe to travel disguised as father and son.

When they checked out of their room, Amanda was puzzled by the old man at the desk, who laughed and gave her a jaunty salute. She looked at Daniel and he shrugged.

Obviously they had a private joke between them she did not understand.

The ride into Richmond was uneventful. They saw no military traffic on the road, only farmers and merchants. She felt far calmer than she had anticipated as they approached the center of the city. At least they hadn't had to pass the Shipley plantation on their way. Amanda had no wish to see that horrid Blythe Shipley or anything associated with her ever again.

She tried to concentrate on what Daniel was saying. ". . . quick in and out. I have to drop something off at St. Stephens. Father Thaddeus is a friend, but we won't take the time to call on him." Amanda realized he was waiting for her response.

It was unusual for Daniel to repeat himself, and she vaguely recalled he had mentioned his friend the priest at breakfast, too.

"If you want to see your friend after you finish your business, Daniel, I can wait. I'm feeling much better, really."

He was being so careful of her feelings. She knew he still felt guilty over leaving her alone in the barn.

Daniel looked skeptical. "We'll see how things work out."

He pulled his horse to a stop in front of the Spotswood Hotel. A young Negro in livery stepped forward to hold their mounts. Daniel gave him instructions to stable the animals for the next few hours, and they entered the hotel.

The lobby smelled of stale cigar smoke and had a slightly shabby appearance. Daniel directed her to a chair beside a pillar. "Keep your hat low and your eyes open. This shouldn't take long. If you recognize anyone, get up and go out to the stables."

"When I get to the top of the stairs, if you're not in your chair, I'll know you spotted someone we need to avoid and meet you out back."

She nodded and sat, watching him climb the main staircase. From under the brim of her hat she studied the few people who came through the main doors. As time wore on she grew fidgety and squirmed on the hard seat. She was less sore now than she had been earlier, but a little padding on the chair would have helped.

She turned her attention for a moment to the men setting up long banquet tables just inside a set of wide double doors to her left. Grasping a linen tablecloth by two corners, a waiter snapped it expertly into the air. The fabric billowed open and unfurled like a sail, then settled dead center on the table. The neatly hemmed edges fluttered evenly to the floor. She watched him move from table to table. Every time he did it, she expected him to miss. He hit the tables dead center every time.

Amanda felt someone staring at her and looked up to see the desk clerk glaring in her direction. She supposed he didn't like scruffy people dressed as she was cluttering his lobby.

She jammed her hands deep in her pockets, making an effort to sit still, and came across a coin. Pulling it out, she realized it was the penny Daniel had tossed into her lap while they sat under a tree at John Martin's farm. That idyllic day seemed so long ago.

Amanda held the coin until it warmed to her hand. Flipping it, she caught it on the fly, the phrase ''penny for your thoughts'' going round and round inside her head.

She heaved a sigh of relief when she caught sight of Daniel at the top of the stairs, missing the coin on its downward flight. It bounced once and rolled across the lobby carpet and under one of the banquet tables.

Knowing he had spotted her in the chair, she went after the coin. She could retrieve it before Daniel reached the lobby.

Amanda scooted beneath the cloth and was groping in the dark when she heard the unmistakable shrill voice of Blythe Shipley. Her heart lurched inside her chest.

''That's him, I tell you, that's him! Arrest him!'' Amanda's blood pounded in her ears.

This isn't happening, she thought frantically. *Tell me this isn't happening.* She peered out from under the cloth and saw Blythe Shipley standing just inside the open front door of the hotel. Two soldiers stood beside her, their rifles pointed at Daniel's chest.

Amanda clasped her hand over her mouth to keep herself from crying out. Not knowing what else to do, she cowered under the cloth. The general murmur of voices in the lobby grew to an uproar.

Mrs. Shipley's strident tones were discernible above it all. "He was traveling with a woman. Did he come in here with a woman?"

The soldiers and Mrs. Shipley had moved closer to where she hid. She could see their feet. So far she had not heard Daniel utter a word. She wondered if he had seen her crawl under the table.

What a terrible coward he must think her. What could she do to help him? she thought frantically. She had no weapon, no way of causing a diversion.

"No, ma'am. He came in here with a boy." Amanda supposed that voice belonged to the desk clerk.

"Well, where is he?" Mrs. Shipley was doing all the talking.

It seemed to Amanda as if Blythe Shipley had expected to find Daniel and her here. Surely the woman didn't travel around Richmond with an armed guard. How did she know? John Martin was the one who had given Daniel the information that had brought them here, along with the notice in the paper. Amanda couldn't believe that the gentle farmer would betray Daniel.

"I dunno. He was here a minute ago."

Blythe Shipley muttered something Amanda couldn't hear. Huddled under the table, peeking out through a slit between the cloths, she saw one of the soldiers tying Daniel's hands behind his back. Her stomach churned and threatened. She stuffed a fist in her mouth and sank back. The receding sound of footsteps and the banging of the front doors told her they were gone.

She stayed where she was for a long time, huddled up, rocking herself gently back and forth, desperately trying to decide what she should do.

Amanda had no idea how long she sat huddled under the table. *Get ahold of yourself,* she thought fiercely. *You're not doing Daniel any good under this table.* But what was she going to do? Amanda had no idea where they would take him, let alone how she could help Daniel.

Had he expected something to happen? She wondered if that

was why he had mentioned his friend the priest twice before they had arrived in Richmond.

Sitting in the dark, she thought of the tender way Daniel had treated her the last two days. He had saved her life, then stayed with her every minute, offering comfort and solace. Her soul felt twisted and small. She should have spotted Blythe Shipley and warned him.

"I'm sorry Daniel. I'm so sorry." She whispered the words.

When she peeked out again from behind the cloths, she could see two soldiers standing and talking by the main door. The first clerk was gone and there was a different man behind the desk.

She watched the lobby for some time, and noticed waiters, carrying trays, coming out of a hallway to her right. Crawling to the end of the tables, she waited until the way was clear to scoot out. She hurried down the hall and around the corner toward a pair of swinging doors.

Pushing through, she found herself in a steamy kitchen. She hunched her shoulders and ignored puzzled looks from the cooks as she headed out the back door onto a service porch. A wagon was pulled up, off-loading a delivery of produce.

She crept around the side of the wagon and saw another soldier at the entrance to the stables, talking to the Negro who had taken their horses for them.

Damn, she thought to herself, she wouldn't be able to take the horses, but she needed the saddlebags. Amanda skirted around the back of the stables and found a door that opened out to the alley. She listened for a moment, then stepped inside. The warm stable smelled of animals and hay, reminding her of the barn where Bodin had attacked her. She pushed away a feeling of panic that threatened to engulf her.

Desperate, Amanda made silent little deals with God. *Please,* she vowed, *keep Daniel safe and I'll be good and go home and behave myself for the rest of my life.*

She moved as quietly as she could from stall to stall and finally found their horses, still saddled. She eased the saddlebags off and was heading out the door into the alley as she heard someone asking about their mounts.

Amanda shouldered the bags. Wanting so badly to run, she remembered Daniel's advice about attracting attention. Keeping her pace steady, she concentrated on putting space between herself and the hotel. She would find a way to help Daniel no matter what she had to do.

Chapter 27

Amanda stood just inside the sanctuary doors of Father Thaddeus's church. Through her haze of black netting veil, she watched as the soft glow of sunlight through stained glass dappled the wooden pews.

She wiped her sweating palms on her black skirt and waited quietly, unsure of what to do. She knew nothing of the mysterious rituals of the Catholic faith.

Amanda had had time to think and plan in the room she had secured near the church. A newspaper article on the front page the day after Daniel's arrest recounted the incident, and described Daniel as a "suspected embezzler and impostor, now imprisoned at Libby Warehouse."

After reading the article, Amanda had suffered complete despair. Cash Walker's troops guarded Libby Prison. He would recognize Daniel as a spy. If Daniel stayed in prison long enough for the authorities to investigate him, someone would recognize who he really was. When the Confederates found out he was a spy, they would hang him.

A soft rustling sound caught her attention. Amanda turned

to see a nun approaching, her long black habit stark against her old wrinkled face. Faded eyes regarded Amanda solemnly.

"Do you wait for someone?" Her voice had a faint lilt to it, Irish perhaps, Amanda thought.

The woman's kindly face helped to put Amanda at ease. "I need to see Father Thaddeus. Is he here?"

The nun glanced warily around the church, lowering her voice to a whisper. "He'll hear your confession in a few moments." She gestured to a row of three narrow doors set into the wall.

"Wait on the end of this pew and I'll tell you when he's ready." As she spoke, the nun took Amanda by the arm and showed her where to sit, then turned and moved down the aisle to the back of the church.

Confession. Amanda considered the word. How much should she tell this man about Daniel? She knew very little about the priest, only a passing comment or two from Daniel.

Well, *she* had plenty to confess, she thought, feeling a touch of hysteria. Perhaps taking Daniel from her was God's punishment.

She gripped the edge of the pew, fighting to get control of herself. The last few days had been a living hell, and her nerves were stretched to the breaking point.

There was no one else but Father Thaddeus she could question about Daniel without drawing attention to herself. She had no choice but to come here and trust this priest.

She studied the narrow doors spaced along the wall. They looked too close together to lead into separate rooms. Where did they go? Would he be waiting behind the door? She tried to judge the distance from where she sat to the outside entrance. How quickly could she get out of the building?

Amanda grasped her hands together in her lap. *Stop it right now*, she scolded herself. *You have to trust him. There's no other way.* She was so busy with her thoughts she didn't hear the nun approach. When the woman touched her shoulder, Amanda jumped.

"Father is ready now. You go in here." She indicated the

door closest to Amanda, then turned and left again, her robes rustling in the silence.

Amanda reached for the handle with a trembling hand. Never had so much rested on what she would say and do.

She said a silent prayer, entreating the Lord to help her to do the right thing. The door opened into what appeared to be a small empty closet. She hesitated for a moment, then went in, closing the door behind her. In the darkness she stumbled over a footstool.

There was a scraping noise and a panel slid open in one of the walls, just above a small shelf, revealing a filigreed screen. Amanda could see movement behind the partition. She held her breath, her heart pounding.

"Kneel down, my child." The hushed voice was friendly and sounded kind, easing her fears a little.

"How may I help you?" This man's voice contained the same lilt as the nun's.

Amanda hesitated for a moment. "Are you Father Thaddeus?"

"Some call me by that name." There was a small pause. "What is it you need?"

"A friend sent me. He said if I was ever in trouble I should come to you."

"What kind of help do you seek?" The voice had a wary edge to it now.

Amanda sensed he was being as guarded as she, trying not to say too much. "It's not for me, really. It's for my friend. He made a mistake and now he's in trouble." Amanda reminded herself she had to trust him. There was no one else.

"What do you think I can do?" This man sounded so calm it irritated her already raw nerves.

"I don't know! Daniel just told me to come and see you!" *Damn,* she thought. She hadn't meant to mention Daniel's name.

"Would that be Daniel McGrath, lately of Libby Prison?"

Amanda didn't know whether to feel alarmed or relieved that Father Thaddeus knew of Daniel's plight.

She spoke hesitantly. "Yes."

"I was hoping he had another friend here in Richmond. Go out into the church and sit for a quarter of an hour. Then leave by the front door and walk east until you get to a small park. Wait for me there." The panel slid shut and Amanda was alone in the dark.

She did as Father Thaddeus told her. While she waited in the church, she felt relieved knowing he knew where Daniel was, but the words "Libby Prison, Libby Prison" echoed through her, filling her anew with dread each time she thought about it.

The small park was only two blocks away. A few children played as their Negro mammies sat together chatting on one of the benches. She chose a bench near them. Amanda had a sudden longing to see Lubirda again.

After a few minutes she had the sensation that someone watched her. She glanced in the direction she had come, but saw no one dressed like a priest. She noticed a short, middle-aged man with bright red hair. Dressed in a dark coat and trousers, he stood alone under a tree. She was sure she had never seen him before, but there was no doubt he was watching her. She felt goose bumps raise up on her arms.

I'll leave, Amanda thought. *I'll see if he follows me.* Then she remembered the priest. If she didn't follow his instructions, Father Thaddeus might not be willing to meet with her again.

She tried to decide what she should do. When she glanced again at the man, he was headed toward her. She stayed where she was, pretending not to notice his approach.

He stopped by the bench where she sat. "Would you care to walk with me?" She recognized the voice. He was Father Thaddeus. Amanda felt relief sweep over her. She stared up at him stupidly as he offered his arm.

"I'm sorry, Father Thaddeus, I didn't realize it was you." She rose and took his arm.

He chuckled. "That, my dear, was the point. Please, don't use the name Thaddeus any more. My name is Father Paul."

They walked slowly back toward the church. She could see its twin spires standing against the cloudless sky.

She flushed. "Of course. I'm not usually so stupid. The last three days have been difficult."

He patted the hand resting on his arm. "I know. I read about his capture, but only heard news of him today. What's your name, lass?"

"Amanda. Amanda Giles." She stopped abruptly and faced him. They were about the same height. "Is he all right? Who did you speak to?"

"That's not important. He's well, but that could change rapidly. The place is a hell hole." The priest's voice sounded angry. His mild features stiffened as he spoke.

Amanda felt dizzy and sick to her stomach. She leaned against him and clutched at his arm for support. *Oh, Daniel, please be all right. Please.*

"Are you feeling unwell, lass?" He gripped her arm, steadying her.

"I'll be fine." She took a deep breath. "Please tell me everything you know."

Paul kept a firm hold on her as they walked. He told her what little information he had. Daniel had been brought directly to the prison and questioned. He had refused to give them his real name, insisting he was Lord Ashton.

Normally Libby Prison was only for enemy officers. He didn't know why they were keeping Daniel there. The last Father Paul had heard, Daniel's jailers were holding him in the main part of the prison.

He stopped walking and turned to her. "I'll be guessing I don't need to tell you what will happen if they find out the truth of why he was in Richmond?"

This man knew so much, he probably knew that too.

Amanda nodded. Only last month the Confederacy had executed two men for treason after a short, sensational trial. The story had been followed in great detail by the newspapers. Daniel had worked with both men.

Amanda voiced a plan she had considered since Daniel's

arrest. "I can go to the authorities as Lady Ashton and vouch for him."

The priest looked appalled. "Absolutely not! We have no idea what they really know. You'll not risk yourself so."

Amanda fought to overcome the despair in her voice. "The man in charge of the guards at the prison has met us."

The priest stopped walking. "As the Lord and Lady?"

"Yes."

"Then he knows no more than the authorities. But that means you will have to be extra careful. I doubt he is there much, with his other duties."

It sounded like Father Paul knew of Cash Walker. "Will they have a trial?"

If she could get false documentation from Washington, perhaps the Confederates would free him.

Father Paul patted her hand as she gripped his arm. "Well, I'm not knowing the details of that, but I am allowed to visit the prison every once in a while to give spiritual comfort. The officer in charge of the prison is a member of my parish. I could arrange for you to accompany me. Perhaps while we're there we'll see another way."

"Could you? How?" This was too good to be true. She could see him. She could see Daniel. For the first time in three days Amanda felt some hope.

"With a change of clothes and a little instruction, I think you might make a satisfactory Sister of Mercy. The disguise should be adequate, even enough to fool Captain Walker. Are you up to it?"

"Yes." Amanda could feel the tears on her cheeks, but her voice was steady. "When?"

Father Paul gave her a thoughtful glance. "As soon as I can arrange it. Have you ever been to Mass?"

Amanda shook her head, worried her answer might cause him to change his mind.

"I say Mass every morning at seven. Come and watch, but don't try to see me. Wear the veil you wear now, sit toward the back where you won't be noticed and pay attention to the service. Learn the way of it.''

Amanda agreed.

"Good.'' He patted her hand. "After Mass, wait by the confessionals. If I have any news I'll send for you. Have you sent any messages to Washington about what happened?''

"No. I didn't know how to safely.''

The priest reassured her. "Don't worry. The story has been in the papers so they probably know.''

"Thank you.'' She squeezed his arm before he walked away.

Amanda had attended Mass every day for almost a week, watching the nuns perform their duties, waiting for a signal from Father Paul. At the end of the first service she had tucked the missal into the folds of her skirt and carried it back to her room, reading it cover to cover. Stealing from a church. She hoped God understood.

After studying and observing Mass several times, she felt more familiar with the ritual. As instructed, she always waited after the service. Days had passed with no word from the priest. Her nerves were stretched to the breaking point.

Amanda sat quietly in the silent, empty church, reticule in her lap, trying not to fidget. Mass had been over almost ten minutes.

There had been no further mention of Daniel in the papers. Amanda had read them cover to cover every day.

She heard Sister's approach, and glanced up when the old woman touched her shoulder.

"Father will hear you now.'' She indicated a different confessional door than the one Amanda had used before.

The interior of the confessional, slightly larger than the first one she had been in, held a chair rather than a stool. A full-length curtain hung across one side wall. Amanda lowered herself into the chair to wait. Within moments, she heard a door open and Father Paul pulled the drape aside.

Taking her by the arm, he helped her up from the chair. "We must hurry, Amanda. Come with me."

He led her down a narrow passage, briefly rapping on a door as they passed it without stopping. He opened a second door and Amanda followed him into the room. Hooks along one of the plain white plastered walls held garments, and two benches were pushed up under the clothes.

"Today? We can go today?" Amanda sounded breathless.

"I ask permission to say Mass every few days. The last time I was allowed was two weeks ago. I only heard this morning they will let me come today." His eyes twinkled with excitement.

A young novice about her own age entered the room. Father Paul smiled at her.

"Ah, it's quick you are, Sister Darda. This is the friend I told you of. She will be Sister Mary-Margaret while she is with us. Help her dress. We must leave within the hour."

The energetic little Irish priest was out the door before Amanda could say another word.

Sister Darda nodded and set about quietly and efficiently transforming Amanda into a Sister of Mercy. She seemed to be accustomed to Father Paul's quick comings and goings and showed no reaction to his unusual request.

The sister showed Amanda how she should wear the robes and wimple. She explained they were a nursing order and there would be some medical supplies in the wagon with them.

" I don't know anything about nursing," Amanda told the young woman.

Sister Darda reassured her. "Don't be worrying about what you'll do. We're allowed to give little to the prisoners beyond tablets for dysentery and lotion to soothe the bites of fleas and lice."

Amanda paid rapt attention to the little nun. Daniel's life depended on how successful she would be in freeing him. Time was their worst enemy. Her hands trembled as she tried to smooth the fabric of her veil.

"Here, my girl, if your hands will shake so, do this." She

showed her how to grasp her own wrists with both hands and let the long loose sleeves of her habit cover them completely.

"And if it's your face that needs hiding, just bow your head a wee bit and the veil will do the trick. Folks seem to think if they can't see your face, you aren't listening to them. You might stand to learn a lot by adopting this pious pose." Her face reflected her amusement.

"Thank you." There were tears in Amanda's eyes. "I know helping me puts you all in some danger."

"Nonsense. I'm only doing what needs to be done." Sister Darda looked around as if expecting to see someone else in the room. She lowered her voice to a whisper.

"Some of the things we do here started long before the war. Besides, the Lord's work can make for a quiet life, and, God forgive me, I enjoy the excitement." She crossed herself and the gesture reminded Amanda of someone warding off an evil spirit.

Impulsively, Amanda hugged the nun, then took several gold coins tied securely in a handkerchief out of her reticule and slid them into a pocket of her habit. If she could slip the money to Daniel, it would help. She had written a brief note of encouragement on the fabric. No matter what their plans might be, the gold would make his stay easier.

Father Paul had told Amanda most of the guards were not above bribery.

Sister Darda smiled and took her by the arm. "Father Paul will be waiting, and he's a dear man, but patience is not one of his stronger qualities. Come along."

Amanda followed her out into the yard, behind the church buildings. They found Father Paul hitching a mule to an old wagon. He nodded at the two women, then helped Amanda up onto the seat. Sister Darda returned to the sanctuary.

The wagon moved slowly, giving the priest time to go over again and again what would be required of her. He indicated the box in the back and they reviewed the ceremony and the items he would use.

"Father Paul, how can you be sure we'll see Daniel?" The question had bothered her terribly.

"The prison commandant, Major Turner, has already been informed that Daniel is of the faith, with a request he be included this morning. We can only pray he will be there. It was the most I could do without rousing suspicions."

His voice became very serious. "Girl, you've not been to a place like this. You must brace yourself. I don't want you to do anything that might draw attention to us."

He reached over and patted her hand. "The less you are noticed, the better. Keep your head down and follow me." As he finished speaking, they pulled up in front of the prison.

Amanda had only seen the building from a distance. She had walked within a block of the place almost every day, daring the risk to be near Daniel. Aside from the bars on the windows and the armed guards out front, the huge rectangular brick building looked like the warehouse it had been before the war.

They were ushered into a reception area, where they registered their names and the box Father Paul carried was searched.

The large room was bare of furnishings except for a desk. The raw wood floor was badly stained and the air was heavy with the smell of old tobacco and unwashed bodies.

Amanda stood quietly beside Father Paul, her head down and hands tucked up inside their sleeves, watching warily for Cash Walker. To her relief, she saw no sign of him.

The formalities of their arrival taken care of, they were shown into a room adjoining the reception area. Two armed men stood at the back. Father Paul busily set out items from his box on a makeshift altar, a board placed over two tall sawhorses. Quietly he told Amanda what to do. The guards looked bored and leaned against the walls, paying them very little attention.

As Amanda and Father Paul finished setting up, Amanda heard the shuffling of feet outside. The guards moved away from the wall, looking more alert.

An armed man opened the door and ushered in the prisoners. Their shackles clanked noisily against the bare wooden floor as they entered the room. Most of them appeared ill, their clothes hanging on thin bodies, cheeks sunken in gray faces.

And they smelled, a terrible sick smell that went beyond a lack of bathing. Amanda felt outrage. If this was how they treated the officers, she wondered how the common soldier was to survive captivity.

Amanda stood behind Father Paul and searched for Daniel among the men. He was one of the last to enter. She fought to hold back her tears of relief when he finally appeared. Dirty and unshaven, he had never looked better to her. He was thinner, but looked healthy. So far. A few of the men were so weak they needed help to walk.

Daniel didn't know she was there yet. He was busy studying the guards. She could see him glance around the room. She knew how his mind worked. He was judging distances, strengths, possible weaknesses. She wondered with dismay how she would manage to free him. The prison appeared to be very secure.

Amanda kept her head down far enough so the veil shadowed her face as she watched him. She longed to throw off the veil and rush to him, to take him in her arms.

She stifled a hysterical giggle. That would surely surprise them all, wouldn't it? A nun rushing to embrace one of the prisoners. Amanda didn't realize she had made a noise until Father Paul laid his hand on her arm.

"Sister, are you all right?" His grip was firm and he squeezed hard, bringing her back to her senses.

"Yes, Father." She whispered her response, afraid to trust her voice.

He leaned very close. "Kneel down now while I begin, then follow what the men do."

Amanda nodded and dropped to her knees, forcing herself to pay attention to Father Paul. The men, linked together by their chains, also knelt.

Father Paul moved from man to man, hearing their brief, whispered confessions. Amanda peered out from under her veil,

but could not see Daniel in the back of the room. She shifted
slightly and leaned to one side, catching sight of him.

He was looking directly at her. He inclined his head ever
so slightly, and winked, then turned and watched the priest
impassively.

The relief at seeing him made her glad she was already on
her knees. She wasn't sure she had the strength to stand.

Countless times since she had seen him being led out of the
lobby of the hotel by armed soldiers, she wished she could
have just one moment with him. Just a chance tell him how
she felt about him, to tell him how much she loved him. Now
they were here in the same room and she would not be able
to speak to him.

Father Paul ended the brief Mass and prepared to give communion. Amanda knew what she was to do and readied herself
to help him. Following along behind the priest, she held the
tray. When they got to Daniel, she bent over him and slipped
the small, tightly wrapped bundle of coins down the sleeve of
his jacket as he folded his hands under his chin, ready to accept
communion.

The expression on his face did not change, even when, to
her horror, Amanda saw her tears drip onto his wrist. She hadn't
realized she was crying. She bowed her head, thankful for the
veil, and moved to the next man.

After communion, a guard followed her around the room as
she distributed medications. She had no chance to speak to
Daniel. Too soon, they were finished and the prisoners were
ushered from the room. Father Paul and Amanda packed up
their box and left through the front door.

As they loaded their wagon, Amanda watched a carriage,
driven by an old Negro, pull up near the entrance. Three well-
dressed, pretty young women descended from the vehicle carrying baskets covered with linen cloths. The guards leaned their
rifles against the building and stepped over to greet the women.

Father Paul and Amanda climbed into the wagon. Amanda
lost her composure completely as they pulled away from the

prison, sobbing into her hands. She took the handkerchief offered by the priest and blew her nose.

"Come on girl. Pull yourself together. We have plans to make," he chided her gently.

"I don't know what we can do," she hiccuped. "There are so many guards, and bars on all the windows." Amanda had never felt such despair. "What did Daniel say to you during confession?"

Father Paul studied the reins in his hands. "He said the place was as tight as a . . ." He flushed and cleared his throat. "He didn't see any weaknesses."

Father Paul's voice was reassuring. "That gold you slipped him will surely help." He patted her hand. "Where there's a will, there's a way! Think!"

She blew her nose. "Are they chained together all the time?"

"No, only on special occasions." His voice was grim.

"When can you go and say Mass again?" Amanda's head felt stuffy from crying. She forced her brain to function.

"No good. They only let me come every few weeks. We can't risk taking that much time." He scratched his head. "There's no way to free him by force. We have to think of something else. You know, last month one of the prisoners, who was a tailor, was asked by a guard if he would repair a torn uniform coat. The prisoner agreed, and after he finished the job he put on the coat and simply walked out past the guards, wishing them a good night."

Amanda listened to the story and remembered the girls in the carriage and the guards who so readily abandoned their weapons to greet them. A plan began to form in her head.

"Father, do you know the story of the Trojan Horse?"

Chapter 28

Amanda fussed with the low-cut bodice of the yellow silk party gown. It certainly didn't cover much of her bosom, which looked fuller than it ever had before. Then she did her hair for the third time.

Answering a knock on her door, she admitted Father Paul. He greeted her and immediately started to pace back and forth.

"For heaven's sake, sit down. You're making me nervous." Amanda removed an untouched supper tray from a chair and glared at him until he sat.

She was lost in her own thoughts as she patted rice flour under her eyes to hide the evidence of another sleepless night. Thank goodness Daniel had brought gold with them, a good deal of it. Confederate money was becoming worthless, and with gold the merchants in Richmond were willing to give her whatever she wanted, and on short notice.

The gown she wore now was the latest style in France, and had come in through the blockade a few days before.

It would all be over tonight. The plan was sound and it would work. It had to.

Father Paul's exasperated voice interrupted her thoughts. "Do you really think this is a good idea?"

"It's a little late to worry about that now! Besides, can you think of a better one?" They had become good friends and she was irritated that he had so little confidence in what she planned to do. "Have a little faith."

He laughed at her comment. "It's not just catching you I'm thinking of. Being out alone and dressed like that in a town full of soldiers is a clear invitation." He flushed and looked away. "I'm fearin' you'll never make it to the prison."

He sounded like her father. "Thank you. That is exactly why I'm dressed like this, remember? It would be a little difficult to be a distraction to the prison guards in a nun's habit!"

Amanda softened her tone, feeling guilty for snapping at him. "Look. I have been driving to that place every day for the last four days. First I inquired if there was anything the guards might need in the way of socks, on behalf of the 'Greater Richmond Ladies' Knitting Society.' Then my carriage just happened to break down in front of the place. Yesterday I went back to deliver the socks. The guards know me. They aren't going to be suspicious when I show up tonight."

She also knew every time she went near the place she risked running into and being recognized by Cash Walker.

"Daniel would never forgive me if . . ." His voice trailed away.

"Daniel understands what needs to be done." Amanda put on a lace shawl that did nothing to conceal her bare shoulders. She laughed. "Besides, Daniel would be the first one to tell you I generally do what I want, regardless!"

Then, as she finished getting ready, she told him briefly of how she met Daniel in the first place. Standing at the window, she became very quiet, staring out into the gathering darkness.

"Having second thoughts?" Father Paul sounded hopeful. "I could find someone else to go tonight."

Exasperation got the better of her and she whirled to face him. "No! And if I had known what an old lady you really are, I would have told you to stay at the church! Besides, we don't have time to change plans.''

He made a gesture of helplessness. ''All right! If I can't talk you out of it, let's go over what you're doing one more time.'' Relieved, Amanda flashed him a smile as she slipped a derringer into her reticule.

''Just in case,'' she said in reaction to his startled look. Two pistols and a rifle lay under the seats of her hired rig, but she felt better knowing she could keep this gun with her.

Amanda and Father Paul went over the plan one last time. She would arrive at the prison around ten that night. The timing was good because the guard changed at eleven, and the shift leaving was responsible for removing the bodies of any prisoners who had died during their watch.

They had observed this gruesome ritual twice from the dark alley behind the prison. Through a source, Father Paul was able to find out which guards would be on duty, and who usually handled the detail.

Generally two guards and two prisoners were assigned the task. One of the guards was offered gold tonight to make sure he volunteered and chose Daniel as one of the stretcher-bearers.

Father Paul refused to tell Amanda who his contact was inside the prison, but he insisted his source could be trusted.

The bodies were carried through the wagon yard at the rear of the prison and left outside the walls, in the alley, beside an outbuilding. A detail in the morning took care of the burial.

If their plan worked, Father Paul would free Daniel once he was outside the walls.

It was Amanda's job to distract the guards at the front of the prison, to help keep Daniel's escape secret.

Amanda would meet Daniel later that night near a landing on the James River. They would make their way overland to the Potomac and cross into Washington. It would work if all the pieces fell into place at the right time.

She had a basket of sandwiches, cake, and several half-full bottles of wine, laced with laudanum. If it worked so well on Sylvie's children, it would work on the guards.

Amanda felt out of control. She hated the fact that the information and bribe money had to be passed through so many hands, but it was the only way. Knowing none of the people involved except Father Paul, she had to accept on blind faith that everyone would do their part.

Amanda wasn't sure how much Daniel knew of the plan. No one needed to tell her what the consequences would be if they failed. Prisoners who were caught trying to escape were chained to the walls inside the prison.

"It's time I left." Amanda glanced one last time in the mirror.

"Where is the basket?" He stood up and moved beside her.

"In the carriage." She took him by the hand. "Thank you for everything. If all goes well, I won't see you again. How can I ever thank you?" She held a handkerchief to her brimming eyes.

"Enough of that, now. You need to look pretty when you get to Libby." He patted the hand that held his. "I'll be going now. We mustn't leave together. God be with you, girl. Just tell Daniel hello for me when you see him."

She kissed Father Paul on the cheek. "I will. Good-bye."

Amanda brushed away her tears as she watched him leave the room. A simple thank you seemed inadequate when the man had risked so much for them.

The short trip to the prison over the dark roads added to Amanda's jitters. She spoke calming words to the horse, who didn't need them.

Four days ago, at the livery stable, she had chosen this lightweight buggy because it was in good condition, and the gelding because he showed some spirit, but was easy to handle.

After putting money down on the rig she drove into the country and fired a shot over the animal's head, making sure he wouldn't bolt at the sound of a gun. The last thing they needed if something went wrong was to be left on foot.

She could see the solid rectangular shape of Libby Prison

looming ahead. The only light showing in the building was at the main entrance. Amanda slowed her horse to a sedate walk.

"Halt!" The voice startled her. She couldn't see who it belonged to in the darkness. "Identify yourself!"

The voice sounded familiar. "Corporal Smithson? Is that you?" Amanda drawled, peering into the darkness.

"Yes, ma'am." He approached the carriage and she could see the smallpox scars on the familiar young face. She heard other footsteps.

He recognized her and tipped his hat. "Excuse me ma'am, but what are you doin' out so late alone?" He lowered his gun.

Her voice took on a whining quality. "Our driver has run off to join the Yankees. Stupid nigger!" She fanned herself. "And I made a solemn promise to myself before Mama's party tonight that if there was any leftover food, it would go to the brave men guarding at the prison. I just couldn't break a promise, now could I?"

She urged the carriage forward, stopping directly in front of the door in a splash of light. The young man trotted along beside her. Wrapping the reins around the brake, she tugged off her gloves.

"Well no, ma'am, I guess not, but it ain't safe to be out so late." By now there were six guards gathered around.

"Oh, fiddle! I'm just fine! Help me." Two of the men handed off their weapons and lifted Amanda down.

Her hooped petticoat flipped just enough on the way down to expose her ankles and a fair bit of her silk-stockinged legs. She heard someone whistle under his breath.

By the time she walked to the rear of the carriage, all the guns were leaning against the steps.

She turned to the two men closest to her and laid her hands on their arms. "Would y'all be so kind and lift that basket out for me. It's mighty heavy."

Amanda had easily loaded it herself not two hours ago.

To a chorus of "Yes, ma'am," the basket emerged. "Set it there, just on the step." She smiled engagingly at the soldiers.

Amanda called into the open door. "Anybody in there hungry?" Several more men came out of the building.

Bending low over the basket, she made sure the cut of her bodice was strategically displayed. She glanced around and saw she had their full attention. Out came the food and wine. Settling herself on the steps, she invited them all to join her, between delicate nibbles of cake.

She found swallowing difficult and small talk almost impossible. Fortunately, the men did most of the talking. She glanced around, but could see no sign of anyone beyond them in the dark or inside the building.

Amanda was delighted as they finished off the wine, passing bottles from man to man. The more they drank, the better. She pulled several more open bottles from the basket. No one seemed the least bit suspicious of the amount she brought. She strained to hear any noise coming from the rear of the building, but heard nothing.

When she inquired about the time, one of the soldiers produced a pocket watch and angled it up to the light, informing her it was ten forty.

"Goodness. I should be on my way." She directed them to load the basket.

Several of the men implored her to wait a few minutes until they went off duty so they might see her home, but she refused the offers, assuring them again she would be just fine.

Amanda stood to say good night and saw several of her companions come to attention. She turned and glanced over her shoulder.

Cash Walker stood framed in the light that spilled from the open door.

Amanda felt as if a fist had smashed her in the belly.

"Evening, ma'am." He smiled and tipped his hat.

She couldn't answer. Maybe he didn't recognize her, she thought wildly, and then dismissed the thought. How could he not?

"Are you gentlemen finished with your refreshments?" His

voice held an edge of sarcasm. He nodded at the chorus of
"Yes, sir!"

"Then perhaps you should return to your posts. I will see
the lady safely home."

Amanda stood rooted to the steps, stunned with fear. He
took her by the elbow and pulled her gently toward the carriage.
She stumbled and he pulled her up close, tightening his grip.

Please, oh please, give Daniel enough time to get away. She
tried to think of something to say or do, but was afraid any
action on her part might make the situation worse.

He helped her climb up on the seat, pushing at her skirts
to work the hoop down behind the splashboard. One thought
comforted her. If he was with her, he wouldn't see Daniel
escape.

He didn't say a word as he climbed up beside her. She
trembled so the harness rattled. He took the leather reins out
of her nerveless fingers and snapped them smartly over the
horse's back.

She sat beside him, mute.

To Amanda's horror, he turned off the road and down the
alley that led to the wagon yard. She thought to leap from the
carriage to distract him, to make him stop, when she heard
shouting from the front of the prison. She could see smoke
billowing over the roof. She rose up slightly, and her whole
body tensed.

Now! If she jumped now and ran toward the smoke it would
take him away from Daniel. She thought like an animal pro-
tecting her young. Walker's hand closed on her upper arm in
a tight grip.

He jammed her back in the seat. "Stay just where you are."

"But the fire, the prison." She gestured at the smoke. He
didn't answer, or even look in the direction she pointed.

She glanced down the alley and saw no one. Perhaps Daniel
had had time to get away. Hope swelled within her.

Walker pulled up beside a mound of firewood stacked against
the prison wall.

"Get down, now. We don't have much time." He yanked her roughly from the seat as he spoke.

She didn't understand what he was doing. Amanda stumbled, then righted herself, wondering what he was talking about. He wasn't making sense.

Then she forgot about him as she realized what lay on the ground. Not a stack of firewood but a pile of bodies. Bile rose in her throat and she turned away.

"Oh, no you don't. We don't have time. You can be sick later. I need your help now." She looked at him without comprehension.

He motioned to her as he began to drag a body away from the tangle of limbs. Her mind closed in horror. It was Daniel. She sank to her knees, her hands covering her face. She didn't want to look, didn't want it to be true. Her stomach heaved.

Walker's voice was harsh and agitated. "Stop that and help me get him into the back."

He shoved the basket aside and waited impatiently for her, then walked over and, cupping his hands under each elbow, lifted her to her feet.

She fought to get a grip on herself. Yes, Cash was right. They must take his body away from here. She couldn't bear to think of him lying in an unmarked grave for the rest of her life.

Walker let go of her and grasped Daniel under the arms. His head lolled back and his arms flopped outward. Amanda took his feet, and with difficulty they lifted him, rolling him into the rear boot. Walker covered his body with a lap robe.

He came around to help her up and found her searching the ground.

"What are you doing?" He whispered impatiently.

She looked at him blankly. "His boots. I'm looking for his boots. They must have fallen off."

He put his arm around her. "Someone took them. Probably one of the fellows who dumped him. Maybe the one who hit him. It doesn't matter. Come on. We don't want anyone to catch us here." He started to hoist her up on the seat and her skirt billowed around her. "Wait a minute. Take off that damn hoop."

He turned his back while she loosened the ties with shaking fingers and let the cumbersome garment slide to the ground. He picked it up and stuffed it behind the seat.

"Better." He announced as he pushed her up into the carriage.

"Why are you doing this?" The night had taken on an unreal quality and made no sense to her. She could hear the crackling of flames and smell the smoke. "What about them?"

"Who?" He urged the horse into a trot.

"The fire. The men still inside."

"The prison isn't on fire. It's an abandoned building across the street."

Father Paul, she thought. Had he planned a second diversion? She wondered if Father Paul would ever know he had been too late. But how did Walker know?

As she pondered, she heard Walker talking, but she was having trouble paying attention. She felt herself slipping away, the way she had after Bodin and those men had attacked her.

Walker's words began to register only when they were punctuated by a groan from the back of the carriage. ". . . and get him a doctor to look at his head."

It took her a moment to understand what Walker was saying. Daniel was alive! He was alive!

Amanda whirled around on the seat and was scrambling over the back when Walker grabbed a handful of her skirt and pulled her back down onto the front seat.

"For heaven's sake, just sit still until we get to someplace safe. And if we meet anyone the road, you be quiet and let me do the talking. Right?" He waited for her response.

Fear replaced numbing grief. Amanda was craned around, trying to pull at the robe covering Daniel.

Walker grabbed her by the arm and jerked her around on the seat again, his voice tense. "Look. There's nothing you can do for him just now. The plan has gone haywire and unless you do what I say we'll never get the forty miles to

Tappahannock before dawn. If they catch us they'll hang him whether he's conscious or not, understand?'' His fierce whisper finally got her attention.

"But he can't breathe under that robe."

"He'll be fine for a while. Leave him be." He pulled her hooped petticoat from behind the seat and flung it into the woods beside the road. She watched it billow and settle over some brush, a ghostly form in the faint moonlight.

"We have a long way to go and two rivers to cross."

For the first time she really looked at him. "Why are you helping us?"

"I have my reasons." He said no more.

Gone was the lighthearted, smiling young officer who had flirted with her at the Shipleys' ball. She knew who he was. He was the man in the sketch, the man Andrew had described as he lay dying. The contact she and Daniel had tried to find on the riverboat.

They drove on in silence.

Chapter 29

The long ride to the Rappahannock River crossing at Tappahannock was a nightmare. Daniel groaned and mumbled once or twice, assuring Amanda he still lived, but her concern for his condition only increased with time.

Two hours out of Richmond, when Daniel thrashed about, causing the carriage to sway, Walker stopped long enough to allow her to check on him. She cradled his battered head in her hands as gently as she could, and gave him some of the wine laced with laudanum from the picnic basket.

Later, they stopped again. He was still unconscious. She didn't know if it was due to his injury or the drugged wine. The warmth of his whisker-roughened face against her palm was precious to her, and she held his cheek cupped in her hand as she stroked his forehead. It seemed to settle him.

"You really love him, don't you?" There was such regret in Walker's voice, she turned to look at him.

"Yes." Her answer was filled with conviction, and she realized it was the first time she had admitted to the emotion out loud.

"Cover him up and get back up on the seat." Walker's voice was low and urgent.

Amanda heard the hoofbeats as soon as he finished speaking. She tucked the robe over Daniel and hurried back to her seat. He watched her slip the small brown medicine bottle into her purse.

"What's in that bottle?"

She answered as she watched the approaching riders. "Laudanum. It'll help keep him quiet."

He threw her a sidelong glance. "Do you always carry it with you?"

"No. I put it in the wine for the guards."

He stared at her, saying nothing.

The patrol came toward them and pulled up in front of their rig. The five men and their horses looked worn and weary in the early morning light.

The lieutenant peered into the carriage and recognized the captain's bars on Walker's shoulders. He gave a tired salute as Amanda pressed back against the seat, heart pounding. She could feel the perspiration on her face in the cool air.

"Captain. Ma'am." He tipped his hat to Amanda. She watched in disbelief as he signaled his men and rode off.

She turned, wide-eyed, to Walker. He shrugged. "They've been out all night and want to get back to their camp." Her shoulders slumped with relief. "Besides, they're heading into the city. We'll have to worry when a patrol is going the same direction we are."

He didn't have to explain. "How long until they realize he's gone?" She wondered how much time they might have.

"Maybe they won't."

"What do you mean?"

He paused for a while before answering. "I don't know exactly what happened back there. If he's listed as dead, they won't miss him when they count the prisoners. If somebody hit him and dumped him without changing his classification, then he'll be missed."

"When?"

Walker turned toward the east. "Right about now." The pink of dawn shown along the horizon.

After another hour on the road, Amanda felt stupid with fatigue. They pulled off to check on Daniel and give him water, but succeeded only in soaking the collar of his shirt. Standing at the back of the carriage, they ate what was left in the basket. It felt good to be on her feet after sitting all night.

"How much longer?" Amanda had her hand under the robe, resting on Daniel's chest.

He was quiet now, but he felt too warm. Exhaustion and fear combined to bewilder her, and she felt overwhelmed.

"Bray's Fork is about a half hour from here.

"Can we cross there?" He wasn't paying attention to her. "Cash?"

"Hush." He turned his head toward the way they had come, like a dog scenting an intruder.

She watched his face as he listened intently. She could hear nothing besides the early morning sounds of the open country.

"Cover him up." Amanda tucked the robe firmly around Daniel.

Walker checked the ammunition in his revolver. She held her breath as he spun the cylinder of the handgun, then flipped it into place and snapped the loading gate closed. Now she could hear what he heard. It sounded like a dozen riders coming fast.

"Unbutton your dress."

She stared at him stupidly. "Pardon me?"

"Just do it." His voice was fierce.

Impatiently, he pushed her trembling hands aside and unbuttoned her to the waist, pulling the dress down over her arms. She gaped at him, unresisting. Looking over their team she could see the riders. When he moved to undo her chemise, she shoved his hands aside and backed away.

He took her by the shoulders and shook her. "No time! Don't do or say anything, just trust me!" She wanted to do as he said, but the memories of the men who had attacked her in the barn were too fresh.

Trust him? she thought, shaking. *We are on a public road with men coming and he's taking my clothes off.*

He had her undergarments down around her waist. There was no time to unlace her stays. He pulled her to his chest and, placing her arms around his neck, spun them both around so her exposed back was facing the approaching patrol. With one hand low on her spine and the other in her hair, he pulled her head back and was kissing her when the first rider came around the buggy.

Walker's voice barked out at the sergeant. "Mister, you are putting the lady in a most embarrassing position!"

"Excuse me, sir!"

Amanda couldn't see him, but she could hear chagrin in the man's voice. Amazed that it didn't seem to occur to the sergeant that Walker was really responsible for her discomfort, she remembered Daniel's words of advice about putting the other person on the defensive.

Well, she thought, feeling her face flush warmly, *his diversion worked.* The riders retreated a short distance from the carriage, and Amanda could hear a low buzz of conversation. She buried her face against Walker's neck in genuine discomposure.

Daniel picked that particular moment to stir.

Amanda wrenched away from Walker, and hugging her clothes to her breasts, threw herself against the rear boot where Daniel lay hidden.

She began to wail at the soldiers in earnest, bumping up against the carriage to cover any sound or movement Daniel might make. Walker made a brief show of comforting her, then removed his jacket and placed it over her shoulders.

He retreated to where the soldiers sat on their horses gawking open-mouthed at the entire scene. After an explanation Amanda couldn't hear, they rode off.

At the sight of them leaving, Amanda's knees buckled and she sank to the ground. Walker hurried over to help her up. Under the cover of his jacket she turned her back to him and struggled into her clothes.

"Are you all right?" he asked with concern.

She nodded. "What did you tell them?" Her fingers trembled, making it difficult to redo the buttons.

"That a man answering the escaped prisoner's description passed us on the road hours ago and asked directions to Bowler's Wharf, down river."

"So they are looking for him. How did you explain me?"

"I didn't. Thought I'd give them something to wonder about." He grinned and she saw a flash of the old Cash Walker.

If he says one teasing thing to her about this she'd hit him, Amanda thought. Walker had enough good sense to remain quiet.

They reached Bray's Fork outside Tappahannock. He pulled up at a dilapidated house on the edge of the little town, unharnessed the lathered, blowing horse, and turned him into a corral. He told her to stay with the rig before he disappeared inside.

Amanda uncovered Daniel and tried to rouse him, but he was still unconscious. She stroked his hair, then let her hand rest against the steady pulse in his neck, finding it reassuring. She felt conspicuous in the early morning light of this tiny town dressed in a wrinkled, dirty, yellow silk party gown.

Within moments Walker was back, hitching a sorry-looking mare to the buggy. Before Amanda could question him, he announced they could not cross here and would head up to Port Royal.

Giving in to exhaustion, Amanda slept against Walker's shoulder for the rest of the trip.

"Wake up." Someone was shaking her arm. Amanda tried to push them away, wanting only to sink back into blissful sleep, but her tormentor was insistent.

Disoriented, she rubbed her eyes and for a moment wondered where she was. Then she remembered. It was dark and they were at a wharf.

Jumping to the ground, she went to the back of the carriage and shoved aside the robe. Daniel lay unmoving in his cramped space.

"The Potomac?" Amanda questioned as Walker approached her.

"Yes, ma'am. That shore that you can't see over there is Union territory." She heard the slap of oars against water.

"Cash?"

"What."

"Thank you." Putting her arms around him, she kissed his cheek, unable to express the depths of her gratitude to this man.

He had given Daniel to her. She refused to think of an unhappy ending. He held her for just a moment before breaking the embrace.

The sound of the oars ceased and two long, low whistles reached them over the water. Walker answered in kind. Within moments the boat docked and three men alighted and helped Walker lift Daniel out of the carriage and carry him to the craft.

Cash assisted Amanda on board and disappeared into the dark. She raised her hand in a hopeless gesture of good-bye, knowing he would not see her. So inadequate, she thought, considering what he had risked for them. She huddled in the damp bottom of the dory beside Daniel's still form. The men rowed silently, not speaking to her or each other.

A wagon and team waited for them on the northern shore. They settled Daniel, his head in Amanda's lap, on blankets in the back of the wagon. One of the boatmen climbed to the driver's seat, and like Cash, the other two disappeared into the shadows before Amanda could thank them.

She wondered what Walker would do now. Could he go back to Richmond without anyone finding out what he had done? Daniel distracted her when he groaned and jerked his arms and legs. Amanda knew his limbs would be cramped after being confined the way he was, and she rubbed his muscles until her hands ached.

He mumbled a few words, and she was heartened that he seemed to be waking up.

It was just after dawn when they reached Washington. The wagon pulled up and stopped in front of a tidy row house.

"Why are you stopping here?" She spoke to the broad back of the driver.

He turned and with a big beefy hand indicated Daniel. "You don't want him in no hospital. Them places are full of disease. You can nurse him here. You're expected. I'll go for the doctor as soon as they know we're here."

She eased Daniel's battered head off her lap. Two figures appeared in the doorway. Even in the weak early morning light she recognized Lubirda and Tobias.

With a cry of joy, Amanda bolted from the back of the wagon and into their arms. "Birdie, Tobias!" He caught her on the fly.

"Missy, you done brought him home." He pulled away from her embrace and tenderly scooped Daniel up in his huge arms, carrying him up the steps and into the house. Amanda quickly thanked the driver without letting go of Lubirda, and followed the men in.

The two women closed the front door and paused in the large entry hall. "Birdie, oh, Birdie!" Amanda had the woman captured in another fierce hug.

"We been waitin' on news of you." She backed off enough so she could see Amanda's face. "We was mighty worried."

"So was I Birdie. So was I." She hugged her again. "I can't tell you the number of times I wished you were with me."

To Amanda's chagrin, she started to cry, great gulping sobs that shook her whole body. Birdie patted and soothed her, telling her she would be all right, saying all the nonsense words a mother whispers to a hurt child. Amanda calmed and was about to ask where Tobias had taken Daniel when there was a knock at the door.

Birdie led Amanda to an umbrella stand with a small seat in the entryway and ordered her to sit. She opened the door and admitted a spare, lanky man carrying a satchel. He tipped his hat to the women and without a word went up the steps to the second floor. Amanda rose to follow him. Birdie caught her by the arm.

"You leaves him to the doctor. I gots coffee and food waiting, and you shore looks like you could use it." She squeezed the arm she held. "Lost some weight."

Birdie was muttering to herself about gals who couldn't take enough care while she pulled Amanda down a hallway and into a kitchen.

The yeasty smell of the warm room welcomed her. Amanda sank down on one of the straight-backed chairs and gratefully accepted the coffee Lubirda offered. It felt so good to be safe again.

Unable to swallow much food, Amanda spent a number of minutes pushing it around her plate, glancing up more than once to see the dark-skinned woman eyeing her strangely. Amanda told her briefly of what had happened since they had parted, then rose to leave the room.

"Jes' where you think you going?" Lubirda asked her, hands on hips.

"I must see Daniel, and talk to the doctor." Amanda faced her friend.

"Sit down."

They were still facing off when Tobias stuck his head in the door and informed them that the doctor was leaving.

Amanda bolted out of the kitchen, past Tobias and down the hallway to the entry. The doctor was headed out the door.

"Sir, wait." She caught his coat sleeve and he gave her an annoyed look.

"He'll be fine, miss. He is gaining consciousness as we speak. All he needs is some rest, some good food, and a bath. He has lice." He tipped his hat and was gone.

Amanda was so relieved at what he said she failed to be annoyed at his brusqueness. She turned to Lubirda and Tobias and said, "Did you hear? Daniel is all right."

Then Amanda promptly crumpled in a heap at their feet.

Chapter 30

Amanda drifted up through hazy layers of awareness, not willing to come fully awake. The bed, soft and clean, was more comfortable than anything she had experienced in days. The warm, quiet state of semi-wakefulness was preferable to the nightmare of her recent past.

But that past included Daniel, and she roused herself, anxious to see him. She pondered briefly on how she had come to be in this bed. Finding no immediate explanation in her memory, she let it drop.

"You feelin' better?"

Birdie's voice startled her. She thought she was alone. "Yes, much. How's Daniel?" She scooted up against the pillows and sank back, not ready to leave her cocoon.

Birdie sat in an overstuffed chair pulled up beside the bed.

"He doin' jes' fine. Sleepin', eatin' and takin' a bath. You I more worried about."

Amanda turned her head to look at her friend. "Me? Why? I'm just tired."

She looked down and was surprised to see she was wearing

a nightgown. When had she changed? And why did Birdie look so mad?

"How long you been breedin'?" The black woman sounded positively fierce.

Amanda sat up, her spine as stiff as a board. The abrupt question took her by surprise. She opened her mouth to deny what Birdie had said, then slumped back against the pillows and closed her eyes.

She faced the possibility she had been trying to ignore for the past month. Daniel was safe. It was time to think about all those signals her body had been sending her.

Tears rolled from under her closed lids. "I don't know."

Birdie left her chair and gathered Amanda against her chest.

Birdie's tone was much softer. "The captain know?" She smoothed Amanda's hair back off her forehead.

"No, and that's the way I want it for now."

Birdie blinked with surprise. "Why for now?"

"I'll tell him when I'm ready." She needed time to get used to the idea herself.

Lubirda took both of Amanda's hands. "You having his child. You better get ready soon."

"I won't be pressured into a quick marriage because of a child."

She recalled his hurt and anger all the times she had refused his offers of marriage. And the fact that the offers had stopped. "Besides, I've hurt him, and I'm not sure how he feels about me."

"He gots the right to know. It's his choice too."

"And I'll tell him. I will." Amanda wiped her eyes with the handkerchief Birdie provided and kicked back the covers.

"Where you goin'?" Birdie pulled the quilt back up over her legs.

"I want to see him."

"Well you can jes' rest a bit more, then. He's back asleep." She tucked Amanda in and smoothed the pillows.

"I'll stay here if you promise to wake me when he stirs."

Birdie nodded in agreement and left the room. Amanda snuggled down into the linens that smelled as if they had just been dried in the sun. She tried to decide how she felt about the idea of a baby and fell asleep before she could reach a conclusion.

Amanda awoke to the sound of gentle snoring. Daniel sat sprawled in the overstuffed chair by the bed, his bandaged head crooked to one side.

In the fading light Amanda could see his hair was damp and he had shaved. Relief flooded her. He really was going to be all right.

With a curious ache around her heart, Amanda thought of the baby she carried and wondered if she was going to be all right, too.

She watched the steady rise and fall of his chest as he slept. She pushed back her covers and leaned over the arm of the chair to kiss him lightly on the lips, forgetting his queer ability to come instantly awake.

Before she had time to pull away he hooked an arm around her waist and dragged her onto his lap, holding her tightly.

"I was so afraid for you," he whispered into her hair.

"Me! You were the one in danger." She nestled against his shoulder and reveled in the smell of him. "How is your head? Shouldn't you be in bed?"

"Sore, no real damage done. Feels like I have a hammer and anvil inside my skull. I hope you don't mind that I came in while you were sleeping."

Mind? she thought. Why did he sound so stiff and formal? When would she ever mind being near him?

She knew that now, after losing him once. Had she learned too late?

Daniel shifted her to a different position and she could see he was uncomfortable.

Amanda climbed out of his lap and he didn't try to stop her. She scooted onto the bed and sat cross-legged as she answered his questions about her time in Richmond. In turn he was non-committal about his experience inside Libby Prison, but his features looked drawn as he spoke. She had seen for herself a little of what kind of hell it must have been.

"But what happened to your escape?" She had wondered over and over what had gone wrong.

"I don't really know. I got a message on a scrap of paper. All it said was 'be ready tonight.' I didn't even see who slipped it to me. Then a guard told me I was on the body detail. I went with him and one of the other guards to the rear door, and somebody hit me from behind. When I woke up Tobias was undressing me." He dropped his head into his hands and rubbed his temples.

"Father Paul arranged a bribe to get you out." Daniel wasn't acting like himself and she worried that he had tired himself out talking.

She called for Tobias to help Daniel to his own room, and Daniel didn't object. "We can talk more about this later."

"I suppose they took the bribe money and what gold I had left. Thank you for taking the risk to get that to me." His tone sounded detached.

Strange, she had expected some teasing from him about her dressing as a nun. Tobias arrived and propped Daniel up on his strong arm for his trip down the hall. She tried to convince herself that the distance she sensed in him was due to the fact he felt unwell.

Lubirda came in to help her dress, but Amanda ignored her inquiring looks. One thought held her mind captive, repeating itself, nagging at her. He had not even tried to kiss her.

Dinner that night was a cozy affair, with just Amanda, Daniel, Tobias and Lubirda at the table. Daniel insisted he felt well enough to join them and declared he would not remain another minute in bed.

There was so much to talk about, the hour was late when the four of them rose to leave the table. Amanda picked up some dishes, following Lubirda to the kitchen. Tobias intercepted her and took the plates out of her hands.

"You tired. I helps dat gal with dis. You go on upstairs."
She thanked him and went to find Daniel. The front door was
open and he was on the porch, staring out at the city. She
could see the Capitol Building as she glanced beyond him. The
bandage at the base of his skull stood out in the darkness.

"What are you doing out here?" She slipped a hand through
his arm and he tightened it up against his body.

"Enjoying the fresh air. And the freedom of walking out a
door." She laid her head against his shoulder.

"We could go for a walk tomorrow, if you feel up to it."
Amanda was anxious to spend time with him, to get used to
the idea of them being together. She liked the feelings that
came with those thoughts.

He stiffened slightly. "I need to go to the War Department.
I got a summons from Secretary Stanton's office today."

"Word travels fast." Again Amanda sensed his distance,
and had to fight to overcome an intense urge to cry.

He pulled away from her and gave a big stretch. "I'm tired.
Are you ready to go upstairs?"

Her heart leapt. She tried to keep her voice steady. "Yes,
I'm ready." Those simple words held so much meaning for
her. She was ready, and had thought all through dinner about
being with him tonight. She wanted the right moment to tell
him about the baby.

Amanda climbed the stairs ahead of him, unsure where to
go. She decided on her room, mainly because she didn't know
which room was his. She stopped at her door, heart pounding,
and turned to invite him in. Before she could speak, he kissed
her briefly on the forehead, murmured "good night," and
walked off down the hall.

She watched him go, feeling desolate, wanting to call to him,
to follow him, but her pride wouldn't let her. The distance she
had sensed in him earlier was because he had stopped loving
her.

Amanda went into her room and undressed, crawling into
bed. Finally letting go, she cried herself to sleep.

* * *

How he wanted to go back to her room, to take her in his arms and make love to her until she cried out her pleasure. Force her to see that their love was more important than her sketches, or her aspirations to be independent. But he had made a promise to himself.

She would be unhappy if he tried to pressure her into accepting the life he longed for. He knew the extent of her talent. All those long hours in prison he had had to think about her. Because he loved her so much he couldn't be that selfish.

Perhaps after she went to New York and made a name for herself as an artist she would consider his offer of marriage, children, standing at his side as his wife.

That was his dream, not hers, and he would have to wait until she was ready. After the war was over, he would find her and convince her.

Over and over Amanda had made her feelings clear. She didn't love him. Now was the best time to leave her. She was protected now, here in Washington. Free to go to New York.

In prison he had suffered much more from not knowing she was safe than from his personal ordeal. Finding out she was with Paul had helped, but as he watched her sleep this afternoon he knew he could never allow himself to put her in jeopardy like that again. The army could hang him before he'd let them use her again as a spy.

His head ached almost as furiously as his heart as he lay in bed trying to sleep.

In the morning Amanda stayed in bed until she heard Daniel leave for the War Department. She didn't want to see him until she decided what she was going to do.

Lubirda arrived with the breakfast tray Amanda didn't want, and proceeded to fuss around the room, driving her crazy.

"Will you stop that!"

Birdie turned to her, an innocent look on her face. "Stop what, child?"

She shook out a dressing grown and hung it in the wardrobe.

"Just stop looking at me!" Amanda knew she sounded childish and petulant, but she didn't care. "Go away and leave me alone! And take this tray." Birdie shrugged and left the room.

Amanda flipped over onto her stomach and cried into her pillow, still damp from the night before.

She bathed her puffy red face with cool water before dressing, but the traces of her tears were still evident. Going downstairs, she found Tobias and Lubirda whispering together in the hallway leading to the kitchen. From their guilty looks and abrupt silence, she knew they had been talking about her.

Daniel's "hello" sounded from the entry hall. Amanda turned and stepped into the doorway so she could see him.

He looked much fitter than he had yesterday. She thought back to a time she had tried to talk herself into considering him an ordinary man. What a fool she had been.

"Good morning, Amanda. May I see you in the parlor?" His formal request surprised her.

"Of course." She followed him into the front room.

He stood apart from her, looking over her shoulder at some distant spot on the wall. "The War Department is grateful for everything you've done. There will be a commendation from the President."

"Lincoln?" As soon as she said the name she realized how idiotic it sounded. How many presidents were there, anyway? She noticed that Daniel failed to tease her, and only nodded, as if he wasn't listening to her response.

"I also told them what you told me, that you wanted to go home." He still wasn't looking at her.

She stared at him blankly. "I did? When?"

"Before we went back to Richmond. You said after that you wanted to go home."

She had no memory of telling him that, but the time he spoke of was a vague memory. Thankfully. She couldn't read the look on his face as he spoke.

"Have you changed your mind?"

She waited for some sign from him, some hint he wanted her with him. There was nothing. "No, I suppose not."

"I have a new assignment." His statement was particularly singular. There was no "we" there. She was afraid to ask him what it was. He would probably refuse to tell her anyway.

"You can go any time you wish. Lubirda can go with you." His voice remained detached and impersonal.

She wanted to scream at him that she didn't want to go anywhere without him, but she wasn't going to embarrass him or herself. Not now. Not after the way he had kissed her on the forehead last night and walked away, leaving her standing alone in her bedroom doorway. His actions made his feelings for her clear.

"Thank you." She couldn't think of anything else to say.

"Amanda, do you feel well?" He looked directly at her for the first time.

"Yes, thank you, I'm fine." *Stop saying "thank you" and leave,* she scolded herself. "If you'll excuse me . . ."

He nodded politely. "Of course."

She turned and left the room, heading up the stairs. Birdie was already in her room, waiting for her. Amanda began gathering the few things she had.

"What you doin'?" Birdie stood with her hands on her hips, watching.

"I'm getting ready to leave."

"You two can't leave now. You and the captain needs to rest." Birdie took the dressing gown off the bed and for the second time that morning hung it up.

Amanda ignored what Birdie was doing and sat on the bed. "Birdie, the captain is not going, just me. And you can come along with me if you like. I would love to have your company."

Birdie's expression changed from confusion to anger. "You didn't tell him, did you?"

"No, and I'm not going to. At least not right now." Amanda heard someone pounding on the front door.

Birdie ignored the noise from downstairs. "You gots to

tell him, missy. The captain, he deserves to know." Amanda watched as surprise registered on the woman's face, and turned to see what she was looking at.

Daniel stood in the doorway. "Tell me what?"

Amanda was glad she was sitting down as she felt the color drain from her face.

Tobias shouted from downstairs for Daniel, who ignored the summons. He repeated his question.

"That I, I mean. . . ." Too upset and exhausted to think clearly, she couldn't think of a suitable lie.

Without a moment's hesitation, Birdie stepped into the void. "Tell you that she be carrying yo' child."

After blurting out the truth, Birdie covered her mouth with both hands, looking stricken. The silence was awesome, broken after a moment by another shout from Tobias.

"Oh God," he finally whispered. "What have I done?" Daniel stood unmoving and stared at Amanda as she sat slumped on the end of the bed. He looked helplessly between the two women, then took a step toward Amanda, his arms outstretched. "Amanda, I'm sorry."

Amanda put up a hand to stop him from coming any closer as her shoulders began to heave with sobs.

Birdie threw him a furious look, then barreled toward the door. Daniel took a step back.

She slammed the door in his face as she said, "You best leave us be for now."

"Men sure is one of God's stupider creatures," she muttered as she returned to the bed and tucked Amanda in under a quilt. "Don't you worry child, he just troubled in his spirit. He think about it and feel better."

Amanda felt too numb to argue. She had seen the horrified look on his face at her news. She huddled under the cover, drained, not believing he was going feel any better when he thought about it.

* * *

Daniel leaned heavily against the wall outside her bedroom for support. How she must hate him for this. No wonder she had been acting so distant. He straightened up. In spite of how she must feel about him now, a spark of joy burned in him. She was carrying his child. That alone would help change her mind. In time.

He had decided in prison he could make the painful sacrifice and let her go, but this changed everything. Now she would have to marry him. Oh, she might hate the thought at first, but he would make it good for her. He pushed away from the wall and with a feeling of anticipation he knocked on her door.

Birdie opened the door a crack and peered out. He could see Amanda curled up on the bed across the room.

"Go away!" Birdie whispered harshly.

"Birdie, I need to talk to her." He didn't want to force his way in the room, but he was annoyed by her blockade. He could hear Tobias pounding up the stairs.

The expression on Lubirda's face softened, along with her tone. "She all wore out. You come back later." She reached out through the crack in the door and patted his hand. "An' brings some flowers."

"Captain, suh, fo' you." Tobias stood behind him.

Daniel took the note from Tobias's hand and read it quickly. The President had summoned him to the White House. "I'll be back as quickly as I can, Birdie. Make her rest."

He turned to leave, amused by the annoyance in Birdie's voice. "I knows how to take care of her!"

A uniformed officer waited in the entry to escort him to see President Lincoln.

Amanda was tired of listening to Birdie. "If you say one more thing you can leave this room!"

She stuffed the hem of a petticoat into the valise and snapped it closed.

Birdie's face showed her distress. "But he say he be back soon."

"Well, I can't wait. The train I plan to take leaves in one hour, and I intend to be on it." She plopped down on the bed and stared at the best friend she had ever had. "Change your mind and go with me?"

"I can't. I gots things to do too, you know!"

Birdie was angry with her. Amanda didn't want to part this way, but she had no choice. She was desperate to get away before Daniel returned to the house. She needed to think, to decide what she was going to do.

Tobias had returned from the train station with the schedules. She was taking the noon train to New York City. It would mean a long layover in Baltimore, but she didn't care. At least she would be away from Daniel. The pain she felt when she remembered the look of dismay on his face the last time she had seen him was too hard to bear.

"What you gonna tell folks? You think they not goin' to be noticin' the changes in you next few months?"

Amanda had done a lot of thinking on that subject. "I'll tell them I'm a widow."

Women everywhere wore black. No one would question her status. She would find a place to live in New York and she could continue her sketching and care for her baby.

Hands fisted on her hips, Birdie made a snorting noise in response to Amanda's plans.

"I'll write you with my address. I want you to come and stay with me when you get finished with your business here. I'm going to need you."

Lubirda had stubbornly refused to tell Amanda what she was doing to keep her in Washington. Amanda suspected she was there just for Tobias, Daniel and herself.

Amanda handed Birdie an envelope. "This is for Daniel. Will you see he gets it, please?"

Lubirda took the offered papers stiffly, then surrendered to a hug. "Gonna miss you, missy."

Amanda choked back more tears. They seemed a way of life for her lately. "Me too. But you will come to stay with me."

It was not a question, but rather a statement. Lubirda nodded and carried the valise downstairs for her, where Tobias waited with a carriage to take her to the train station.

The street in front of the depot was crowded. Tobias finally found a place to pull up, then helped her from the carriage. Amanda gave Tobias a hug, ignoring the startled disapproving glances of two older couples waiting on the curb, and sent him home with the assurance she would be fine. Heaven knows she had proven she could take care of herself.

After purchasing a ticket for New York, Amanda located the correct platform and found space on a bench to wait until train time. The noisy, dirty station added to her discomfort. She felt numb with fatigue and hoped she would be able to sleep in her seat.

Amanda thought she heard her name being shouted and turned to see Daniel striding through the crowd. Briefly she considered trying to avoid him, but he had already spotted her.

She thought about the first time she had seen him in a train station, in Baltimore. She remembered his kiss and her throat ached and her eyes stung. Oh, dear, she was going to start crying again.

"What the hell do you think you're doing?" His furious shouting created a stir. People turned to watch them. Amanda felt as if everyone in the place listened to what they were saying.

She mustered her courage and stood up before him. "I'm going to New York."

"You can't!" He was shaking with anger.

She had only seen him like this once before and it frightened her. She remembered that night in front of the campfire after she had suffered the wound in the raid. She took a step back but was halted as the bench caught her behind the knees.

"Yes I can!" Her embarrassment was making her angry, too.

She held up her ticket as if it were a talisman that could ward him off.

He lowered his voice a little. "You're going to stay here!"

"Why? You have an assignment." One that didn't include her.

"It's here, in Washington."

"I have a ticket!" It sounded like such a silly reason.

He loomed over her, menacing. She leaned back as far as she could.

His voice was low and had taken on a silken edge. "Shall I tell all these people why you need to stay, and marry me?" Amanda glanced around at all the curious faces.

"Oh, no Daniel, please!" she whispered, mortified.

He was going to tell everyone she was pregnant. She felt herself go crimson with shame.

He surprised her by dropping to one knee. He took her hand.

"Amanda, you have to stay because I love you, more than I can begin to say." His voice, clear and resonant, carried to the crowd, which seemed to hang on every word. "I have loved you from the beginning. I want you to stay, and marry me, and be my wife." His eyes pleaded with her. "You can have your dream. I'll never stand in your way. Please Amanda, say yes."

Her knees buckled and she sat down hard on the bench. She stared at the earnest expression on his face and knew without a doubt in her heart his proposal felt right, more than anything in her life ever had.

"Yes."

The crowd let out its collectively held breath in a cheer. Amanda remembered where they were as Daniel rose up, pulled her up into his arms and kissed her soundly. The crowd cheered again. He circled her waist with one hand and supported her elbow with the other as he hurried her from the station.

"Daniel, please." They were in a public place. She tried to put some space between them.

Abruptly he stopped. "I'm not going to let go of you until we're married.

She laughed for the pure joy of the moment. "That might prove to be a little awkward for the next few weeks."

"Weeks? We're getting married today. Now."

"Now? But . . ."

What could he be thinking of? You couldn't just get married. At least she didn't think you could.

"Be quiet. I outrank you."

He propelled her up into a hired hack, handed the driver a slip of paper, and told her again how much he loved her. He kissed her fiercely and Amanda felt all her dismay of the last few hours fade away. He pulled her into his lap and ran his hand up under her skirt while he kissed her again. She had half the buttons on Daniel's shirt undone when the vehicle began to slow.

Amanda peered out the widow. They had stopped directly in front of the President's mansion.

"Why are we stopping here?" She caught sight of Lubirda and Tobias on the portico. They waved and disappeared through the door. "What are they doing here?"

He smiled at her while he buttoned his shirt. "Someone has to stand as witnesses for us. I can't think of anyone I would rather have. Can you?"

Maybe the blow he took to his head had addled his thoughts. Someone was going to come and lock him up when they found out how crazy he was.

Daniel led her into the house, nodded to two young men standing by the door, and pulled her by the hand down a hallway. He stopped and waited so she could precede him into a room. Lubirda and Tobias stood by a lovely fireplace with an elderly, gray-haired man in a clerical collar.

She said hello to Lubirda and Tobias, both of them grinning, obviously delighted with their part in the surprise.

"When did you arrange all this?" She turned to Daniel in wonder.

"This morning. Two hours ago. Mr. Grady is pastor of the Presbyterian Church. We met here this morning. He agreed to come back with a license."

Amanda nodded to the stooped little minister.

"Then I came home and found out I had forgotten one detail. You." He picked up a bouquet of roses and handed it to her. "Ready?"

"Daniel, I love you," she said, weak at the thought of what her pride had nearly cost her.

The tender smile he gave her almost broke her heart.

She slipped her hand into the crook of his arm, afraid this was all a dream and she would wake. But she could hear the minister as he began the vows, smell the roses, and feel Daniel holding her hand. If it seemed like a dream, it was only because it was so perfect.

Late that night, lying up against the comfort of Daniel's warm, sleeping body, wrapped in his arms, Amanda knew with a sense of certainty she was just where she belonged, and all her dreams would come true.

ABOUT THE AUTHOR

Jill Limber has been telling stories all her life. She lives in San Diego with her husband and an assortment of cats and dogs. She has a degree in sociology and two grown children. Her favorite pastime is to gather friends and family together for good food, conversation and laughter.